W9-CEL-810

SORROW ROAD

ALSO BY JULIA KELLER

SORROW ROAD

JULIA KELLER

MINOTAUR BOOKS ✠ NEW YORK

This is a work of fiction. All of the characters, organizations, and events portrayed in this novel are either products of the author's imagination or are used fictitiously.

SORROW ROAD. Copyright © 2016 by Julia Keller. All rights reserved. Printed in the United States of America. For information, address St. Martin's Press, 175 Fifth Avenue, New York, N.Y. 10010.

www.minotaurbooks.com

Designed by Omar Chapa

The Library of Congress has cataloged the hardcover edition as follows:

Names: Keller, Julia.
Title: Sorrow road / Julia Keller.
Description: First edition. | New York : Minotaur Books, 2016. | Series: Bell Elkins novels ; 5
Identifiers: LCCN 2016008510 | ISBN 9781250089588 (hardcover) |
    ISBN 9781250089601 (ebook)
Subjects: LCSH: Women private investigators—Fiction. | Murder—Investigation—Fiction. |
    BISAC: FICTION / Mystery & Detective / Women Sleuths. | GSAFD: Mystery fiction.
Classification: LCC PS3611.E4245 S67 2016 | DDC 813/.6—dc23
LC record available at http://lccn.loc.gov/2016008510

ISBN 978-1-250-08959-5 (trade paperback)

Our books may be purchased in bulk for promotional, educational, or business use. Please contact your local bookseller or the Macmillan Corporate and Premium Sales Department at 1-800-221-7945, extension 5442, or by email at MacmillanSpecialMarkets@macmillan.com.

First Minotaur Books Paperback Edition: July 2017

10   9   8   7   6   5   4   3   2   1

To John L. Phillips, U.S. Air Force veteran, and to Elaine H. Phillips, the light of many lives

The thin grey line of a road, winding across the plain and up and down hills, was the fixed materialization of human longing, and of the human notion that it is better to be in one place than another.

—Isak Dinesen

Prologue

She lurched across the table at the old man, grabbing the collar of his shirt and coming up with a crinkled fistful of blue polyester. She was out of control, and she knew it. It was totally inappropriate—she knew that, too—but she could not stop herself. The sight of his face enraged her: The heavy-lidded, half-closed eyes, as if he couldn't be bothered to open them wider to make sure it was really *her* he was looking at, and not some random stranger. The saggy chin. The unstrung mouth. The ridiculous ears. The flaky-pink forehead, flat as a landing strip.

God, she thought, seconds before accosting him. *I can't stand it that he just—he just* sits *there. Smiling.*

And so she had bolted forward, launching herself across the little round table, knocking off the game-ready checkerboard somebody had left there. The red and black plastic coins bounced soundlessly across the carpet. The old man did not flinch. He let her snatch his collar and tug him toward her, until their faces were so close that she could smell his sour, yeasty, old-man smell.

"Say it," she said. Her voice was breathy and wet, as ragged and sopping and lost as something left out in the rain overnight. It had a rasp to it as well, a rasp of desperation. "Say you're sorry. Say it. *Say it,* you bastard."

He blinked at her. If he felt any discomfort from the force of her grip, or any recognition of who she was, he did not show it. He had no fear of her. No fear of anything. He'd forgotten fear, just as he'd forgotten everything else.

It was infuriating, but there it was.

Then, all at once, her equilibrium returned to her. The madness—the madness that had her in its grip, just as surely as she had a hunk of blue polyester in hers—passed.

Janie let go, opening her hand and releasing the fabric, which meant she released him, too. She was appalled by what she had done, ashamed that she had lost track of herself that way. She had promised herself that she would never do it again—never touch him in anger, never give them any excuse to say she could not come back. She needed to come back. He was her touchstone.

She despised him, of course, but he was her past. And she was his.

She took a quick, nervous look around the visitors lounge, to make sure it was still empty and no one had seen her. Sometimes other residents slipped in, silent as fog, and drifted into the corners. Or an aide, taking a break, might come in to take advantage of a comfortable armchair. You were never alone in this place. That was one of its chief horrors.

Her father's smile held steady. He had smiled when she first sat down here with him, and the nature of his smile—impersonal, abstract—did not change, even after she said, "It's Janie, Dad. Do you know who I am?" His smile had already lasted too long to be anything but an automatic response to stimuli, like an amoeba going from a comma to a period in reaction to light.

She endured that smile as long as she could. Today's limit turned out to be a bit less than five minutes. At that point she had lunged, grabbed his collar, confronted him, and then recovered herself.

She let her shoulders relax against the back of the chair. She looked around again. It was fine; no one had seen her. Good thing. This time, they would probably press charges. She had been warned.

Funny, she thought. Parents can beat the crap out of their kids as often as they like, but lay a hand on a geezer these days and they slam you for elder abuse. She chalked it up to the private-public thing. Kids were locked away in their parents' homes, with no witnesses and no one the wiser; old people were mostly penned up in public facilities, where nosy bureaucrats were always watching, writing things down.

"You bastard," she repeated. Softly this time. There was no anger in her voice anymore. Only weariness. It was a bland statement of fact, not an accusation.

His smile stayed put. Once it established a beachhead on his face, it rarely gave up any ground. The smile was unrelated to pleasure or amusement or even interest in what was going on around him. It just was.

"You bastard," she said for the third time.

She would have no satisfaction from him, no outraged denials, no savage counterclaims. None of the things that, if this were ten, twenty years ago, she might have had.

Janie Ferris knew this was a fool's errand. She had known it before she left her house early that morning, before she had made the three-hour drive to Muth County, West Virginia, before she parked in the lot attached to Thornapple Terrace, before she paused at the sign in front of the facility, the cheerful white wooden one with the bright green letters assuring her that the place offered MEMORY CARE—tricky euphemism, that. She had the same thought each time she came here, the same grudging respect for words that obscured grim realities.

She had known it before she opened the front door and checked in at the circular reception desk, asking to see Bill Ferris.

"Bill Ferris," the woman at the desk had repeated back to her, making sure she had it exactly right.

"Yes," Janie said. "That's it."

"Yes," the woman said.

This repeating thing—was it, Janie wondered, some kind of tic? Some sort of aphasia? Or maybe it just automatically happened to you when you worked at a reception desk in a place like this, a place with no hope, a place where time had essentially stopped. Why bother coming up with an original reply? You probably got used to echoing whatever people said to you. They said, "Good morning" and you said, "Good morning" back. No more, no less. They said something, and you repeated it.

Janie had lost touch with her father for many years. The need to find him and talk to him had come upon her suddenly about six months ago; it was like a mysterious ache that just shows up one morning. You start to Google symptoms, book a specialist, and then you think: *No, I'll take care of this myself, with vitamins and exercise.*

The receptionist turned away. She had to stretch to her right, to the far corner of the desk, poking out a stubby arm to fetch the clipboard on which the residents were listed in alphabetical order. Bill Ferris had been here two years now. The regular receptionist, a woman named Dorothy, never had to check. This woman was new, or maybe she was just a substitute, which is why she had to look at the list.

Had Dorothy been on duty, Janie would never have been alone with her father in the visitors lounge today. Dorothy would have called someone from security or from the nursing staff to sit with them.

That was the rule. Everyone had signed off on it—the executive director, Bonita Layman; the head of security and maintenance, Mike Ford; the sheriff's deputy who had responded to the call that other afternoon, Clifford Wilkins; and Janie.

Because of what had happened two months ago, because of "the incident," as they insisted on referring to it still, Janie was not supposed to be alone with him when she visited. She had signed an agreement to that effect. If she had not signed it, they were going to press assault charges against her.

But today's receptionist, a hefty woman whose name tag said HELLO! I'M SHERRY, didn't know Janie. She didn't blink or frown when Janie gave her the name of the person she was here to see.

HELLO! I'M SHERRY simply repeated the name, and then reached for the clipboard on the far side of the desk.

When she leaned that way, the fabric under the arm of her pink smock pulled and bunched unbecomingly. Janie noticed things like that. The smock looked as if it had once fit but now did not—owing, no doubt, to the steady expansion of the woman's body, a thing, Janie knew, that happened in middle age to everyone. Except her. She had been very thin as a child, alarmingly thin, and even thinner as a teenager, when a cardboard cradle of fries and a can of Mountain Dew— bought for her by her boyfriend, Kenny Huffman—often constituted her entire food intake for three or four days at a stretch. She had been thin throughout her twenties and her thirties and forties and now into her fifties. Her body was not like other women's bodies. People thought she was lucky, but they were wrong. Her body never quite seemed to get the knack of absorbing nutrients. It was as if the very idea of sustenance—the taking in of nourishment to prolong life—was strange and hateful. Sometimes she wondered why she was even still here at all. She had never really reconciled herself to the idea of existing.

She blamed him for that.

She blamed him for everything.

She had driven here today knowing full well that no matter what she said, he would not react. He would just sit there looking placid and content, as he always did. She could scream, she could pound the table with her fists, she could shout accusations, she could roll up the sleeves of her blouse and show him the scars on her arms from the times when he had put out cigarettes on her skin after she had *dared* to talk back to him, after she had *dared* to stand up for herself and for Nelson, her little brother—and it would not matter.

Not one bit.

He would smile. He would blink. He would cross his legs at the knee. He would fold his hands and place them in his lap. He would look at her and say, "Hello there, sweet thing"—and you might think she'd be flattered, touched, maybe even nudged toward some tentative form of forgiveness, but the truth was that he said that to everyone he encountered, all day long, from the nurses to the housekeeper to the receptionist. The phrase had no meaning.

Nothing he said had any meaning.

She had made the trip again, knowing that, again, she would get no satisfaction. Knowing that, again, she would leave here frustrated. She came at least twice a month. Sometimes three or four times. Perverse as it sounded, the more remote the possibility that he would ever respond, would ever remember what he had done to her and to Nelson, the more she craved a response from him. Apology or excuse or justification or rationalization or ridicule or threat—whatever. She did not care. She wouldn't even care if he denied the whole thing. She wouldn't mind if he called her a crazy bitch and told her to get a life. She would take it.

She just wanted *something.* Some reaction. And the less likely it became, the deeper her need. As time went by, as his mind continued to shrivel, the fiercer the desire grew in her. It was, she had decided, like playing tennis with no one on the other side. You kept furiously swatting balls over the net and no one ever hit them back. Again and again and again, you hit the ball with a nice clean stroke and it landed and it bounced a few more times and then it rolled harmlessly to the edge of the fence. The balls all waited there, a fuzzy yellow line of utter pointlessness.

She wanted a return hit, she wanted the chance to volley, but she got nothing. She wanted him to say what he had done to his children.

She wondered if Nelson, wherever he was, wanted it as much as she did. Or if he'd given up by now and never even thought about Bill Ferris. Janie had not spoken to her brother in twenty-five years. He never said why he was going away. She thought she understood why, without him telling her. He was a good boy. A caring boy. Sensitive, but also tough. He could endure his own wounds, as deep and indelible as they were; what he could not endure was having to look at her wounds, knowing that she suffered as much as he did. And so he had left West Virginia right after high school. She might not even recognize him anymore.

Well, if he rolled up his sleeves, she would. They could compare scars.

Did Nelson ever dream of getting a reaction from the old man, as she did? Did Nelson ever fantasize that their father would suddenly remember what he had done to them and either acknowledge it or deny it—or do *something,* something that would make revenge even possible? Did Nelson, too, yearn for payback?

Across the table, the old man continued to smile. Then he winked at her.

"Hello there, sweet thing," Bill Ferris said.

Chapter One

"Drugs."

Darlene Strayer nodded. "Copy that," she said. "So what's second?"

"Drugs."

"And third? Fourth? Fifth?"

"Drugs. Drugs. And drugs."

"I'm sensing a pattern here." Darlene offered a brief, tight smile. She picked up her shot glass and moved it around in a small level circle, making the river-brown liquid wink and shiver. The whiskey did not slosh; it trembled. Barely.

Darlene had no intention of finishing her drink. Bell Elkins was sure of it. She had used the technique herself on occasion. Order a drink—because not ordering one is too conspicuous, especially when your invitation had been casual but specific. *Hey, want to meet for a drink?* Take one tiny sip. No more. You needed to keep a clear head. Use the glass as a prop, as a thing to do with your fingers, to stop those fingers from fidgeting. Lift the glass, tilt it, let the liquid move. Lower the glass. Pretend to be just about to take a second sip. But somehow, you never do.

This little get-together, Bell had recognized right away, had nothing to do with alcohol. Or with friendship—the friendship between them was nonexistent. And it certainly had nothing to do with a desire to spend time in the Tie Yard Tavern in Blythesburg, West Virginia, a tattered, ramshackle bar as overstuffed as a sausage casing on this Saturday night in February, filled with too many people, too much bad country music, too much loud talk, and too many peanut shells on the painted concrete floor. Annoyingly, you crunched with every step.

So what *was* the actual purpose of this rendezvous, which had come about as the result of Darlene's phone call two days ago?

Bell had no idea. She was letting Darlene run things. It was her show. Her choice of venue. Bell had indulged her opening question—*What's the number one problem that county prosecutors face in the state today?*—even though they both knew what the answer would be.

It was always the same. Prescription drug abuse and its following swarm of illegal activities had upended life in the hills of Appalachia, turning ordinary people into addicts, and addicts into criminals. Unlike meth, unlike heroin or cocaine or Molly or all the other sexy-sounding, forbidden substances that people pictured when they heard the word "drugs," pain pills had ushered in their very own, very special version of hell.

"Asked you the same thing the last time we talked," Darlene said. "Four years ago, remember? You gave me the same answer."

"Things stay pretty consistent around here." Bell raised her own glass. "Consistently hopeless." She smiled as if she was making a joke, which they both knew was not the case. Then she set the glass back down again, also without drinking from it. The liquid in her glass was clear: Tanqueray and tonic. The darker pond in Darlene's was Wild Turkey. But the differences between these two women went far beyond their choice of drinks they weren't drinking.

Bell and Darlene had been classmates at Georgetown Law. During the subsequent two decades, Darlene became a federal prosecutor based in Northern Virginia, and had handled, over the years, the kinds of major criminal cases that landed her unsmiling, *this is business* face in photographs on the front page of *The New York Times* alongside the equally grim mugs of the attorney general and the FBI director. Bell was the prosecuting attorney for Raythune County, West Virginia. The closest she had ever gotten to the front page of the *Times* was when she managed to dig up a copy in rural West Virginia and read it over breakfast.

Oddly, as Bell found herself musing now and again over the years, anyone who had known them back in law school would have expected each woman to live the other one's life. Both had grown up poor in rural areas—Bell right here in Raythune County, Darlene in Barr County—and yet it was Belfa Elkins who had seemed destined for a glittering career in a big city, surrounded by tall buildings and knotted traffic and a magisterial sense of importance, while Darlene Strayer was the misfit, the shy, slightly awkward and even somewhat gauche girl who was never able to shed the small-town veneer of earnestness and yearning. Her clothes were never quite right; her hairstyle was always a few years out of date. She had talked endlessly about returning to her hometown and using her law degree to help the people there escape the poverty and hopelessness that engulfed them.

Dang. Just look at us now, Bell thought, glancing across the battered wooden booth at the woman who, once again, had lifted her glass in order to not drink out of it.

Darlene was the one in the cool black suit. The one who owned the elegant Massachusetts Avenue town house along Embassy Row and the Sanibel Island condo. The one whose life was as smooth as a fitted sheet.

Bell was the one in the jeans and turtleneck sweater. The one who lived in Acker's Gap, West Virginia, in a crumbling stone house built more than a century and a half ago. The one whose life was as rumpled as that same sheet, after a passel of rowdy kids has used the bed as a trampoline.

It was as if, late at night just after graduation from Georgetown, they'd met in some secret location and agreed to swap ambitions. And lives.

"I suppose I thought things had improved a little bit," Darlene said.

"Really. That's what you thought." Bell did not even try to keep the skepticism out of her tone. Darlene, she knew, had access to more and better crime statistics than any county prosecutor could ever hope to obtain. Those stats were grim and getting grimmer by the minute.

"Well, maybe it's what I hoped," Darlene said. "Let's put it that way." She started to bend two fingers around the glass one more time, preparatory to another pointless lift. But Bell had had enough. She reached across the table and stopped her hand.

"Hey," Bell said. "Let's cut the small talk, okay? You're busy. I'm busy. You drove a long way in some pretty lousy weather to get here tonight. So come on—why am I here? What do you really want?"

"Fine." Darlene slipped her fingers out from under Bell's grip. They did not like each other. They never had. They were cordial, but just. Two social encounters in twenty years—one in D.C. four years ago, at a class reunion, and now this—strained the outermost limits of each woman's politeness allocation.

"Truth is," Darlene went on, "I need your help."

"Forgive me, but I'm trying to imagine how a federal prosecutor who routinely takes on special assignments from the attorney general of the United States could *possibly* need any assistance from a small-town DA in West Virginia."

"I'm not a federal prosecutor anymore. I resigned last month."

"Really."

"I'm taking a little time off, and then I'll be heading the litigation department of a D.C. law firm." Darlene told her the name of the firm, but she didn't have to; it was exactly the sort of practice that Bell would have expected her to join. It rivaled the snooty splendor and cool exclusivity of the law firm at which Bell's ex-husband was a partner. Darlene and Sam Elkins would be like bought-and-paid-for bookends: two very talented attorneys who spent their time massaging the egos of millionaires.

It was not Bell's idea of personal satisfaction, but it didn't have to be. Free country, she reminded herself. To each her own.

Bell waited for Darlene to say more. When she did not, Bell began to speak.

"Listen, I've got to wind this up pretty soon because—"

"*Jesus,* Bell. Give me a minute, okay? Just hold on." An exasperated Darlene shook her head. Her soft dark hair was cut so stylishly short—it looked like a velvet bathing cap, Bell had thought when she'd first spotted her across the crowded expanse of the Tie Yard Tavern— that not a strand moved. "Jesus," Darlene repeated.

She took a brief sip of her drink. She coughed. She shook her head. Her shoulders rose and fell. She seemed to be recalibrating herself. "Look, Bell. This is about my father. Harmon Strayer." She coughed again. Bell was surprised, but remained silent. Whatever it was that her former classmate needed to say to her, she would say it when she was good and ready.

In the back of Bell's mind there stirred a vague recollection of a story she had been told a few years ago by another Georgetown alum. A story about Darlene Strayer's father, a diagnosis of Alzheimer's, and the long, lightless road to nowhere that the disease brought about.

"He died last week," Darlene finally said. "He was almost ninety."

"Sorry to hear that. Always hard to lose a family member."

"Yeah. It was rough toward the end. Hell—it was rough all the way through. He was living in Thornapple Terrace. Do you know it? An Alzheimer's care place over in Muth County. Pretty close to his home— although why that even mattered, I don't know, because he didn't have a friggin' clue where he was. He'd been there about three years. Ever since it opened."

"I think I've heard of it." Bell was being polite. The name meant nothing to her. That was not surprising. New elder care facilities seemed to pop up monthly; an aging population riddled with end-of-life issues such as Alzheimer's made such places the only growth area around here. Bell couldn't keep track of them all. Typically they were christened with names like Sunnyside and Brooksdale and Willow Walk and Friendship Bay—happy, soothing, cheerful names. Names that tried to gloss over the reality of what went on past the pleasant lobby and the carpeted corridors: a swan dive into decline and a ragged death. Such places were located at the end of one-way roads paved with sorrow. But that was better, she supposed, than what used to happen years ago, when a deteriorating older relative was left to rot in a back bedroom with a portable commode and the blinds pulled shut.

"Thornapple Terrace," Darlene said, "is supposed to be one of the best."

"You don't sound convinced."

"For the past several months, my father had gotten more and more agitated. We used to sit in the visitors lounge, but he didn't want to go there anymore. He wanted to stay in his room. Something—or someone—was bothering him. He couldn't tell me—he didn't talk very often—but I knew. I just felt it. And when I tried to have a chat with the director about it, she—"

An argument suddenly erupted in the booth next to theirs, a tangled snarl of voices jump-started by beer and bad manners. Bell had seen the trio of twentysomethings on her way in. She could not see them now—the back of the bench seat rose too high—but she got the gist of the fight based on the spillover noise.

Two women were quarreling—shrieking, really—over whether or not the man across from them was, as one of the women had just eloquently dubbed him, a shithead, because he had been dating them simultaneously, without either one knowing about it. Until tonight. "He is *too* a shithead," the woman said, and the other countered wittily, "Is *not*."

This went on for a few more dreary minutes, while the man said nothing. Bell couldn't see his face, but she imagined he was lapping up the attention, even though his evening would probably end with a Bud Light bottle smashed over his head and a lot of blood loss.

Violence was always lurking just below the surface in a place like this. It made up its mind, moment by moment, whether to rise up with a bellow and a roar, or to lie in wait, biding its time, eager for an opportunity to do the most possible harm.

Then, as quickly as it had begun, the loud part of the argument stopped. The voices dropped to inoffensive mumbles.

Darlene waited until she was sure it was over, and then spoke. "Anyway, it really bothered me—seeing my father upset like that. Not much I could do, though, unless I wanted to move him, which would have been a major ordeal. I didn't think he was up to that." She paused. "It was a lot of responsibility. All the decisions were mine. I'm an only child. My mother died when I was in grade school. So it was all on my shoulders."

"I'm sure you did your best." Bell had no idea if Darlene had done her best or not, but it seemed like the kind of thing you were supposed to say.

"You're sure of that, are you?" Darlene shot back. Her tone was cold, belligerent.

Bell had a flash of recollection about this woman, from back in their Georgetown days. Darlene Strayer hated bullshit. She brutally dismissed well-meant clichés and platitudes like a soldier waving around a saber at a batch of flies. Trying to console her was a dangerous business. You might very well come away with flesh wounds.

"From the little I know of you, Darlene," Bell said carefully, "you're a woman who would do right by her father. That's all I meant."

"Yeah. Sure." The sarcasm in her voice was heavy and dark. She rearranged her elbows on the wooden tabletop. There was a restlessness in her movements, an ill-concealed frustration.

"What's really going on?" Bell said.

Darlene did not look at her. Instead she dropped her eyes and studied the tabletop. It was the color of mud, and it was shiny from repeated coats of shellac, which only served to preserve the undesirable, like a fly trapped in an ice cube. The surface had been roughed up over the years by the assorted shitheads and their assorted girlfriends who had occupied this booth, and used it as a scratch pad for their switchblades. It had absorbed their spilled beer and sopped up their unused dreams.

The tabletop, Bell thought as she watched her, did not belong anywhere near Darlene's present life—a life defined by the sleek haircut, the elegant wool suit, the pressed white silk blouse, the necklace of tiny pearls. Yet it was still a part of her, too, still a part of her deep and abiding past. Darlene, like Bell, had tumbled out of a scuffed-up, stripped-down childhood. She had risen above all that—far, far above it, and good for her—but when Darlene glanced down at the creased and greasy-looking tabletop, Bell guessed, it probably came back to her, all of it, just for a moment. And a moment was long enough.

"When we were in law school," Darlene said.

Bell waited.

"When we were in law school," Darlene repeated, needing to start again, "I didn't like you very much. I'm sure you figured that out." She lifted her head and looked at Bell with a solemn, unblinking stare.

Bell shrugged. "If there was one seat left in the Williams Law Library, and that seat was next to me, you'd leave the building. Find somewhere else to study."

"Was I really that bad?"

"I'm exaggerating. But, yeah—I picked up on your attitude and just steered clear."

"We come from the same place. And *I* wanted to be the Appalachian success story, you know? *I* wanted to be that woman. I didn't care to share any of it with you. Plus, I was jealous."

"Oh, come on."

"I mean it. You had a handsome husband and a cute little baby girl and a life—a real life. You know what I had? I had a studio apartment and a rusty bike and a debt total that was rising so high and so fast I couldn't see over it anymore." Her voice shifted, lightened, lost its load of bitterness. "And my dad. I had my dad." She smiled. The smile chased the bleakness out of her face. "He believed in me, Bell. As little as he had, he gave it to me. So that I could make something of myself. And not just money. He'd send me these amazing letters twice, three times a week. That's what kept me going—seeing that West Virginia postmark. I'd run home after class and I'd tear open those letters and I'd read every word. Just standing there, holding my books. I was hungry and tired—it didn't matter. I'd still stand there, reading every damned word. I couldn't wait. I craved those letters. Needed them. Turns out *that's* what I was really hungry for."

"Just takes one."

"One what?"

"One person who believes in you," Bell said. "The rest of the world can go to hell—as long as you've got one person in your corner." Darlene did not ask, but if she had, Bell would have told her that for her, the one person had been Nick Fogelsong, former sheriff of Raythune County. He'd known her since she was ten years old. He'd seen her through all the major phases of her life, good and bad. Without him, her life would have been . . . Well, she did not want to finish that sentence. "Your dad must have been pretty special."

"He was. He really was. Anyone who knew him will tell you that. He'd never been out of Barr County in his life and then—*boom*. Right after Pearl Harbor, he runs down and he enlists. Him and his two best friends. He was only fifteen, so he had to lie about his age.

Served in the Navy. He was part of the D-Day landing. Never talked about it, but I got the story from other people over the years. He was a great man. A truly great man." Darlene swallowed hard. "Which is why you're going to be surprised at what I came here to tell you tonight."

"What's that?"

Darlene leaned across the table. Her face had changed. The look in her eye was unsettling.

"I killed him," she said.

"You—"

"I didn't pull a trigger. But I saw there was something going on. I should have *forced* that director to get to the bottom of it. I'll regret that for the rest of my life. Because now my father is dead. He trusted me to take care of him, and I let him down." Her jaw tightened. When she spoke again, her voice had a lost and pleading quality to it. "If you don't help me—someone's going to get away with murder."

Bell stood alongside her Ford Explorer in the dark parking lot. She watched the snow come down in a furious, wind-driven swirl, the millions of bits briefly illuminated as they intersected with the thin triangle of light provided by the single bulb fastened to a pole alongside the lot.

By now the snow completely covered the gravel. It piled up in sugary peaks and tufts against the tires of the cars. It smothered windshields like grave blankets.

Back in the bar, she had listened to the rest of Darlene's story. It was long on accusation, short on evidence. They had discussed options, strategies, possibilities. Then Darlene settled the bill. They looped thick scarves around their necks and buttoned up their heavy coats and tugged on gloves and left the low-slung, cinder block building, exchanging the crunch of peanut shells for the crunch of snow in the parking lot.

Because they had arrived here almost simultaneously, their vehicles were parked side by side. Darlene paused at the driver's door of her midnight-blue Audi. She brushed the snow off the shoulders of her coat, and then she opened the door, slid in, and pulled it shut. Bell waved. She said the thing she always said when anyone departed in winter, when snow added yet another treacherous element to mountain roads that were pretty damned perilous to begin with: "Be careful."

Darlene's window was rolled up, so she could not hear the words, but Bell hadn't really meant them for her. The words were aimed at the universe, at whatever distant, brooding force controlled the destinies of people forced to live in dangerous circumstances. "Be careful" meant: Be careful with the souls in your care. They had suffered enough, most of them.

Hell. All of them.

As Bell watched, Darlene backed the Audi out of its spot and then pulled forward, leaving the lot in a wide, slow, wary turn. The snow was thickening so quickly that her tire tracks disappeared almost instantly.

Bell was consoled by the fact that Darlene knew these roads as well as she did, including the switchback halfway down that had caused more deaths than a serial killer. Yes, Darlene had moved away a long time ago—but some things, you never forgot. Mountain roads in winter definitely made the list.

She continued to stand by the Explorer. She didn't want to leave right away. As cold and dark as it was, as furiously as the snow was falling, Bell wanted to wait here for just a few minutes more and contemplate what Darlene had told her. She needed to figure out what—if anything—she should do in response to it. The snow boxed in her thoughts, sealing them off. It temporarily kept distractions at bay. Soon, of course, the snow would be its own distraction; Bell would have to negotiate the switchback, too, and trust the Explorer to get her safely down the mountain.

But for the next few minutes, she wanted to watch the snow as it faithfully coated every object, obscuring edges and differences, making everything look the same. Simplifying the world. She felt the flakes melting in her hair.

Darlene was still grieving her father's death. Bell did not know her well, but she did not need to know her well to understand that. Darlene was stunned, angry, turned inside out with the kind of despair for which there was no antidote. Grief was something you simply had to get through, howsoever you could. Grief was brutal, and it was cruel, and it lasted as long as it lasted. Grief could turn even the calmest, most poised and rational person into an emotional mess. And when grief was mixed with guilt—the guilt that burned and surged and twisted inside you because you so futilely wished you'd done more for your loved one, wished you'd stopped in more often and paid better attention when you did, wished you'd hugged him just once more during that last visit, and told him just one more time that you loved him, although, God help you, you did not *know* it was going to be your final chance to do that, to do anything—then you were in for trouble.

Bell had listened to Darlene. She had heard the pain in her voice. She had nodded. But she'd made no promises to her old acquaintance, beyond an agreement to look into the matter. Informally. Discreetly.

In some ways—and Bell knew she didn't have to explain this to Darlene—a prosecutor had less power than an average citizen, not more. When a prosecutor made a casual inquiry, it wasn't casual anymore. It couldn't be. A clanking, wheezing, cumbersome bureaucracy always came along for the ride. Unless she was prepared to initiate a formal investigation on the basis of what seemed to Bell to be fairly skimpy evidence—or, more accurately, to persuade Muth County Prosecutor Steve Black to do so, being as how Thornapple Terrace was on his patch—she had to tread very, very lightly. She'd probably have to let a surrogate do the gentle probing.

"Surrogate" was a euphemism for Rhonda Lovejoy, her assistant prosecutor, who specialized in just this sort of sideways, not-quite-official errand. Rhonda's roots in the region ran so deep that when she asked questions, people just assumed she was collecting contact information for a family reunion. It was easy to forget that she worked in the Raythune County prosecutor's office.

Didn't Rhonda have a cousin or two up in Muth County? Bell was almost sure of it. She recalled Rhonda talking about a branch of the Lovejoy clan that had shifted northward, following a rumor of jobs, as prospects in Acker's Gap had steadily dwindled. Maybe Rhonda could, under the guise of visiting her relatives, stop in at Thornapple Terrace and have a look around. Nothing overt. No big deal. And then maybe, if the opportunity presented itself, Rhonda could find a chatty employee and hang out long enough to ask about Harmon Strayer's fate.

A cell ring tone sliced into Bell's thoughts. It was the ring assigned to her twenty-one-year-old daughter, Carla—Adele's "Hello"—and so, with fingers that felt paralyzed with cold despite the protection of gloves, Bell fished the phone out of her purse with extra urgency.

"Sweetie?"

"Hi, Mom."

"Is everything all—"

"Fine. It's *fine*. Why do you always ask me that, first thing? It's like you're expecting to hear that I've screwed up."

"No, I . . ." The conversation needed a reset. Bell changed directions. "It's snowing like crazy here."

"Here, too. Has been for hours. CNN says they might shut down Reagan National. Dulles, too."

Carla lived with five roommates—and an untold number of mice and other anonymous freeloaders—in a tilting, fraying three-story house in Arlington, Virginia. Before that, she had lived with her father, Bell's ex-husband, Sam Elkins, in a condo in Alexandria. She'd spent her senior year at a private school, transferring from Acker's Gap High

School after the terrifying night when she almost died at the hands of a killer whose real target was Bell. Carla had decided to postpone college for a few years, a decision that Bell found keenly disappointing, but she capitulated after sensing Carla's resolve. *Pick your battles,* was the advice everyone had given her. Made sense—for moms as well as for prosecutors.

"Are you home?" Bell asked.

"Yeah. Just watching the snow from my bedroom window. Can't even see the pavement anymore. How about you?"

"Actually, I'm standing in the parking lot of a bar in Blythesburg. Getting ready to head home. Met an old friend for a drink."

"Mom, *come on*—hang up and start driving. That's what you'd be saying to me."

"You're right. I would." Bell turned around and opened the Explorer's door. "Kind of nice, though. Being out in it. Peaceful." She scooted in and pulled the door shut.

"Peaceful, my ass. Go home, Mom. It's a long way from there back to Acker's Gap. With the snow, you're looking at an hour or more."

"Surprised you remember." Bell started the engine, wanting to warm it up before she headed out. She'd have to wait, anyway, for the wipers to shove aside the snow that had congregated on the windshield.

"Oh, I remember all right. And I also remember almost skidding down the mountain when I was driving back home once with Kayleigh Crocker," Carla said, naming one of her best friends from Acker's Gap High School, a young woman whose wildness had continued into adulthood. Bell knew that because, as a prosecutor, she'd had several encounters in court with Kayleigh Crocker and a revolving cast of worthless boyfriends clearly bound for much more significant trouble. "Trash magnet" was the category in which Bell placed Kayleigh Crocker.

"We went to a party in Blythesburg," Carla added. "Winter of junior year."

"Stop right there. Retroactive worry is a mother's prerogative—even though it's totally pointless."

She waited. There had to be more. Her daughter didn't need a specific reason to reach out—Bell loved their casual, spontaneous conversations, and had told Carla so, many times—but she could feel the looming weight of whatever it was that Carla had called her to talk about.

"Sweetie?" Bell said. "What's going on?"

A pause, a brief throat-clearing, and then a flying wedge of words: "I need to come home, Mom. Right away. To Acker's Gap. For good. I'll be there tomorrow."

"But this weather—can't you wait until Monday or Tuesday?"

"You're not *listening* to me. I have to come *now*. Roads will be clear by late morning. Promise I'll be careful."

"One day can't make that much diff—"

"See you tomorrow, Mom."

Chapter Two

Snow fell throughout the night. Behind it came a ferocious cold. The cold set in with a vengeance, sealing the snow in place like quick-drying mortar.

The sun rose on a motionless world.

Bell stood at her living room window, mesmerized by the transformation. She'd seen it before, of course, having lived through many winters—too many, she thought, feeling a stiffness in her right knee and a tweak in her left shoulder that testified to her four-and-a-half decades on the planet. But a total whiteout like this one was always a spectacular surprise.

She was dressed in a pair of red plaid flannel sweatpants and a gargantuan gray sweatshirt. The sweatshirt was rubbed clean through at both elbows, one sleeve was ripped and the collar was unraveling. It was a look she did not even like to share with her mirror. But the getup was warm, dammit. And comfortable.

It was just after seven a.m. She had a mug of coffee nestled in her cupped palms like a battered chalice in a low-rent religious ceremony.

She tried a sip. Too hot—and so she blew on it, and then sipped again. Still too hot.

Well, no matter. Throats could heal, right? Sure they could. She needed the coffee, and she needed it now.

Down the hatch.

She winced, instantly repenting of her decision to face the pain and drink it anyway, and then, as the deliciously bitter black coffee branched through her body like a liquid wake-up call, she repented of her repentance. She was ready now. Ready to face whatever the day might bring.

She took another drink. She did not notice the heat anymore. She had a lot on her mind, and snow was the perfect backdrop for thinking. It was the original blank canvas.

Carla would be arriving today.

Today.

The idea made Bell feel a little dizzy. There was still a slightly dreamlike quality to the idea of her daughter's return, a gauzy, *Can it really be so?* sense of unreality. The fact that the actual picture spreading out in front of her was so altered from its usual state—it was a tidy, homogenized wash of white, not a tangled, unruly mess of brown yards and gray street and broken sidewalks—added to the surreal feeling, the feeling of a landscape and a life unplugged from their usual sources of color and action.

Bell had yearned for Carla's return for so long now that she had forgotten what it felt like to live without that fierce desire, that ache in the very center of her being. She had never told Carla how deeply she missed her, because she did not want her daughter to feel guilty about her choice. Bell never discussed it with her ex-husband, either, or with her best friend, Nick Fogelsong. It was the most profound truth of her life and she had kept it hidden, as if it were a guilty secret.

And so the sadness had tunneled deeper inside her. Life closed back over it.

Carla was coming home to reassess things. Okay, not just "things"—*everything*. That's what she had told her mother last night toward the end of their phone conversation, after announcing that she simply had to drive there Sunday. No delay. She needed new skies. Well, new-old, anyway. She'd quit her job. Found someone to sublet her room in the Arlington house. Her car was already packed. She would hit the road first thing tomorrow—now, today—and point her Kia Soul in the direction of Acker's Gap. She knew all about driving in heavy snow, she said. She'd checked the tread on her tires, had all the fluids topped off. She'd be fine.

Bell was thrilled at the prospect of Carla's return. Of course. Of course she was.

But part of her wondered—she *had* to wonder, it was her *responsibility* to wonder—if a small, fading, isolated and economically bereft town in West Virginia, a place from which a lot of people seemed to run screaming the very first second they had the chance, was really where Carla belonged, long-term. Or for however long her daughter ended up staying.

Clearly there was a lot more to this abrupt homecoming than Carla had let on; something had happened in the young woman's life, something that Bell would have to question her about, slowly and carefully, once she was settled in. It was not the kind of detective work that Bell relished. But it was necessary.

Carla's bombshell had shoved everything else out of her mind, including Darlene Strayer's request. Now it came back to her. She felt a touch of guilt about having forgotten so easily. She would talk to Rhonda Lovejoy. Ask her to spend a few hours poking around the care facility, asking questions.

Done.

Back to Carla.

She envisioned her daughter's long narrow face and short dark hair. The set of her chin. The sound of her voice. Carla had a lot of Bell in her, but she had a lot of her father in her, too. She had Bell's stubbornness and grit but she had Sam's analytical skills. And his sense of humor. And his charm—that golden charm that accounted for so much of his success. Carla had her mother's eyes and she had her father's chin. She had parts of both of them. The combination was mysterious and wonderful and slightly daffy and mildly exasperating and—well, it just *was*. It was.

Her love for Carla was like an underground river, sweeping along so fast and so deep inside her that she took the slight humming sound in the background of her life for granted. It was always, always running.

Another swallow of coffee. Her throat, she hoped, had built up enough scar tissue in the last minute or so to handle the heat. Bell realized that she had been looking at the snow without actually seeing it. Now she squinted out the window, exploring the particulars.

She gauged the snow's depth to be about fifteen to eighteen inches. Not impenetrable, especially not for the heavy-duty, all-wheel-drive vehicles favored by people who lived in the midst of mountains—but something you had to consider, to factor into your plans, before leaving your house. Not a single tire track had yet marred the street's frozen perfection. A county road crew would come along eventually. The slowpoke snowplow would do what it could. But the crew, quite rightly, would focus on the main arteries first. They might not reach the residential streets until late this afternoon.

Now there was activity. Bell watched as a black Chevy Blazer fought its way through the thick drifts that striped Shelton Avenue like nature's speed bumps. Every few feet the Blazer stalled out and fell back, stymied by ridge after ridge of stubborn snow. The driver was forced to put it briefly in reverse and then attack the street from another angle. The sound of the engine—the chopped-up *vrrrr vrrrr vrrrr* of its constant revving—had a kind of seething frustration embedded in it, and an *Are you freakin'* kidding *me?* weariness, too. Bell assumed it was just channeling the feelings of the driver.

The Blazer stopped in front of her house. "Stopped" was a generous interpretation; it really just stalled and then quit. The door flapped open. A man in a thick black overcoat and knee-high black boots fought his way out. He shuddered briefly at the cold. He closed the door behind him. Bell took note of what she'd seen a second ago but had willfully chosen to ignore: the round white county seal on the door, encircled by the words RAYTHUNE COUNTY SHERIFF'S DEPARTMENT.

No question about it. This was official business.

Bell scarcely had time to set her mug on the mantel and pull on a ratty, dignity-preserving bathrobe before the knocks came, a bluster of four serious-sounding assaults on the ancient oak door. There was a doorbell in plain sight, but for some reason, Deputy Jake Oakes—she'd recognized him as he lurched and plunged up the long front walk, or at least in the general vicinity of what constituted his best guess as to where the walk might be lurking under the snow, and then struggled up the porch steps—always preferred to knock, loud and long. He had been a Golden Gloves boxer in his youth, he'd told her once, and she wondered if he secretly missed using his fists on a regular basis.

She opened the door. The deputy's nose and cheeks were cherry-red from the cold. His blue eyes watered profusely. He seemed slightly stunned by the ordeal of having traveled on foot just a few yards in this weather. His lips, she saw, were cracked and flaking.

"Sorry to barge in on you like this," he said.

Bell nodded. She did not know the details of the situation that had prompted his visit, but she was sure its essence could be summarized in a single word:

Trouble.

Darlene Strayer's body had been found just before sunrise. That's what Oakes told her, his words flat and informational. He knew she preferred to hear it that way: cold facts arranged in chronological sequence. She didn't appreciate hesitation. She didn't like it when people hemmed and hawed and hedged, trying to pretty things up, temper the blow.

A trucker named Felton Groves had come upon the mangled wreckage off to the side of the road. Darlene had been ejected from the Audi when it slammed into a pine tree about twenty yards beyond the tight interior curve of the nasty switchback. Groves was negotiating that same *Help me Jesus* stretch of the descent when he spotted the carnage, his headlights splashing up on the crusty white snow like a flung bucketful of some glittering substance.

That description, Oakes said, glancing up from his notes, had come from Groves himself. The trucker fancied himself a bit of a poet.

Groves had immediately realized what he was looking at: a driver's fatal misjudgment. The vehicle, going too fast around the curve, had sailed clean off the road in a long solemn arc until the tree put a sudden stop to its progress. Groves pulled over, yanked on his emergency brake. He approached the scene. One quick glimpse was all he needed. The Audi's front end was a corrugated mess. A torqued body lay facedown on a mound of snow about ten yards from the drastically foreshortened car.

At that point, Groves said, all the poetry fled from his mind. He called 911. He did not check for a pulse. "Maybe I should have," he'd murmured uncertainly to Deputy Oakes, once the paramedics had trussed up the driver on a gurney and slotted the gurney in the back and taken off. The light on top of the van spun around and around, draping the landscape in dire pulses of red, but the paramedic behind the wheel had to exercise restraint; the road surface was compromised by the heavy snowfall as yet untouched by any plow, and by at least an inch of ice under the snow. It was strange, Groves remarked to the deputy, to see an emergency vehicle just creeping along like that, tentative, reined in, only moving forward in small cautious spurts. "Yeah," Oakes had said. "Sure is."

He still had nightmares, Groves had added—unprompted—to Oakes, on account of an accident scene he'd once come upon near Macon, Georgia, fifteen years ago. Eight kids, two parents, nobody wearing seat belts in a van that for some unknown reason had gone left of center and ended up smashing headfirst into a tractor-trailer rig. He'd stopped his truck that time, too, and jumped out. Once again, it was before the cops had gotten there, and the air was still quivering from the ferocious impact, as if the earth itself still could not believe what had just happened, the violence of it, the terrible surprise. The bodies looked like laundry tossed every which way in a ditch. He would never forget the sight.

That was why he'd kept his distance when he saw the body in the snow, he told Deputy Oakes. That was why he hadn't gone closer, hadn't looked for signs of life, hadn't called out, "Hey—you okay?" He knew she wasn't okay. And frankly, he was worried about his sleep. For the rest of his life. He could not take on yet another reason for insomnia, another trigger. But it bothered him, just the same. "Maybe she was still alive. Maybe if I'd . . ."

"No," Oakes had replied. He was matter-of-fact about it, tapping the eraser end of the little pencil back into his shirt pocket, and then rebuttoning his overcoat against the phenomenal cold. You could not use a pen in these temperatures; the ink froze. "Guaranteed—she was dead when she hit the ground. Never had a chance."

Odd to find that consoling, Oakes would think later. Odd that instant death sounded like a blessing.

But it was. Given the condition of the body, it was. Definitely, it was.

They had found Bell's name on a handwritten note in the victim's coat pocket. That was why the deputy was here now. He had written down the words of the note in his little spiral-bound book; the original was in an evidence bag, stowed in a locked room at the courthouse. This was not a criminal investigation—it was an accident, plain and simple—but they did things right in Raythune County.

"The paper said, 'Bell Elkins. Eight p.m. Tie Yard Tavern.' And then your cell number." Oakes looked up from his notebook to meet Bell's eye. "Car was registered to an Alice Darlene Strayer. Nobody's made the formal ID yet—we're having a hell of a time locating a next of kin, there's no answer on the home phone—but the body matches the photo on the driver's license. And on her federal ID. Looks like it was expired—the federal ID, not the license—but she still had it in her purse."

"Yes," Bell said.

She was too stunned at first to offer more than one word. It was impossible to believe. Just a few hours ago she had been sitting with her in the bar. She could remember the way Darlene's hand looked when she lifted the whiskey glass. She could remember the sound of her voice, the expression on her face. And now all of it—the hand, the voice, the face—was gone. Darlene Strayer was dead.

Bell realized that she and Oakes were standing in the foyer, facing each other, in radically different states of attire. She wore a pink chenille robe and sweats and slippers. He wore a brown uniform and a black wool greatcoat, and a black toboggan instead of his usual flat-brimmed hat. The snow was melting from his boots onto the wide-plank flooring. Already two pools had formed around his feet.

In other circumstances, the disparity in their appearances would have amused them. Neither commented upon it now. Not even Oakes, who presumably kept a few choice wisecracks on ice just in case he ever encountered a prosecutor in a bathrobe.

"Anyway," he said, "I needed to notify you ASAP. And get a few basic facts for the timeline."

"Yes. Of course."

He sensed her shock and kept his demeanor businesslike. Normally, Jake Oakes was a joker, a scamp, a cutup; he and Bell often clashed over his reliance on the inappropriate quip as his primary communication tool. Not today. He was suitably serious. She appreciated that.

"We met at the Tie Yard last night," Bell went on. "I know Darlene from law school. Haven't seen her in years. She's originally from Barr County. Lives in D.C. now. But she wanted to get together. She left the bar just a few minutes before I did. And she's a good driver, far as I know." Bell realized she was still in the grip of the present tense. It was too soon to change.

"Right." He wrote some words in his notebook.

"And like I said, she left before me. Why didn't I come across the accident? It doesn't make sense."

"Can't say."

Bell put her left hand on the newel post of the stair railing close to where she stood. She needed to hold on to something. Oakes knew better than to offer assistance.

"What was the cause, Jake? I mean—yeah, the roads were in bad shape, with the snow and all. That switchback can be a bitch. And it was dark. But Darlene knows her way around these mountains. Was there anything else? Any other contributing factors?"

Oakes looked at her.

"Ma'am?" he said. He seemed slightly perplexed.

Bell waited. She did not know what was going on, and waited for him to enlighten her.

"Ma'am," Oakes repeated. He was tentative now, as if she might be testing him. "We don't have the toxicology report yet, of course, but it's an easy guess. There was a strong smell of alcohol on the body. And vomit in the car. She was drunk. That's how she lost control and hit the tree. She was impaired."

"No." Bell's objection was sharp and quick. "No way. I was with her. She had a few sips from one drink. That's it. She was *definitely* not drunk."

"Ma'am, I've already checked with the bartender at the Tie Yard. He was none too happy to have to answer his door first thing on a Sunday morning, but he remembered her right away. Recognized the picture. He served her four shots in a row. Some guy came in and sat down next to her at the bar, he said. Looked like they hit it off right away. The guy bought her a few more. By that time, she was slurring her words. Bartender finally had to cut her off."

Bell was irritated now. "And I'm telling you he's wrong. I was *there*, Jake. He's got her confused with somebody else. Darlene had one drink. And we walked out together—just the two of us. She was *fine*. Totally sober."

The deputy flipped a few pages in his notebook, finding the passage he wanted. "What time did you leave the bar?"

"Nine thirty at the latest. I was home by ten forty-five."

"Well, that's our problem, right there." He tapped the page. "Bartender says he came on duty about ten. She was already there, shotgunning her drinks. She didn't clear out until after one. She was pissed as hell when he told her she'd had enough."

Bell let the information settle. "She must have gone back. She must have pulled over somewhere and waited for me to pass—and then doubled back. Returned to the bar."

"Could be."

"Still doesn't make sense. Even back in law school, I never saw Darlene touch so much as a beer. I mean—*never*. And nobody gossiped about her having a problem with alcohol, either. Believe me—if she did, there would have been talk."

Oakes frowned. "Okay, well—there was something in her other coat pocket. A blue coin. About the size of a poker chip."

"What was it?"

"A sobriety medallion. From Alcoholics Anonymous. Represents one year's sobriety. Looks like your friend might have been hiding a secret or two."

Aren't we all, Bell thought grimly. *Aren't we all.*

Three Boys

1938

Their names were Harmon Strayer, Vic Plumley, and Alvie Sherrill, and they were always together.

If you saw Harm, you knew you'd see Alvie, and if you saw Vic, you could set your watch by the fact that Alvie and Harm would be coming along less than a minute later. They lived on the same block and they were roughly the same age. They had each been born in 1926, and so the milestones of life—first day of school, first paying job, first kiss—came to them at the same time. They were each other's reference points and touchstones of memory. Later, when they were middle-aged men, if one of them blanked on a date or a detail, one of the other two could fill it in for him. So nothing was forgotten.

They lived in Norbitt, West Virginia. It was a small town and a dingy one, the county seat of Barr County. Barr County, too, was small and dingy. Town and county echoed each other's insignificance, like two smudged mirrors set face-to-face, forever reflecting back a third-rate version of eternity.

It was a town that did not matter, in a county nobody cared about, in a state that people overlooked except when they were making jokes about it.

But that was about to change.

There was a darkness gathering in the skies, a darkness that soon would swallow up the world. Places like Norbitt were about to become as important as the great cities—London, Paris, Vienna, Moscow—because the men who rescued the future were born here. They were born in the small towns of West Virginia, and in the small towns of Kentucky and Arkansas and Kansas and Maine and Oklahoma and Montana and Pennsylvania. The fact that most of the world had never heard of these towns would not matter anymore.

These three boys, like boys from other threadbare, soiled towns in threadbare, soiled states, were just a few years away from the great adventure of their lives: saving the world.

Vic Plumley was the restless one. The hungry one. The one with the most potential. He was big and handsome, with thick dark hair and eyes that had started out as pale, almost translucent blue, but by the time he was in junior high school, had turned a deep indigo shade that made the things he said seem earnest and sincere, even profound, if he looked at you a certain way when he was saying them.

His father, Frank Plumley, was a salesman, and he was richer and more successful than the other fathers. His mother, Vivian, was prettier than the other mothers. So Vic had a sense of himself *as* himself—as, that is, a real person, a person with desires and a destiny. And he wanted out. He had been led to believe that he could achieve things in the world, real things. Norbitt would never be big enough for him. Barr County would not be big enough, either. The whole state of West Virginia, as a matter of fact, was too small to hold all of Vic Plumley's aspirations. He once complained to Harm that being born in West Virginia was like buying the wrong-sized suitcase. You got it home and then you looked at everything you needed to fit in there, and you realized you'd made a mistake. You needed something bigger. It was infuriating.

On the day of Vic's twelfth birthday—Alvie had turned twelve the month before, and Harmon would turn twelve in a few months—the three of them sat on the back stoop of Vic's house. It was a Saturday morning in the early spring. The air felt rinsed and clean, which was unusual; typically the air in Norbitt smelled as if it carried flecks of something foul in it. Some of the mothers wouldn't even hang their family's wet clothes outside to dry on the line because, they said, the smell would get in there and stick. You'd have to wash those clothes all over again. And again after that. But today—ah, today was glorious, as if a seine net had been dragged across the sky, catching all the dark particles, separating them out, leaving only the clarity, the sparkle.

In the distance, the mountains were silver-black triangles. The peaks looked as if they had been dusted with confectioner's sugar.

Three boys: Vic, Harm, and Alvie.

Vic was short for Victor. Harmon was commonly known as Harm. Alvie, though, was always Alvie. Some people thought it was a nickname—a diminutive for Albert, say, or Alfred or Alvin—but it was not. The name on his birth certificate was Alvie Sherrill. No middle name. The Sherrills did not believe in middle names. Middle names were too fancy. Too showy. Too sissified. Alvie's father, Leonard Sherrill, was a Baptist minister, and he knew the devil could smell pride on a person, and use it to get his red hooks into that person's soul, the way a wild animal is instantly aware of a garbage can with the lid left off, even if it's miles away.

Vic had already gotten his birthday present from his father: a two-year-old Ford pickup. Vic had been driving since he was nine years old. His father would put a Charleston phone book on the seat so that Vic could see over the dashboard of the family Packard. Frank Plumley rode along, too, on those initial journeys, sitting sideways in the passenger seat so that he could watch his boy at the wheel. Frank kept his right arm thrust straight out, bracing himself against the dash. Just in case. He had a lot of faith in Vic's abilities—the kid had great reflexes and crack eyesight—but still. Nine years old.

Now Vic was twelve, and there would be no stopping him. First thing that morning, as he had just related to his two best friends, his father had come downstairs and sort of burst into the kitchen. He threw something at him. Vic did not know what it was, and so he turned his head, not wanting to get beaned, and the keys landed in his corn flakes. The milk splashed all over the tablecloth.

"You're kidding," Alvie said. He laughed through his nose, in and out, like a snorting horse rejecting his feed. "What'd your mom say?"

"She was damned upset, tell you that," Vic replied. The cursing he had always done in private had recently made its debut in public. Harm and Alvie were deeply admiring; they, too, often said damn or hell or shit or cock or fuck or even the most taboo of all—goddamn, notorious for its blasphemy—in conversation with each other, but they still lacked the courage to utter a curse word out in the wide world. At school, for instance. It was an especially high hurdle for Alvie, the preacher's son.

But Vic had done it. He had started a few weeks ago, and now every other sentence was spiced with a damn or a hell. He didn't care who was listening. His foul mouth just added to his legend.

"And then what?" Harm said.

"My old man said, 'Whaddaya think those keys go to, son?' "

"And what did you say?" The question came from Alvie.

"I said, 'I don't know. Why don't you tell me, Pop?' "

Alvie squirmed a little in his place on the stoop, half in pleasure, half in apprehension. He knew what would have happened if he had ever talked that way to his own father, and he could not help but picture it. The Reverend Sherrill would have unloaded on him. No question. Alvie had been warned to keep a civil tongue in his head. To speak with respect to his elders. Something as fresh as "Why don't you tell me, Pop?" would have netted him a fist-sized welt on the side of his face, a face so gray and narrow that Alvie had been told more than once that he looked like a rat. And he did, too, but not just because of the color and shape of his face. His front teeth protruded brashly, and he had small eyes and a pointy nose.

"And what did your father say to that?" Harm said. He, too, was enthralled.

Vic leaned back. He was on the second step from the top, and he arched his back against the front edge of the top step and spread his elbows, balancing himself. He stretched out his legs and kicked the back of his sneakers against the wood of the third step down. First one shoe, and then the other shoe. Harm and Alvie sat on the top step, on either side of Vic. They scooted over, to give him room to sprawl. Vic liked to sprawl.

"Pop said, 'Well sir, I heard a rumor it was somebody's birthday. That true?'"

"And what did you say to *that*?" Harm asked.

"Lemme guess," Alvie said, breaking in eagerly before Vic could answer. He was giddy with certainty. "I bet you said, 'Hell, yes, it's somebody's birthday. It's *my* fucking birthday.' Right? Ain't that what you said?"

Alvie had overstepped. He had gotten caught up in the story and forgotten himself. He knew it right away. Vic did not say anything for a long time. It was probably no more than a minute, but it felt like forever to Alvie. He could swear he felt his life leaking away, like a glass of milk he'd accidentally knocked over. He'd have to make it up to Vic somehow. He was a fool.

"No," Vic said. His voice was no longer lazy and no longer amused. It was cold. "That's not what I said. What I said was, 'You know whose birthday it is, you fat old man, and if those keys belong to a car, it damned well better have gas in the tank.' That's what I said."

Neither Harm nor Alvie believed for a second that Vic Plumley had talked that way to his father. Vic was just showing off. But you could not challenge him.

"And then," Vic said, and once again his voice had that smug, lazy sound to it, "he took me outside and he showed me what was parked in the driveway." Vic sat up straight. "He'd parked it right over there. So's I could see it, first thing."

They all looked. They were awestruck, just as they'd been when they arrived here today and Vic came out the back door, slamming the door behind him, and they saw what was sitting in the Plumley driveway, the widest driveway on the whole block: a cream-colored 1936 Ford pickup with red trim. It was a beaut. That was the word Harm used when he first spotted it, and Alvie started to make fun of the word but then Vic said, "I like that word, Harm. A beaut. That's just what it is," and so Alvie had to say that he liked the word, too. It was the perfect word: beaut. Vic's birthday present was a beaut.

The pickup had a flathead V8 with a three-speed transmission and a 12-volt electrical system. Its top speed was just over 80 mph. It was not brand new, but it was only two years old, and that was fine. That was plenty close enough to new.

Harm and Alvie were agog. They had not even ridden in it yet, and they were almost speechless with admiration.

There were only two rules, Vic told them: He had to let his father know when he was going to drive it. And he couldn't take it past the Norbitt city limits unless his father was with him.

The legalities of a twelve-year-old driving a car were not a concern. The state of West Virginia had been issuing driver's licenses since 1917, but only began testing drivers—the test was a formality, nothing more—in 1931. You were supposed to be sixteen to get a license, but driving without one was a ho-hum offense. The deputies didn't care. They had other things on their minds. Besides, if you were wealthy enough to have a car, then you—and your family—were the kind of people whom the deputies went out of their way to please.

Suddenly Vic's mother was there. She startled them, opening the screen door and initiating the drawn-out creak of its tired hinges. They had been gazing at the Ford and were ignorant of her presence until they heard that creak. Then they turned and looked up, taking in the shape of her, the way she held her arm out straight to prop open the door. Her other hand was curled and perched on her hip. Her hair was long and thick and blond. Harm felt his heart jump in his chest like a fish.

"You boys have your breakfast yet?" she said. She had a low, soft voice, a voice with a purr in it. That voice had a peculiar effect on Harm. He felt, along with the flopping heart, the heat rising in his cheeks and a flush moving across the back of his neck. And that was not the only thing that happened to his body when he was in the presence of Vic's mother. The other thing he couldn't talk about, not even with Alvie—and God knows he would never discuss it with Vic.

Harm's mother, Sylvia, swore that Vivian Plumley rehearsed that voice of hers, trained it, so that it would sound sexy and "drive the men wild." That was Sylvia's exact phrase: "drive the men wild." Like most of the women in Norbitt, Sylvia did not like Vivian Plumley. Harm had overhead his mother and some of the other mothers talking about Vivian, claiming that she had been observed at the edge of the woods a few months back, standing by her car, shouting until she was hoarse, trying to permanently lower her voice. Make it sexier. Was it true? Maybe. Harm didn't know. But the other things about her— her jutting breasts and her full hips and her mouth, a mouth that was never without a generous splash of red lipstick—had nothing to do with shouting at the woods.

Harm could not think about her too much. If he did, things happened to him, confusing things. Things he could not control.

"Yes, ma'am," Alvie said. "I had my breakfast."

"Harmon? How about you?" Vivian Plumley said, looking down at him.

"Me, too, ma'am."

She seemed a little disappointed. Harm wondered if he should have said no. If he had lied, she would have invited him into the kitchen and he could have been in the same room with her for as long as it took him to eat a second breakfast. Oatmeal, probably, is what it would have been. Or maybe pancakes. Hard to say.

The screen door closed. She did not slam it. Only kids slammed screen doors, Harm thought.

For some reason, he wished she had slammed it. Just let it go. That would have put something final and absolute between the moment when Vivian Plumley was there, and the next moment, when she wasn't there. A dividing line. A boundary. But without the slam, it was as if she might still be there behind him, waiting at the screen door, watching. He knew she wasn't—she never spied on them, not like his own mother did—but without the slam, she *could* be. She could still be standing there, with that slight smile on her lips, a smile of faint amusement but not ridicule or mockery. Without the slam, she continued to be present. It was as if she spent the day with him. Invisible—but still there. Distracting him.

Harm thought about Vivian Plumley lots of days, of course, but this day was one that he would remember for as long as he remembered things.

Because this day—the day of Vic's twelfth birthday—was the day they committed murder. The three of them did it. Each boy was equally responsible.

Okay, well. Maybe Vic was a *little* more responsible. That's what Harm and Alvie both thought later, and who could say it wasn't so, but they kept that conclusion to themselves. Because it seemed grubby and small and disloyal. In the event, they agreed that the blame would be apportioned equally, that they would think of it one way and one way only, and that was how they would learn to live with what they had done.

Chapter Three

The snow rose high on both sides of the road. The plow had been out here early, its blade pushing back a thick continuous curl of snow like a razor slicing through shaving cream on pitted gray skin. Carla had not actually seen the plow—that was hours ago—but she could imagine it doing its work based on the size of the ramparts lining the road: the heavy scraping sound, the patient, straight-ahead effort.

She was grateful for the clear road. She needed to make this journey in a hurry, before she changed her mind.

She had stopped just once.

"All outta Diet Dr Pepper." The old woman behind the counter at the little store had offered five words and no smile. She wore an oversized flannel shirt. Her hair was a runaway blaze of white fuzz. She looked very tired. Everything sagged—her face, her breasts, the skin on her neck. "Got Coke and Sprite and Dew, though."

Carla wanted a can of Diet Dr Pepper. No: She *had* to have a can of Diet Dr Pepper. It was a symbol, not a liquid. It was her reward to herself for having gotten this far, and it was her incentive to keep going. As her agitation had increased, she'd persuaded herself that if she could just get a can of Diet Dr Pepper, she'd be okay. It would be a sign—a sign that she was on the right track.

After that, she told herself, her mind would lie quietly for a while. She'd be able to make it the rest of the way home. And once she was home, she could figure out how to fix the mess she'd made of everything.

She had spotted the store on the right-hand side of the road just after she crossed the West Virginia state line. JUNNIOR'S, the sign said. A misspelling, she surmised. Or the petty revenge of a sign painter who had yet to be paid for the last job he'd done for Junior. Or maybe it really was how the guy's mother had spelled his name on the birth certificate. Could be. Anyway, Carla turned in. She parked between ruts of snow. She struggled through the shin-high mounds of it that Junior or Junnior—or whoever was in charge here—had not bothered to clear away from the entrance.

She headed for the rumbling cooler in the back. She searched in vain for a white-and-maroon can of Diet Dr Pepper. There had to be one, right? She picked through the assortment. Her distress was growing.

Dammit. They were out.

Maybe they had more somewhere else. In a back room, maybe. Maybe it was just a matter of replenishing the stock.

Carla returned to the front of the store. The old woman was having a frisky go at a thumbnail with a pair of rusty clippers, grunting with satisfaction at each tiny snip. She finished her grooming, such as it was, before looking up. Carla had to ask twice about the Diet Dr Pepper. The first time, the woman frowned and shook her head, as if whatever language Carla was speaking was not spoken here.

Then the clerk delivered the blow: No Diet Dr Pepper.

Carla felt a rising panic. She knew she was being ridiculous—*for God's sake,* she told herself, *it's a freakin' can of pop*—but she had been so focused on getting it, so intent on procuring this one small token as a sort of reward for the progress she had made on the drive, that this bulletin that it would not be forthcoming had devastated her.

The panic gave way to outrage. How the hell could they be out of Diet Dr Pepper? A dump like this was *supposed* to keep staples in stock. It had an *obligation.* Why else would it even *exist,* except to assuage specific cravings for items with no nutritional value? Carla took a quick disdainful glimpse around the dilapidated store and its three rows of plywood shelves, shelves featuring little more than a couple of pyramids of dusty Spam cans and six jumbo rolls of Hefty paper towels and a shiny red clutch of Wavy Lay's and several packages of Double Stuf Oreos.

"We got fresh coffee if that'll help," the old woman added.

At least she was trying. But that made Carla feel even worse: Was her fragile emotional state *that* obvious? The surly old woman would not be offering alternatives had Carla not seemed right on the edge— ready to faint or puke or pitch a fit. The clerk surely did not want any trouble in her store this morning. The snow was bad enough. Who needed to deal with a lunatic in a rage because they were all out of Diet Dr Pepper?

"You okay, honey?"

This time the old woman's voice broke into Carla's thoughts like as broomstick crashing through a plate-glass window. The clerk seemed honestly concerned about her.

Carla flinched. The unexpected kindness had caught her off-guard. And so, just like that, she started to sob.

The first hour of her trip from the D.C. area had been on the interstate. Plenty of traffic, even on a cold Sunday morning, with plenty of places to stop. Carla did not stop. She kept right on going.

The exit showed up a little before she was expecting it to. It dumped her out on another four-lane highway. Not an interstate, but close. Forty minutes later, she made another turn. Now all resemblance to an interstate disappeared. She felt as if she had driven off the edge of the world—and landed, weirdly, not somewhere in outer space, bobbing amidst stars and planets and dark matter, but in another universe altogether. A universe with its own special brand of dark matter.

This road was a shortcut to Raythune County, used by natives or by people whose GPS systems had spitefully betrayed them.

Gone were the outlet stores with their endless iterations of brand names—Chico and Nautica and Pottery Barn—and the soulless strip malls offering tax prep and pizza by the slice and tanning beds and picture framing and PC repair. Gone, too, were the fast-food places that tended to pop up in multiples, as if the initial one had released spores that lodged in the soil and grew a new franchise every month or so, just to keep the first one company.

The back roads of West Virginia were very different from the interstates that coiled around big cities. That was obvious. But it was the *degree* of the difference that always astonished Carla, even though she had made this trip so many, many times, first as a child in the backseat of her parents' car and now as an adult driving her own car.

How could everything change so quickly, so absolutely? She meant the road—but right now, the same question could be applied to her life.

She was surrounded by dense white scribbles of woods and by the occasional gray zipper of a train track. In the distance, the mountains crowded along the horizon, sheepish-looking giants doing their best to meld seamlessly with a sky that arched over this remote and mysterious world. Today those mountains had snow on their shoulders, a mantle of white that helped them disappear into the bleak winter backdrop.

Yes, Carla knew this road well. And yet she was struck anew by its absolute singularity. Interstates were ubiquitous; driving on an interstate, you could be in St. Louis or Phoenix or Atlanta or Dallas or Baltimore. You could be in Miami or Chicago. Anywhere. A back road, though, had its own flavor and color and character. Its own brand.

It was more than a matter of what you saw out the window. It was also a feeling. Leaving the four-lane highway, she could have sworn she had felt a shift in the barometric pressure. There was a raw new element in the air once she headed down the road to Acker's Gap.

To her home.

Granted, she had not lived there for several years—but it was still home. It would always be home. Had her mother tried to convince her of that, back when she had first decided to leave Acker's Gap and go live with her father, Carla would have rejected the idea, instantly and fervently. She might have even been nasty about it, sprinkling in a few profanities, just for the shock value.

No, she would have declared hotly to her mother, scowling, pouting, *don't you* dare *say that. Don't you* dare *try to tell me that this hellhole is my home, my destiny. It's* not. *I don't belong here. Maybe you do, Mom—but I don't. And I never will, okay?*

She did not feel that way anymore.

Now Acker's Gap was her only hope.

The headaches had started about four months ago. Furious, merciless headaches that created a sort of nonstop mayhem in her head, a relentless expansion and contraction, expansion and contraction. After that came the insomnia. It made her crazy. One of her roommates, Kurt Leftwich, gave her one of his Ambien tablets. He meant well, but it was a disaster. She woke up on the back porch at three in the morning, screaming and flailing. Kurt and his girlfriend, Beverly, heard the commotion and ran out and caught her fists, subdued her, brought her back inside. They settled her down. Or at least they tried to.

What she did not tell them—what she did not tell anyone—was that she was having flashbacks. Was that the right word? It didn't sound right. Because she did not relive the events themselves, the terrible events from four years ago.

She did not see, once again, three old men murdered in a fast-food joint.

She did not see, once again, her best friend, Lonnie Prince, dying as the bullets pierced his chest. She was not forced to watch his eyes one more time as the light fell out of them.

She did not have to repeat the moment when the shooter tied her to a chair in the middle of an abandoned building and pointed a gun at her face.

No. Her flashbacks were not like that.

What she relived were the emotions. The *feelings* were what came pounding back, splitting her, like hard stakes driven into the softest parts of her brain. The memories were all sense-memories: panic and fear and an acid-drip of dread.

Her mother had saved her life. Her mother had rescued her from the drug dealer who called himself Chill, the punk with the gun. And Nick Fogelsong saved her, too. He was sheriff at the time, and he was the one who'd fired the shot at Chill. Carla had been woozy and confused from a severe concussion, but she had roused herself in time to watch Chill stagger and fall, blood bubbling from his perforated torso.

For the next few years, things had been okay. She had dealt with the memories. Pushed them back. Locked them away. She was helped by a good counselor, a woman her dad had found for her. Carla saw her twice a week. Three times, if she needed it. And a lot of times, she needed it. Being away from Acker's Gap made a difference; that was Carla's theory, anyway. She was in a new place with a new life.

She graduated from high school. She had good friends. She had a serious boyfriend—his name was Greg Balzercak—but neither one of them was sure about where things were going, or where they wanted them to go. So they were taking a break. He was in Paraguay now, in the Peace Corps. They kept in touch. Sort of. Who knew what would happen when he got back? She had decided that college was not what she wanted right now. Maybe later. Half-sick with apprehension, she had told her mom about her decision. She knew Bell wasn't happy about it, but she did not argue. Same with her dad: disappointment, but no fireworks. *Your life—your call.* That was the essence of what both of them said. It was a relief.

She had moved into the house in Arlington. She had an okay job. Eventually she quit that one and got a better one. Everything was going fine.

And then, as of four months ago, it wasn't. It wasn't going fine at all.

The symptoms hit: the headaches. The insomnia. The feeling-flashbacks. With no warning the world would lurch sideways, and when it did, she ended up doing odd things to try to shock it into getting upright again. Things she had never done before. Bad things. One *especially* bad thing. She knew better, but she could not help herself; she was desperate, and she had to do something to steady herself. Something outlandish. Something to knock her crazy spinning thoughts back into a normal rhythm. Something wild and shocking and hard.

Something that would serve as a sort of emotional defibrillator. That was how she rationalized it. She needed something to stun her back toward normalcy.

She lost weight, because she could not eat, because the thought of food revolted her, and instead of expressing concern, most of her friends asked her what her secret was: Atkins, South Beach? Vegetarian? Vegan?

Many times, out of the blue, she could not catch her breath. She would be at work or hanging out with her housemates and she would start sweating. She could not focus. She thought she was going to pass out. She was barely twenty-one, but the first time it happened, she was pretty sure she was having a heart attack. The second time, too. And the third and fourth. The moment eventually passed, but that did not matter.

The fact that it wasn't a heart attack the last time it happened did not mean that it wasn't a heart attack *this* time. Or maybe a stroke. Or something.

Saturday afternoon, she had crawled under the thick down comforter on the bed in her tiny room. She closed her eyes. She waited to die.

She did not die.

A few hours later, she got out of bed and fired off an e-mail. About a job she'd seen advertised. A job in Acker's Gap. And then she called her mother and told her she was coming home.

Sunlight smacked the peaks of piled-up snow lining the road, bouncing back into her eyes and momentarily blinding her. Carla adjusted the visor. She hadn't brought her sunglasses. She hadn't brought a lot of things. In fact, she had left a ton of junk behind. More than just sunglasses. She'd only taken her laptop and a makeup kit and a couple of books and some bras and panties and an extra pair of jeans and a few sweaters. She'd just stuffed everything into her backpack and thrown it onto the passenger seat and taken off. She'd text Skylar later. Skylar had the room next to hers. Skylar would dump the rest of her stuff in a box and ship it to her in Acker's Gap. No rush, she had told Skylar. Whenever.

This was a rare straight stretch of road. Carla was able to see a long way down it. She had left the store an hour ago. She'd finally finished crying, wiping her nose with the sleeve of her coat. *Gross,* she had thought, even while she was doing it. The clerk watched her. Then the old woman forced her to take a can of Diet Coke, even though Carla didn't want it. *Here, honey, c'mon—it's free, okay? You don't look so good and you need sumpin'. Here.* She had pushed the cold wet can into Carla's flaccid hand. *Sorry we don't have no Dr Pepper but this'll do ya right 'til you can get summa that.*

And then Carla was back out on the old country road, which for the most part wound around and around in tight corkscrews, wriggling and twisting around frozen-over creeks and snow-matted fields and abandoned barns that looked seconds away from total collapse. That's why this sudden stretch of straightness felt like a gift. For once, she could actually see where she was headed.

The bumpy walls of snow on both sides of the road created a kind of tunnel effect. Instead of feeling closed in or trapped, though, instead of feeling suffocated, Carla found the narrowing to be . . . *comfortable*. Peaceful. It cushioned her. Protected her.

She was going home.

Kurt and Skylar, two of her roommates she liked the best and was closest to, had tried to argue her out of it, telling her that she was going back into what Skylar called "the belly of the beast"—returning to the very place where all the bad things had happened, and where things never changed. Skylar was an African-American woman from Brooklyn, New York. She had family members, she told Carla, who lived in places where a black face was an anomaly—and not a welcome one. On her visits to those relatives, she explained, she had realized that you can't make people be what they don't want to be. You just have to live your life somewhere else. It's not worth the energy to be angry and upset all the time. Skylar could not imagine why *anybody* would want to go back to a tiny mountain town in the middle of nowhere, once she had managed to get out.

Especially not after Carla told her what she had gone through there.

But Carla persisted. "I'm going," she had said. "First thing tomorrow. It's what I have to do, okay?"

She did not tell Kurt and Skylar the rest of the story: *I'm afraid I'm losing my mind.* And when she did lose her mind, she wanted to be in a place where they knew her. She wouldn't be able to tell her mother what was really going on—Bell would feel responsible, she would feel guilty about it all, and Carla could not do that to her, and nor could Carla deal with her mother's apologies and her sadness—but she wanted to be home.

No. She *needed* to be home.

Her cell rang. When she'd started out that morning, Carla had flipped it onto the passenger seat, and it landed on top of her backpack. The backpack was surrounded by a fringed blue flannel scarf and a pair of gloves and, as of an hour ago, an unopened can of Diet Coke.

She took a quick glance at the lighted screen.

The caller ID made her shudder.

She did not touch the phone. The rings continued. Carla had intended to shut off the damned thing, but forgot. She stared straight ahead with an extra intensity, like someone ignoring a heckler.

She had made a mess out of everything. An absolute fucking mess. She could blame the chaos in her head, but the truth was, a few days before, she had done something really, *really* stupid. More stupid than usual. That's what this call was about.

She knew she would have to face the consequences. Eventually.

For now, all she wanted to think about was the big stone house on Shelton Avenue. She pictured the wraparound front porch, and the lopsided porch swing, and the ginormous wooden door with the tarnished brass knocker that sometimes reminded her of the one in the *Christmas Carol* movie—the one that morphed into Jacob Marley's pinched and squinty face. The knocker on the door at Shelton Avenue, though, was not creepy. It was not forbidding. It was heavy and old-fashioned and sort of cool.

And the sight of it would mean she was home.

She wondered if her mother had shoveled the long front walk yet. Carla hoped not. The moment she got back, she wanted to plunge into something physically demanding, even grueling, something that would leave her totally wrecked with exhaustion, blitzed with bone-deep, brain-numbing fatigue, so that at long last she would have a chance—unlikely as it seemed right now—to actually sleep all the way through the night. Just one night, freed from her memories. That's all. That's all she wanted.

Those memories would be waiting for her the next morning, of course, ready to pounce. She knew that. But she would be stronger, after a long good rest. She would be able to deal. To fight back. Yes, she would.

Wouldn't she?

Chapter Four

There were two kinds of drunks. The first kind lurched through the world with no shame. They made no attempt to hide the extent of their dependence on alcohol, a dependence that had begun the very first time they took a drink and felt that astonishing calm that canceled out all of their anxieties, pushed away all of the awkwardness and the insecurities; it left them shining, elevated, the true self revealed at last.

And the second kind was—

Bell paused. *Damn,* it was cold out here. Deputy Oakes had left an hour ago, having exhausted his supply of bad news, and now she was trying to clear the front walk. With every shovelful, she tunneled deeper into the heart of her thoughts about Darlene Strayer. Which meant she also chipped and picked her way past her convictions about alcoholics, with which she'd had, to her displeasure, far too much experience.

Time for a break. She stomped her booted feet. She stabbed the business end of the shovel into a nearby mound of snow. It stayed upright without a fuss. She slapped her gloved hands against the sides of her black down jacket, encouraging her circulation to work a little faster. She opened her mouth and took a deep breath. The cold air was instantly painful, a pain that reached deep into her chest. Yes, she should have been expecting it, but for some reason, she wasn't; it took her a few seconds to recover. She blinked back the water that sprang into her eyes. Then she dislodged the shovel and got back to work. Back to her thinking.

The second kind? The second kind were the subtle drunks.

They were the sly, hidden ones, the ones who were convinced of their own cleverness when they refused a glass of wine at a social occasion, making a great noble show of sliding a hand over the top of the glass when the waiter came by—*Oh, no thanks, none for me!*— and then later, in the privacy of their own homes, finishing off a fifth of Jack straight from the bottle and getting stinking, puking, shit-faced drunk. They awoke hours later to a battering-ram headache and up-ended chairs and shattered glassware and a large lurking pocket of nothingness where the memory of the night before ought to have been.

Darlene Strayer had been the second kind. No doubt about it. Because Bell had never had the slightest inkling of a problem. There were no hints, no rumors. Yet the evidence seemed pretty clear. The sobriety chip, for one thing. And for another, nobody drove drunk on a winter-slick mountain road except somebody who could not help it, somebody who had given up command and control over herself a long time ago when it came to drinking.

Between the two kinds of drunks, Bell preferred the first. Public drunks made no bones about who they were. You knew what you were dealing with. The second kind—the sneaks—were far more challenging. She'd had a friend in high school, Mindy Brewer, whose mother was the second kind. Linda Brewer showed the world a smiling, cheerful face, and was fond of reciting homilies about self-reliance and facing up to your problems and the sacred gift of each new day, but in private—Mindy confessed this to Bell one night when they were seniors, as they sat in Mindy's silver Mustang after clocking out from the Hardee's—Linda Brewer drank vast quantities of vodka every night, and ended up in a sloppy rage. They were all her mother's co-conspirators, Mindy said, herself included. Everyone kept the secret: her dad, her little brother Arthur, and her mother's sister Paige, who came over sometimes to help when Linda could not get out of bed because she had "the flu."

Yeah, Mindy said. The flu. Like *that* fooled anybody.

The first kind of drunk was a nuisance, and they annoyed you. The second kind broke your heart, over and over again.

And over and over again after that.

With each accumulating thought, Bell thrust the shovel forward, hooking it up underneath a too-big hunk of snow, bending over to lend an extra oomph to her maneuvers. As she straightened up, the shovel came up with her, along with its fresh burden of snow. She grunted. She turned, dumping the load next to the sidewalk. At first she'd tried tossing it, but the snow was too heavy, and she ended up just letting it slide off the side. Then she inched forward and did it again: bend, thrust, hook, lift, grunt, dump. Repeat.

Years ago, when she lived in D.C. with Sam and Carla, they had hired a landscaping service to keep the walks and the driveway clear after heavy snowfalls. And the few times since her return here that a major storm had come barreling in, Bell paid a kid in the neighbor-hood, Ben Fawcett, to handle the aftermath. Trouble was, Ben was away this weekend on a ski trip with his Boy Scout troop.

Standing at her front window just after the deputy's departure, she had decided at first to ignore the snow on the porch steps and the walk and the sidewalk in front of her house. Just let it be. No one would blame her; her neighbors understood how busy she was, how the pros-ecutor's post is a 24/7 deal, how she needed a little down time. They never judged her. It would be okay, right?

No. It would not.

As she had continued to watch, people began trudging out of their houses up and down Shelton Avenue, encased in big plaid coats and thick corduroy pants tucked into blocky black boots and furry hats and earmuffs and insulated gloves, toting shovels and brooms and old blue-tin Maxwell House coffee cans full of salt, attacking the porch steps and sidewalks with a gritty gusto. When they exhaled, their breath was instantly visible. There were moms and dads and small children. There were grandmothers and grandfathers. Even the can't-miss-a-Sunday churchgoers were out here, digging and clearing. The fancy clothes stayed on coat hangers back in the closet. This was the priority. The pastor would understand.

I'll be damned, Bell had thought, *if I'm going to hang out here at this window and just watch.*

She needed to pitch in. She *wanted* to pitch in. There was something about dramatic weather—a big snow or a shingle-snatching wind or an epic rain—that brought a neighborhood together. Shared misery was a great unifier. And so she had gotten dressed, opened the front door, stepped outside. A clear dome of cold had settled over everything, like a lid on a jar. The air was as crisp as a finger-snap. There was a black-and-white simplicity to the world that Bell found appealing. Snow was the only meaningful reality.

She finally remembered where she had left the shovel—it was propped up against the side of her house, buried in snow up to the handle. She wrenched it loose and got to work.

She didn't know what time Carla would be arriving. Between now and then, she had a lot to do to be ready, outside and in. During the past year or so she had begun using her daughter's old room as kind of spillover area for things that would not fit anywhere else: the 12-speed bike she had bought so that she could accompany Clay Meckling on long rides down the county back roads; plastic bins filled with out-of-season clothes; boxes of notebooks from her law-school days that had outlived their utility but that she could not quite bear to throw away, either. Bell envisioned Carla stepping hopefully into the room that

had been her beloved sanctuary until her junior year in high school—
and coming to a dead halt when she spotted the box marked ENVI-
RONMENTAL LAW/PROF JEFFCOAT in purple Sharpie or the
one on top of it that bore the label TORTS/PROF STANLEY.

"Hey, Bell! Betcha woke up and thought you'd moved to Canada,
right?"

She knocked the snow off her shovel and looked to her left. Hank
Bainbridge, Myrtle Bainbridge's youngest son, was waving a heavy-
gloved hand at her from the driveway two houses over. He was round,
like his mother, and in that puffy white parka he resembled a human
snowman garnished with a tuft of gingery hair on top.

The Bainbridge boys had been in high school the same time as
Bell. Hank was a year younger, George was her age, and Wyatt was a
year older. They had been wild things back then, surly hell-raisers who
seemed destined for the jail or the cemetery or both, the second shortly
after the first. Funny: They were all middle-aged now, like her, and
you could not find more sedate, respectful, law-abiding men. It was as
if the wildness had been knocked off them along the way, like the
caked snow on Bell's shovel. They had gotten it out of their systems.
The three of them now took excellent care of Myrtle, who had a revolving drama of health problems. There was always a Bainbridge
brother around to drive her to a doctor's appointment or help her with
her weekly shopping at Lymon's Market.

"Hey, Hank," Bell yelled back.

"You need any help over there?"

"I got it. Thanks."

He waved again and went back to his slow excavation of his
mother's driveway.

Bell leaned an elbow on her shovel and checked her progress. It
was pitiful. She had made such a small dent in the preponderance of
snow that the few inroads looked almost accidental—and yet her palms
were stinging and her back had already filed multiple complaints. At

this rate, she would finish clearing the walk just in time for the spring thaw.

Occasionally it still felt strange to her, this being a part of a neighborhood, a community. Having people to wave to, people who waved back. People who looked out for her. Most of her childhood had been spent in foster homes, where she had never been able to put her full weight down, and as a young married woman in D.C., she moved frequently, as Sam's promotions and career jumps had propelled their rise into better and better areas. They never established roots. Sam did not want roots. Roots were for losers. Roots were for people with no ambitions. Stuck people.

And during all those moves, Bell had begun to notice a peculiar thing: The more dazzling and exclusive and ritzy the neighborhood, the less it felt like a neighborhood at all. Nobody ever seemed to be home when she knocked on a neighbor's door to say hello. Nobody took walks. In the last home she and Sam shared, just before she had filed for divorce, she looked around one day and realized she did not know the names of any of the people on their street. Not one.

Well, wait. That wasn't true. She did know one name. A former secretary of commerce lived on the corner in the overgrown Tudor behind the high hedges—at least when she wasn't flying all over the world, giving speeches about altruism and other Christian virtues for fees that equaled the annual GDP of a medium-sized country. Bell had never met her, and she had never met her children or her husband or her personal assistant or her nanny or her gardener, but she knew the woman's name, because Sam had told her. It was the besotted way he said the name—with a sort of holy-grail gleam in his voice—that annoyed her.

All these years later and here she was, shoveling snow. Not a former cabinet member in sight. And that was just fine with her.

But would it be fine with Carla? Would her daughter, that is, miss the racket and the romance of a big city, a city filled with the things that everybody else in the world seemed to think were madly desirable?

Bell yanked the shovel out of the snow mound. Her break was over. Using her other gloved hand as a visor, she gave the sun a quick, vicious squint. Why the hell couldn't it help a little bit, melting some of this crap? The question was purely rhetorical because she knew the answer: It was just too dang cold. The sun was a stage prop today. Nothing more.

Her mind was suddenly and unexpectedly filled with an image of Darlene Strayer's face, the way it had looked the last time Bell saw her: sitting across a wooden table in a booth the night before at the Tie Yard Tavern, her dark eyes going from troubled to calm when the topic switched to her father, Harmon Strayer. And then back to troubled again when she announced that she was responsible for his death, because of her negligence. Because of the hunches she had not pursued. Because of something. Or nothing.

Was Harmon Strayer's death worth looking into? It would stand as Darlene's last request of her, but still—the man was nearly ninety. He suffered from Alzheimer's, for God's sake. Plus multiple health problems. Heart disease, diabetes, hypertension, peripheral neuropathy. Name your ailment and, according to Darlene, Harmon Strayer could have checked the box.

Now Darlene herself had died violently, victim of a fate that Bell would never have foreseen for such a careful, conscientious woman. She had died on a road she knew well, during conditions she had endured many times before. If the toxicology report backed up Deputy Oakes's surmise, then Darlene had succumbed to an old demon, a secret one, one she had kept hidden from Bell and from other classmates at Georgetown.

But why had she slipped back into her addiction last night, of all nights? Was it sorrow over her father's death? What had sent her over the edge—in both the literal and metaphorical sense of the phrase?

"Hey there."

The familiar voice belonged to her neighbor on the other side, Larry Jenrette, a systems analyst for the gas company. He'd come out on his front porch while Bell was contemplating Darlene Strayer's fate.

He had a desk-sitter's body: pendulous gut, soft hands, rear end that seemed to spread wider by the week. He took a deep, shoulder-raising breath and surveyed the white tomb that the world had become. He held his shovel out to one side, as if he wasn't quite certain what he was supposed to do with it and didn't want it too close.

"Morning, Larry," Bell said. "You and Angie okay?"

Angie, his wife, had multiple sclerosis. She had recently given in and started using a wheelchair, a concession to reality that did worse things to her spirit, Bell knew, than anything the MS could do to her central nervous system.

"Fine and dandy," Larry said, as he always did. Then he grimaced, but in a comical way to let her know he was teasing. "Well, it's colder than bejesus out here, but other than *that*—fine and dandy. Heard your shovel scraping the walk and figured I better not shame myself in the eyes of my neighbors." He pulled a red stocking cap out of his coat pocket and used it to smother most of his head, including the entirety of his ears. "We'll just be doing it all over again tomorrow morning, way I hear it. Coupla feet more supposed to be comin' down."

"Yep," Bell said. She had already resumed her bending and grunting.

Larry used his shovel like a ski pole, pushing off against each step as he descended from the porch and prepared to deal with the snow on his own front walk. "Hey," he said, before getting started. "How come Clay's not doing this for you? Don't tell me you're letting him sleep in today, the lucky so-and-so."

And that, Bell reminded herself with a silent flourish of unwelcome insight, was the not-so-charming side of living in a place where everybody knew you—and knew your business. And knew that you were dating a man named Clay Meckling. And knew that he almost always stayed over on Saturday nights.

You got asked questions like this one: Where's Clay?

"He's out of town," she said, and then she turned her back on Larry Jenrette, ostensibly to move on to another section of sidewalk, but her ultimate intention was to cut off the conversation.

She was not lying. Yes, Clay was out of town. That was a fact.

But the facts rarely had much to do with the truth. She knew that from her job as prosecutor, and she knew it, too, from her experience of being human—and of feeling, over and over again, how inadequate the facts were to explain something as savagely complicated and chronically illogical as love.

"You already did it."

"Did what?"

"Shoveled the walk," Carla said. "I was sort of hoping to do it myself."

"You're in luck. More snow predicted for tonight."

They stared at each other for a few seconds, Carla poised in the doorway and Bell standing just inside it, as if each needed to be sure that the other was real and not some holographic projection. Not some wishful hallucination. Then the moment passed and practicality returned. It was too damned cold for dramatic pauses on thresholds.

"For heaven's sake get in here, you," Bell said. She held open her arms, the universal summons for a hug. "You've got to be frozen."

"Pretty much." Carla took four steps forward. She shut the door behind her. She dropped her backpack on the floor and leaned awkwardly into her mother's embrace.

The small talk had been a ruse, a way to keep intense emotion at bay. Both of them were complicit in the scheme, because both of them felt it—felt that surge of tenderness and vulnerability at the sight of the other, after having gone so long with phone calls and Skype sessions as their only points of contact.

It was just after three p.m. Bell had heard the Kia grinding its way up the street—an hour ago the plow had whittled a path up Shelton Avenue roughly the width of a single car—and she leapt up from her chair and raced over to open the door. By the time she got there, Carla was already crossing the porch.

The moment Bell touched her, it was all over. Carla's stoicism crumbled. She wept, just as she had done in the little roadside store. Her body trembled, caught as it was in accelerating waves of an emotion too intense to be held inside a second longer.

"Mom," Carla whispered. She was about to say the thing she did not want to say, because her mother was the bravest, strongest, steadiest, steeliest person she knew, and to admit this to such a person— even if the person loved her, as Bell unquestionably did, and did unconditionally—was shameful, ridiculous, unthinkable.

But also necessary. If, that is, Carla wanted to be able to take another breath. If, that is, she wanted to live past this moment and on into the next one, and then the one after that.

"Carla, sweetie—what is it? Is there anything I can—"

"I'm scared, Mom. I'm just really, really scared."

And so they talked. Naturally, that's what they did: They assumed their familiar positions in the living room as if no time at all had passed, as if this were four years ago and Carla was still a junior in high school and Bell still a fledgling prosecutor, both of them feeling their way through new roles in a new place that was also an old place. A known place. Bell automatically went for her favorite spot, the dilapidated armchair with the coffee-stain tattoos on all visible surfaces, and Carla's straight-line path took her to the green couch, in the middle of which she plopped down and yanked off her boots and settled back against the nubby, pilled, all-but-worn-out fabric.

Carla closed her eyes. She took a deep breath, and only let the air out in staggered stages.

Bell looked at her daughter.

Home, Carla's expression said, more eloquently than any words. *I'm home now. Nothing else matters.*

But the truth was, of course, that plenty else mattered. Time had passed. Too much time, really, for the illusion to last that being home could fix everything. Carla was a young adult now, not a teenager. The brief moment at the door—when Carla had dissolved in Bell's arms, amid a frantic avalanche of tears and babbled, incoherent talk about having ruined everything, *everything*—was over. It had passed now. They were different people than they had been when Carla moved out, and even Bell's furious love for her daughter was not enough to win the fight against all those years, all those changes.

So as Bell sat and waited for Carla to tell her the reason for her tears, she realized that no matter what Carla said, most likely it would not be the real story.

It would not be a lie, but it also would not be the real story. Carla would be vague, and she would give her the short summary version. The real story would be a while in coming—days, maybe, or even weeks. Carla, she knew, would understand that she owed her mother *some* explanation for having kicked over the barn of her current life and winding up in Acker's Gap on a cold winter afternoon—but the long story, the thorough one, the one with all the loops and turnings, was not going to be forthcoming. Not today, anyway.

Carla opened her eyes. She offered Bell a tiny smile, a sheepish one, one that seemed to say: *Can you even* believe *what a ridiculous baby I was just a few minutes ago? Crying like that? I mean—Jesus.* Her cheeks were still shiny-wet with the ghost trails of the tears.

"God, Mom—sorry I lost it there for a minute."

"It's okay." Bell let her eyes rove over Carla's thin face. Her eyes seemed slightly sunken, ringed by smudges of fatigue. "You're exhausted."

"Yeah."

Bell waited. With Carla, you could not come on too strong. You did not push. Pushing was counterproductive. It irritated Bell sometimes, having to be patient until Carla finally decided to open up, but this was the only way.

"In fact," Carla said, adopting a breezy tone out of the blue, "that's the problem. I'm, like, *really* tired. I could barely keep my eyes open on the drive over. The thing I said about being scared—that's just drama queen stuff. I'm not really scared of anything. I'm just whipped. I haven't been sleeping very well."

"So you came all this way for a nap?"

That was a mistake. Carla shook her head. She sighed; she was annoyed. She spoke to an invisible witness in the room. "Same old Mom."

"Look." Bell leaned forward. She reached across the distance between them and touched Carla's knee with two fingers. "You don't have to tell me anything. Not unless you want to. You're always welcome here, no matter what. You know that. But you can't blame me for asking a few questions. And if there's anything I can help you with, anything I can do or—"

"There's not." Carla's voice was as blunt and non-negotiable as a DEAD END sign. "I just want—I just want to chill. I don't know for how long. I want to move back into my old room again and just *be* here, okay?"

"Okay."

Carla was plainly ready to change the subject. She looked around. "I kind of thought you'd have another dog by now."

"A dog."

"Yeah. I mean, you and Goldie hit it off so well."

Last year Bell had kept a dog that belonged to a defendant. Initially she had been reluctant to invite a strange animal into her home, but by the time the man—now exonerated—returned to collect his companion, Bell had grown to love Goldie. Watching her leave that day had been an excruciating emotional ordeal. Many people had predicted that Bell would be haunting the Raythune County Animal Shelter the very next weekend, searching for a new pet.

But they didn't understand. She could no more have replaced Goldie than she could have gone out and found another stubborn, smart-talking teenager to replace Carla once the latter left for D.C. It didn't work that way. Loved ones weren't like interchangeable parts. Love was a singular event, and every love was different. That was what made it special.

"I go out and see her from time to time," Bell said. She hadn't really addressed Carla's point, which was a deliberate strategy. "Royce lives way out in the middle of East Jesus, but it's worth the drive," she added, naming Goldie's owner.

"Bet she goes crazy when she sees you, right?"

Bell nodded and smiled. "Oh, sure. Just about licks me to death." That was true, but the reality was—a reality she did not share with Carla—that with each visit, Goldie's enthusiasm waned a bit. Goldie was letting go. Gradually, she was forgetting about the time she had spent with Bell, and at some point in the future Bell would be just another visitor, her arrival greeted with curious barks and mad sniffing and then a reassuring tail wag: *You're okay,* the wag would imply. *I've thoroughly vetted you. Feel free to advance at will.*

"One of my roommates has a dog," Carla said. "She's sort of annoying."

"The roommate or the dog?"

"Both, come to think of it." Carla grinned. The grin looked good on her face, and Bell hoped it would last a while longer. It didn't. "So you're okay," Carla went on, "if I just hang out for a while? Stay in my old room?"

"Of course."

Bell waited for more, even though she sensed there was not going to be more. Not now, anyway. And not, for the time being, about anything that really mattered. They sat silently for a brief run of seconds. They were like two cars stuck in snow.

At last Carla said, "So what's been going on around here? Other than the crazy weather?"

"Plenty," Bell said. Briefly, she told her daughter about Darlene Strayer's death the night before. She had mentioned Darlene to Carla over the years. Tracked her success. Sitting at the kitchen table in this very house and seeing a wire story in the paper about a significant case and how instrumental Darlene had been in seeing it through, Bell would tap the headline with a finger and murmur, "Local girl." Hoping Carla got the message: *You can be from here and go anywhere. Do anything.*

"So it was the same road you'd just gone down a few hours before your friend's accident," Carla said. She seemed a little shaken by the idea.

"Yes. But I wasn't drunk."

Carla reacted with her eyebrows.

"Won't sugarcoat it," Bell said brusquely. When Carla was in high school, Bell had lectured her and her friends endlessly about driving while drunk or stoned. As far as she knew, Carla had never done so. But there was a lot that mothers never found out about, unless a night ended in disaster. Bell knew that. Lecturing about dangerous things was one of those activities that mothers were hardwired to do, effective or not. "Turns out," Bell added, "Darlene probably had an alcohol problem going way back to law school. Or maybe before. I don't know. She kept it hidden. And kept herself under control."

"Until last night."

"Until last night." Bell nodded.

More silence.

"Do you see much of Aunt Shirley?" Carla asked.

"Not as much as I'd like." Shirley was Bell's older sister. She had returned to Acker's Gap after serving a long prison sentence for an act of violence. The violence was thoroughly justified, but the law didn't see it that way. Now she lived two counties away with her boyfriend, an aspiring songwriter named Bobo Bolland. She worked as a clerk in an auto parts store. She hated it but, as she'd once told Bell and Carla when the three of them were having dinner, you were *supposed* to hate it; it's when you stopped hating that kind of job, when you settled into it without a fight, that you needed to start worrying.

"She posts a lot of funny stuff on Facebook," Carla said. "Bobo has a fan page."

"Really."

"Yeah. He's got a bunch of Likes." Carla checked out the living room with her gaze, as if she needed to make sure it was still the place she remembered: fireplace, picture window, bookshelves, coffee table. Then her eyes came back around to her mother.

"How's Clay?" Carla asked.

This was tricky, and so Bell hesitated. Carla knew all about her relationship with Clay Meckling. That wasn't the tricky part. The tricky part was that Bell could not answer Carla's question—because she had not spoken to Clay in a week and a half. Not since the moment when her lover had caught her so completely by surprise, when he had startled her so profoundly that she had been forced to wonder: Who was the real Clay Meckling? Was it the gentle good man with whom she had fallen in love four years ago—or was it the man who had stood before her in that shattering moment, having just revealed a part of himself that she had never suspected could live inside him, amidst all the decency and casual gallantry?

"He's fine," Bell said. She would tell her the truth later—or part of the truth, anyway. As much as Carla needed to know. Too much truth could be as bad as too little.

Jesus, Bell thought wryly. *And I wonder where Carla learned about evasiveness and the artful deployment of partial facts.*

Carla's voice was apprehensive. "And he'll be okay with—with me, like, living here again? I mean, I won't be in the way or . . ."

"Sweetie." Bell's eyes blazed with conviction. "This is your home. Your *home.* That's the only thing that matters, okay? So it doesn't matter who else is in my life. Doesn't matter how long you've been gone. This place will always be here—*right here*—waiting for you. This house—and me. Clear?"

"Clear." The word sounded muddy. Carla needed to get something out of her throat. "Clear," she repeated. Stronger this time.

"Good," Bell said, reaching out and giving Carla's knee a light double-pat at the same time she said it, as if to seal the deal. "You remember that."

"Mind if I take my stuff upstairs?"

" 'Course not."

They rose in unison. There was so much more Bell wanted to ask her, so many questions she had about the reason for Carla's return and the source of her daughter's emotional tumult—but she reminded herself that she could not do it all at once. She'd have to bide her time. Pick her spots.

There would have to be a few house rules. Some structure. All of that could be worked out in the days to come.

"So I'll see you later," Carla said.

"At dinner. Chicken okay?"

"Sure." Her daughter turned and started trudging toward the staircase. She retrieved her backpack from its spot by the door. She didn't sling it over her shoulder. She held it at her side by the thick strap, so that it dangled like a hunter's bounty.

"Hey. One more thing." Bell had to speak. Their entire conversation had felt stilted, unnatural; just a little while ago Carla had been sobbing in her arms. Now she was nonchalant. The change was jarring. Something was wrong. Just because Carla would not tell her what it was did not mean that it wasn't important. "The offer stands, okay?" Bell said. "I mean—to talk about whatever's bothering you. Whenever you feel up to it."

Carla had paused at the initial "Hey." She had not turned around; she simply stopped walking.

Now she did turn. She looked as if she was about to say something, but had lost her nerve. "Can I, like, just live my life for a while, Mom? With no questions until I'm ready? Promise I won't be in your way. I'm going to get a job. Already have an interview set up for tomorrow morning."

"Fine. But at some point, I'd really like to sit down and have a good long talk about—"

"Got it, Mom." Carla gave her a thumbs-up sign. "Full disclosure. Soon."

She did not mean it, and Bell knew she did not mean it, but an important part of parenting was stopping yourself from saying, "You don't mean it." Because an even more important part of parenting was perpetual hopefulness, the abiding belief that Carla really *would* decide eventually to tell her what was going on in her life.

Bell listened to her daughter's steps as she climbed to the second floor. Those steps sounded slow and ponderous and heavy—heavier, certainly, than should have been the case for someone as light as Carla, someone who used to make short work of that staircase, taking two and three steps at a time, never touching the handrail, a lively, black-haired blur on fire with ideas and passions and crushes and *everything,* everything that caught her eye or snagged her heart, which could mean a book or a boy or a song or a social cause or all of the above.

Not now. Now she moved with a dull, deliberate plod that sounded like the aural embodiment of dread. She was carrying a lot more these days, Bell thought uneasily, than just a backpack.

Only one thing could account for the invisible weight. Only one thing was substantial enough to be burdening Carla to this extent: a secret. Or several secrets.

What the—

Bell, blindly thrashing, knocked the alarm clock off her bedside table. Her head was still under the covers. She had heard the landline ring once, twice, three times, and then on the fourth ring, her right arm poked out from under the edge of the blanket and began swiping the air in wild pissed-off arcs. She struck the clock. It made a solid *thunk* when it hit the hardwood floor. Finally she located the receiver.

"Elkins," she muttered.

She heard breathing, and then a slight rustle. The breathing was thick and clotted. The caller had been weeping. Bell knew that sound well. Once, just for sport, she'd tallied up the number of times that a crying person had called her; the total was in the double digits. County prosecutors were akin to priests, in some people's eyes, and the phone was as good as a confessional.

"Elkins," she repeated. She did not say it impatiently; she wanted to give the person time to recover. She looked around the dark room, seeing nothing. God, it had to be the freaking middle of the freaking night. Another time, she'd added up the number of occasions that she'd been yanked out of a heavy sleep by a phone call.

Again: double digits.

"I need to talk to you," the caller said. "It's urgent."

"Who's this?"

"You don't know me." A slow intake of breath. "My name is Ava Hendricks." Another pause. "Darlene Strayer was my partner. We'd been together for fourteen years. And she told me that if anything ever happened to her, I should get in touch with you right away. You'd know what to do." Another deep breath and then a much longer pause, as if more courage had to be retrieved from some distant storeroom in order for her to continue. "I just got the notification about Darlene. I wasn't home and they had to find me first. Track me down." She stopped talking. Her breathing was heavy, rusty-sounding.

"I'm very sorry for your loss." Bell sat up, pushing away the blanket. Her thoughts were starting to clear, like a foggy windshield after the defrost has been activated. "Where were you? Why couldn't anyone reach you?"

The caller's voice snapped to attention. Gone was the soft anguish. "I'm a neurosurgeon, Mrs. Elkins. I spent the day removing a glioblastoma multiforme from the brain of an eight-year-old girl. It was an extremely complicated procedure. I wasn't reachable until an hour ago."

Bell switched on the lamp by her bed. Instantly a small area of light leapt to life inside the black room, like a struck match held between cupped hands.

"I'm so sorry about Darlene," Bell said. "Never easy to get that kind of news."

Her mind was working fast: Had she known Darlene was involved with a woman? Or with anyone, for that matter? No. She hadn't. It did not matter, one way or another, but it reminded Bell all over again how little information she had ever really had about her former classmate. The alcoholism wasn't the only surprise on this night of surprises.

And the surprises just kept on coming.

"The thing is, Mrs. Elkins," Hendricks said, "Darlene was convinced that someone wanted to kill her. The same person who killed her father. This wasn't an accident." No emotion in her voice. Just a cold certainty.

Suspicion kicked in. How could Bell be sure this woman was who she said she was? Anyone might call her and claim a close association with Darlene Strayer. Until she had confirmation, she would only say what was already public record.

"Look," Bell said. "The facts are pretty clear here. Darlene missed a turn on a snowy road and crashed into a tree." She did not mention the blood alcohol level. She wouldn't, unless Hendricks persisted. Hendricks surely knew about Darlene's issues, and there was no point in piling on until she had the lab report in hand and could use it to swat away the protests and denials. "That's all. And I've not had a chance yet to look into her concerns about her father's passing. I will. But for now, all I can offer you are my condolences."

"That's not enough."

"Well, it'll have to be. I hope you'll let me know when any services are planned. I'd like to attend. And if you want a copy of the accident report, you're welcome to call my office at the Raythune County Courthouse and request one. My secretary's name is Lee Ann Fri—"

"No." It was a slap, not a word. "And frankly, I'm rather surprised at your attitude. Darlene always said you didn't like her. I told her that probably wasn't true. Now I believe it."

Hendricks might have been a neurosurgeon, but she would've made a dandy psychiatrist, Bell would decide later, when she looked back upon this conversation—one that proved to be so crucial to all that came after.

Because nothing got to Bell Elkins faster than the galling accusation that she was letting her emotions cloud her professional judgment. Nothing riled her up quite so much. Or guaranteed that she would do everything she possibly could to prove it wasn't so—to prove that she took each case as it came, and made her decisions about it based on rigor and cool rationality, on evidence and precedent, and not on the wildfire of her feelings.

Hendricks had sensed that. Or maybe Darlene had told her enough about Bell for her to figure it out. In any case, Ava Hendricks played her. It was for a good cause, as Bell would later acknowledge to herself—and to Hendricks, too—but she had played her, just the same. Hendricks knew exactly which buttons to push, and she pushed them at exactly the right moment.

"You don't have *any idea* how I felt about Darlene," Bell snapped. She couldn't keep the fury out of her voice. "And it doesn't matter, anyway. It doesn't matter *who* is involved. If there's even a hint of a crime—if there's even a single unanswered question—we investigate."

"Prove it."

"I will." And just like that, Bell realized, she had committed herself to taking a second look at the death of Darlene Strayer.

Chapter Five

Rhonda Lovejoy leaned over Bell's desk from the opposite side and deftly executed a document dump. The tall stack of printouts hit with a wallop. The top several pages slid to one side like a drifting snowbank, bumping up against Bell's coffee mug.

"Everything you ever wanted to know about Ava Hendricks," Rhonda declared.

It was just after eight on Monday morning. The overnight snow hadn't materialized, after all. Good thing: The town was still digging out from under what was now commonly referred to as the Saturday Night Massacre. It snowed every winter in these mountain valleys, but rarely did it snow this much all in one go.

In the downtown area, the plow had pushed the snow into tall piles that brooded over the corners of major intersections, creating a mini-Stonehenge effect. Driving to the courthouse that morning, Bell could have sworn she saw a couple of Druids chanting and gesturing oddly at the base of an obelisk, but it turned out to be adolescents in gray hoodies with floppy sleeves who were posing for selfies next to snow piles.

"And by the way," Rhonda added. "Real sorry about your friend. That road's bad news in the ice and snow. Curves'll sneak up on you."

"Thanks." Bell moved the mug so that it wouldn't be in the way if the stack shifted again. "What'd you find out?"

"Hendricks is a big deal. Head of neurosurgery at George Washington University Hospital. Pretty amazing credentials. I found a ton of stuff on the Internet—interviews, profiles, award citations."

"So she's solid."

"Solid? Yeah, I'd say so." Rhonda lifted her eyebrows and lowered her chin, her standard *Wait'll you get a load of this* pose. "Born in Boston. Everybody in the family's a doctor. Even the cat, I bet. Oh, and then there's—um, let me see here—oh, yeah. Columbia med school, residency at Mass General, surgical fellowship at Johns Hopkins. A ton of commendations for community service. There aren't a lot of neurosurgeons, period. And *female* neurosurgeons? We're talking *really* rare. Endangered-species rare."

Two chairs faced Bell's desk. Rhonda picked the one on the left. She was a large woman who moved with nimbleness and grace. If Bell had been asked to come up with a phrase that defined her assistant, she would have said that Rhonda was comfortable in her own skin. She possessed a distinctive sense of style that Bell admired without ever feeling the slightest desire to emulate. Today her assistant wore a white wool cable-knit sweater with flecks of red and gold thread, an orange scarf, and purple wool slacks. Her bright blond hair was stacked on top of her head and secured there by a combination of hope and hair spray.

After a brief pause to enable Rhonda to situate herself, Bell spoke.

"Did you enjoy your weekend?" The topic-switch was abrupt. And the words sounded rehearsed, because they were. Bell was trying to be friendlier to her staff these days. Lee Ann Frickie had recently used the words "prickly" and "moody" to describe Bell's behavior as a boss, and it bothered her, so much so that she had lashed out at Lee Ann—thereby proving her secretary's point.

"I mean," Bell added, "with the snow and all."

Rhonda was flummoxed, and looked it. Bell did not make small talk, especially small talk about the *weather,* for God's sake, and this felt an awful lot like small talk. About the weather, no less.

What was going on?

"It was fine," Rhonda said. Cautiously.

"Good." Social niceties over, they could get back to business. Bell placed a hand on top of the stack. "Looks like you were thorough."

"I brought you anything even remotely relevant. Hick finally fixed the printer in our office, so I didn't have to run all over the courthouse looking for one I could cabbage onto. Last week they almost threw me out of the assessor's office. I tied up their printer for an hour and a half, trying to print out all those motions in the Vickers case."

Hickey Leonard was Raythune County's other assistant prosecutor. Bell was fortunate to have two. Most West Virginia counties as small as this one had only a prosecutor and no assistants at all. It wasn't a question of workload; there were always plenty of cases. It was a question of money. Pressured by a steady drop in revenue as coal mines shut down and businesses closed up and families moved away in multiples, the majority of counties could not afford the luxury of assistant prosecutors.

But Bell was lucky: Two-thirds of the Raythune County commissioners owed their political success to Hickey Leonard, and he never let them forget it. He had lived every second of his sixty-seven years in Acker's Gap, as had his father and mother before him. He knew which skeletons rattled in which closets belonging to which commissioners, and if there was ever any talk about cutting the budget for the prosecutor's office and maybe getting rid of him or Rhonda, all Hick had to do was show up at a commission meeting and, while the minutes of the last meeting were being read, tug a small spiral-bound notebook out of the inside pocket of his suit coat and thumb through the first few pages he came to, brow furrowed, mouth bunched in a thoughtful frown as if he had forgotten the particulars of some especially heinous incident but—oh, my!—here those particulars were, written down in all of their lurid shamefulness. And then he would look up and catch the eye of one of the commissioners—Bucky Barnes, say, or Sammy Burdette or Carl Gilmore or Pearl Sykes— and, still holding the eyes of that suddenly nervous person, he would lick his finger and use it to turn to yet another page of the notebook, slowly, slowly, while shaking his head ever so slightly as if to say, *You think you know a person, but no. No, you don't. Not when you see what they're truly capable of, when no one's looking. Or at least when they* think *no one's looking.*

It was a form of soft blackmail that once upon a time would have disgusted Bell, but she was a different person now from the one she had been when she first came back to Acker's Gap, stuffed uncomfortably full of idealism and judgment, in addition to being headstrong, snippy, and quickly notorious as a know-it-all. She had changed. She had been forced to change, if she wanted to accomplish anything. Now she appreciated Hick's regularly scheduled performance. It meant that Bell was able to keep him and Rhonda Lovejoy on the payroll, and she needed them. More to the point, the county needed them.

And besides: She'd had a peek at that notebook of his. The pages were blank.

"I appreciate you pulling all this together so fast this morning," Bell said. "I'm sure Dr. Hendricks will be paying us a visit. Apparently she and Darlene were together a long time. And a grieving spouse is going to want some answers."

"Yeah. Well. About that. Jake Oakes said that when he finally reached her—apparently you have to go through about twenty-eleven layers of hospital bureaucracy to even get her on the phone—she was, like, 'Okay, thanks.' Pretty weird, he said. For somebody whose whole life just changed."

"People grieve in their own way."

Rhonda put a funny squint on her face. "I do sort of wonder about them."

"Wonder what?"

"About—well, you know."

"Not a clue. Wonder what?"

"I mean . . ." Rhonda discovered a phantom speck of lint on the sleeve of her sweater that she needed to remove. The gesture took a very long time. Too long. She was stalling.

"What are you getting at?" Bell said. Her voice was brusque. She had a full schedule today. And she had asked Carla to meet her for lunch at JP's, the diner down the block from the courthouse, after her job interview. The list of things Bell had to accomplish between now and the moment she slid into a booth at JP's, clamping her hands around a mug of hot coffee, was dauntingly long.

"Well," Rhonda said, "I just mean that—well, usually you think that women who are—well, *together,* you know, in that way, you just assume it's because . . ." She was struggling.

At this point Bell understood perfectly well what Rhonda was trying to say, and was determined not to help her out. She was surprised at her assistant's attitude, but then again, except for Rhonda's time at West Virginia University and then its College of Law, she had lived all thirty-three years of her life within a stone's throw of the Raythune County Courthouse, in the shadow of which diversity did not exactly flourish.

Still, Rhonda was a bright woman, and usually an open-minded, wide-souled one, and Bell was disappointed in her. Bell consoled herself with the thought that everyone had to start somewhere.

"Explain," Bell said curtly.

"You just naturally assume," Rhonda said, starting again, but haltingly, "that it's because they can't get a boyfriend or a husband, right? And so they finally just give up and get involved with each other as a kind of—well, I mean—"

"As a kind of what?"

"As a kind of substitute. Next best thing. But your friend—she was really pretty. And this woman . . ." Rhonda gestured toward the stack of printouts she'd left on Bell's desk. "This woman's a *brain surgeon,* for heaven's sake. And she's attractive, too, if those photos got it right. Bet she doesn't have a lick of trouble finding men who want to go out with her. But somehow the both of them ended up . . ." She didn't know how to finish the sentence.

Bell did it for her. "They ended up with each other. By conscious choice. Not desperation."

"Totally." Rhonda looked relieved. "So you *do* get what I mean."

"No, I don't."

"Come on, Bell. You know the point I'm trying to make."

"Maybe you'd better enlighten me."

Her assistant looked around the room dismally. She was clearly regretting the topic she had introduced. Major blunder. She'd just remembered that Bell, despite being born and raised in Acker's Gap, was not really One of Them. Bell had started out that way—but then she left. When she came back, she wasn't anymore. That was how it worked.

Bell read the sentiment right off Rhonda's distressed face. And waited.

"Okay, fine," Rhonda said, peeved at being put on the spot. "But would *you* ever want to be in a relationship with a woman?"

Bell smiled. "Sorry, but I'm already spoken for. Anyway, I don't believe in workplace romances."

"No—wait—I didn't mean . . ."

Bell let her sputter and blush for a few seconds. Then she reached for a file folder on the far side of her desk. She opened it. "Let's get back to work."

For the next hour they went over the latest developments in the county's case against a man named Charles Leroy Vickers. The charge was aggravated assault. There was a simpler phrase for the fancy label "aggravated assault," Bell had learned after her first few years as a prosecutor in these parts: using a broken-off beer bottle during a bar fight. The trial had been postponed several times. First Vickers grabbed his gut in his jail cell one day, claiming illness; his attorney demanded that he be hospitalized. After several weeks of tests and Jell-O, Vickers decided that he was feeling much better, thanks. Next came a string of frivolous motions by the defense. "It's like they think we'll just get frustrated and give up and go away," Rhonda had said last week, as she and Bell went over strategy. The Vickers case was the first one that Rhonda had been assigned to handle all on her own—not as second chair to Bell or Hick Leonard.

Now there was a new trial date—a week from today in Judge Tolliver's courtroom. "Unless," Rhonda said, as she accepted the transcript of a deposition that Bell was handing her, "Charlie-boy gets a toenail fungus and we have to wait for him to heal up." She had read this transcript multiple times already. She had made notes about her notes. And then more notes about *those* notes.

"Pretty good chance you'll actually be starting next week," Bell said. "You feel ready, right?"

"I've been ready for three months."

"Good." Bell set aside the legal pad that contained her prosecutorial to-do list on the Vickers case. "So you'll have some time this week."

"Absolutely. And I'd appreciate another assignment. Take my mind off things while I wait for the trial."

"Glad to hear it." Bell gripped the arms of her chair and leaned back. She let her gaze wander around her office for a moment, taking in the glass-fronted bookcases and their brood of maroon law books, the painted plaster walls that always looked scabby and slightly damp, and finally the tall leaded window that looked out on the snow-beleaguered streets of Acker's Gap. Few people strolled those streets today. It was too cold. Fronds of bright white frost were printed across each pane, a curt reminder of the outside temperature and the perils of poorly caulked windows. "You up for taking a little drive this afternoon? By yourself, I mean? I can't promise it'll be easy. Some of those county roads haven't been cleared off yet."

"Let me at 'em," Rhonda said eagerly. "I've been using my cousin Rodney's truck to get around in. He's got a brand-new Silverado. The tires alone are higher than any of those snow piles out there. Where am I going?"

"The place where Darlene Strayer's father died. That new Alzheimer's care facility over in Muth County."

"Thornapple Terrace."

"So you know it?"

"My grandmother's best friend, Connie Dollar, is the assistant head of housekeeping."

And that, Bell reminded herself with satisfaction, was the great glory and verified value of Rhonda Lovejoy: She either knew or was related to a good four-fifths of Raythune County and the counties adjacent to it, which meant she could slide with ease into places and conversations without disturbing the surface area.

She was a good assistant prosecutor, now that Bell had cured her of unfortunate habits such as procrastination and a tendency toward verbosity when nervous—but she was a great investigator. And every prosecutor needed a great investigator. Not every prosecutor could afford one—but every prosecutor needed one. In an office as small and as poor as this one, the fact that Bell could rely on Rhonda to do the digging—and to do it discreetly and reliably and effectively—was a blessing beyond measure.

Bell was still disappointed by Rhonda's bigotry toward lifestyles that did not look like those she saw all around her every day—but she could teach Rhonda to be more tolerant. That would come. What she *couldn't* teach—to anybody, including herself—was the subtle art that made Rhonda a dogged bloodhound of an investigator. It was a gift.

"Excellent," Bell said. "I'd like you to poke around a bit. Talk to the staff about Harmon Strayer's death. If there's any blowback, you can reassure the director that it's just a routine inquiry—because, quite frankly, that's what it is."

"Do you remember the news stories about that Alzheimer's place back East? Couple of years ago? Turns out this crazy nurse wanted to put the patients out of their misery. So she added a little something—a *lethal* something—to their morning orange juice. Her motives were pure. But she still went to jail."

Bell shook her head. "As a friend of mine used to say, there's only room for one God. And the job's already taken." She moved the stack of papers. It was a signal to Rhonda that the meeting was almost over. "Strayer's death certificate said natural causes. Nothing suspicious. So this is probably a waste of time. But I'll still feel better if we go through the motions. Maybe we can help Darlene's partner find some peace—once she knows that both deaths were accidental. So just gather up any details you can find about the old man's passing. And anything else that's going on out there."

Rhonda used a thumb and a finger to flash a small round *O* of acknowledgment. "If it happens at the Terrace," she said, "you'll know about it." She turned at the door. "Oh, and I meant to ask—how's Carla doing? She's back, right?"

Bell had not said a word to her about Carla's return. Rhonda just knew it, the way she knew about everything. Sometimes a gift could be a nuisance, too.

It took Carla a good five minutes to shed all the winter gear in which she'd wrapped herself in a futile defense against the cold. She lifted off her earmuffs, pulled her knit cap off sideways, unwound her scarf, struggled out of her long wool coat, peeled off her mittens, and untucked her trouser cuffs from the tops of her sopping-wet boots. It felt to her like the slowest and least-sexy striptease in the history of the world as she removed one heavy item after another and then hung it on the coat tree next to Sally McArdle's desk.

"I think," Carla said, "I'm melting on your carpet." The snow sliding off her boots was steadily darkening the beige.

"Don't worry about it. Winter's winter."

McArdle hadn't gotten up when Carla came in. Carla knew why. She knew because she'd grown up in this town, for the most part, and when you'd grown up here, you knew things like the fact that Sally McArdle had had her left leg amputated on account of her diabetes on the day after her fifty-eighth birthday, which was ten years ago. Getting up and down was difficult for her.

Wow. I know two different people who've had a leg amputated, Carla suddenly realized. The other was Clay Meckling, her mother's boyfriend. He had been trapped beneath a heavy beam after an explosion. Two people: What were the odds? Infinitesimal, probably. Well, maybe not in Acker's Gap.

Why hadn't it struck her before? Maybe because she never thought of either one of them—not Clay, and not this old woman—in terms of lack. They were strong, both of them. You did not focus on what wasn't there. You focused on what was.

Or maybe it wasn't as noble as all that. Maybe she was just obtuse. Inattentive. Preoccupied with her own problems—such as the fact that, while she'd slept better last night than at any time in the past six months, she'd still woken up with a cold feeling in the pit of her stomach, like something dark and greasy that hadn't gotten washed down the drain when it should have.

"Have a seat," McArdle said. Her voice was gruff, but it was an abstract, professional-grade gruffness. It didn't mean that she didn't like you. Carla knew that, too. She had spent a lot of her Saturday mornings here when she was in middle school and the first two years of high school, rooting through the stacks, searching for a book for a class assignment—or, more desperately, for a book that would verify that there really *was* a world beyond this one, a world beyond the narrow streets and throwback attitudes of a small mountain town.

McArdle used a stubby finger to point to the gray folding chair alongside her desk. "Sit," she said, repeating the order.

Feeling a bit like a cocker spaniel in an obedience class, Carla sat.

The Raythune County Public Library consisted of a single room in an old brick building across the street and down the block from the courthouse. The last three library levies had failed by large margins, which surprised nobody; it was hard to argue on behalf of books when half the county roads were crumbling to mush. The library, though, somehow hung on, battered but unbowed. The interior walls were dull brown sheets of trash-picked paneling, the bookshelves had been donated a decade ago by the Lowe's up on the interstate, and the carpet had been salvaged from a tobacco warehouse torn down in the 1950s. Water stains spread out across the drop ceiling like a child's drawing of pumpkin-colored clouds.

Right now the room was deserted except for the two of them. You could hear the ticking of the large round clock on the south wall—it was white with thick black numbers—as it went about its business, each bundle of ticks synched up with a faint forward tremor of the minute hand. Carla knew that clock, and she knew that ticking, and she knew the movement of that minute hand. She and the clock were old friends. Well—acquaintances, maybe. The clock had never done what she'd asked it to do: speed up when she was waiting for her mom to pick her up, or slow down when a guy from her biology class happened to come in and Carla hoped he'd notice her and say hi. No: That damned clock always played it straight, dispensing its rough justice minute by carefully measured minute. It never cut any corners. Never did you any favors.

Carla was surprised that no one else was here yet. Almost always there were at least a few other people in the library, reading a book or a magazine at one of the three long metal tables or poking at the keyboard of the single public computer on a card table in the corner. Sometimes the older people in town would actually hang out in front of the building before 9 a.m., waiting for Sally McArdle to come limping along with her Snoopy key ring.

Not this morning. Must be the weather, Carla thought.

"So," McAdrdle said. "You want to apply for the job." Her desk doubled as the circulation desk. She was the sole paid employee.

"Yeah."

McArdle looked down at the sheet of paper that Carla had handed her. It was her résumé. Carla had updated it on her laptop that morning.

With McArdle's head bent like that, Carla had a perfect view of the Z-shaped part in her yellowish-white hair. She wondered why old ladies like McArdle kept their hair so long. Why not just whack it off, instead of letting it dribble over her rounded shoulders like bleached-out moss draped across a rock? McArdle must have been young once, but Carla could not envision her any way other than this: dumpy, wrinkled, suspicious, her heavy black-framed glasses sliding down her blobby nose. She'd probably looked the same way at nine. She'd probably look the same way at ninety.

"I have several other applicants," McArdle said. She lifted her eyes from the paper. She glared at Carla. "And I don't play favorites. You know that. Doesn't matter to me who your mother is."

"Of course."

McArdle peered at her for a few more seconds, and then went back to reading the résumé. Carla waited. The clock hand moved.

It moved again.

"And you know," McArdle said, looking up once more, "the position is temporary. It's grant money. For a single project. A onetime thing. That means that when the job's finished, that's it. I couldn't keep you on even if I wanted to. There's no budget for that. So we're talking maybe a few weeks. A month, tops. An hourly rate—not a salary. No benefits. Are you sure you understand?"

"Yeah."

The old woman returned to the résumé. Carla sneaked another glimpse at the minute hand.

McArdle's face popped up again. "You'll be going," she said, "into some pretty remote areas. The grant covers five counties. Not only private homes, but hospitals, too. Trailer parks. Apartments. And nursing homes."

"Yeah."

"You'll have to input your notes at the end of every day. Keep good records. That means a lot of nighttime work. No putting it off."

"I understand."

"It'll be boring. Repetitious. Asking different folks the same questions, over and over again. Getting them to answer those questions when they're too shy to do it."

"No problem."

"And it's old people. People who talk slow and don't hear so well. People who'll repeat themselves. Go off on tangents. Pause a lot."

"Sure."

"You still think you're right for this?"

"Yeah."

"Why?"

"I know the area."

"So does everybody else who's applied."

"Yeah, but I know it from both sides." Carla had not thought about this before, but now that she had said it, she realized she actually believed it. "That's what sets me apart. I've lived here, yes—but I've lived away from here, too. It'll make a difference. To how I do the job."

She felt the sweat inching down the center of her back, gluing her sweater to the metal folding chair. She was perspiring not because she was nervous—well, not *only* because she was nervous—but also because this was winter. That was the thing about the season: You were freezing cold, but you had to wear so many damned layers that you were also burning hot and sweaty-gross under your clothes.

She really, *really* wanted this job. She had been cavalier about it until just a few minutes ago—it had sounded like a nice stopgap, a way to pass the time while she hid out from the complications of her life back in D.C.—but now she realized just how intensely she wanted it. She wanted to talk to people about how they had done it: How they had handled their lives. How they had made decisions and then stuck to those decisions. And it had to be strangers. She could not talk to her mom about it. Or her dad. Because they loved her. That tainted everything they said.

Carla leaned forward. "I can handle this, Mrs. McArdle. Better than anybody else. I've done some canvassing for nonprofit groups in D.C., so I know how to engage people. Get them to talk. And I know how to listen. I'm really good with computers, too—I worked for a year and a half in Web design—and so when I'm not out in the field, I can also be a sort of informal tech support for the computer over there in the corner. When people have problems." She saw the gleam in McArdle's eye. Patrons were *always* having problems with the computer, Carla knew, and when they did, they clogged up the area around the circulation desk with their agitated inquiries about control-alt-delete and all the rest of what Sally McArdle considered to be rank nonsense. A No. 2 pencil, a fresh notebook, and a 1968 edition of *The World Book Encyclopedia* were still the best research tools around: Carla had heard the old woman make that point on numerous occasions. Things that had happened after 1968 were just variations on a theme.

"That," McArdle said mildly, and Carla could tell she did not want to betray her delight at the idea of somebody else handling computer issues, "would be a big help."

Now McArdle frowned. She worked her tongue around the inside of her mouth. She stared hard at her, as if Carla was the last line on the eye chart. "I need to know something," McArdle said. "You left. Now you're back. Why? I mean, you went through a rough time four years ago. We all know that. That horrible man who kidnapped you—it must have been terrifying. Everybody understood why you wanted to go away. But here you are. And I need an explanation. Because I can't hire you and then have you change your mind and leave again. I have to make sure you will finish the project."

Carla had assumed this question would be coming. It was a natural one. It was a fair one. She wasn't ready to talk about the extent of her struggles—if she were, she would have confided in her mother. But Sally McArdle deserved at least a partial explanation. A few broad strokes. She was an intelligent woman, Carla knew, despite her aversion to new technologies, and she would be able to fill in around those details on her own.

"When I first left," Carla said, "I wasn't thinking about what happened that night. I couldn't. I just blocked it out. It was the only way I could function. And it worked. For years."

McArdle nodded. Unlike most people, she did not smile encouragingly and get all warm and gushy when Carla alluded to the kidnapping, or to the reality that she had witnessed the violent death of her best friend. McArdle remained silent. She continued to look at Carla without blinking. It felt like a compliment.

"Anyway," Carla went on, "they're sort of bothering me again. The memories, I mean. I guess I'm tired of running away from them. I want to deal with them straight up. Head-on. Full force." *Sort of like the way you're staring at me right now,* Carla was tempted to say. But she didn't, because it might have come across as smart-ass, and the only thing that annoyed Sally McArdle more than the mindless worship of computers was the smart-ass quip. Carla had seen her throw people out of the library for the unforgivable sin of replying to her with a wisecrack.

"Understood," McArdle said. She rearranged her large bottom on the chair. She always had trouble sitting comfortably. The clock's minute hand moved before she spoke again. "Want to know what I hear when you tell me those things?"

Carla nodded. She had no choice.

"This," McArdle said, "is your home."

Four hours, five meetings, nine phone calls, and three cups of coffee later, Bell stood up. She crossed the room to retrieve her boots for the walk to JP's. It was only a block and a half away, but the sidewalk surfaces were choppy and rutted with snow and topped off by a thin pernicious layer of ice. Even with last night's no-show by a second major storm, the effects of the first one still had to be reckoned with.

She was leaning over, one boot on and the other one just sliding up over her toes, when Lee Ann came in.

"Before you go—you have a visitor," Lee Ann said. She was almost seventy, but only diabolical and sustained torture would ever have gotten her to reveal it. Lithe, white-haired, and wool-suited, she had been a secretary in this office going back through five prosecutors; her domain was just outside Bell's, a spot that enabled her to screen people as well as calls.

She stepped to one side. Deputy Oakes ambled into Bell's office. His cheeks were less red than they had been yesterday morning, but not by much. He had wadded up his toboggan and pushed it under his arm for safekeeping. His black hair stood straight up from his head in multiple spots, the tufts frozen in place. He smelled of cold and wood smoke and something else, too, something ineffably male, with gasoline and a trailing hint of tobacco as the rich bass notes.

"Was just about to return your call from this morning, but had to come back to the courthouse, anyway," he said. "Thought I'd stop by. Looks like you're on your way out, though."

"I have time. Hold on." She finished with the second boot and stood up. "How're things going out there?"

He knew she meant the county back roads, the territory he patrolled every day.

"Spent most of my time so far this morning just pushing stuck cars out of ditches," Oakes said. He slapped at his chest, where the wool was marked with mud and damp. "Oughta see what happens when those wheels get to spinning and grinding—and me behind a car, rocking it back and forth while I'm hollering, 'Gun it! Come on, you sonofabitch!' Driver always assumes I'm talking to the car when I yell that." He laughed. Oakes had a deep genuine laugh. "Only good thing you can say about a big snow is that it cuts down on crime. It's enough of a chore just getting from place to place. Folks're not much inclined to act up."

She nodded. "Sounds about right." She reached for her coat. "Quick question. Where did they tow Darlene Strayer's car?"

"Impound lot over behind Leroy's place. Same as always. All four counties—us, Collier, Steppe, and Muth—use that lot. Until there's been a final determination by the coroner, that's where it'll stay."

"Good." She knew about that lot, but the knowledge had been shoved to another part of her mind after new things came in and commandeered the space.

He waited. She had more to say. He had worked with her long enough now to know that. He could sense the intensity of her thinking.

"Jake," she said. "I know we've already gone over this, but I have to ask again. Any possibility at all of foul play? Even a hint?"

He shook his head. "Nope."

"You're sure."

"Like I told you. Worst curve on the whole mountain. Bad weather. Evidence of driver impairment. Nothing at all to suggest anything but an accident. Tragic—but there it is."

"Okay. Just needed to double-check. I've heard from the family. Apparently Darlene thought somebody wanted to kill her."

The deputy's eyes widened. "She'd been a federal prosecutor—was it maybe related to that? Some kind of retaliation?"

"No idea. I only had a single conversation with Darlene's partner. A neurosurgeon named Ava Hendricks. She's convinced that someone wanted Darlene dead."

Oakes had no reaction to the gender of Strayer's partner. That pleased Bell. It was unexpected. In a choice between Rhonda Lovejoy and Jake Oakes as to who would be automatically accepting of people and who they were, she would have easily picked the kindhearted, salt-of-the-earth assistant prosecutor, and not the flashy, flirty, good-ole-boy deputy.

That'll teach me, Bell thought.

"I can ask Leroy to take a look at the Audi," Oakes said. Leroy Perkins ran a towing and salvage business as well as leasing the land to the counties for the vehicle storage site. He was also the best mechanic in the southern half of the state, Bell believed. Because of his expertise with anything that had an engine attached, he had performed some forensic work for her on previous occasions. And he had testified in several trials.

"Appreciate it."

"Right away." He started to reapply the black cap, squashing his ears in the process. "Can I give you a lift somewhere? I'm headed back out to the Blazer."

"Thanks, but I'm just walking over to JP's. Meeting somebody for lunch."

He waited for her to identify her lunch date. She didn't. He gave her a lazy smile and then a two-fingered salute, and he walked out ahead of her. His smile was easy enough to translate: *Okay, fine— don't tell me who you're meeting. Doesn't matter. I'll know in about ten minutes, anyway. Word'll get 'round. This is Acker's Gap, re-member?*

"I got the job." Carla had promised herself that she would be blasé about it when she told her mother, impassive, but she could not keep the pride out of her voice.

"Hey—that's wonderful, sweetie. Oh, and I'm sorry I'm late. Had to take care of a few things before I could leave the office."

"That's okay." Carla never expected her mother to be on time. Which was a good thing, because she never was. "Anyway," Carla added, "I start tomorrow."

The small diner was crowded and lusty with noise, but Carla appreciated that; the racket conferred a jury-rigged privacy on the booth that she had staked out an hour ago and defended against the glares of other people who were forced to settle for seats at the counter. Carla felt a little guilty about hogging a booth—the most desirable locations in the place—but then she remembered how loyal her mother had always been to JP's, and how she just about single-handedly kept it in business during rough patches in the beginning, and the guilt disappeared. While she waited, she had gone over the paperwork that Sally McArdle had given her, the details of the oral history project.

Each time the door had opened and a customer came in, a punch of frigid air came in with her. One of those times, the new arrival was Bell. Seeing her mother's face, seeing the light in her eyes when she spotted Carla and waved, Carla felt a brief needle of guilt. She considered telling her everything—such as the real reason she had fled her life in D.C. The thing she had done. The crime she had committed.

And what she was going through, from the unbearable headaches to the gut-churning panic to the constant anxiety.

No. She couldn't tell her. Her mother would try to fix everything—including Carla—and Carla did not want that.

So instead she broke the news about the job, and about how she would be starting right away.

Bell tossed her coat on the far side of the bench seat and slid in. Carla had hung up her own coat on one of the wooden pegs over by the cash register, but Bell knew better than to risk it; by now those pegs were thoroughly overloaded and tilting dangerously downward. Any second now, the jumbled hump of parkas and hats and long scarves would end up on the wet floor.

"Tomorrow seems kind of soon, don't you think?" Bell said. "I mean, you just got here."

"It's not like I need to ask directions. I grew up in Acker's Gap, Mom."

Before Bell could muster a counterargument, she had to say hello to Jackie LeFevre, who had stopped by the booth. Jackie had a plate of fried eggs in one hand and a bowl of white beans in the other. She was delivering the food to the next booth over. The owner of JP's was a tall, rawboned woman with a sharp angular face and thick black hair kept under tight control by a blue bandana. She wore a red-checked apron over her sweater and jeans. She also wore Birkenstocks, her footgear of choice no matter what the weather was. The Birkenstocks had provoked intense whispered conversations when Jackie first opened the diner five years ago. Now, nobody cared.

She frowned at Bell's empty coffee cup.

"I'll send Martha over with the pot," Jackie said. "Some things are sacred." At JP's, there was a facedown coffee cup on every place mat in every booth and table. If you did not want coffee, you moved the cup to one side. If you did, you flipped it over and tried to catch the waitress's eye to give her a hopeful grin.

"You all know what you want?" Jackie added. "I'll tell Martha that, too. So we can get your order going. I know you're in a hurry,

Bell. You always are." It was a dig, but only a mild one. Jackie had mellowed over the years since she'd first opened the diner, but there was still a coldness at the core of her, Bell thought, a permanent aura of aloofness, and a hint of distance and reserve in her manner. She had known sorrows—some that Bell knew about, and some, Bell was sure, that she did not. It was the same with everyone. But with Jackie, you had the sense that the sorrows were still calling the shots, no matter how automatic her smile.

"Good to see you, Carla," Jackie said.

"Yeah. Same here." Carla dipped her head. She didn't know what else to say. Well, maybe she did. "Cheeseburger for me. Mom?"

"Sounds good. Make it two."

"Two cheeseburgers," Jackie said. "Okeydoke. Well, I better get these lunches to their rightful owners." She used her chin to indicate the plate and bowl, and then she was off.

"So I'll be starting with Raythune County," Carla said, picking right back up again with the news about her job. "I have a list of people who've agreed to be interviewed. I can finish up here by the end of the week. And then get over to Muth County by early next. After that, I move on to Collier. Oh—and one of my stops in Muth County is that new place with the Alzheimer's patients. Apple-something."

"Thornapple Terrace. Darlene's father was a resident there." Bell frowned. "Hold on. How do you interview people with Alzheimer's?"

"Not the *patients,* Mom. The *staff.* Turns out they hire a lot of older folks. Aides, housekeepers, maintenance staff. That's our target demo— people over sixty-five."

"What do you ask them?"

"Everything. These are people who have lived their whole lives here. The idea is to get a sort of general sense of how and when they made the decision to stay in West Virginia."

As if they had a choice, most of them, is what Bell wanted to say. But she didn't. She had read a few articles about the project in the

Acker's Gap Gazette. Public libraries throughout the state had received grants to record brief autobiographies of longtime residents, after which the videos would be posted to a Web site that anyone could access.

Who leaves, who stays—that was always the central question around here, Bell thought. It was the question that haunted them all, as if the same ghost lived in every attic.

Darlene Strayer's face instantly came into her mind. Darlene Strayer, whose desire to go had been fierce enough to enable her to achieve escape velocity. And then she had died in the very place she'd fought so hard to leave behind.

"Earth to Mom," Carla said. "Your coffee's getting cold. And you don't like it unless it leaves third-degree burns on the roof of your mouth."

Bell looked down. The waitress had apparently come by, filled her cup, and probably traded a few banalities with Carla, all without her noticing.

Jesus, Bell thought. *I'm more affected by Darlene's death than I realized.* Although perhaps it was not only her death, but also Ava Hendricks's insistence that it was the result of a deliberate act, not of a dark night and a slick road.

"Oh. Okay." Bell took a drink. She barely tasted it. Was it hot? She could not have told you, seconds after.

"You were thinking about Darlene, right?"

"How'd you know that?"

"I didn't. Just a guess." Carla took a sip of her own drink, a Diet Dr Pepper in a tall green-tinted glass shaped like an hourglass. "I wonder what your friend would have said. About leaving West Virginia, I mean. Do you think she ever regretted it?"

Bell was ready to utter an emphatic and definitive "God, no." But something made her hesitate. Maybe it was the memory of Darlene's face at the tavern that night, when she talked about her father and how much he meant to her. About how important his belief in her had been, propelling her forward, giving her hope in future dreams that frankly were pretty outlandish, when you considered the distance that had to be traveled, the obstacles overcome. Darlene must have missed her father terribly, once she settled in D.C. And when he became ill, when his capacity for thought began to recede and finally wink out like a star in the dawn sky, her sadness must have been profound.

"Mom?"

Bell shook her head. She had always disliked people who could not manage to be present in the moment, and here she was: the worst of the lot. And with her own daughter.

"I think," Bell said, "Darlene probably regretted a lot of things. We all do. The trick of it, I guess, is learning how to live with those regrets. Finding a place to store them so that you can get on with things. You know?"

Carla eyed her glass. She poked at the ice cubes with the tip of her straw, making them bob and spin. "Yeah," she said. "So what're you going to do?"

"About what?"

"About your friend's death."

"Not much I *can* do. Pretty open and shut. All the facts say it was an accident." She had not told Carla about the disturbing call from Ava Hendricks. It hardly mattered; Hendricks would surely be showing up in person any minute to keep tabs on the investigation. "I'll take a second look at the report," Bell went on. "Just to be thorough. Have somebody go over the car—make absolutely sure it wasn't tampered with."

"I don't mean as a *prosecutor*," Carla said. She made a face when she pronounced her mother's job title. "I mean as a human being. I mean as somebody who was her *friend*. How are you going to deal with it?"

All at once Bell understood the motivation for the question. Four years ago, Carla had watched a friend—her best friend—die. She had seen him die a savage and horrible death. Given Darlene's ties to Bell, the news of the fatal accident must have brought back a nasty, swarming gang of memories for Carla, memories that cut and burned. Memories that wounded.

But then again, Bell asked herself, were there any other kind?

"I don't know," she said.

Lee Ann Frickie had left for the day. Her desk when Bell passed it was tidy, with the tidiness of the buttoned-up and battened-down. There was only one item on the polished oak surface, a piece of ruled notebook paper on which Lee Ann had written a single word: *Dark*. Bell understood. It was only 3:37 p.m., but given the state of the roads, her secretary wanted to make it home in her less-than-reliable Chevy Impala before the pure, hard darkness of winter overwhelmed the world. Lee Ann had a long drive ahead of her. Dusk had already begun to creep across the landscape, the slow-closing-of-a-coffin-lid blackness of winter that seemed to arrive earlier and earlier, day after day, throughout this meanest of seasons. It was the only time of year that Lee Ann asked for special favors.

Bell sat down at her desk. She wanted to finish an e-mail to Jim Ardmore. He was a state legislator, and he had asked her for an opinion about his idea for a new program. The goal: getting newly paroled people into drug and alcohol rehab programs. It was a good idea. Like a lot of good ideas, though, it lacked one essential feature: the money to implement it. Bell knew Ardmore was right when he noted that, in the long run, it was much cheaper to pay for treatment than to deal with the inevitable crimes of desperate addicts. But West Virginia was a place that seemed to specialize in the short run.

Her cell rang.

"Elkins."

"Hey, boss." It was Rhonda, her voice pitched low and snagged in a nest of static.

"You're out at the Terrace, right? How's it going?"

"Had to call you right away." Rhonda spoke quickly. Bell heard what she had missed before: the agitation in her assistant's tone.

"Rhonda, what—"

"There was another death here this afternoon." She lowered her voice even more. "I'm out in the lobby now. Took forever to get some privacy. They've been sticking pretty close to me ever since it was announced. Afraid of the bad publicity, I guess." She paused. Bell could imagine Rhonda looking around nervously, making sure no one was listening. "I was sitting in the director's office when the nurse came in and said an aide had found her. The dead woman's name was Polly Delaney. Eighty-eight years old. Only been here a week. They think it's natural causes—but it's just weird, you know? Three deaths so close together? Even if Harmon Strayer and Delaney *were* older than dirt—and suffering from Alzheimer's to boot—it's still a hell of a coincidence, timing-wise."

"You said three."

"Yeah. Turns out there was *another* death here about three weeks ago—a woman named Margaret Jacks. Same deal. She was in her early nineties, she'd been suffering from Alzheimer's for a long time. No family. Lots and lots of health issues—any one of which could've taken her down any minute—but still."

Bell did not respond right away. She closed her eyes. An ominous feeling was rising inside her, a dark tide of dread. Maybe it was just this latest news from Rhonda. Maybe it was residual shock over Darlene's death. Maybe it was the persistent chill of winter, which she never quite managed to shake off until midway through the spring. Maybe it was the darkness that seemed to prowl around just outside her window, nosing the lock, probing the seal.

Or maybe it was something else.

Chapter Six

I don't have time for this. And it's none of my business, anyway.

That's what Bell had been telling herself since 9 a.m., over and over again, as she drove along the fog-misted two-lane road the next day. After forty minutes she crossed the Muth County line. Ten minutes after that, she pulled into the large parking lot of Thornapple Terrace. By now the fog was beginning to break apart, departing this earth one misty bit at a time, drifting fitfully up toward a white sky that looked as if it might, at any second, unzip into a snow sky.

Bell did a quick exploratory visual of the scrupulously well-plowed space. She was here for a conversation with Bonita Layman, Thornapple's executive director, even though—as Bell reminded herself again—this was officially none of her business.

Which Layman, if she were so inclined, would be fully justified in pointing out to the Raythune County prosecutor, perhaps with umbrage in her voice—again, fully justified: This was not Bell's jurisdiction. Moreover, even if it were, there was no evidence of any crimes having been perpetrated on the premises, nothing that would give Bell the right—legal or moral—for any sort of inquiry, formal or informal.

Rhonda, after delivering the bulletin yesterday about another resident's death, had added that she'd found nothing unusual or suspicious about Thornapple Terrace. The staff, she said, was somber at the news of Polly Delaney's passing, but no one had taken her aside to whisper a warning that something untoward was afoot. Delaney, Strayer, and Jacks had been old and sick. Their deaths were perfectly normal. Perfectly plausible.

Bell had to agree.

Yet here she was.

She had engaged in a modicum of professional courtesy at her office that morning before setting out. At her request, Lee Ann had gotten Steve Black, the Muth County prosecutor, on the line. He was in his mid-sixties, and had occupied his office for three and a half decades. His greeting to Bell was effusive and overloud and far too familiar, just as she had expected it to be, because it always was:

"Belfa Elkins! Lady, it's been *way* too long." His Southern drawl had a cartoonish edge to it, as if he'd learned his accent not from his upbringing down near the Virginia border but from *Hee Haw* reruns.

"Hi, Steve. Sorry to interrupt your day." She had put him on speaker. She needed to twirl a pencil between her fingers as she talked, a way of diverting the surge of distaste she felt at the sound of his voice.

"Interrupt my day? Lordy, Miss Belfa, you just *made* my day. What can I do ya for?"

"I was thinking about heading over to Thornapple Terrace this morning. To have a chat with the director. Just wanted to keep you in the loop, in case I run into anything you need to know about."

There was silence on the line. When Black spoke again, his voice was a tick less friendly. "Really. Well, I know I don't need to tell you this, darlin', but that place is the first new business we've had starting up in this county in—hell, I don't know *how* long. Years, for sure. They employ a good number of folks. Pay a nice big tax bill, too, which is a mighty welcome development. I wouldn't want any trouble stirred up out there for no reason. Wouldn't want them to regret having located themselves in Muth County." That was a lot for Black to say all at one time. He stopped, and took a few makeup breaths. "So I'd like a little more detail, if you don't mind sharing. Whaddaya think you might find?"

"Probably nothing. But the father of a friend of mine recently passed away there. And I've heard about two other recent deaths. I thought I'd take a look around."

"This friend of yours. What's her father's name?"

"Harmon Strayer."

"Strayer." He seemed to taste the word as he repeated it. "Lady by that name died over the weekend, yes? Coming too fast down the mountain in that godawful weather on Saturday night—that was a Strayer, too, right?"

"Yes. Darlene was killed in a one-car accident."

"Oh, Lordy. Thoughts and prayers're with you, Miss Belfa. And with the lady's family. Thoughts and prayers. Lots of 'em."

"Thank you." Bell let a moment pass. "In our last conversation, she asked me to look into her father's death. Just thought I'd poke around a bit, ask a few questions. Out of respect for her memory. Nothing official."

"Forgive me, darlin'—I hate to even bring this up, but I need you to relieve my mind." Black really did sound reluctant. "This inquiry of yours—it wouldn't happen to be a sort of unofficial payback, would it, for the parent company picking Muth County over Raythune? I mean, we won it fair and square. We made a good deal with 'em. Had the perfect spot and all."

"Steve. Come on." It was too outlandish even to prompt a decent amount of ire. "You know better than that."

"I do. I do." He sounded pleased, though, to have her denial on the record. "What's the coroner say about Harmon Strayer?"

"Pretty much what you'd expect. An old man died in his sleep. Complications from Alzheimer's caught up with him."

Before Rhonda had ended her workday yesterday, she had faxed Bell the Muth County coroner's reports for the first two deaths. Early this morning, Rhonda stopped by the coroner's office in person to pick up the third one, the moment it was ready, and faxed that one, too. It had reached Bell before she asked Lee Ann to dial Black's office.

Natural causes. Natural causes. Natural causes.

"Those folks at the Terrace," Black said, "are already in pretty bad shape by the time they get there. The fact that a few of 'em pass away from time to time—well, it doesn't really call for an official investigation, you know what I mean? If we jumped into action every time an old man with Alzheimer's passes away, we'd have no resources left over to handle the real crimes. Just last month, we had four gas stations held up at gunpoint. Took a boatload of cash. Robbers're still at large. That's an *actual* threat, Belfa. We're just scrambling here to keep folks safe."

"Yes, of course. But you know what, Steve? This is the last thing I can do for my friend. She loved her father deeply. He was old and sick, and she knew that, but she was having trouble getting her head around the fact that he could just—just *go* like that, you know? After everything else he'd been through?"

"Gotcha. Makes perfect sense, honey." Black's voice was instantly cordial again. Playing the family card had worked. In these parts, Bell knew, sentimentality was as effective as a glue trap used to catch a mouse. "I'm not at all surprised that you're honoring your poor friend's memory by granting her final request. You're that kinda woman. You help folks out." His voice began to inch toward the lascivious, which is what usually happened at this point in any conversation with him. "Matter of fact, I've always hoped you might be willing to—well, to help *me* out a little bit, you know? I've got a few suggestions as to how that might be accomplished, if you ever find yourself feelin' lonely on one of these here cold winter nights." He chuckled. He was a man who parlayed his age and his position into a free pass for his sexual harassment and innuendo. If ever called on it, he would claim—while an expression of outraged innocence seized his wobbly, many-chinned face—that he'd been grievously misunderstood.

The fact that he was married and had six children was just an add-on to the disgust Bell felt after most contacts, on the phone or in person, with Steve Black. But she could not show it. Alienating a fellow prosecutor would only make life harder for her; there was always a fair bit of horse-trading and deal-making and favor-granting between country prosecutors, with goodwill as the necessary emollient.

And so she had headed on out to the Terrace—not exactly with Black's blessing, but at least he'd been notified.

Bell parked her Explorer in the second row of spaces. She backed in, so that she would be facing the facility. There were only three other vehicles in the lot. They probably belonged to staffers, she thought. In this weather, the number of visitors surely suffered a precipitous downturn.

Arms squared over the steering wheel, she took a moment to appraise the exterior. The main building was a large two-story redbrick box with decorative white shutters framing the second-floor windows, apparently to give it a homey touch. There was a smaller, one-story structure off to one side, also brick. It was linked to the main building by a winding concrete path that had been shovel-cleared; the strokes were still visible in the frosty residue glittering in the muted winter sunshine. A sign indicated it was a skilled nursing and rehab adjunct to Thornapple Terrace. A third structure on the other side, much less grand, appeared to be a maintenance shed.

Overhanging the main entrance was a dark green awning that jutted out at least two car widths, with the letters *TT* in swirling white on the front. If anyone was being dropped off or picked up here, they would be protected from the elements. Indeed, protection seemed to be the real cornerstone of the place, Bell decided. The bricks rose in straight rows, the edges met in sharp points, the roof was weather-tight. Quiet calmness prevailed. It was all very tasteful, and orderly, and civilized.

Yet on this day, a day of bone-white sky and insinuating cold, the Terrace also had a mildly sinister feel, as if rampant unruliness lurked just out of sight, waiting to break ranks and smash through all that carefulness, all that neatness, all that steady poise. Most people were brought here against their wills, angry and confused, by family members at the end of their tether. Their minds were disintegrating, piece by piece, like that early morning fog as the day advanced, and the internal violence of the loss—the terrible whirling flight of reason, the fleeing of memory—should somehow be palpable, Bell thought. There should be panic radiating from the outer walls like a heat signature on an infrared map. No one ought to give up the core of themselves without a struggle. No one should let the memories go without a fight.

But the fury and the desperation were all subdued, struck down by time and by futility and by the very fact of institutionalization— the dull soothing sameness of routine. Bell had a rough idea of what she would see on the inside of the Terrace. She would see women and men in baggy clothes shuffling slowly through carpeted corridors. Their faces would be blank. Their eyes would be like clear lakes in the wilderness, reflecting the sky above but not the depths below. There were no depths below. Not anymore.

Bell hated the idea that someone could be defeated by something as miniscule as plaques and tangles in the brain, that memories could be stripped away, layer by layer, until the only thing left was a spongy once-bedrock of nothingness. A wiser part of her, however, understood that it was not a matter of defeat, or of weakness. It was not a matter of will. It was just what happened.

She opened the double doors.

A receptionist behind a circular wooden counter looked up, offering Bell a neutral face. The lobby was otherwise deserted; no one sat on the couch or chairs. That surprised Bell, even considering the weather. Fifty-seven people lived here, she had learned from her research, and you'd think at least a few of them would have visitors waiting to see them. Or be walking through the lobby themselves. Then she reminded herself that this was not a regular nursing home. It was a place for people with Alzheimer's. She saw the thick green metal door leading to the hallway, and the keypad on the wall next to the door. There would be an identical keypad on the other side, Bell knew. The code was usually simple—1,2,3,4—but it was enough to keep vulnerable residents inside.

"I have an appointment with Bonita Layman," she said.

The receptionist, an older woman with short gray hair that glinted with bobby pins, nodded. She stood up, smoothed down the front and sides of her pink smock, and came out from behind the counter. She led Bell toward the executive director's office on the other side of the lobby.

Layman was waiting for her. She stood behind her desk. She got rid of the receptionist with a curt, "Thanks, Dorothy."

The woman in charge of Thornapple Terrace was not what Bell had anticipated. For one thing, she was young, perhaps no more than thirty, with a round cocoa-brown face and close-cropped hair that lay in tiny flat circles across her scalp. Gold hoop earrings shifted when she leaned forward to shake Bell's hand. Layman's dark eyes snapped with alertness and intelligence. And she seemed to be cheerful, whereas Bell had suspected that anyone who dealt daily with the tragedy of Alzheimer's would of necessity be somber and glum. Dressed exclusively in dark garments. Prone to deep sighs and frustrated frowns. Layman, though, wore a pale green skirt topped by a cream blouse and yellow cardigan, and her smile looked genuine, if a trifle wary.

One more time, Bell gave herself a quick private talking-to about expectations and stereotypes. She had fallen into some bad habits. Bad—and dangerous, too, for a prosecutor.

"I appreciate your time this morning," Bell said. She sat, taking off her gloves and her coat. She draped the coat across her lap.

The office was simple to the point of austerity. A red Keurig coffeemaker and a square black printer were the only items atop the credenza along one wall. On the opposite wall, two medium-sized prints offered ubiquitous mountain scenes, one set in daffodil-rich spring, the other in iron-gray winter. The director's desk featured a monitor and keyboard, a small brass lamp, a phone console, and a black mug bristling with sharpened pencils arranged in a tilting spray, each one equidistant from the one next to it.

"As I told you on the phone," Bell said, "and as I'm sure Rhonda Lovejoy mentioned yesterday, Darlene Strayer was a friend of mine. Shortly before her death, she asked me to look into the circumstances surrounding her father's passing."

"I saw the story online about Darlene's accident. It was shocking. Totally shocking."

"So you knew her."

"Oh, yes. She came by frequently to visit her father." Layman's small brown hands were clasped on the top of the desk. Her attitude was affable but puzzled. "Your assistant seemed startled yesterday by the death of Mrs. Delaney, but I'm not sure why. Our residents are quite elderly. Many are also gravely ill, in addition to having Alzheimer's. Sadly, we do see some deaths here. It's not uncommon."

"Some, yes," Bell said. "But three in such a short span? Surely that's unprecedented."

Layman cocked her head to one side. Her thinking pose. "We're a relatively new facility, Mrs. Elkins. We opened about three years ago. So there's really no precedent here yet. For anything. But based on the statistics at our other facilities, it's not an anomaly. We sometimes have clusters of deaths. And then there might be a long span—several years, in fact—with none."

"So you're a chain?" Bell asked. She knew the answer, having had Lee Ann Frickie do a Google search on the company yesterday, but she wanted to keep the conversation matter-of-fact, focused on numbers, before heading into the hard part.

"Yes. American Care Network is based in Dallas. We have twenty-seven facilities in fifteen states. We expect to open a dozen more by the end of next year," Layman declared, in a voice that knew its way around a PowerPoint presentation.

"No problem filling the rooms, I suppose."

"Quite the contrary. We have a waiting list." Layman offered a small, perfectly timed frown. "Alzheimer's is the coming storm, Ms. Elkins. Roughly half the population over the age of eighty-five has been diagnosed with it. It's on track to overwhelm the resources of our health care system—not to mention the patience and stamina of caregivers. In the next forty years, the number of new cases could very well triple. The cost of that? Twenty trillion dollars is the latest estimate I've read."

Bell nodded. Time to move past the bullet points. "Can you tell me a bit about the three people who died?"

"Of course." Layman reached into a desk drawer and pulled out a file folder. She opened it and used an index finger to find her place on the fact sheet. "Polly Delaney had just recently joined us. She was deteriorating rapidly, I'm sorry to say. One of our aides found her in her bed. She immediately called the front desk, and Dorothy notified the sheriff, which is always our procedure, even when there's nothing even remotely suspicious about the death. Deputy Wilkins came right away. The coroner immediately informed us that—just as we thought—Polly died of natural causes. It's a common progression with late-stage Alzheimer's. First they lose the ability to walk, and then they stop eating or holding up their head. Next the heart stops. It's usually a very quiet death—and it was for Polly Delaney. The same for Margaret Jacks. Three weeks ago, she was wheeled back to her room after dinner. She'd not been feeling well. She was found later that night by an aide. Margaret, too, had died in her sleep."

"Same aide?"

"Pardon?"

"Was it the same aide who found both residents dead?"

Layman searched the sheet. "Why, yes. Yes, it was. Marcy Coates. One of our best employees. Very reliable. Been with us since we opened."

"And who found Harmon Strayer?"

This time Layman did not need to look down. "That was Marcy as well."

"I'd like to speak to her."

The director frowned. "She's already been interviewed by Deputy Wilkins. And it's really not something she enjoys talking about, Mrs. Elkins. It was quite traumatic."

"I'll try my best not to upset her. But it's important."

A beat. "Fine," Layman said. "I'll get a phone number for you. She has the next few days off. It was the least we could do." She hit a few keys on her computer. "Yes. Here it is."

Bell put the number in her cell. "Thank you."

Now she waited. When Layman did not speak, Bell filled the silence herself. "How did Harmon Strayer die?"

Layman closed the file folder. She re-linked her fingers on top of it. Her dark eyes moved to the single window in her office. It looked out on another parking lot at the side of the building, a gray rectangle in which only two cars were parked, on opposite sides of the lot. At the edge of the space was a long pile of frozen snow, shoved there by a plow and heaped up. It wasn't much of a view.

After a few seconds Layman looked back at Bell.

"That was difficult," she said, her voice grave. "And it's even sadder, given what happened to his daughter this weekend. Harmon was a favorite with all of us. He was very respected around here. Respected and loved. Did you know he served in World War II? He was part of the D-Day landing. The thing about Alzheimer's, Mrs. Elkins—and maybe this is old news to you—is that you often lose short-term memories but not the longer-term ones. Not the oldest ones, the ones that you've had for decades.

"So Harmon couldn't tell you what he had for breakfast five minutes after his meal—but he *could* describe every detail of being on a U.S. Navy ship on D-Day. I mean *everything*—the gray color of the sky, the smell of the ocean. The way the Normandy coast looked as they got closer and closer. They weren't part of the original landing force—their ship was there to search for survivors. Or for any soldiers, alive *or* dead, who were still in the water. They were going to take them home."

"Did all those details come from Harmon?"

"Some. And some came from Darlene. She and I had a lot of conversations about her father. She'd grown up hearing the stories about his experiences on D-Day. And I got the rest of it from his oldest friend, the Reverend Alvie Sherrill, who also visited here quite often. Twice, three times a month. He'd sit with Harmon in the lounge. Always brought a checkerboard. I guess he hoped they'd play a game. That was never going to happen—Harmon was well beyond the ability to play checkers. But that's what they had done, for so many years, and so the reverend brought the checkerboard. It was a kind of symbol, he told me. Of what they'd meant to each other. Finally he just left the checkerboard here. Said he didn't need it anymore.

"He and Harmon would sit there at a little table in the lounge, hour after hour, with that checkerboard between them. When Harmon first came to live here, you might hear some conversation, but in the last few months, Reverend Sherrill did all the talking. That's what happens, Mrs. Elkins. Most of our residents don't talk at all anymore. I can tell you this, though. Harmon was blessed—blessed to have a loyal friend like that, as well as a devoted daughter. Harmon was one of the lucky ones."

"And the cause of death?"

"Same as the others. Natural causes. Harmon just didn't wake up one morning." Layman paused. "You would think we'd be ready for it," she said. "I mean, our residents are in their eighties and nineties, for the most part. And in the final stages of Alzheimer's. Their lives are basically over. But Harmon's death hit us hard."

"How did Darlene take it?"

"Not well. I was concerned about her. She seemed so—so torn apart, really. The news just destroyed her. She was definitely having trouble accepting it. Asked me a million questions. Demanded to talk with the staff. She told me she'd been a federal prosecutor—and wow, did it ever show! She could argue like nobody's business. It was her way of coping, I suppose—charging around, getting all the facts. But you know what? I'm going to miss her."

"Doesn't sound like it."

"Oh, don't misunderstand. She was tough on me, sure. But I'd rather deal with irate family members all day long than have to think about the residents who are truly alone. The ones nobody makes a fuss over. The ones nobody ever comes to see. The ones nobody cares about."

"I can understand that."

Layman laughed a quiet, soon-concluded laugh. "Well, I'm not sure my *staff* understands it. They get pretty weary of being screamed at by children or grandchildren or spouses who stop by once in a blue moon and want to know why Daddy's shirt is on backward. Or why Grandma's trying to flush the forks and spoons down the toilet. They don't understand. They're not here often enough to know how much their family member has deteriorated. And so when they do come by, and they see someone who looks an awful lot like their father or their husband or their great aunt—but who is acting like a demented stranger, they're shocked. And then they feel guilty. Guilty people have to find somebody else to blame. Lashing out is a pretty typical response."

I like this woman, Bell thought. *And I admire the way she handles her job.*

Liking and admiring, however, did not automatically equate to trusting.

"So you had a few run-ins with Darlene," Bell said.

"Nothing serious. We always worked it out. Everything she did was in her father's best interest—and it's hard to argue with that." Layman looked as if she was trying to find a way to describe the Darlene Strayer she had known. "I think what impressed me most was how she let Harmon have his dignity. She refused to treat him like a child. No matter how much he'd declined."

"How so?"

"Well, a few months ago, she found out that one of her father's best friends had been killed. A hit-and-run accident in Bluefield. A man named Victor Plumley. They'd all grown up together in a little town called Norbitt—Harmon, Reverend Sherrill, and Plumley. As teenagers they'd joined the service together. They were all on that ship on D-Day. After the war, they settled back in their hometown. Anyway, Darlene came to me with the news about Plumley. Asked if I thought she should tell her father. I told her not to. All it would do at that point was upset him. See, the thing about Alzheimer's is—he was likely to forget about his friend's death in about two minutes, anyway. So why tell him? Why put him through all that grief for nothing?

"But Darlene didn't agree. She thought about it a little while, and then she said, 'I have to tell him. Vic was his friend. Even if he forgets it a few seconds after I break the news, he deserves to know.' She wanted to honor her father with the truth. For Darlene, it was always about the truth."

Hardly, Bell thought. She pictured the small blue chip Deputy

Oakes had found in her friend's pocket, revealing the secret of her alcoholism.

The phone on the desk rang. Layman held up an index finger. "Just a sec," she said to Bell. "Yes. Yes. No," she said into the phone. "I'll have to get back to you on that one." Pause. "Okay, then—if you have to know right now, then no." She hung up. "This job has toughened me up considerably. My new motto is, 'She who hesitates is ignored.'"

Bell rose. "I'd better let you get back to work."

"One thing." Layman kept her seat. "I've answered your questions. Will you answer one of mine?"

"Sure."

"Why did you come here today?"

"I told you. Darlene asked me to."

"It's more than that, though. Isn't it?"

"I don't know what you mean."

"I mean," said Layman, who by now had decided to rise, too, putting herself at Bell's level, "that it wasn't easy for you to get way out here. I know what those roads are like. You could have just called. And I also know that county prosecutors don't have a lot of spare time. I don't think you would have gone to all this trouble just to hear about a death from natural causes. And anyway, it's old news now. It's history."

Bell let a few seconds go by. "Are you from the area?"

Layman hesitated. Her face indicated that she wondered if this was some kind of trap.

"No," she finally said. "Born and raised in Indianapolis."

"I'm not surprised. If you were from these parts, you'd understand that there's no such thing as history."

"I have no idea what you're talking about."

"There's no such thing as history," Bell went on, "because it's all still right here. The past never goes away. It's in the air. It's all around you, every second. It's just another name for the present."

"Still don't understand."

"Stick around long enough," Bell said, "and you will. Thanks for your cooperation." At the doorway, she turned. "Mind if I give myself a quick tour?"

"Not at all. I'd be happy to escort you, but I have a conference call with corporate coming up. Can't miss it." Layman gave her the code for the keypad.

For the next twenty minutes, Bell walked through the corridors of Thornapple Terrace. She did not doubt that Layman really did have a conference call scheduled. But she also knew that letting a visitor nose around without a chaperone made a compelling point: The staff here had nothing to hide.

A muted calm pervaded the place like an odorless scent. The carpet was a light plum shade. The ceiling was creamy white. A waist-high wooden rail ran the length of both sides of the hall, broken only by the doors to the residents' rooms. Most of the doors were open, and most of the rooms were occupied. The person inside either sat in a straight-backed chair next to the single bed, or stood by the window, looking out at the gray-and-white world of deep winter. Sometimes they noticed Bell, and offered her a face devoid of curiosity. Mostly, though, they did not notice her.

In one room, a lanky man in overalls and work boots was balanced on a stepladder. He was reaching up with a screwdriver to make an adjustment to the sprinkler head, which extended from the ceiling in a small silver ring. He appeared to be in his late forties or early fifties, hence Bell speculated that he was most likely an employee and not a resident. His movements were fluid and assured, and there was a seriousness of purpose in those movements, the kind of focus that was, Bell knew from her reading about Alzheimer's, generally no longer possible for the people who lived here. He looked down at her and nodded. He had the kind of face she liked—weathered, resolute. No fake smile. She gave a slight wave. She moved on.

She passed an emaciated woman of perhaps eighty or so who had stopped in the hall, feet spread, body bent and tense. She clutched the wooden rail with both hands, as if she were stranded on a high bridge and afraid of falling. Those hands were as twisted as tree roots. She called out to Bell. Bell turned.

"Yes?"

"I have to go home," the woman said. She wore a black turtleneck, black sweatpants with a white stripe down the side, and white tennis shoes. Her short white hair was combed straight back from her forehead. Her face had collapsed in on itself, the features receding into a conical basket of wrinkles. Her eyes were startlingly blue. But it was an empty blue, the blue of endless sky.

"I'm sorry," Bell said. "I can't help you."

"I have to go home," the woman repeated. "I'm late."

"I'm afraid I can't—"

"I said I have to go home! *I have to go home!*" And just like that, the old woman's agitation clicked in, and she reached out to claw at Bell's arm while she screamed. "Now! Now! Now! Now! Now!"

A woman in a pink smock and white polyester slacks swiftly appeared; she had been in one of the resident's rooms. She artfully wrangled the old woman, securing an arm around the hunched shoulders while prying the desperate hand from Bell's sleeve.

"Stop it, Millie," the aide commanded. Her voice was firm. Coddling would not get the job done. "Let's go. Come on. Back to your room." She gave Bell a bleak smile. She looked almost as old as the woman she was subduing, but her eyes were inhabited; they carried rich notes of awareness, of sentience. Duty mingled with sympathy in those eyes, Bell thought. Fatigue, too.

By now the maintenance man had come into the hall as well. "Everything under control, Amber?" he said.

"Got it, Travis," the aide replied. "Thanks, though."

"Okay. Just give a holler if you need me."

Bell continued her journey. She passed more residents up and down the hall, walking or standing, women and men who seemed as faded and diaphanous as pastel scarves tucked away in a forgotten drawer, their hair wispy, their skin dry, their spines crumbling under the steady assault of gravity and time. Most of them ignored her; some glared. A few smiled. One woman laughed, too loud and too long, and then stopped abruptly. A man cried—softly, with no emotion, and the only way you could know he was crying was the wetness on his papery cheeks. These people seemed like ghosts who returned again and again to a place that was supposed to be familiar, but somehow wasn't. Ghosts who haunted themselves.

Bell felt a gradual recognition of memory as more than simply an assemblage of known facts and mastered capacities and recalled experiences, and more, even, than personal identity, but as the very tent pole of life, every life, the solid vertical rod at the center of things. When it collapsed, the fabric gathered in folds around your feet; if the wind blew, everything was swept away. And the wind was always blowing.

There was sadness here, to be sure, but it was a benign, thoughtful sadness, a sadness that was nobody's fault. So different from a courthouse, she told herself, where the tragedies were vicious and deliberate, the wretched fates almost always self-imposed.

If Layman was hiding something diabolical, she had hidden it well.

In the lobby, the receptionist was dealing with a skinny, middle-aged woman who leaned aggressively over the desk, jabbing a finger in her face. As Bell passed them, she heard the skinny woman unleashing phrases like "know my rights" and "hearing from my attorney" in a dark, threatening voice.

The receptionist, however, was holding her own. To every point the visitor tried to make, she shook her head slowly, continuously, like a white-haired, pink-smocked metronome. "I'm sorry, Miss Ferris," the receptionist said, in what was clearly a practiced spiel, "but you know the requirement. You agreed to it. Unless we have a staff member available to accompany you and your father to the lounge, or unless you bring along a third party, you have to stay here in the lobby. We won't allow you to be alone with him. And one of our employees just went home sick, so we're shorthanded. I'm sorry, but we can't accommodate you today."

"I don't have to put up with this crap," the woman muttered. "You know what, lady? I got nobody to bring with me. I got friggin' *nobody,* okay? I used to have my brother Nelson, but he—" She broke off the sentence. She shook her head. "Stupid friggin' rules."

An elderly man waited at the other end of the reception desk. He was slender, and his clothes had a slouchy-casual look about them, giving him the relaxed aura of a retired golf pro: checkerboard driving cap; loose-fitting, yellow V-neck sweater; cuffed khaki trousers. Hands resting lightly in the pockets of those trousers, he seemed oblivious to the quarrel taking place just inches from him. *Must be a resident here,* Bell thought, basing her assumption on his vacant eyes and abstract, mindless smile, his lack of normal affect.

Before she had quite reached the front entrance, Bell took a quick look back. The old man winked at her.

"Hello there, sweet thing," he said.

Chapter Seven

Digital recorder.

Check.

Notebook.

Check.

Pen.

Check.

ID.

Check.

Brochure explaining the oral history project.

Check.

Had she forgotten anything? Carla switched off the engine. She'd had no trouble finding a place to park along the run-down, curbless street on the west side of Acker's Gap.

She wanted to wait a few more minutes before she got started. She sank back against the car seat. She closed her eyes and recalled her meeting with Sally McArdle yesterday morning. Especially the last part, right after McArdle had said, "Okay, fine, you're hired. Don't make me sorry I picked you." McArdle then scooted around in her chair so that she could reach into the bottommost bin of a file drawer. Grunting from exertion, she had drawn out a sheet of paper with a checklist on it. She read the items aloud to Carla—"You might want to be writing some of this down, Miss Elkins, if it's not too much trouble"—and Carla had brushed aside the sarcasm and did as she was told. Sarcasm was Sally McArdle's chief means of discourse. She didn't allow it in others, but she gave herself permission to indulge at will. It was her shield, her way of deflecting the world's gaze—a gaze either judgmental or pitying, and both were equally repugnant to the old woman. Carla knew that, and was prepared to deal with it in her new job. Sarcasm and Sally McArdle were old pals. They'd gotten acquainted right after McArdle's leg was amputated and now they were inseparable.

Carla thought about the items McArdle had enumerated yesterday, matching them up with her own list: Got it, got it, got it, got it . . . Had she skipped anything? Oh, right. The release form. McArdle had handed her a stack of pages. The people Carla would be interviewing had already agreed to participate, but she still had to have them sign the form. It authorized the library to post the material on its Web site.

Carla grabbed her slumping backpack from its place on the passenger-side floor and hoisted it up on the seat beside her. She rummaged through the motley contents—billfold, paperback copy of *1984,* ChapStick, an extra pair of gloves, cell charger, earbuds, tube of moisturizer, oatmeal raisin Clif Bar—until she found the release forms. She fingered one from the top of the stack. The paper was wrinkled, a natural consequence of having been thrust into a backpack. She smoothed it out against her right knee.

She was actually excited. She looked out the car window at the small brown one-story house set back from the narrow street. The house needed a new roof, and new siding, and a new front porch that did not tilt violently sideways, but the same was true of just about every house in this neighborhood. And all of them, Carla knew, had an equal likelihood of getting those things—a likelihood which stood at zero.

According to the list of names and addresses McArdle had given her, this was the home of Jesse and Annabelle Harris, aged seventy-five and seventy-eight, respectively. He was a retired employee of the Jiffy Lube over in Blythesburg. She was a retired cafeteria worker from Acker's Gap High School.

Maybe I'll recognize her from school, Carla thought. Abruptly, she wondered if that was okay. Or was she only supposed to interview people she'd never met before? Would that somehow taint the interview? Dammit. Why hadn't she asked Sally McArdle about that?

Before she'd switched schools for her senior year Carla had probably passed through the lunch line—what, two hundred times? Three? She tried to recall the face of a single cafeteria worker. Just one.

Nope. All that came to mind was a blur of hefty women in hairnets; in white uniforms that ballooned out like tents; in hard, black, lace-up shoes that must have been hell on swollen feet. Women with hairy forearms and big hands, ladling out beans and corn and Brussels sprouts into square indentations stamped into beige plastic trays. Women who never reacted to the insults and complaints from teenagers dreaming of fries and Diet Cokes.

I don't remember any of those cafeteria workers, Carla told herself. *Not one. I was too selfish, too self-absorbed. I can't even remember if their faces were black or white or brown. I won't know her.*

She was troubled by this epiphany, and then she was relieved by it. She was free to do her work. Annabelle Harris *was* a stranger to her—even though she'd probably passed the old woman many, many times, day after day, in the cafeteria of Acker's Gap High School, a place that smelled like ammonia and burned tater tots and sometimes—when the flu was at high tide—vomit.

Yum, Carla thought.

She suspected that Sally McArdle's sarcasm might be contagious.

She gathered up her equipment. She had already put on her cap and buttoned the top button of her coat—it was monstrously cold out there, or as Carla had described it in a text to her mom that morning: *friggin FREEZING*—and she might very well be shivering on that porch for a while, if Jesse and Annabelle were slow in getting up to answer the doorbell. Creaky arthritic limbs can't be rushed, right?

Her cell rang. Carla slipped off a glove and dug a hand into her coat pocket. It was probably her mom, checking to make sure she was okay. Carla would act all perturbed at the overprotective parent stuff—but the truth was, she kind of liked it. She liked the idea that Bell was there.

She looked at the caller ID.

She recognized the number—but it wasn't her mom.

Carla felt a hard torque of panic in her stomach. The blood rushed out of her head, or so it felt, as if somebody had pulled a cord and emptied the lot. The rigid chill that overtook her had nothing to do with the temperature.

She had to get hold of herself. She had to do her job. She had to carry on. She *had* to. And so she did what she'd been doing for the past week and a half, which was to ignore it, to pretend it wasn't happening.

I can do this, she said to herself. Chanting it, really: *I can do this. I can do this.*

She turned off her cell. She opened the car door.

Ava Hendricks was waiting for Bell at the courthouse. She sat on the small butternut couch across from Lee Ann Frickie's desk, feet flat on the floor, hands flat on her lap. Bell had never met her. She'd never seen her picture. But based on their brief phone conversation two nights ago, and on the extraordinary poise she witnessed now, the name "Ava Hendricks" came into Bell's mind the moment she saw the visitor.

"This is Dr. Hendricks," Lee Ann said. Her secretary did not get up. She was typing on her computer keyboard, and she simply lifted one hand and motioned toward the couch. "She's been waiting an hour and a half. Wouldn't let me call you."

And I bet she hasn't moved a muscle in all that time, Bell thought.

Ava's expression did not change. "I know how annoying it is to be interrupted in the middle of work," she said to Bell. "I didn't mind waiting."

She had crinkled, shoulder-length black hair that widened out from the top of her head in a frizzy A-frame, a small flat nose, and wire-rim glasses with lenses the shape of slender ovals. Bell put her age at somewhere between forty-five and fifty—same as her own. Same as Darlene's. Her suit was royal blue. An expensive-looking winter coat was folded on the seat beside her.

"I thought you might come yesterday," Bell said.

"Remember that eight-year-old? The one I told you about?"

"You operated on her."

"Yes. She took a turn for the worse. I had to go back in. I wasn't free to leave the hospital until today."

"Come into my office," Bell said. She glanced at Lee Ann, knowing her secretary would understand: no calls.

As soon as they'd resettled themselves, Bell offered coffee.

Ava grimaced. "I don't drink caffeine. It's been definitively linked to hypertension and gastrointestinal motility."

"Yeah, well—I guess I like to live on the edge." Bell rose and fussed with the curmudgeonly Mr. Coffee machine on top of the file cabinet. There was no sink in here; she kept a full carafe of water by the pot, ready for service.

A few seconds later the space was invaded by a loud hissing wheeze that sounded like a row of old men simultaneously blowing their noses. Then the lapel-grabbing aroma of brewing coffee hit the room.

"Damn," Ava said. "That smells pretty good. Maybe just this once."

Bell gave her a thumbs-up sign and scrounged in her desk drawer for a second mug. *Good,* she thought. Ava was human, after all. Her perusal of the hyper-impressive biographical information that Rhonda compiled had made her doubt it.

"I want to tell you again," Bell said, "how sorry I am about Darlene."

Ava did not answer. Bell was mystified. There were indeed all varieties and manifestations of grief, as she had pointed out to Rhonda, and it was true that each person grieved in her own way, but this was downright peculiar. An observer with no information would have assumed that the person named "Darlene" had been a causal acquaintance. Nothing more.

She handed Ava the filled mug. "It's hot. Be careful."

Her visitor nodded. "You know," she said, "we were probably two of the most mismatched people in the world. But I knew right away. And so did Darlene."

She stared at the front of Bell's desk. Her voice was low and soft, imbued with the faint tremolo of reminiscence that often comes, Bell knew, when people talk about the past and its most precious elements. Once again, she was knocked off balance by Ava's behavior.

"I'm very calm," Ava went on, as if she had read Bell's mind. "Restrained. I have to be. My work requires it." She said nothing about the challenge of being a woman in a field dominated by men, but Bell was sure it was not easy. "Darlene, though," Ava said, "was a hothead. She had a fierce temper. And she needed to be in motion all the time."

Ava looked meaningfully at Bell, who by now had taken her own seat behind the desk.

"You knew her," Ava declared. "You know what I mean. She couldn't sit still." She sampled the coffee. Nodded. "We never talked about it, but if I had to guess, I think that's what alcohol did for her— it settled her down. Smoothed her out. She didn't drink to feel good. She drank to feel normal. Like the rest of us."

"You said I knew her. I have to be honest—I don't think so. I never knew about her alcoholism." *Or about you,* she wanted to add, but held back.

"No one did. I didn't know myself, until we moved in together."

Bell gave her a surprised look.

"It's true," Ava said. "Once she trusted me, she told me the story. She realized she had a problem when she was still an undergraduate. Joined AA right after she started law school. There were . . ." She was trying to decide how to phrase it. "There were times when she went back to it. She fought it with everything she had, but sometimes it got the better of her. When she read stories about problems back in West Virginia, for instance. I think she always felt a bit guilty about not going back and helping, once she had her law degree. Or when her father was diagnosed with Alzheimer's. Emotions—she had a hard time with those. Facts in a court brief, she could handle. Feelings— not so much." Ava's voice grew more thoughtful, with a baffled- sounding awe at the back of it, like the wind in the sail. "She was a very different person when she drank. Completely transformed. I still loved her with all my heart—but I barely recognized her."

Bell let a brief period of silence settle over the room. She consid- ered the things she might say to this woman—about how no one ever really knows another soul, no matter how much you try or how close you are to each other—but the words, even unspoken, sounded inadequate to her, and far too glib. Almost insulting in their assump- tion that a relationship could be summarized in slogans, and that grief could be assuaged by homilies and aphorisms.

The great mystery at the heart of the world, Bell reminded herself as she regarded Ava's impassive face, was why people did what they did—not only the bad things, when they seemed driven by demons, but also the splendid things, the lovely, mysterious things, such as when and whom they chose to love. Psychology and probability could only take you so far. After a certain point the science broke down and simple magic took over. How else to explain how Darlene Strayer, a driven and haunted lawyer from Barr County, West Virginia, had fallen in love with Ava Hendricks, a brilliant and accomplished neurosurgeon from Boston, Massachusetts?

The truth, Bell believed, was that it could not be explained. And even if it could—would you really want it to be?

Truth. The word lay like a lead weight on Bell's mind. On her way back into town she had checked in with the Raythune County coroner, Buster Crutchfield. Time to tell Ava what she'd learned, as hard as it might be for this woman to hear about the partner she had cherished and respected.

"I know Darlene was active in AA," Bell said, "but the investigating officer believed alcohol was a factor in her accident. The coroner confirmed it. Her blood alcohol level was twice the legal limit."

"Yes," Ava said. "I know."

"How do you—?"

"I spoke to your coroner this morning. At length. Don't look so shocked. I'm a physician, Mrs. Elkins. And so is he. There's a thing called professional courtesy. Anyway, he told me about the blood work and toxicology report. Darlene was obviously impaired. Getting behind the wheel of a car in the state she was in—well, it was reckless and irresponsible. No question."

"So if you know all that, what makes you think her death was suspicious?"

"Darlene was afraid. She'd had some threatening calls."

"Did she contact the police about them?"

Ava placed the mug carefully on Bell's desk. "No. She didn't. I advised her not to. She had no proof, no recordings—it was only her word about the calls—and I told her they wouldn't believe her."

Bell felt a faint itch of impatience. "Okay, I'm still in the dark here. Who was supposedly threatening her—and why? And you just acknowledged that the evidence proves she was drunk when she started down that mountain Saturday night. So how could foul play have been involved?"

Ava answered the second question first. "Both could be true. She was drunk—*and* someone ran her off that road. Or tampered with her car."

"Look, Dr. Hendricks, I—"

"Call me Ava. If we're going to be working together, we need to lose the formality. I'll call you Bell."

"Whatever." Bell's impatience was growing. She would deal later with the "working together" fallacy. There was nothing to work on. "So I'll ask you again. Who might have been threatening her? Someone she prosecuted in federal court? Someone in organized crime, maybe?"

"No. Nothing like that."

"Then who?"

"Darlene believed that someone at Thornapple Terrace was complicit in her father's death. Maybe it was just negligence or maybe it was outright murder—she didn't know. She was collecting evidence. Interviewing the staff. They knew she was getting close. So they killed her, too." Ava's composure slipped for a moment. Her lip quivered. She swallowed hard. By the time she spoke again, she was back in control of herself. "I don't have a lot of details. And no description of the calls—just that the caller was male, or sounded that way to Darlene, anyway—and that he warned her to stop asking questions about her father's death. She wasn't sure why Harmon had been targeted. Maybe it wasn't personal. Maybe he'd been picked at random. She didn't know. Her investigation had just started. Darlene didn't tell me much more than she told you on Saturday night."

"Why not?" *For God's sake,* Bell wanted to exclaim, *you were her partner, right? Why the hell did she hold back? Why didn't she give you every speck of information she had uncovered thus far?*

Ava's eyes softened.

"Because she loved me," she replied. "And she didn't want to put me in danger. The more I knew, she said, the greater the risk. Given what happened to her up on that mountain, I'd say her apprehension was justified."

"Or it could be," came Bell's sharp response, "that she was paranoid, and her judgment was clouded by grief, and her suspicions were baseless, and she was beginning to realize that and was embarrassed by it, and so she was wallowing in self-pity on Saturday night, and after talking to me she just decided to get drunk in a bar and—in effect— kill herself. It could be that, too."

Bell hated her own harshness, but she was tired, and the world outside her window was getting colder and darker every minute, and there was no way to do anything more for Darlene Strayer than to mourn her and to wish that she had been able to accept her father's death from natural causes. Yes, Bell had promised Ava to look into the accident, but her visit to the Terrace that morning had yielded nothing of note. The additional deaths were explicable. Everything made sense.

It was time to be honest with Darlene's partner.

It was time to stop indulging the highly unlikely notion that a conspiracy was brewing at an Alzheimer's facility in Muth County, West Virginia, a conspiracy to do—what? To rid the world of octogenarians with bushel-baskets of serious health problems and the inability to recall which end of the toothbrush they ought to use?

No. The truth here was not dramatic or sinister. It was ordinary: A very old man with a very bad disease had died. End of story.

Ava seemed taken aback by Bell's brusqueness. Her umbrage was almost immediately superseded by a kind of snippy stoicism. "All right," Ava said. "Then I don't suppose there's anything more for us to discuss. Thank you for your time." She stood up, tapping the rim of the mug with two fingers as she did so. "And for the coffee."

Bell watched her gather up her coat and her purse. "You'll let me know the date and time for Darlene's service?"

"Yes."

"It'll be back in D.C., I suppose."

"Yes."

"And that eight-year-old." Bell had to know. "She died, right?"

"What?"

"The child you operated on. You said there were complications."

"There were."

"So I'm guessing she passed away."

"No. She's holding her own. Chances are, she'll make a full recovery."

I have to remember, Bell thought. *I have to remember that happy endings do exist. It's easy to forget. Because I've seen so few of them lately.*

By seven p.m. Bell was thinking not about crime and punishment, but about spaghetti and meatballs. She had promised to make dinner for her and Carla. So she stopped at Lymon's Market on her way home to pick up the ground beef and the tomato sauce and the spices. Her intention had been to leave the courthouse much earlier—but that was always her intention, and it was usually an unfulfilled one.

Lymon's parking lot was almost empty. When Bell opened the door of her Explorer, a freezing wind fought her for control of the handle. Twice she skidded on the icy pavement, barely catching herself before she ended up flat on her ass. Opal Lymon constantly harangued her staff to keep this lot cleared and well-salted, but even when they did, once the sun went down and the temperature dropped, the melty runoff from a day's worth of parked cars froze into a dangerous black glaze. Moreover, snow had started again, a thick continuous shimmer of flakes that rapidly stacked up. By the time she reached the front door and watched it slide open automatically, Bell's hair was wet.

God, she thought. *I hate winter.*

It was nearly closing time, so she had to be quick about her business. She'd just put a jar of Ragu into her cart when her cell rang. She made a quick bet with herself that it was Carla. What else would her daughter be reminding her to pick up at the market? Of course: Cap'n Crunch. Carla had been disappointed to discover that, once she'd moved out four years ago, her mother did not still keep multiple boxes in stock in the pantry.

"Hey," Bell said. She jammed the phone between her ear and an upraised shoulder. She needed to keep shopping while she chatted.

"Boss." It definitely wasn't Carla. "I'm over at my grandmother's house. Grandma Lovejoy."

"Hi, Rhonda." Bell was holding up a second jar of Ragu. Should she? She could always freeze the extra batch. *Yes: two jars, definitely.*

"I hate to bother you, but Grandma's kind of upset."

"What's wrong?"

"Well, she's been trying to call her friend for the last few hours. Connie Dollar."

Bell did not want to be rude or impatient with Rhonda, but she needed to finish her shopping and get home. And she was unclear as to why this was any of her business.

"Rhonda, I—"

"Connie works at the Terrace, remember? She's in housekeeping. She's gotten to be good friends with an aide named Marcy Coates. Marcy's the one who found those residents who died. They gave her a few days off—she's been real upset about it, and no wonder. Well, Grandma was calling Connie because she knew Connie was worried about Marcy. And that Connie planned to go over to check on Marcy tonight."

Bell's head was starting to hurt. The maze of relationships in

Rhonda's world often had a byzantine quality that you tried to chart at your peril. "I'm a little busy here. Can we talk later?"

"Bell, listen. Please. Grandma talked to Connie's husband, Luke. Turns out Connie went over to Marcy's house three hours ago. And nobody's heard from either one of them since. It's over off Hanging Rock Road. Marcy doesn't answer her home phone. Neither one's answering her cell."

"Maybe their cells are down in the bottom of their purses. Happens. And the landline's out. Has anybody gone over there to check?"

"That's why I'm calling you. Luke drove out to Marcy's place. We just heard from him. Says Connie's car is there, and Marcy's, too, but there's nobody home. The front door's wide open. Cold as it is, that doesn't make any sense. Luke says the door is just swinging back and forth on the hinges. Says he found signs of a struggle inside—chairs on their backs, dishes knocked off the kitchen table. The home phone's been pulled clean out of the wall."

Bell did not like the sound of this. She felt a tingling in her fingertips.

"Call Sheriff Harrison," she said. "Right away."

"I did. She's on another call. So she's sending Deputy Oakes."

"Good." She didn't realize how hard she was gripping the handle of the grocery cart. She looked down. The knuckles of her hand were drained of color. "Rhonda, call Luke back and tell him to get out of there. Get out of the house. Just go sit in his car—with the doors locked—'til Jake gets there." By now the tingling was moving through the rest of her body, splitting into separate filaments, branching out. She had been feeling cold all day but now she was even colder. It was a different kind of cold. It was the cold of foreboding.

"Bell, what do you think is going—"

"Just call him, Rhonda. Just tell him to sit tight, okay?"

"Okay."

"Good. And you stay there with your grandmother. Don't leave her." *She's going to need you,* Bell thought. *If the news is as bad as I think it might be, she's definitely going to need you.*

They found the dog first. Marcy's rambunctious border collie, Nadine, had had her throat cut, and then, based on the blood trail that Luke Dollar missed in the darkness but that the deputies would later discover, had staggered crookedly out of the house in a daze of mortal pain. She collapsed in the snow about a dozen yards from the front porch. Later, the people who had known Marcy Coates would say they were not at all surprised at the dog's behavior; Nadine was a noble and resolute warrior. Whoever had gone after the women would have had a real fight on his hands, getting past Nadine.

It took Oakes and a second deputy, Charlie Mathers, another twenty minutes to locate the bodies of Connie Dollar and Marcy Coates. The deputies had searched in an ever-widening radius with the house as the center point, moving through the densely packed snow in which they repeatedly sank to the tops of their boots. They fought for visibility through the silvery haze of snowfall. They wove their way between the trees, trees that looked like black stakes jammed randomly into the snow as if searching desperately for its heart.

And then the heavy-duty flashlights illuminated a gruesome tableau. The two old women lay on their backs at the base of a tree about three-quarters of a mile away, on a white mound of snow, limbs twisted like an Egyptian hieroglyphic. They were holding hands. By now, the snow had almost covered them over.

Connie had been shot twice in the chest. Another bullet had caught Marcy full in the face. The sight of the carnage caused Deputy Mathers to stagger backward a few steps, lurch to his left, and vomit up his dinner—pork chops, applesauce, and corn bread—in the snow, after which he dragged his wrist across his mouth and apologized, an apology to which Oakes responded: *Forget it. Only reason I didn't upchuck myself is 'cause I ain't had my dinner yet.*

The women were not wearing coats, only the long-sleeved wool dresses and support hose they'd been wearing when they were surprised—or so the investigators would later theorize—by the intruder. They had not had time to grab their coats or their boots. While the dog held off the assailant as long as possible, until her throat was slashed, the women had bolted out the back door, making a run for it through the fast-falling snow.

They must have blundered and crashed across the freezing woods as best they could—Marcy with her bad hip and her peripheral neuropathy, and Connie with the extra sixty pounds she'd been carrying since the birth of her third child, forty-one years ago, and a painful lack of cartilage in her right knee—and given up only when it became clear that they had to. They were at the end of the line. They must have been able to hear their pursuer as he chased them, getting closer and closer. They might have been able to hear his breathing. Certainly, they would have heard him thrashing through the woods just as they had done a few seconds earlier, only much, much faster, batting away the snow in front of his eyes, tearing at the vines and branches. Relentless.

And then, the evidence appeared to show, they had understood that they were not going to be able to escape. At that point, they had turned and faced their attacker. They joined hands. Connie's friends would smile at that detail—later, months later, once those friends had gotten over the shock and the grief and could finally contemplate a thing like smiling, which at first had seemed impossible—and say, *Yes, that's our Connie, that's exactly what Connie would have done.* With the end so near, with death a certainty, she would have reached out her hand and taken her friend's hand, so that neither one of them would face it alone. Connie's husband Luke Dollar said so, too. She'd have done that. That was pure Connie, he said.

Holding hands, looking their killer straight in the eye through the whispery scrim of snow, they waited for the shotgun blasts that had not been long in coming—or so their loved ones hoped, knowing the agony of anticipating the grimly inevitable.

Chapter Eight

She needed to talk to Nick.

Two days had passed since the night when Connie Dollar and Marcy Coates were found dead at the base of the tree. Heavy snowfall had obscured any usable clues. A search of the house and repeated sweeps of the area had turned up nothing.

The conviction had gripped Bell suddenly: *I have to talk to Nick Fogelsong*. So even though she had just settled herself at her desk on Friday morning, she sprang up again, pulling on her coat, ignoring Lee Ann's perplexed and even slightly alarmed look as she left.

She parked in front of the long, low, cedar-shingled house and walked around the north side, heading for the backyard. The walks bore no evidence of the week's repeated bouts of snow; they were cleaned down to the quick. Nick was a demon with a shovel.

She was not in the least concerned when she heard the *pop!* of a gunshot as she rounded the back corner. She had expected it. It was the quality of the sound, not its presence, that intrigued her. Cold air changed everything. Sound waves traveled faster in warmer air than in cooler; the cold muddied the sounds, knocking the sharpness out of them. She heard another *pop!* and then two more in succession: *pop-pop!*

The regularity of the shots—the way they were spaced out, the orderly rhythm of them—meant target practice, not random gunfire. Nick was trying to get his marksmanship skills back. A year ago he'd had an injury, a serious one, and the nerve damage in his right arm was a hill he just might not be able to climb. Ever. But no one said that to his face.

"Hey," Bell called out. She knew better than to sneak up on a man with a gun. You made your presence known, loud and clear and often. If she'd had a bugle, she would have tooted it.

He lowered his weapon. He turned around. He grunted a greeting.

Nick was wearing a gray plaid Woolrich coat and boots, a workingman's clothes, but the dress pants were the giveaway. He had a desk job now, an executive position. Until recently, he had been sheriff of Raythune County. He had held that position for many years, and for the last portion of them, he had been Bell's confidante and partner in keeping peace in the region—but not anymore. He had gone another way. She had finally forgiven him, but it was a long time coming.

"Heard about those poor old ladies out on Hanging Rock Road," he said. "Any leads?"

"No." She crossed her arms, jamming her hands up into her armpits. "It's damned cold out here, Nick. Can we go inside to talk?"

He nodded. "One more?"

"Sure."

He turned back to the cardboard target he had suspended from a pair of thin black cables that traversed the back of his property. On the target was a sketch of the top half of a man's body; the man was crouching, a revolver in his hand. Tiny circles with numbers on them radiated out from the man's center of gravity, the numbers getting smaller as the size of the circles increased. Nick bent his knees, brought both hands up on the Glock, held his arms out in front of his body—not rigid, but relaxed and natural—and aimed and fired. The *pop!* ricocheted off the white-hooded mountains in the distance, but in the frigid air, it never achieved the wincing sharpness of a classic echo.

The target jumped and shuddered. He holstered his pistol and pulled at the parallel cables, hand over hand, until the target came close enough for him to snatch it off the line. He checked it out. He had hit it very close to the center.

"Not bad," Bell said. With Nick Fogelsong, you had to keep the compliments to a minimum. Anything that reeked of gratuitous praise would send him into a two-day brood. She had learned that the hard way.

He shrugged. It was good. He knew it was good. But he also knew that it did not really mean anything. Not yet. He had a long, long way to go before he was anywhere close to where he had been as a marksman. He was fifty-six years old. Even without the injury that had almost taken his life—he had been shot last year by a drug dealer—he would be fighting time. The fine motor skills that had made him a crack shot were the first to go. He hated that. But hating a fact did not make it any less true.

They sat down in the kitchen. It was a bright, well-kept one, with clean countertops and a white tile floor. Bell piled up her outerwear on a third chair. Nick gestured toward the coffeepot. She shook her head.

"Already had a full pot before I left home this morning. 'Bout to float away as it is," she said. "Where's Mary Sue?"

"She's been volunteering at the school." He did not need to specify which school; Bell knew he meant Acker's Gap Elementary. His wife had taught third grade there for many years until mental illness forced her to take disability leave. She was doing better now, with the right balance of medication. And with a diligent daily attention to routines, such as keeping a kitchen spotless. But she wasn't able to teach third grade anymore.

"She likes being back there," Nick went on. "Helps out with the math classes. Goes in on Fridays, when I'm home in the morning. I give myself a half-day off. She claims that otherwise we'd be tripping all over each other, both of us home on a weekday morning. Probably true." He was head of security for the Highway Haven chain—a good job, a job coveted by a lot of people, but not the one he'd done for most of his adult life. And not the one he wanted.

It struck Bell—not for the first time, certainly, but with a poignant force today that she had not felt before—that Nick and Mary Sue were in the same boat now, trying to work their way back into their former lives, trying to recover some essential part of themselves that they had lost along the way. There was a kind of quiet heroism about that. But at what point, she had begun to wonder, did it start to be counterproductive, robbing the present because your hopes were fixed so passionately on the future?

Unclear. And frankly, she knew she was in no position to be giving life advice to anyone.

"I need your help, Nick," she said. "I'm just frustrated as all get-out."

"This about the old ladies?"

"Sort of. Pam Harrison is pretty well convinced it was the same perpetrator who's been holding up gas stations in Muth County." Harrison had been deputy sheriff under Nick Fogelsong, and then, with his endorsement, was elected to the top spot.

"And you're not."

"That's a hell of an upgrade—going from robbing gas stations to committing murder," Bell declared. "And why take the chance? Marcy Coates's house was a run-down piece of crap. Her TV set was about a thousand years old. And there were no other electronics. No jewelry. Who'd target her in the first place?"

"What does Harrison say?"

"She says beggars can't be choosers. She says the assailant probably just found himself out there on Hanging Rock Road. Maybe he was cold and hungry. Maybe he saw the light in Marcy's window. Stopped by to take what he could get. Maybe they resisted. And that's what got them killed."

"Two old ladies. Resisted."

"Exactly," Bell said, smacking the tabletop. "You see my point. Those women were—and forgive my bluntness here—old and fat and helpless. The chances of either one of them putting up a fight? Nonexistent. And anyway, these were good people we're talking about here. If a stranger came along and asked for a sandwich, they'd fire up the stove and ask him if he wanted his grilled cheese on white or wheat."

"So you figure it was on purpose. Somebody wanted one or both of them dead."

"Maybe. Makes more sense, anyway, than the idea of two old ladies sneering at a knife-wielding, gun-toting maniac and saying, 'Make my day.' I mean, come on." She shook her head. "The good news is that Jake Oakes isn't giving up. He pointed out that the killer would have had to check and make sure Coates and Dollar were really dead. Couldn't take a chance on surviving witnesses. So our man might have gotten some of their blood on his shoes when he did that. Just a drop or two, maybe—and he could very well have burned his shoes afterward—but it might give us an angle if we take someone into custody."

She filled him in on her visit to Thornapple Terrace, and on the fact that Marcy Coates was the aide who had found each of the three deceased residents. He knew about Darlene Strayer's death on Saturday night; Bell had mentioned her name to him in the past, when Darlene was involved in a run of big cases.

"I'd been meaning to give you a call about that," Nick said. "Express my condolences."

"Well, now you've got a chance to do more than just mumble some empty platitudes in my direction," she shot back. She knew he would not get mad, but instead would appreciate the point of her visit. "Help me think this through, Nick. Did Marcy's job at the Terrace have something to do with her death? It's tempting to think so—but how to prove it? And even if there *is* a connection somewhere, and Marcy gave Mother Nature a little nudge, so what? Three old people with late-stage Alzheimer's die in their sleep. Not exactly hot news, you know? Not even much of a tragedy. More like mercy."

"And you've still got Darlene's death. And her suspicions about her father's passing." Nick's voice was ruminative.

"Yes. But the truth is, every single thing that has happened—Darlene's accident, the deaths at the Terrace, even the murder of the two old women—could have another explanation entirely. They might not be linked at all. It *sounds* like a lot of bodies, but except for the deaths of Marcy Coates and Connie Dollar, these are probably not criminal justice matters at all. Just happenstance. Inevitability."

"What does your staff say about it?" Nick believed that most people in the world were fundamentally overrated, but he had an abiding respect for Rhonda Lovejoy and Hickey Leonard. He had worked with them on enough cases over the years to know who they were.

"Wish I knew," Bell said.

"Pardon?"

"We haven't had a staff meeting in a while. Rhonda was getting ready to try the Charlie Vickers case, but she needed an emergency family leave. So Hick took over for her. He's up to his ears in trial prep, trying to be ready for next week."

"What's going on with Rhonda?"

"Her grandmother had a stroke on Tuesday night—the night they found the bodies. Not expected to make it. The news was just too much for her to handle. Grandma Lovejoy was best friends with Connie Dollar. Blames herself, apparently, for not trying to reach Connie earlier." Bell shook her head. "She's Rhonda's paternal grandmother. Rhonda's been really close to her since she was a little girl. And you know Rhonda—her family is her life. There's no way I wouldn't grant her the leave."

"Well," he said. "At least you've got the sheriff to talk it over with. Discuss strategy."

Bell grimaced. "I respect the hell out of Pam, but you know how she operates. Makes up her mind early. After that, it takes an act of God or Congress to get her to change it. And neither one of those parties is much concerning themselves with the deaths of a bunch of old folks in West Virginia." Last year, Pam Harrison had persuaded Bell to prosecute a man for a murder that, evidence later proved, he did not commit. The rush to judgment was a habit to which Harrison seemed permanently inclined. It was her only significant flaw, as Bell saw it—but it was a doozy. From that moment on, Bell had relied less and less on Harrison's instincts and perspective. Harrison would never be to Bell what Nick Fogelsong had been. Never again would Bell bring her into the innermost circle of her thoughts.

"And the sheriff," Nick says, "believes it was a crime of opportunity."

"Yes."

"Even though Marcy Coates worked at the Terrace."

"Yes." Bell's frustration showed through in her voice. "I'm going to keep pushing, of course. Talk to Marcy's family. Find out the circumstances surrounding her discovery of those three bodies at the Terrace. But I sure wish I had Rhonda and Hick to help me think it through."

"It's a shame you can't rely on Clay. He's got a good head on his shoulders, that one. But he's a civilian." A slight chuckle. "Hell, so am I, come to that. Better watch what you tell me, young lady. Professional ethics and all."

She was quiet.

"Hey," he said. "I was kidding. I'm grandfathered in, right? As the former sheriff?"

"Right."

Her mind was elsewhere. Should she tell him? Jesus, she wanted to. She wanted to tell him the whole story, right here and right now, because Nick would listen, and he would guide her toward the correct course of action, and she could finally go one way or the other way. She could forgive Clay or she could tell him that she *couldn't* forgive him—not now, not ever—and that they needed to move on, both of them, in separate directions, toward separate futures. No hard feelings.

Feelings. Those were the real culprits. Those were the guilty parties in this mess. If she did not feel what she felt for Clay Meckling—a lively and beguiling sexual attraction, an immense respect for his intelligence and his work ethic and his ambitions, plus a quiet comfort in just being in his presence, all of which added up to the simple fact that she was in love with the man—if she didn't have *that* to reckon with, she would not be in this fix in the first place.

He was all wrong for her in a hundred different ways. He was too young, and he wasn't sure if he wanted to stay in Acker's Gap long-term. They did not have any of the same friends. They had very few shared life experiences. Their relationship over the past four years had been up and down. On and off.

But she loved him, she loved him passionately, and his absence from her life for the past couple of weeks—her idea, not his—had made everything on her prosecutorial plate harder, from the violent deaths of Darlene Strayer and the two old ladies, to the less urgent but still perplexing deaths of three residents of the Terrace.

Damn, Bell thought. *I wish . . .*

What? What did she wish, when it came to her and Clay?

She did not really know.

Nick read her mind. Or at least it seemed that he had, because he said, "Things aren't great, I take it, with Clay. Something happened." Before she could get mad at him, tell him it was none of his damned business—she was just about to do just that, and he knew it—he held up a hand to head off her wrath. "You don't have to confirm or deny. Don't like to pry into your personal life, Belfa. You know that. All I want to say is that Clay Meckling's a fine man. Never known a finer one. Whatever you two are going through—work it out. He's worth it. And you're worth it."

Bell gave him a hard, steady glare, like a Buick with its high beams on. She hoped he would keep up his little mind-reading trick for just a few more seconds and pick up on what she was thinking with all her might:

You don't know. You don't know what it is that he did.

She did not say anything, though. They had strayed too far off the topic of what she had come here to talk about. They both sensed it.

"So," he said. "You'll keep on asking questions out at the Terrace."

"Yes. I've got a hunch that somehow it all starts there. Somebody knows something. So I have to pry it loose. A little bit at a time, if I have to."

"Depressing place. Went there once myself. Mary Sue's great uncle needed a ride to go see an old Army buddy who'd just moved in. We sat in that visitors' lounge for about an hour. Felt like about eight hours, you know? All those sad folks, shuffling along. Asking the same questions over and over again. 'What day is it?' You'd tell 'em, and then a minute later, you would get it again: 'What day is it?' Skin and bones, a lot of 'em. They forget how to eat, is how it was explained to me. They waste away, not remembering the names of their children or the year they were born or where the hell they are. Sure you're ready for that on a regular basis?"

"Of course not. Who could be ready for that?"

"Point taken."

"If those three old people died of natural causes—which is what it looks like—I'll be able to ascertain that quickly and then move on. Get the hell out." Bell smiled a rueful smile. "Until the day they finally stick *me* in a little room over there. For keeps. Or you. Or any of us. No telling what the future holds, Nick. That's the hell of it."

He used his thumbnail to pick at a spot he saw on the table. There may or may not have been an actual spot. Truth was, he did not want to look Bell in the eye right now, because a thickness had come into his throat. He was afraid it might show up in his voice.

"You ever wonder?" he said.

"Wonder what?"

"If it's worth it. Fighting for a long life. Doing everything you can, to last as long as possible. I mean, you either end up like Rhonda's grandmother—flat on your back in some hospital, rigged up to a bunch of damned machines, or you end up like those folks out at the Terrace, with your memory eaten away like a sweater that the moths have had their way with. Living a kind of death in life. Or you get yourself butchered like those two old women in the woods. Be honest here, Belfa—is it really worth it? Any of it?"

"Don't ask me that today. I've got too much work to do."

"When can I ask?"

"Tomorrow."

"And what are you likely to say then?"

She grinned at him. It was a little catechism they went through. He knew what she was going to say—they had been in this place before, the two of them, burdened by duty and sadness and a sense of futility, and sometimes she was the one asking and he was the one answering—but he needed to hear the words from her. Just as, when the roles were reversed, she needed to hear the words from him.

"I'll say, 'Ask me tomorrow.' Best I can do, Nick."

Marcy Coates's granddaughter, Lorilee Coates, sat in the wooden chair in front of Bell's desk. Or tried to.

She could not hold still. She itched and she fidgeted. She coughed. She sniffled. She rubbed her nose and scratched her skinny arms. Left arm with the right hand, right arm with the left hand, left arm against the back of the chair. It was eight degrees outside, and she was wearing cutoff jeans and a pink tube top. Her outerwear—it lay in a slatternly heap on the floor—was a jean jacket that still had the Goodwill tag affixed to it by a dirty string, the giant number visible in slanting Magic Marker: PRICE $3. Lorilee had aimed for the coat hook on the wall. She missed. She did not seem to notice. She was twenty-six years old. She could have passed for forty.

She asked if she could smoke, and when Bell said no, she scowled and mouthed the word *Fuck* and then looked around the room with incredulity. Her disgruntled glance was easy to translate: *No smoking? Really? In* this *dump? Like—why's it even matter?*

She crossed and recrossed her legs. She uncrossed them altogether, placed them flat on the floor. The chunky-heeled clogs hit with a *thwunk.* Then she crossed her legs again, right over left, left over right. She had stringy hair, dyed purple, with a twisting strand of red that looked like drainage from a scalp wound. Her skin was almost reptilian, a carapace of sore and flake and scab. She had a nose ring, and another ring through a piercing in her lower lip. Both holes were infected. The crusty ring of red around each one added a touch of lurid color to her drab complexion.

She was, according to Rhonda, who had heard it from Grandma Lovejoy—back when Grandma Lovejoy could still form sentences—a heroin addict. Grandma Lovejoy had heard it from Connie Dollar, who had heard it from Marcy Coates. Bell really didn't need the provenance of the information; Lorilee Coates was well-known to law enforcement officials in a three-county area, not because she was a criminal mastermind, but because she was so pathetic, and her story such a familiar and depressing one.

Lorilee had started huffing glue, paint, whatever, at twelve. At thirteen she had her first arrest, for drunk and disorderly. At fourteen she'd been caught in the ladies' bathroom of the Pizza Parade over on Oak Street, chugging the plastic dispenser of floral-tinged soap, hotly desirous of the alcohol content. In the years to follow she'd been picked up three times for prostitution out at the Highway Haven, and another two times for shoplifting at various locales. She had slept and giggled and mocked her way through two court-ordered stints in rehab.

She was a total wreck of a human being. She was a rapidly disintegrating mess. She was a walking tragedy. And she was the apple of her grandmother's eye.

Deputy Oakes had found her that morning in a tattoo shop on Route 6, a place called Skin U Alive, begging the owner for a freebie. Oakes had gotten a tip about where she might be. His network of sources was nowhere near as extensive as Rhonda's, but as he often said, "Give me time." He had only been living and working in Acker's Gap for three years. Moreover, his informants were more likely to be from the sleazy side of the line—pimps, addicts, dealers, prostitutes—whereas Rhonda's people were churchgoers and old folks. Different universes. Both important to a prosecutor's office.

"So. Lorilee. Appreciate you coming by," Bell said.

"No choice. Damned deputy made me." Lorilee's voice sounded like she'd been gargling with Clorox. "What the fuck's going on?"

"Your grandmother was murdered two nights ago."

"Like I don't know *that*. I know, okay? They told me." Lorilee sneered. The expression necessitated the flexing of a nostril, the one with the infected piercing, and she winced. "Why'm I here? What's the deal? Ain't done nothing wrong."

"I'm hoping you can help us." Bell knew there was absolutely no point in lecturing Lorilee Coates, in trying to inspire her to lead another kind of life. Her grandmother, Rhonda said, had tried to do that, over and over again, year after year. It never worked. Nothing worked. And so Bell understood that there was no percentage in threatening Lorilee, or cajoling her, or bargaining with her, or reminding her that she was still young enough to change everything. That she could get clean. That she could, once again, see things as they really were, see a panorama of crisp edges and depth of field—not a pinched-off, woozy haze, viewed through a constant stupor.

If Lorilee Coates had not responded to the sweet grandmother who loved her, she sure as hell was not going to respond to the meddlesome prosecutor who most assuredly did *not* love her.

All the young woman could do for them right now was to provide information. Maybe. If she had it, and if she was inclined to share.

"Help you do what?" Loriliee said, her voice chipped and gravelly with *I suspect a trap* tension.

"Figure out why someone would have wanted to murder your grandmother."

Lorilee narrowed her eyes. "Look, if you're trying to say that I had something to do with that—you are *fucked up,* lady. Wasn't even in Raythune County that night."

"I know." Bell had already ascertained Lorilee's whereabouts at the time of the killings so that she could rule her out as the perpetrator. Deputy Oakes had located several witnesses that put her in Room 27 at the Sundowner Motel in Chester with four other people—using her wiles, such as they were, to obtain enough black tar heroin to get her through until morning.

"So if you *know,*" said a newly peeved Lorilee, "then why the hell you asking?"

"Because you occasionally stayed at your grandmother's house, right? For a few days, sometimes a week? When you didn't have anywhere else to go?"

"Yeah. She was good to me, Granny was. Real good. Loved me. After my folks threw me out, she was the only one in the family who'd speak to me." Lorilee looked as if she was going to cry. "The *only* one." Now she did cry, loud, snot-laden tears that surged up out of nowhere. Emotional incontinence, Bell knew, was one of the more common and harmless side effects of chronic drug use. "Nobody else gave a rat's ass," Lorilee went on. "Only Granny. And now she's gone."

Bell handed her a tissue. Instead of using it, Lorilee wadded it up and stuck it in the pocket of her cutoffs. Maybe she thought she could resell it later for cash.

"Did your grandmother keep money or valuables in her home?" Bell asked.

Lorilee snorted. A bubble of snot escaped her left nostril. "Hell, no. She used to—but then she and me had ourselves a misunderstanding, and she didn't do that no more. Didn't keep no money in the house. Little bit she had, she put in a savings account."

The misunderstanding was that Lorilee had robbed her too many times. Bell knew that without having to ask for particulars. She was just about to ask another question when Lorilee spoke again.

"And the thing is, she didn't really *have* no more. Even her savings account was down to nothing. That's what she said. And Granny never lied. See, she wanted to send me to another place. To get me some help. Talked about it all the damned time. But she couldn't. 'Cause she didn't have no more money. She'd heard about this new place out in California. Better, she said, than the lame-ass places 'round here that they're always sending me to." Lorilee nodded, agreeing with herself, her movement as loose and wobbly as that of a bobblehead doll.

"So she needed money."

"Yeah. Real bad. That's how come she was working double shifts out at that place. That place where she worked."

"Thornapple Terrace."

"Whatever. Said that as soon as she got the cash, she'd send me out there. To California. Had her heart set on it. Those places—shit, they cost a ton. Ten, twenty thousand. Just to get you started. More and more after that."

Bell made a note on the pad in front of her. When she raised her head, Lorilee was looking at her expectantly.

"So," Lorilee said. Big smile, revealing infrequent teeth. "We're friends now, right? I mean, I helped you. So maybe you can help me out a little bit? To honor my Granny? With maybe, like, reward money or something like that? For telling you whatever it was that you wrote down there just now?"

"I can have a deputy take you where you'd like go. It's cold outside. Hard day to walk anywhere. Best I can do."

"Fuck you." There was no passion in the curse. Passion required energy. Lorilee tried to stand, tumbled back in the chair. Her long bony legs reminded Bell of a colt's legs, stick-thin and unreliable. Lorilee tried again. This time, she made it up and stayed that way. "Fuck you. Fuck you, okay?"

"Little advice," Bell said mildly. "You really need to brush up on your people skills."

She watched the young woman scrabble for and finally hoist up her jacket from the floor and then stumble away. Bell's mind had already moved past the moment. She was pondering the new information about Marcy Coates: No, the old woman apparently did not have enough money to make her a target. But she had a good reason to *want* money, and lots of it.

Carla did something colossally dumb: She listened to her voice mail.

As long as she ignored it, she could pretend (a) she had not received any messages from anybody back in D.C. and (b) nothing had happened that would have caused her to *expect* to receive any messages from anybody back in D.C. and (c) she had made a clean escape, and the past was past.

None of the three was true. And (c) was the least true of all.

It was late Friday afternoon, and she had just finished her final interview in Raythune County. Next week she would be moving on to Muth County. She sat in her car, head back against the headrest. Seconds ago, she had wedged the clipboard and the recorder into her backpack. She looked over at the apartment complex from which she had just departed.

She had spent the last two and a half hours interviewing the sole resident of Apartment 2-B, an eighty-eight-year-old retired railroad brakeman named Julius Jones. He was an African American. It was her favorite interview so far. Jones told wonderful stories, and when he came to the big finish, he sat back in his oak rocker, tucked his thumbs under his bright red suspenders, pulled the strips forward, and then let them go. They snapped back onto his belly with a deeply satisfying sound, as if he were sending forth the story into the world with a smack on its bottom, like you'd do to a dawdling child.

He told her tales about midnight rides around treacherous curves and across bottomless-seeming gorges, and about a time in the winter in the early 1950s when the tracks were blocked with snow. How much snow? So much snow, Jones explained, that they might as well have been facing the mountain itself—that's how little chance the locomotive had of pushing through the massive chunk, of tunneling out the other side.

So that was that, Julius Jones said. The train stopped and stayed there. He explained things to the passengers, many of whom had places they needed to be that night, important appointments, people to see, businesses to run. But you could not argue with a wall of snow that was taller than the train itself. Frustration gradually gave way to a sort of madcap frivolity. Men in nice suits, men with a net worth of millions of dollars, got out in the deep snow beside the tracks and played with the children, ruining their expensive shoes but laughing about it. They built snowmen and snowwomen (the upper half of the snowwomen, Julius Jones explained with a courtly dip of his head, were covered with shawls borrowed from the elderly female passengers, so as not to confront the indelicate issue of anatomical correctness) and snowchildren. There was a rousing but harmless snowball fight. The adults let the children win, but not so obviously that the children noticed. Finally, energy spent, everyone came back aboard the train and made passable beds out of seats and out of cushions arranged in the aisles. By noontime of the next day, the temperature had risen high enough to enable Julius Jones and the rest of the crew to clear a great deal of snow from the tracks. The train got a running start, and managed to push on through.

The funny thing, he said, was that by the time they got to Pittsburgh, the businessmen were all serious again, and arrogant and buttoned-up and ill-tempered, and when the train pulled into the station they shoved rudely past the same children they had played with so merrily the night before, as if those children were rank strangers, and just obstacles that stood between them and their profits. It was hard to watch, Julius Jones said. He had come to believe in the years since, however, that maybe the night had its own special kind of magic, and constituted an enchanted place, and so it had to stay sealed off forever, and end the way it did: with the businessmen going back to being their mean old narrow-souled selves. It could not last, that magic.

"If we'd tried to make it last," Jones said, rearing back in his rocker, snapping his suspenders, "it wouldn't have been magic. Magic's temporary. Has to be. If it lasts, it ain't magic. It's only reality."

Carla was not sure she understood the logic, but no matter. She loved the story. She could see it, too, in her mind's eye: the vast blackness of night in the mountains; the unassailable citadel of snow that rose up before the stopped train and its astonished engineer; the kids and the businessmen running around, squealing and shouting and bending down to craft yet another snowball, packing it tight, hurling it with giddy joy; the only light coming from lanterns hooked to the outside of the train and from a high yellow moon; and Julius Jones, watching it all, knowing it won't last, knowing it can't last, and knowing, too, that it is the very fact of its not lasting that gives the moment its joy, its singular splendor.

"So why did you stay in West Virginia?" Carla finally asked him. She realized she needed to get back to her script.

"That's a question," he said.

She waited. Finally he started talking again, but he did not pull at his suspenders this time. "I intended to leave. I did leave. Once. Had some relatives in Chicago. We all came from Mississippi, you see. Most of my family kept on moving, and ended up in Chicago. I stayed here, though. And when I visited them, I saw that they didn't have it one bit better than I did. The North was supposed to be so superior to the South, right? Well, that was a lie. I took the train to Chicago. Came into Union Station. Tried to hail a taxicab to get to where my family lived, down in Englewood. No taxicab would stop. They'd just go right on past me. I tried for an hour and forty-five minutes." He stopped. He moved his tongue around his mouth as if he was trying to clear a sour taste from it. "That's right. One hour and forty-five minutes. I finally just started walking. I knew how to do that."

"So you decided to stay in West Virginia."

He nodded. "It's not perfect, Lord knows. And there's never been a lot of folks around here who look like me. I had a good job, though, a job I loved, and I guess that's what matters."

Carla was a little disappointed at his conclusion—she had expected a big dramatic finish, filled with noble words about human equality—but of course she did not say anything about her disappointment. She thanked him and shut off the recorder. She gathered up her materials. She thanked him again.

And then, just as she was leaving his tiny, overstuffed and over-heated apartment, Julius Jones said, "One more thing, miss. About my staying. There's this, too. A lot of my friends—they don't remember anymore. You try to remind them about something that happened, and they just look at you. They're losing their memories. I'm okay, though. For now. I remember almost everything. Especially from the old days. So I'm glad I stayed—because I have to do all the remembering now. For the others. Somebody's got to do the remembering."

Now Carla sat in her car. To her surprise, she was feeling pretty good. She had not had a serious headache in two days. Her appetite was back. At least her appetite for Cap'n Crunch. And that was a start, right? Her mother was going through a rough time—everybody was talking about the two old ladies who had gotten killed, and there was a ton of other stuff going on, too—but the truth was, there was *always* a ton of stuff going on with her mother's job. Her mother could handle it.

In the library the other day, when Carla was giving her daily report to Sally McArdle, she had seen a guy she'd gone to high school with. Charlie Crawford. And it was fine. It wasn't embarrassing at all. Or awkward. Charlie said, "Hey," and she said, "Hey" back, and that was that. He was not any more inclined to stick around and answer questions from her about *his* present life than she was inclined to answer questions from him about hers. She had been dreading an encounter like that one, with somebody who'd known her before, but it was okay. It was really okay.

And then, because she was feeling good, because she was feeling stronger and more centered and focused, and much calmer, even, than she'd been feeling in a long, *long* time, she decided to listen to her messages.

It was a mistake.

The first one was time-stamped on Monday, the day after she'd left Virginia. It was from Skylar: "Okay, like, I've been calling and *calling.* You don't answer. You don't want to talk to me? Fine. But I thought we were *friends,* Carla. What the hell is going on? Some kind of investigator showed up here today. From the prosecutor's office. Kurt got rid of them. He told them we don't know where you are. But they'll be back. They said so. And they have your cell number, okay? I don't know how—I sure as hell didn't give it to them, and I didn't confirm it was right when they rattled it off—but they've got it. And so they'll be calling you, too."

There was also a nervous-sounding message from later in the week from the highly excitable Kurt: "You've been getting a *shitload* of calls here. I need to know what to tell them, okay? I mean—I'm totally in the dark. Which is okay. It's your choice. But these people are *serious.* What the hell did you *do,* girl?"

A flurry of additional messages had come in just a few hours ago. The first one was from a sergeant with the Arlington, Virginia, police department.

So was the second. And the third, fourth, and fifth.

Bell sat at her kitchen table. Sometimes—not always, but sometimes—she liked to sit in the dark. The thickness of it, the way it surrounded her on all sides, helped to direct and clarify her thinking. No distractions.

It was just after eight on Friday night. She did not know what time Carla would be coming home. House rules were still in the discussion phase. Bell had suggested a midnight curfew—"curfew" was not the right word, because Carla was an adult, but Bell had pointed out that she would prefer not to be awakened out of a sound sleep by the noise of the front door opening and closing, and be forced to wonder if it was her daughter or an ax-wielding maniac. So if Carla intended to stay out later than midnight, fine—but Bell expected a courtesy text with an ETA. Fair?

Sorta, Carla had answered. Could they maybe talk about it again later? Renegotiate?

Bell agreed, but in the meantime: midnight. Or a text that indicated approximately when.

She had only been home herself for about ten minutes, just long enough to pry off her boots and dump her coat and briefcase and then head in here. She had started to switch on the overhead lights, but didn't. She'd considered making dinner, but realized she wasn't hungry.

She had an image in her mind. She needed to go over it again, every detail. Interrogating it, in effect, by giving it close attention.

It was a silver-framed photo of Marcy Coates and her grand-daughter, Lorilee. A latex-gloved Deputy Oakes, assisting the crime-scene unit sent over from Charleston, had taken it from a table in Marcy's house. The actual photo resided in a locked room at the court-house where evidence was stored for trials, but Bell did not need the actual photo. The picture was in her head. It would always be in her head from now on, because it was the kind of image that stuck with her. It was so vividly emblematic of this region and its tight family bonds, those sticky connections that could be either uplifting and inspiring—or grim and imprisoning:

A stubby, heavyset woman with short gray hair and a round red face, smiling broadly and hopefully, dressed in a pink smock and white Dickies pants and white lace-up shoes—the uniform she wears at Thornapple Terrace. Her right arm is locked around the frail, knobby shoulders of her granddaughter. Lorilee's head is tilted away from her grandmother and her skinny face is puckered, as if she's smelling the contents of a backed-up sewer drain. The tiny hands at her side are drawn up into fists. Her body has that *Wish I was anywhere but here* shudder to it. She is wearing a tight white T-shirt with a ripped collar

JULIA KELLER

and denim short-shorts. Her face is thickened with rouge, eyeliner. Her sloppy mascara is clumping so badly that it looks as if she is weeping toxic sludge in lieu of tears.

The two women seem to be occupying different universes. Granny, heavy and rooted, as stolid as a fence post; Lorilee, fragile and skittish, ready to bolt.

And yet of the two, it is Marcy Coates who is gone, while Lorilee lives. Lorilee, in the end, is the tough one. The survivor. Marcy is the vulnerable one, the one at risk.

Bell shook her head. She had to let Sheriff Harrison and her deputies do their work. It was their investigation. She had already called Jake Oakes and passed along what she had learned in her conversation with Lorilee. He would check out the granddaughter's known associates, he said. Find out if maybe one of her skanky pals had stopped in to paw through Granny's cookie jar for spare change—and while there had committed double homicide.

Sure, Lorilee had claimed that Marcy was broke, and doubtless passed along the intel to her jittery brethren. But junkies don't trust other junkies. They know—far better than non-junkies—what desperation can do. A lie about Granny's finances would hardly constitute breaking news in Lorilee's dark world.

So if it wasn't just a random crime of opportunity—if the killer had not just blundered along that road until he saw the light from Marcy's window and decided to take advantage of the house's isolation—then why? Why had Marcy Coates been chosen? Who stood to gain from her death?

And was Connie Dollar an intentional target? Or had it been just a case of wrong place, wrong time? They both worked at Thornapple Terrace. Was that a factor or—

A knock at the back door.

Bell was startled. Could it be Carla? No, she'd use the front. And anyway, Carla had a key.

She opened the door. She'd forgotten to turn on the back porch light, and so she based her instant identification of the visitor solely on his silhouette. Clay Meckling was six feet four and a half. And lean. His physique was a direct consequence of hauling around roof trusses and eighty-pound bags of Quikrete all day long.

She flipped on the outside light. The switch for the kitchen light was right next to it. She flipped that on, too.

"Hey," Clay said. "I know you asked me to leave you alone. Give you time to think." He was talking very fast, the spurts of his breath visible in the super-chilled air. "But I need to say something, okay? If you want to throw me out after that, then fine."

Bell pulled him inside by his jacket sleeve. The jacket was stiff with cold. "It's freezing out there. Come on." She shook her head. "I can't throw you out. I'd face charges for reckless endangerment. Was that part of your diabolical plan?"

He was surprised by her jocularity. She could see it on his face. The last time they had spoken, here in this very kitchen, Bell was trembling with anger, with outrage, laying down the law: *Leave me alone. I have to decide—decide if I can have you in my life. Don't call. Don't come by. Don't text. For God's sake—I have to process things, Clay. I have to find out if I can deal with this. Or if I just need you to go away for good. So—please. I'll call when I'm ready. Not before.*

What had changed?

Nothing. Nothing had changed.

Only that it was a cold night, and some time had passed, and she cared about him, and even though he'd ignored a direct request to give her space, she was not going to shut the door in his face. God, no.

"Coffee?" she said.

"I'd pay a million bucks for a cup of coffee right now."

"Sounds like a yes." She went to the cupboard to get the fixings. The moment was emotionally charged, and she tried to defuse it. "I'll take that million in cash," she said.

"My check's no good?"

"Only if you've got ID."

She turned around. She had not realized how fast he had come up behind her. He gathered her in his arms and gave her a driving, passionate kiss. His mouth was cold, but the cold did not last.

He let her go. "Will that do?"

And then he stepped back, more embarrassed at what he had said than at what he had done. It was a corny bit of banter from a usually serious man. Under other circumstances, she would have groaned and asked him which Hallmark TV movie he had swiped the line from. But she was still reeling from the kiss.

She sat down at the table. He took the seat beside her. He reached for her hand. She shook her head, drawing her hand away.

"That was never our problem, Clay. That part, we did just fine with."

"Then what *is* our problem? Damned if I can figure it out."

"You know." An edge to her voice now. He was playing dumb, and he was hardly a dumb man.

"I apologized."

"Yes. You did. And I accepted that apology. But it still happened. I'm going to need some time."

Restless, he rose from his chair. For the first time tonight, she was aware of his prosthetic leg; mostly she forgot about it. He moved so smoothly, so nimbly, that it was easy to do. Only when he made a sudden move—like bolting up from the kitchen table—did she remember. Clay had lost his leg three years ago in a building collapse. The collapse was caused by an explosion that rocked downtown Acker's Gap. But with physical therapy, and with the kind of determination that still left her in awe, he had fought his way back. Now he cycled, he kayaked, he climbed mountains, he supervised a crew for his father's construction company. He was a whole man again.

She corrected herself: He had never been anything less than a whole man. But he had needed to persuade himself of that, even when no one else doubted it.

He faced her, arms spread out wide to both sides, hands propped against the counter.

"I'm asking you for a second chance, Belfa."

She knew what this was costing him. He was not the kind of man who asked for things. He was young—fourteen years younger than she was—but he had an old-fashioned self-sufficiency about him. He was, in fact, a lot like Nick Fogelsong. He took care of himself, knew his own mind, went his own way. And no matter what he said, he really did not understand what he had done to her.

It had been an ordinary night. A regular night, the same kind of night they had spent together so many times before. Clay brought over a takeout dinner. Their plan was to eat, watch something on Netflix, and then, perhaps, he would stay over. That usually only happened on weekend nights, when neither one of them had early morning work commitments. But he would be leaving town the next day for a builder's convention in Richmond, and after that, he had some business in Virginia and Maryland. He would be out of town for ten days. Bell was going to miss him. She did not realize just how much until she thought about it, and was surprised to feel an intense, almost overpowering yearning for him, even though he was still here, and would not leave until morning.

Missing someone even before he left: That was new. And unsettling.

But it was a rocky night. They quarreled. She didn't remember why. She'd be willing to bet that he didn't, either. Something silly, trivial. It didn't matter. Even before dinner was over, the tenor of the evening had changed. The mood shifted. Both of them brooded, unwilling to say what was really going on: After four years of casual good times with each other, the relationship had suddenly heated up. Things felt too serious. She was apprehensive about the age difference. And he worried about how much he loved her. Needed her. She knew that, because he had told her: He hated to be dependent on anyone, even someone he was in love with.

And that's when it happened.

She had risen from the table. It was time to clear their plates. He stood up, too, to help her. They were arguing. She said one thing. He countered it. She was moving past him. He reached out and grabbed her arm, harder than he meant to. Startled, she stumbled. The dishes smashed against the floor and she almost lost her balance, lurching against the table as her world turned black.

All he wanted to do was to get her to *listen*. To slow down and hear his point. But at the sensation of a hard hand clenched around her upper arm, the power in that hand fueled by anger and frustration, Bell panicked. Something sprang up inside her like an animal snapping its leash.

"Get the hell out of my house," she had cried, her voice high-pitched and hysterical. She twisted her arm, freeing herself from his grip. Then she lunged at him, almost knocking him over because he was not expecting it. She pounded on his chest with her fists. She was sobbing by this point. Her words came in ragged gasps, in the breaks between the sobs. "Don't you *touch* me—don't you *ever fucking touch me* again—Don't you—Don't—"

Clay had tried to catch her flailing hands, hold them still, not to protect himself but to settle her down. To no avail. She pounded and she sobbed. He had triggered something in her, something so immense that it could not be tamped back down again. He knew the general outline of her life—they had divulged a great deal of personal information to each other, the way lovers tend to do in the perfect security of a shared bed and the sweet languor after lovemaking—but he did not know the true power of those memories, the way they waited inside her, secretly furious, smoldering, like a campfire with red embers still hidden under the ash, needing only a slight sifting and the right wind to flash into flame again.

He knew about her father, a nasty piece of work named Donnie Dolan, and about the night when it all reached a terrifying and definitive climax. The night when Shirley rescued ten-year-old Belfa from him forever by slashing his throat.

But Clay did not know about the other times. The ordinary times. He did not know about the daily swats and smacks and pokes and random punches, the routine kicks and sideways wallops. The times when Belfa would be rounding the kitchen table and, for no apparent reason, Donnie Dolan's arm would dart out like a snake's tongue and snatch her arm, pinching it, yanking her back toward him. She had bruises constantly on her arms. Purple marks, elbow to shoulder. It was one of the reasons her father withdrew her from third grade: He was tired of answering questions about the marks on her arms. *None of your goddamned business anyway,* he would mumble into the phone, jerking her back and forth in rhythm with his words, holding her arm, shaking her like a mop. She did not fight back. She couldn't.

Now she could. She was all grown up, and when those fingers closed once more around her upper arm, she felt the massive force of a sense-memory. The present dissolved. She did not see Clay; she saw the blackness that was Donnie Dolan, and she felt all over again the nightmare of her childhood. She felt threat and menace.

That night, Clay had continued trying to soothe her, center her. He apologized, over and over again. Which only made it worse— because that was what Donnie Dolan had done as well, a muttered, kneejerk, insincere iteration: *Sorry. Yeah. Sorry 'bout that.* Clay was wrong, he knew he was wrong, and all he could say to her was: *I'm sorry.* There was no other vocabulary to use in the wake of such a shattering betrayal, and it wasn't enough. Tonight, though, he was trying again.

"You have to forgive me, Belfa," Clay said.

"I do?"

"Yeah. You do."

"And why's that?"

"Because I don't want to lose you. I *can't* lose you."

"What if you already have?"

He pondered the question. "You warned me about this. When I first got back."

A year and a half ago, Clay had left Acker's Gap for graduate school at MIT. It was a longtime dream of his. Then he returned. He had helped Nick Fogelsong recover from a bullet wound and he had resumed his relationship with Bell, whereupon a mildly pleasant romance had accelerated into a fierce mutual passion. A passion not just for sex—although that part was, as Bell did not mind conceding, especially delicious—but also for their conversations. She loved Clay's mind, the way it solved mechanical and mathematical problems with the same creative rigor that her own mind brought to legal and moral ones. She wondered how she had ever thought she could spend her life with another lawyer, much less a lawyer like Sam Elkins. *No.* She wanted a life with a builder. Not with someone who, like her, just moved words around on a page. Just argued over clauses and sub-clauses.

"You told me," Clay went on, "that as good as this was, you were afraid you'd do something to screw it up. Sabotage it. Because you really don't believe that you deserve happiness. Remember?"

"I do. And you said I was just frightened."

"I think the phrase I used was 'fraidy cat.'" He smiled.

"And I think I told you to quit psychoanalyzing me—or I'd bust out the headlight of that truck of yours, which everybody knows you love more than you could ever possibly love any woman." She smiled back at him, a saucy, playful smile.

"Empty threat."

"Don't dare me, Clay Meckling. You'll be sorry."

"Oh, yeah?"

"Yeah."

He had, she realized, gotten her to a better place, a calmer one. He had restored her to herself. He had a knack for that.

"Look," he said. Serious again. "I want this to work, Belfa. Whatever it takes. No matter how long I have to wait." She could tell from his eyes that he knew they were not out of the woods yet. They might never be out of the woods—not with her past sharing every damned moment with them.

At some point, she knew, Clay might decide it wasn't worth it, having to fight back against that past, the past with its torments and its open wounds. And she might decide that it was not worth it, either, watching him try and fail, and try and fail again, to lift her out of the dark place where that past had left her.

But right now, here in this moment, it *was* worth it. She could see that in his eyes, too. That, and his keen desire for her that provoked an answering vibration in her own soul. And in other places, places that had nothing to do with her soul.

"No excuse for what I did," he said. "Just wasn't thinking. It'll never happen again. My word on that. I was careless and I was stupid and I'd never hurt you or—"

She put a finger on his lips. Then she removed her finger, and kissed him.

"I heard," he said, "that Carla's back. Is it okay if—"

"Yes." Standing so close to him, she could feel the chill that still came off his body. He had been working outside all day. Well, she would warm him up. She unbuttoned the top three buttons of his flannel shirt. She kissed his chest. He moaned. "Just for the record," she murmured, "this won't change anything. It can't. Not for a while. Not until I figure out how to protect myself."

"From me?" he said. He leaned away from her. He was troubled by that idea, and it showed on his face.

"No. From the memories." She rose up on tiptoe and kissed him again. Then she turned around to face forward and, still holding his hand, she led him out of the kitchen and through the hallway and slowly up the staircase.

Chapter Nine

Wow, Carla thought. There it was—alive and kicking.

She had not known if the place would still be in business. She would have guessed not. Seven years was an eternity in the world of dive bars. A month was often long enough for a place to open and close. In the back of her mind, she had fully expected to come upon the usual residue of a once-lively, now-moribund nightspot: an abandoned building tattooed with copious graffiti; busted windows; waist-high weeds stalking the place; a faded piece of orange cardboard stapled to the disintegrating door, its words shouting at you in bullying black capitals: CLOSED BY ORDER OF WV ALCOHOL BEVERAGE CONTROL ADMINISTRATION.

But the Driftwood Bar out on Old Route 37 near the Raythune-Muth county line was still a going concern. And this being Friday night, it was hopping. Everything looked roughly the same as it had four years ago: same sign. Same crude white cinder-block building. Same unpaved parking lot, now crusted and rutted with frozen snow. Same crummy cars, mostly compacts and stripped-down pickups, the fenders pocked and bleached from road salt. Same loud music,

blasting from the doorway each time somebody walked in or stumbled out, music produced by a second-rate sound system that ground
the songs down to static, and then wrapped that static in a pounding
bass beat. Nobody minded, though, because nobody came here to
actually *listen* to the music. You came here to hide in it. To use it as
camouflage. You came here to lose yourself in the loose folds of that
music, slipping in between the notes, hoping to disappear. Maybe forever. But at least until closing time.

The Driftwood was where Carla and her high school friends had
come when they were feeling bored and reckless, when they were about
to climb out of their skins with discontent. The ID check was a joke.
That made it perfect. She'd gotten drunk for the very first time in her
life right here, when she was fifteen years old, after which Kayleigh
Crocker had taken her back to Kayleigh's house. For all Carla's mom
knew, she and Kayleigh were watching *American Idol* and giving each
other pedicures; in reality, Carla had spent most of the night in the
Crockers' bathroom, puking her guts out while Kayleigh held her hair
and dabbed the back of her neck with a cool washcloth. Carla could
not even think about tequila anymore without a twinge of nausea.

And here it was, same place, same compellingly disheveled mess:
the Driftwood.

She parked the Kia and walked with mincing-stepped caution
across the icy lot, grabbing the occasional side mirror so that she
wouldn't slip. It was very cold. Cold permeated the world; it was a force
unto itself, almost prehistoric in its bluntness and lack of nuance. This
was a deadly, no-nonsense cold. If you miscalculated, if you were
trapped outside without protection, it would kill you without a second
thought. Or a first one. That gave Carla an odd solace: This cold was
a reality that didn't mess around. It was direct. It couldn't be bought
off or bargained with.

Somebody had thrown up right next to the front door. The stiff

SORROW ROAD

puddle of orangey-green vomit had frozen solid. It was, Carla decided, the ideal welcome mat for this place. She took a deep breath and reached for the wooden door handle—dark from decades of groping by other people's greasy hands—and entered.

The place was packed. She hit a headwind of darkness and swirling, raunchy smells: beer and sweat and Tommy Girl and aftershave and a sort of clinging, moldy odor that even winter could not dispel. Carla fought her way forward. She glanced around. Some people sat at the small round tables, some danced, some just stood there, trying to look cool. She didn't know a soul, which was just what she'd hoped for. She wanted to be by herself, but not in a quiet place. She wanted distraction. She wanted loud noise and a lot of pointless motion. She wanted chaos. Seething chaos—to match the seething chaos inside her. To balance herself out.

By now she was aware of another level of smell, too, suspended slightly above the alcohol and the body odor and the cologne, a smell that was harder to describe but always present in places like this: the smell of raw human need, mostly sexual but sometimes not, sometimes just the desire not to be alone.

"Hey."

Her path was abruptly blocked by a short, portly man with a big grin and a bad toupee—it was blond, and it lapped down on either side of his face like a pair of fuzzy saddlebags. Carla had been heading to the bar, a long one that ran across the rear wall. Behind it was a tarnished mirror. A hand-lettered sign taped to the mirror read: NO SHIRT, NO SHOES—COME ON IN, COUSIN!

"Excuse me," Carla said. She tried to go around him. He stepped to the right, blocking her way again. She went left; he did, too. His grin got bigger.

"Come on," Carla muttered. "Give me a break, mister. Okay? I just want a beer."

173

"Lemme get it for you. Happy to." He waggled his eyebrows. As noisy as it was in here, as closely packed as the crowd was, she could hear him perfectly well.

She gave him the once-over. She had to, because he would not move. He had bad skin and saggy eyes and a sackful of chins. He was ancient, Carla thought; he had to be at least fifty. He wore a tight blue sweatshirt with WVU across the front in yellow letters, and below that, in small letters: MOUNTAINEERS. He might have been wearing a belt, but it was impossible to tell because his belly flopped over the front of his jeans as if he were toting a bag of something loose and jiggly. Those jeans were so tight that Carla wondered how he moved his legs. And he wore cowboy boots.

Of course, she thought. Had to be cowboy boots. He was about as authentic a bronc buster as Garth Brooks was.

"So whaddya say?" he persisted.

"Just leave me alone, okay?"

Now he frowned. The chins wobbled, settled.

"You think you're too good for the likes of me, that it, princess?" he said. Some preliminary menace in his tone now. He belched. She smelled the last beer he'd had.

I should have known better, Carla thought. *Coming in here alone. Jesus.*

She tried once more to go around him, moving again to her right. This time, he stuck out an arm.

"You gotta pay the toll," he said. The big grin was back. "Wanna know what the toll is?"

No, she did not want to know. She had an idea, but it was too gross to contemplate. She was just about to ask him again to leave her be— more politely this time, hoping that maybe he had a streak of decency in him, although the signs were not promising—when another man stepped out of the sweaty jungle of people.

"Move along," New Guy said, and not in a nice way. He was tall and sinewy, a lean streak of bad attitude. He did not look at Carla. His eyes were locked on Cowboy Boots.

"Make me."

"I don't think you want me to do that," New Guy said. "Do you?"

Cowboy Boots got the point. He dropped his arm. He shrugged. He started to sidle away. His last official act was to glare at Carla and utter the classic bar retort, the pride-restoring words used by every man rebuffed by any woman since the beginning of time: "Goddamned dyke."

Carla laughed. She watched Cowboy Boots melt into the crowd. By the time she turned back, New Guy was gone. She was disappointed. She wanted to thank him. Oh, well.

Nobody else bothered her. She drank a beer while standing at the bar, letting the essence of the place seep into her while she observed it. The sheer density of all the assembled bodies made it very warm in here. At first she faced the mirror, seeing nothing, not even her own reflection—the mirror was cloudy, and the room was dark. Then she turned around, elbows against the wood, and watched the people. The tightly coiled knot inside her stomach was gradually loosening. It was partly the beer, she figured. And partly the place.

This was what she had needed. A place filled with strangers, where she would be cushioned by other people. None of them knew her, and so none of them would be likely to come up and say how disappointed they were at what she had done or not done in her life. Mission accomplished. She turned back around. The bartender pointed to her empty glass. She shook her head. No, she didn't want another.

Outside, the cold felt exceptionally good on her flushed face. She took a deep breath, appreciating the way the cold reached deep inside her chest with its icy fingers, waking her up, layer by layer. It was invigorating. She had just rounded the corner of a black Dodge Charger and was halfway to her car when she saw him: Cowboy Boots. He was leaning against a red truck at the end of the sloppy row of parked cars, lighting a cigarette.

Spotting her, he suddenly straightened up as if someone had punched him in the small of the back. He flung aside the cigarette.

"Well, well," he called out. "Whadda we got ourselves here? Little princess don't have her prince around no more."

In the bar he had seemed pathetic, not scary. But here in the parking lot, it was a different story. There was no one else around. The meager light from a bulb clamped to the side of the building caused the vehicles to cast crazy purple shadows across the frozen, snow-rutted ground, and amidst the crooked striping, he radiated a kind of crazy, anything-goes menace. He laughed. His laugh was low and sharp, with no amusement in it.

Carla ignored him. She kept walking. *Any minute now,* she thought, *somebody else will be coming out of the bar. A witness. He won't touch me if there's anybody else around.*

No one came.

She had her keys in her right hand. She was within three feet of her car when Cowboy Boots grunted and lurched forward, pushing off against the side of the red truck. He was coming after her. Startled, Carla dropped her keys. She looked down, but the ground between the parked cars was a shadowy no-man's-land. The keys must have bounced and landed—where? She didn't know.

Her last weapon was gone.

Panic overwhelmed her. Cowboy Boots was mumbling as he barreled forward, and while she couldn't understand his words, she didn't have to: the tone was enough of a tip-off to his mood and his intentions. He might have been fat and old, but he was big, and she was small.

She would make a run for it. Yes. That was what she would do. Dark snowy fields surrounded the lot. No trees to provide cover, but the snow was deep enough to give her an advantage in a foot race: She was much lighter than he was. But if he caught up to her, the advantage would be reversed. His bulk would work in his favor.

"Hey."

Another voice. Where had it come from? Carla's head whipped around.

It was New Guy. A cigarette was slung in his mouth, which explained why he was out here. He came at Cowboy Boots from the other end of the row.

"Help you with something?" New Guy said.

Cowboy Boots sized him up. New Guy was slender, but he was wiry, and wiriness can possess the strength of steel. Cowboy Boots seemed to understand this.

"Don't need no help from the likes of you."

"In that case," New Guy said, "why don't you get the hell out of here? Like, right now?"

Cowboys Boots offered up a sneer. "Shit, mister, she's all yours. I'd check her for crabs, though. Looks pretty skanky to me." He laughed a manufactured laugh and left. His mutterings blended with the scrape and chop of his heels against the stiff mini-drifts of snow.

Carla looked at New Guy. She didn't know what to say. "Thanks" seemed lame. And it occurred to her, as she searched for a proper way to acknowledge his help, that at no point in his two exchanges with Cowboy Boots had New Guy's voice risen above a conversational tone, or acquired even the beginning of an angry edge. There was a gentleness about him, almost a courtliness, that Carla could not quite fathom; it wasn't weakness—his presence alone had intimidated Cowboy Boots—but it also wasn't the sort of dumb machismo that generally won the day in these parts. She decided that she would not be surprised to find out that he was from somewhere else.

"Hey," she said.

"Hey."

He was older than she'd thought. Maybe even older than Cowboy

Boots. He wore a thick plaid parka, cargo pants, work boots. He had a hard, angular face that had once been handsome. She liked a memory of lost handsomeness, she decided, even better than the kind that was still there. His hair was hidden under a watch cap.

"You really helped me out," she said. She had to say it, lame or not: "Thanks."

"No problem." When he drew on the cigarette, his cheeks caved in. The red tip of the cigarette glowed. She could not take her eyes off it. He blew out the smoke, lifting his chin as he did so.

She waited for him to say something else. A wisecrack, maybe, about Cowboy Boots. A funny insult. A joke. Hell—she'd settle for anything.

She was freezing her ass off. Why was she still standing here?

Because there was something compelling about this man. Something very different from the men she'd known. A kind of quiet integrity or calm strength or—whatever. She could not put her finger on it.

"Guys like that," she said, "give dive bars a bad name."

He smiled. Okay, so he had a sense of humor.

But then he ruined everything. He peered at her and said, "You're kind of young to be hanging out in bars, aren't you? Dive or otherwise?"

"Yeah, right," she said. She was disappointed. Crap. Was *everybody* a narc these days? She'd make him pay. "Thanks, Grandpa. Thanks a lot. Appreciate you looking out for me. Oh—isn't it past your bedtime?"

"Forget it." He flipped the cigarette into the snow. "See you around."

"Wait." She did not want him to go. She really, *really* did not want him to go.

What was she doing? What was she playing at? She had a boyfriend, right? Greg Balcerzak. Well, a sort-of boyfriend. Things weren't all that great. The night before he left for Paraguay, they'd made love, or tried to. It was awkward, and bad. Well, had it ever been good? She and Greg didn't work. Was it really that, though? Or was it the fact that every time she tried to talk to him about what had happened to her four years ago in Acker's Gap he just said, "Thank God you're out of there now," or asked her if she'd been in love with Lonnie Prince, which wasn't the point. Of anything. Not even close.

"What is it?" New Guy said.

"It's pretty cold out here."

"Can't argue the point."

She had spotted her keys on a snow mound next to her left front tire. She bent down and retrieved them. When she stood back up again, she took a deep breath. She felt like she was on a high dive, her toes curled around the front edge of the board. She was spreading out her arms on either side of her body. Looking way, way down at a blue expanse of pure possibility.

"Want to sit in my car and, like, talk?" she said. "Just for a couple of minutes?"

A beat. "Okay."

She put out her hand. "Carla Elkins."

"Travis Womack."

She started the engine to get the heat going. The first thing he told her was his age. She'd been right; he was old. Forty-eight. *Jesus,* she told herself. *That's not just old. That's* old.

Older even than her mom. But—okay.

They were several minutes into their conversation when Travis made a confession: He had feared her motives when she asked him to chat in her car. He fully expected her to try to buy or sell drugs. "And I was going to tell you," he said, "not to be an idiot."

"Great. Another authority figure. I don't have enough of those in my life." She made a scoffing noise in the back of her throat.

"Hey. I've seen what that shit can do."

She had a fleeting urge to tell him about her mother, the Raythune

County prosecutor who had made it her one-woman mission to stop the drug trade in these mountains. But, no. She did not want to talk about her mother.

"You're not the only one," Carla said, "who guessed wrong. I thought maybe you said yes because you were going to—well, you know."

"Take up where that fat asshole in the Tony Lamas left off."

"Yeah."

He smiled. The smile creased his face but did not reach his eyes. "You're a nice kid. And I can tell you need somebody to talk to. Somebody who'll just listen. Do I have that about right?"

She started to cry. Just a bit. She did not sob, the way she'd been doing lately, at the drop of a hat. Two teardrops slid down her face. She wiped them off quickly.

He did not react to her tears, which pleased her; instead he let a little time go by. And then he spoke, temporarily relieving her of the responsibility to keep up her end of the conversation. She was absurdly grateful for that.

"Been there," he said. "When I was your age, and going through a rough patch, I didn't know how to handle myself. Didn't know what to do with the things I was feeling—a lot of anger and hate, mostly. All I wanted was to find somebody to talk to. Somebody I'd never met before."

"And did you?"

"Nope." Not a trace of self-pity in his tone. He was dispensing information, not asking for sympathy. "There was a family member who wanted to help, who would have done anything in the world for me, but that's not the same. Family's too close. Too much shared history. I wanted what you want—a neutral observer. I think it would have made a hell of a difference." He paused. "So whatever you want to say—say it. Or not. Don't say it. Either way's okay with me."

And so, with the pressure off, she talked. She talked about how, when anybody asked, she said everything was fine—really, really fine—but it *wasn't* fine, not at all, and about how, as a consequence of all those things she had stuffed in the back of her mind, like junk you cram in your closet until one day you try to get out your tennis racket and everything falls out on top of your head, she did something bad.

"How bad?" Travis said.

"Bad."

She told him about how the memories now came back to her at periodic intervals, and how she could not control them, and how they sort of took over her brain, and she could not focus on anything else except how it had felt to see Lonnie Prince drop to the carpet, his chest opening up. The color of the blood. Lonnie. Her friend. And the three old men, dying right in front of her. That, too. It all came back, over and over again.

Not so much the actual *events,* but how it felt to recall those events. She remembered the memories. And that's what she could not get out of her head: the memories of the emotions, which were like the shadows of the events themselves. How weird was *that*?

He nodded. He did not look at her or say something stupid like, "I feel your pain" or "It will all work out"—and somehow that made it okay for her to keep on talking.

She told him about losing control in that store in the mall a week and a half ago. Why did she do it? She did not know. It seemed like the only thing she *could* do. Like she had to do something totally insane. Something stupid, something she'd never done before, something that was *not like her at all*. The opposite of her, as a matter of fact. It was the only thing that would get her anywhere close to equilibrium again. Balance. And after that: peace.

With both hands, she explained, she'd started grabbing junk off the racks—scarves and blouses and earrings and belts—and stuffing some of them in her purse and some of them in her pockets. Other things, she dumped on the floor.

Why? She did not know. She just did not know.

And then, when the cops showed up, she still did not settle down. She yelled a lot. She even took a swing at the officer. She did not connect—she was just flailing around, like a toddler in a bathtub who's just discovered what a splash is—but still.

I almost hit a cop.

Why? She did not know that, either. She was sorry right away, but by then it was too late. Way too late. The cop cuffed her. Read out her rights. Marched her to the mall parking lot and put a hand on the top of her head and shoved her into the back of a squad car.

"Must've been a sight to see, you having a fit in the mall," Travis said mildly.

She appreciated the fact that he wasn't appalled. Nor was he titillated. He did not treat her like she was some kind of freak, or some kind of hero, either. He just listened.

"And so," Carla said, winding up her story, "I came here. To Acker's Gap. I had to. The trouble back there—God, I don't even want to think about it. I *can't* think about it. Somebody from the court keeps trying to call me, but I don't answer. My roommates, too. But I can't deal." She shuddered. "I'm hoping I can just hang out for a while. Maybe it'll all blow over." She knew it wouldn't, but just saying it made her feel better.

"Could be." He shifted his feet. He did not think it would work, either—by now she could read his body language—but he still said it. "So what're you going to do? Get a job?"

"Already got one." She told him about the survey, about asking old people why they had decided, back when they were young and had a choice, to stay in West Virginia. "I'll be starting over in Muth County on Monday. I'm supposed to go to Thornapple Terrace. The Alzheimer's place."

He had lit another cigarette by now. He removed it from his mouth before he spoke. "That's where I work. And I guess I'm wondering—

how much usable information do you really expect to get from people who have Alzheimer's?"

"Not the patients. My interviews are with the staff. Most of the people they hire are old." She clicked her tongue sheepishly. "No offense."

"You're right. The aides, the custodians, the office assistants— there aren't many of us under sixty-five. At the Terrace, I'm one of the younger ones."

"What do you do?"

"Maintenance. Keep the place up and running. Electrical, plumbing—if it needs fixed, I'm the go-to guy." He took a long drag on his cigarette. "Forgot to ask if it's okay to smoke in here."

"Not a problem." She wrapped her arms around her shoulders. "Did you know that woman? The one who got killed? Who worked at the Terrace?"

"Sure did. Marcy Coates. Fine woman. Loved talking about her dog. And she really cared about the people at the Terrace. You could just tell. She'd watch their suffering and she'd just shake her head." He shook his own. "Marcy had some problems, though. Like a worthless granddaughter who'd show up every few weeks, begging for money. I hated to see that. Drove Marcy crazy. She deserved better. But she had a real blind spot when it came to that girl. She'd do anything to help her." He nodded, agreeing with his own point. "Damned shame about what happened to that sweet old lady."

"Yeah." Carla shuddered.

He let a moment pass. "Getting late. I better go." He looked out the windshield, not at her. "So you're okay to drive home?"

"Fine." She liked his profile. It was reassuring somehow, the set of his chin, the long straight nose. The fact that he was older. He'd been through things, too—and survived. "So I'll see you Monday," she added. "At the Terrace. When I come to do my interviews. It might take me a few days to finish, so I'm sure we'll run into each other."

"Probably," he said. He tried to stretch out his legs. They had been jammed up under the glove box. There was not much room to stretch, but he did his best. "Except," he added.

"Except what?"

"You'll be going back to D.C. any day now, right? To make amends for the damage you did in that store?"

His voice was casual, but still she felt ambushed. Okay, so in the end, he was just like everybody else: trying to tell her what to do.

"Maybe," she said. She rubbed a thumb against the steering wheel. It was cold. Hell, everything was cold tonight. Cold and pointless.

"Your choice," he said. "Just a thought."

So he was not going to push her, after all. He was not going to give her a lecture. He had redeemed himself. She felt a peace returning, even a fragile optimism. "Look, Travis, I'm glad you were here tonight. I don't know what I would have done if you hadn't—"

"You would have been fine. You're a strong woman, Carla. You can take care of yourself. Saw that right away."

When he said her name, her stomach did a funny little flip.

"I wish I could repay you somehow," she said. "For taking the time. For listening."

"Not necessary."

"I mean it, though." Carla needed to make him understand. "It's like—even though I just met you, I can tell you know what I mean. You've been through it, too. You've seen things. You've been through something terrible, something that changed you forever. And the memories—they just keep coming at you, right? And so you have to do things that you wouldn't—things that you'd never believe you could . . ." She gave up. She had to hope he would get what she was trying to say. Even if he didn't, though, it would be enough that he tried.

She had never had this feeling before, with anyone: Like he understood her, without her having to explain everything. His calmness was rubbing off on her.

He shifted his feet. He was getting ready to leave. She reached out and patted his arm, as a way of saying good-bye. It felt funny not to have even touched him, after the intimacy of their conversation. Not so much as a handshake.

Mistake. He flinched and pulled his arm away from her, as if she'd hurt him.

Carla felt a sudden sinking dread. She instantly factored it all in: the skinniness, the pale complexion, the flinch.

Shit, she thought. *IV drug user.* His arm was probably tender and sore from all the needles. No wonder he had been suspicious of her motives, the moment she'd asked him to sit in her car and talk. When that was your world, it was all you thought about, all you saw. You assumed it was all anybody else thought about, too.

Disappointment turned her voice into a monotone. "See you around," she said.

He opened the car door. Cold air knifed its way in.

"Yeah," he said. "See you around."

Damn, Bell thought, as the ring tone she had assigned to Sam Elkins cut through her contentment. *Damn, damn, damn.*

Having to take a call from your ex-husband when you were snuggling in bed with your lover, both of you languid and wet and warm and loose-limbed after a mutually satisfying episode of lovemaking, struck her as absolute proof that the universe had a wicked sense of humor.

She reached across Clay's body to retrieve her cell from the bedside table. As she did, her nipples brushed his chest, and the moment was electric; his hands were on her hips once more, and he was situating her on top of him. Bell resisted. Cell in hand, she rolled back over to her side of the bed. She did not want to, but she had to. Sam would not call her this late unless it was important. He was a bastard, but he respected her privacy.

She was brought up short by her ex-husband's tone. It was livid with anger: "Is she there?"

"Sam, I don't—"

"*Is she there?* I asked you a question, Belfa. I'd like an answer. I've been calling Carla's cell for the past five hours. Leaving messages. She's ignoring me."

Bell sat up in bed. She put a hand on Clay's chest. It was her silent way of apologizing to him for the interruption. He placed a hand on top of hers—his silent way of telling her it was okay. No more explanation was necessary. He trusted her to handle this howsoever she saw fit.

God, she loved this man.

"I don't know where she is," Bell said. Carla wasn't home; she would have heard the front door open. She never slept through that. "She's an adult. She can do as she pleases." She could sense her ex-husband's ire ratcheting up, even as she spoke.

"Do as she pleases," he snapped. "Right. *Right.* Well, what if I told you she didn't show up at her preliminary hearing today at Arlington Circuit Court? That she was supposed to be there at four p.m.? That her attorney—and the court clerk—have been leaving her messages all week to remind her?"

"Preliminary hearing? Sam, what the hell are you talking—"

He interrupted her with a savageness that took her aback, almost as much as the information did. "Yeah. That's right. I didn't tell you, Belfa. She begged me not to. Said you'd freak out. Said you had too much going on as it was. Said she'd tell you herself. Later. In her own way. So I agreed. And I got her released on her own recognizance at the arraignment last week. Hired a great attorney—a buddy of mine. He was going to set up the plea deal today." Sam blew out some air. "I was a goddamned idiot, okay? I see that now. I didn't even know she'd left D.C. I only found out tonight when I went by that shack she lives in and started interrogating her roommates. They finally caved. Told me she'd gone back there." He was clearly seething. "She played me. Our daughter *played* me, Belfa, and I'll tell you this—it doesn't feel too good. It feels pretty damned bad, as a matter of fact."

Bell had to restrain herself from pointing out to her ex-husband that, under the circumstances, his feelings were the least of her concerns.

"What's the charge?" she said. A strangeness rose up in the wake of the words when they were applied to her child. To *Carla,* for God's sake.

Was this even happening? Or had she drifted off to sleep after she and Clay had made love, and this was a bizarre and harrowing dream?

It was no dream. Sam's voice on her cell was as bleak as she'd ever heard it.

"Shoplifting," he said. "Destruction of property. And resisting arrest. Apparently she just kind of lost it in some store at the mall. Went off on the sales clerk. Started grabbing things and throwing them around, cramming some stuff in her backpack and slinging the rest of it on the floor. Something like that. The cops got there and she was uncooperative. She told me—she told me she's been having flashbacks, Belfa. For the past few months. Times when she feels out of control. And one day—the day in the store—she got to the point where she thought she was going to break into a million pieces. Just shatter, like a pane of glass. That's how she described it. She doesn't know why she started taking stuff. Or cursing at the cops. Nothing. She can't explain it. She just felt like she was coming apart. Exploding. When she came back to herself, she was sitting in a jail cell. I got her out of there as soon as I could. The court clerk's an old friend of mine. Called me right away."

"Sam—my *God,* Sam—why didn't you tell me?"

His voice softened. "She begged me not to. She said she'd face the charges, do whatever they told her to do. She promised me, Belfa, that if I didn't tell you, she'd tell you herself. In her own way." His voice was almost a whisper now. "She was ashamed. She knew you'd be so disappointed in her. I know I made the wrong decision, not telling you, but—but I was afraid. Afraid that if I didn't agree, she might—do some harm to herself. Our little girl, Belfa."

By now Clay was standing up beside the bed. The room was dark, but his movements were discernable by the brief rasp of a zipper being pulled up on his Levi's, by the rustle of a flannel shirt being put on. He'd caught the gist of the conversation, of the burgeoning emergency. He was leaving. And she had to let him go.

Clay knew the night was lost to them. Because Carla always came first. He had understood that from the first moment of their relationship. Bell had never had to spell it out; it was always there, a permanent and unassailable truth. It was a natural fact of their shared universe: There was Carla—and then, miles down the list, there was everyone and everything else.

She felt his hand on her arm as he leaned over the bed. It was a question: Did she need anything? She lifted his hand and kissed his palm, admiring its hardness, a hardness that testified to the physical labor he did each day, building things, creating things. He would understand the subtext of the kiss: *No, I've got this.*

Another man might have tried to stay, insisting on helping her deal with Carla, but Clay Meckling knew her better than that. She would make love to him, but she would not let him into the deepest part of her life. That, too, was something he'd understood from the beginning.

She heard a brief medley of creaks as Clay went down the old wooden staircase. She heard the back door open and close. If she hadn't had to return to her conversation with Sam and could focus on something else, she also would have heard, in the next minute or so, the distant ruckus of Clay's truck engine as it came to life in her driveway.

"Belfa?" Sam said.

"You did what you thought was best, Sam. But I had no idea—"

"I know, I know." His sigh was a deeply troubled one. And then it was as if he had abruptly slipped the shackles of intense emotion. He was back to his old self. Back in control. He was the hard-nosed, slash-and-burn attorney who had risen from a scruffy upbringing in West Virginia to a position of power in a top D.C. law firm, a man who beat the odds. He was a success because he got things done, dammit. He took care of business. He was a winner. And being a winner meant that he did not coddle losers. Even if the loser in question was his own daughter. "Okay, here's what's going to happen next. No more chances. No more hand-holding. I'm picking her up tonight."

"Tonight." Bell repeated it back to him, so he'd know how ludicrous it was. "It's late, Sam. The temperature's minus seven. We're expecting another foot of snow overnight. In these mountains. And you're going to drive over here *tonight*?"

He grunted his displeasure. "Okay, fine. First thing in the morning. I mean *early*. In the meantime, I'll call the DA and try to get this thing straightened out. I've known him for years. He'll deal. So you tell her to be ready. Packed and ready. You got that? Am I being absolutely clear here? Or should I repeat it? Go slower? Put it in writing, maybe? Send you a text?"

"Don't you dare talk to me like I'm one of your interns," Bell snapped back at him. She'd had enough of his attitude. Enough of his bullying. Yes, this was a crisis; yes, Carla's future was very likely dangling in the balance. But Bell had done nothing wrong. She did not deserve his scorn. If she'd know about Carla's arrest—if he had confided in her, which he damned well should have done—she would have handled this differently.

He knew that, too.

There was a pause. "Point taken," Sam said. It was the closest he would ever come to an apology. Winners never apologized: That was another one of his rules. "I'm just concerned, Belfa. This is a grave situation. I'm about to use up every last favor I have access to. And when that happens—"

"Understood." Without Sam's protection, without his influence, Carla could be in serious trouble. Skipping a preliminary hearing was not like blowing off a dentist appointment.

By now Bell was out of bed. She turned on the lamp. She switched her cell to speaker so that she could get dressed while finishing her conversation. "I'll find her."

"Okay. And Bell . . ."

"Yes?" She was all business now, too. Coldly focused. "What?"

"I wish . . ." He waited. "I wish I'd known how much pain she was in. I didn't know. I mean, she said things were fine. Said she didn't need her counselor anymore. Once she moved out, I didn't see her every day. I just trusted what she told me. We've always been able to trust her, right? I never knew she was suffering, I never knew that . . ." He could not finish. He coughed. Something was in his throat. Yes— that had to be it.

"She's all grown up now, Sam. We don't tuck her into bed at night with Mister Gompers anymore." That was the name of Carla's favorite childhood toy, a purple plush giraffe. "It was up to her to tell us. To keep us informed."

"It's the memories, you know?" Sam said. "Seeing Lonnie Prince get shot. Watching him die. And then the kidnapper. Him, too. God, Belfa, she's been through hell, hasn't she? Our little girl has been through hell. The memories filling her head. Do you think—do you think she'll ever get rid of them?"

"No." Bell was blunter than she'd meant to be. But she had work to do. She could not let herself slide back into the soft enveloping warmth of her bed—or the similar comfort of lies. "Absolutely no chance of that." *If forgetting were possible,* she wanted to say to Sam, *don't you think I would have cut loose the memories of my own roy-*

ally fucked-up past? Wouldn't I have done that, instead of having to deal with them every goddamned day of my life?

"So how can she go on?" he said.

"The way everybody does. You find a place to put them. Lock them up. So they can't hurt you anymore."

"Does it work?" Sam said. His tone was soft and probing. Plaintive, even.

So he did remember. He remembered that she, too, had a past that cut her each time she brushed against it, and memories that lurked in her mind like dirty bombs with ticking timers.

She needed to go. She had to find her daughter.

"Does it work?" he repeated, assuming she had not heard his question.

"Sometimes," she said. "And sometimes not."

Three Boys

1938

It was Alvie's idea. Vic was driving, but it was because of Alvie that they went in the first place. And to say that Vic was driving was a bit misleading, because you could argue that, at the crucial moment, Vic *and* Harm were actually at the wheel.

So: All three boys—Vic, Alvie, and Harm—were responsible.

"Let's take 'er out," Alvie said.

The screen door had just clicked shut. Vic's mother had gone back into the kitchen, to do all those mysterious things that mothers did in kitchens, the things that made families run as smoothly and efficiently as that flathead V8. The comparison came to Harm because they had been discussing analogies in English class the week before and he had discovered that he really, really liked analogies. He found them everywhere now.

"Naw," Vic said. "Supposed to ask my dad first. And he's at work."

"So?"

The air was instantly thick with tension. Alvie's "So?" was a direct challenge to Vic and all the things that made Vic *Vic*: the authority, the swagger, the assumption of privilege and autonomy. Moreover, the fact that this challenge came from Alvie—little rat-face Alvie, whose father was made fun of by everybody, because he'd been fired from his job as pastor of the Crooked Creek Baptist Church, and how often, really, did a *preacher* ever get fired?—added several more layers of apprehension to the moment.

Harm felt slightly sick to his stomach. He wished Alvie had kept his mouth shut. He did not like it when his friends argued. It was supposed to be the three of them against the world. Not one of them against another. In the beginning their friendship had been based on proximity and convenience—on the fact that they all lived in the same neighborhood—but as time passed the very habit and longevity of the friendship had acquired its own significance. Now they were cemented in place, like three stones in a wall.

Vic, for all of his bravado, was afraid of his father. That was a well-known fact, without it ever having to be stated out loud. Frank Plumley was a bully. He had been known to slap his wife when she got out of line, when she said the wrong thing to him at the wrong time. He had even done it in public: once in the bleachers at a ball game, and a few times at the Double-D Diner. Frank occasionally shoved and punched Vic, too, and he did not care who saw him do it, but that was different: Adults could always smack kids around. That was expected. That was fine. But most of the men in town held back when it came to their wives. Sure, they hit them—but only at home, when the drapes were closed. So how did you know it happened? You knew because the next day, the woman would wear sunglasses when she did her shopping, even though it was not a sunny day, or she'd have a slight limp, which meant he had kicked her on that side.

But as Harm's dad always pointed out to him: No man ever hit a woman unless she deserved it. Unless she had asked for it. And if you thought about it, Joe Strayer would add, the blow was really an act of love. A compliment. It meant the husband cared. He thought the wife could learn from her mistakes. There was hope.

Vic did not want to go against his father. Harm could see it in his face, feel it in the way Vic rammed the back of his shoe on the edge of the step, with extra vigor. Vic knew he ought to follow the rule, and wait until his old man came home that afternoon before he took the Ford out for a ride. Ask permission. He knew his dad would say yes. It was a formality, nothing more.

But Alvie's "So?" had gotten under his skin. He could not look weak. The thought of that was unbearable. Truly, truly unbearable. Thus a brief, fierce battle raged in Vic's soul. Harm knew it was raging in there, even though only seconds passed, and even though Vic did not say a word. And even though nothing moved in Vic's face.

Which was worse: defying his father or looking like a chump in front of Alvie Sherrill?

It wasn't even a contest.

"Wait 'til you see me open her up," Vic said. Decision made, he bolted from his lounging position on the back steps. Halfway to the driveway, he turned. His friends were still sitting there. "You coming?"

They wedged themselves into the Ford with a sort of manic, pushing gusto. Vic was at the wheel, of course, and Harm was beside him. Alvie was smushed against the door. Alvie was laughing; his laughter had a faintly hysterical edge to it, like a girl's laugh. Harm would long remember the sound of that laugh. He did not like it then, and he would grow to like the memory of it even less.

Vic was a fine driver. He had a sure hand on the wheel. He did not do what Harm's mother did, which was to lurch forward and then come to a stomach-jiggling stop at the end of every block. The lurch-stop method favored by Sylvia Strayer had sometimes made Harm throw up, when he was younger. But Vic's driving was smooth. He had a sense of the vehicle, and a sense of himself. The two elements—two-year-old machine and twelve-year-old boy—lined up neatly, a truly swell synchronicity.

They kept to the back roads, theorizing that there would be less chance of somebody spotting them and reporting back to Frank Plumley. Everybody wanted to please Frank Plumley. And it worked. Vic drove them from Norbitt to Redville and then back around through Caney-town, and they did not see anybody they knew. Vic stayed completely away from major roads. They passed farms, and they shouted at cows; the freedom made them feel goofy and almost airborne with delight. They yelled greetings at a dumpy old man in suspenders in a bean field. Harm did not recall what they said, but the old man lifted his straw hat in tribute to the Ford. A vehicle as fine as this one was a rare spectacle along the back roads of Barr County, West Virginia.

They were nearly home when it happened.

Vic downshifted. He checked his side mirror as he rounded a curve, having just left the city limits of Caneytown; he wanted to watch the yellow clouds of road dust boiling up behind him. Now he shifted again, and accelerated. Was he going just a touch too fast? Did he, for just the briefest moment, lose control of the vehicle, and of himself, as the exhilaration got the better of him?

An old lady and a little kid—girl or boy, you could not tell which, because the kid had short hair and baggy overalls—were crossing the dirt road. No one would ever know if they saw the truck or not; they did not hesitate at all, or even glance in the direction of the Ford. They just marched right out into that road, the old lady holding the kid's hand and looking straight ahead, the kid looking up at the old lady and talking up a storm. In her other hand, the old lady held a large black purse. Harm remembered thinking—the thought came to him in the final second of what he would come to regard as his old life, his life before the accident—that it was the same kind of purse his Grandma Strayer carried. She kept tissues in there, and coupons, and peppermints.

She always gave him a peppermint from that purse when she saw him, without him even having to ask for it.

The sound was bad, brutal and bad—a deep, resonant *thunk-thunk*—but the feeling was even worse. The vibration traveled from the front of the truck right on through to the steering wheel, a violent shudder.

Harm knew what the wheel felt like because, at the very last moment, he tried to grab it and turn it abruptly, so that they would not hit the old lady and the kid. But Vic had seen the people, too, the pair of them walking so confidently and so obliviously across that road, and he was a good driver, with that sure touch on the wheel, and he had a great deal of strength in his wrists. Had he been left alone, he might very well have been able to execute the swerve, just missing them. The old lady and the kid would have felt the heavy swish of air as the pickup skidded and fishtailed in a vicious half-circle turn around them, and they probably would have blinked and squinted from the dust flying up in their faces. The old lady, maybe, would have frowned and made a fist and hollered something at Vic. About watching where he was going. About letting people cross the road in peace, for heaven's sake.

But Harm was pulling at the wheel, too, pulling it in the other direction, fighting Vic. And Alvie, at the last second, was pushing at Harm, trying to get him to grab the wheel tighter, turn it more sharply. Harm jerked the wheel out of Vic's hands and thus he ended up sending the front of the Ford smashing full-force into the little kid and the old lady, knocking them like bowling pins, *bam bam*.

The kid flew up in the air. If it had been a dog or a possum or a fence post, it might have been amusing: a small object looping up over the hood of the pickup like a ball tossed in the air, then landing in the dirt, now a funny crumpled new shape. The old lady did not fly anywhere; she was slammed into a ditch at the side of the road. Her dress, Harm could not help but notice, was up around her neck. Her knickers—frilly, edged with lace, but slightly yellowed, because nothing could stay true white when it was washed by hand and hung out on a clothesline to dry—were there for all the world to see. She was not wearing a brassiere; Harm noticed that, too. Her flesh was flabby, the fat around her waist puffed out like biscuit dough. Her breasts hung down on her torso.

All was still, except for the roaring in Harm's head.

The dust on the road was yellow-brown.

The liquid mingling with that dust, a liquid that ran out of the old lady's ears and the kid's mouth, was a dull dark red.

The Barr County deputy sheriff who came along about ten minutes later—the boys never knew how he had learned about the accident, and thought maybe it was a coincidence, maybe this was his regular daily route—was named Pete Diehl. Deputy Diehl. He asked the boys to step out of the Ford.

Until the moment when the deputy arrived, they had stayed in the pickup. With the engine still running. They had not moved. They had struck the kid and the old lady and then they just sat there in stunned, flummoxed silence. All three of them. Maybe if they just sat there, it would be as if it had not really happened. The vehicle ended up at a crazy angle, half-in and half-out of the road, but no one else had come along. Until the deputy did. Deputy Diehl.

Vic still held onto the wheel. Harm also had a hand on it. Alvie was leaning against Harm. Vic's mouth hung open and there was drool shining on his chin, but Harm and Alvie never let on that they had seen it.

It was clear that the two people—one in the ditch, one in the road—were dead.

Where had they come from, anyway? An old lady and a kid? There were no houses around here. No stores. Not even so much as a shed. Where the hell were they on their way to?

Deputy Diehl asked them again: *Come on, fellas. Come on out.*

He had checked the bodies first, although the gesture was pointless, a formality. Then he opened the driver's side door of the Ford and spoke to them. His voice was amiable, almost singsong: *Let's go, boys.*

An ambulance came and took away the bodies. The deputy found the old lady's purse. Her name was Gertrude Eloise Driscoll. The kid was her granddaughter, Betty Driscoll. Betty was five years old.

Somehow, Frank Plumley got there in his Packard. Deputy Diehl must have called the sheriff's office on his radio, and someone in the sheriff's office called Frank's office. Harm never knew quite how it happened. All he knew was that by the time Frank arrived, they were lined up against the side of Deputy Diehl's squad car, all in a row, like birds on a wire: Vic, then himself, and then Alvie.

Three boys.

"Deputy," Frank said, touching the brim of his hat.

"Mr. Plumley," the deputy said. He nodded smartly.

It was all arranged, then and there. Frank Plumley had been driving. That was what the report would say. Frank Plumley had been driving, and he had tried to avoid Gertrude Driscoll and her granddaughter, but damned if the two of them had not jumped right out in front of the Ford. Nothing he could do. Nothing anyone could have done.

Maybe, Frank Plumley added, and these words went down in Deputy Diehl's report, maybe Mrs. Driscoll was deaf and had not heard the Ford approaching, and the child did not have the wherewithal—Frank deliberately avoided words like "good sense" or "intelligence"—to look in both directions, being so young and all. It was a tragedy, no question. Two precious lives.

Frank Plumley was a well-known and much-respected man in Norbitt, indeed in the whole of Barr County. The judge would require only a few minutes to decide that he was not at fault. Accidental death: That was the ruling.

Harm never knew how the small details were explained away. The niggling facts. If Frank Plumley had been driving the Ford, then how did the Packard get to the scene of the accident? And what were the three boys doing there?

It turned out that the three boys had not been there, after all. Harm eventually read the report. Their names were not in it. Which meant they were not there. Vic Plumley's future, plump as it was with promise—dazzling, even—would not be imperiled by something as trivial and irrelevant as an old lady and a kid crossing a dirt road on the outskirts of Caneytown, West Virginia.

It would be nice to say that in the aftermath of an event as momentous as causing a death—because of course they carried the truth in their hearts, even if it was never officially acknowledged—the three boys changed. Straightened up. Settled down. Recognized the fragility of life. Displayed the grace of gratitude. Worked harder in school. Were more respectful to their elders.

It would be nice, but it would not be true. Over the next four years, they became even wilder than they had been before the accident. Vic, Harm, and Alvie were trouble, period. They shoplifted, they vandalized buildings, they got into nasty fights. Vic attacked a man in a bar with a pool cue; he ruptured the man's spleen when he shoved it into his side like a Roman gladiator thrusting a spear. The man was strongly encouraged not to press charges, and he did not. Alvie was twice caught stealing cars, and both times, Frank Plumley squared things with the sheriff. The spring Vic turned fifteen, one of his girlfriends, Wendy Devlin, ended up pregnant—it might or might not have been his, but he was glad to claim it, because of the way it burnished his reputation— and he and Harm drove her to Baltimore, so that she could get it taken care of. Frank Plumley knew a doctor over there. The round trip took all night. On the way back, Wendy almost bled to death. Later, Frank Plumley helped them scrub the blood off the leather.

It was as if the terrible shock of the deaths that spring day in 1938 had knocked something loose in the three boys—a wire that attached itself to another wire, and then that wire was supposed to be attached to a conscience—and now the untethered end was like a vestigial limb. They were vaguely aware of it, but they did not need it, and so they tried to ignore it.

They still did a lot of the things they had done as boys: They fished together, and challenged each other to footraces up and down Main Street. They spent summer afternoons over at Crooked Creek, swinging high out over the cocoa-colored water in an old truck tire tied to an overhanging tree by a spindly bit of twine. At the right moment, one of them would yell, "NOW!" and the one clutching the tire—Vic or Harm or Alvie—would let go, legs bicycling wildly in the bright air, and crash down into the water, making a tremendous splash. They did a lot of bad things, irresponsible things, but they still did the playful, ordinary things, too, the things that had defined their friendship for as long as they could remember.

In the late fall of 1941, the boys were fifteen years old. Vic was still the best-looking of the three of them, with his solid shoulders and his blue eyes and his big *I don't care* grin, but Harm was not far behind him now; Harm had dark curly hair, olive-green eyes, and an athletic bounce to his step. Alvie, gray and skinny, still looked like a rat, only a taller one.

On the afternoon of Dec. 7, 1941, the slanting, broken sidewalks of downtown Norbitt began to fill up with people. All kinds of people. There were layers and layers of them, all swirled on top of one another like a parfait dessert. That was the image Harm came up with. He still loved analogies.

A special edition of *The Barr County Herald* was available on every corner. Kids had been recruited to sell it, and they yelled out the headline until they were too hoarse to yell out any longer. The papers were snapped up instantly. The kids could have sold double what they had. Triple, even. The news was so profoundly shocking that everyone wanted every piece of information they could get, every scrap, every rumor. Some women were crying. Some men looked angrier than they had ever looked before in their lives, and they locked their hands into fists and loosened them and tightened them into fists once again, over and over.

"How dare they?" the men muttered, and then spat. "How *dare* they?"

The Japanese, it seemed, had sucker-punched an American military base way over in Hawaii, a place that, until its name showed up in news accounts of the current crisis, was largely mythological to most citizens of Norbitt. There was feverish speculation as well that the Japs had submarines stroking toward the coast of California, vessels vacuum-packed with enemy soldiers, and that this pillaging swarm would hit the beach and then fan out across the country until it reached the streets of Norbitt. These very streets. "My God," the men said.

The three boys watched and listened.

Chapter Ten

It was late. Bell sat in the living room, cell in her palm. This was her favorite chair, and normally it gave her comfort, but the document she was reading right now—or trying to read, because she could only get so far before she had to stop—made any sort of comfort impossible. Minutes after they ended their call, Sam had e-mailed her a PDF of Carla's arrest record.

Bell had not turned on the lights. She didn't need them. The cell gave off plenty of illumination—too much, as a matter of fact. It conveyed too well the glaring reality of what Carla had done, from the list of items she had destroyed in her mini-rampage at the mall to the responding officer's recollection of the epithets she had hurled at him.

What it could not tell her—what only Carla could tell her—was why.

WHERE R U??

That's what Bell had texted to her daughter sixteen minutes ago. Carla's reply:

On my way. Lost track of time

Then there was a frowny-face emoji.

Bell's thoughts kept splitting off from the document in her hand. She was a terrible mother, right? The worst ever. For nearly a week now she had not pressed Carla, had not demanded an explanation for her sudden arrival here. Because Bell didn't want to be the heavy. The bad guy. The nosy, overbearing mom who waggled a finger in her child's face. Because if she pushed, if she hectored and prodded, Carla might go away. She was an adult now. She could do that. She could leave.

That's what I would have done, Bell told herself. If someone had confronted her with something she had done, something inexplicable, she would have booked. Instantly. That was her modus operandi—just take off. When things became too real, too hard, too emotional, she withdrew. She fled.

It was how she'd handled her relationship with Clay, after all. Until tonight. Wasn't it?

So Bell had let things slide. She had not questioned Carla closely about the reason she'd left D.C. The thought that kept rolling around Bell's head was this: *She will tell me when she's ready. She's a good kid. A levelheaded kid. A responsible kid.*

Except that she's not *a kid,* Bell corrected herself. Not anymore. Carla was an adult, with adult problems and adult consequences to her behavior.

And there was more. Bell could not let herself off the hook. It was too easy that way. She knew that her non-interference in Carla's life was more than just a desire not to alienate her daughter. There was another reason that she had not gotten in Carla's face and declared, "I want some answers—*now.*" Bell was busy with her own affairs—with Darlene's accident, with the deaths at Thornapple Terrace, with the murder of two defenseless women. Her job was always in the picture. Always trying to own her complete focus.

It was her job that had put Carla in danger in the first place.

When Carla was seventeen, she was among the witnesses to the murder of three old men in a restaurant in Acker's Gap. Carla thought she had recognized the shooter. She could not reveal that to Bell, however, because of where she knew him from: a party at which drugs had been present. He was a dealer, intent on drumming up new business. Carla should not have been there in the first place. Her mother was a prosecuting attorney, sworn to eradicate the drug trade in Raythune County. Carla was ashamed of having been at that party.

And so she had tried to track down the killer herself. She had enlisted the help of her best friend, Lonnie Prince. And in their confrontation with the drug dealer, Lonnie was shot dead and Carla was kidnapped. Carla narrowly escaped with her life, after a gun battle in an abandoned building.

It was the kind of searing emotional trauma from which Bell had tried so desperately to protect her child. Because she knew those wounds never washed out. She knew about shock and terror. She knew how it felt to stare into the face of an evil that seemed to drench the world in endless darkness. Bell's own childhood—thanks to her father, Donnie Dolan—had been lived in daily proximity to that kind of evil, that degree of darkness. She had promised herself that Carla would never, never know it.

I failed, Bell thought. *I failed my child.*

Her sweet girl already knew the truth about the world: that while it had joy in it, and good people, and hope, it also was a place of sadness and suffering.

Bell thought she might understand why Carla had done what she had done in that store. They had not talked about it, but Bell got it: Sometimes the only way to make the roaring chaos inside your head go away was to create a rhyming chaos on the outside. Match frenzy with frenzy, anarchy with anarchy.

I used to do that, too, Bell thought.

In her case, she did it with running. Endless, insane amounts of running. In high school, in college, she would go for long runs along fearsomely steep mountain roads until she was slammed with exhaustion, half-delirious with dehydration, her legs too weak and wobbly to stand. Until finally she could feel the faint stirrings of an inner peace, an eye-of-the-hurricane calm carved right out of the middle of the emotional maelstrom.

Her little girl, her beautiful daughter, had wrecked a store in a mall for the same reason that Bell had run up and down mountains: to try to heal herself.

She lowered the cell. She did not need to read any more of the police report.

Sam would be arriving in a few hours to drive Carla back to Arlington. Bell wanted to come as well, but her ex-husband had said: *Listen. Maybe it's better to let Carla handle the problem on her own. Face the mess she's created.*

Okay, Bell had replied. She was glad to have Sam make the decisions. Her own judgment seemed highly suspect to her these days.

Sam had spent most of Friday evening, he told Bell, working the phones. Working his sources. Pulling strings and trading a favor now for a reciprocal one to be named later. Warren Etherington, chief counsel for the development company that owned the mall? An old pal from Sam's earliest days as a D.C. lawyer. If the store was reimbursed for the cost of the damaged merchandise, they would agree to drop the shoplifting and vandalism charges. "And if the judge is in a good mood and overlooks the fact that Carla missed the preliminary hearing," Sam went on, "we can probably get her off with some community service." No felony arrest record. A record which could, Bell knew, stand squarely in the way of so many things Carla might want to do with her life someday—law school, business school, law enforcement, a teaching career.

So Bell was relieved. Sort of.

If Sam fixed this for her, smoothed it over, would Carla assume she would never have to atone for the bad choices she made? Would she become chronically irresponsible? Was Sam—with Bell's blessing—dooming their daughter to a life of excuses and under-achievement? Or would Carla make this moment a turning point, and deal with the painful flashbacks, and never get into serious trouble again? There was no way to know. No certainty.

To intervene or not to intervene: That was always the question with someone you loved. Were you creating a monster—or enabling a fulfilling life?

Her cell rang. It was Clay, she saw.

"Hey," she said. She spoke softly, even though there was no one else in the house, no one she would be disturbing. She had a powerful sense-memory of Clay's body next to hers, and the memory made her want to keep her voice silky-low. "You make it home okay?"

"Only spun out half a dozen times. Only got stuck in a few ditches. I'm fine."

She laughed. "Good. I don't know what I'd do without you."

"Do you mean that, Bell?"

She had intended it as the cliché it was, as a throwaway line, and he had taken it seriously. As a declaration. But the fact was, she could not handle that—she could not handle any sort of discussion of their relationship—right now. She had to deal with her daughter.

She ignored his question. "Sleep well," she said, in an even softer voice. He would understand.

"Everything okay with Carla?"

"It will be."

A few minutes later Bell heard a sound from the front of the house. It was a light step, hitting the porch. Carla was home.

Bell watched Sam's car all the way to the end of Shelton Avenue. It was astonishingly cold out here on the porch at this early hour, but she had bundled up for it, knowing she would want to wave until her hus-band and her daughter were officially out of sight; it made her happy to see Carla turning around in her seat and waving back, the gesture just barely visible through a rear windshield stamped with frost.

The car rounded the corner, and then it was as if it had never been here at all. Only the parallel tire marks in the new snow—that narrow herringbone pattern made by the expensive tires on Sam's Lexus—remained behind to suggest that a vehicle had come and gone. Otherwise the world did not stir, locked as it was in the deep freeze of a winter dawn. The neighborhood was still under wraps, the roofs submerged under snow, the yards entombed in it, the curtains shut tight to keep in the heat provided by beleaguered furnaces. No lights were on behind those curtains.

Before Sam had arrived to ferry Carla back to Arlington, she and Bell had had a chance to talk. They assumed their usual positions in the living room—Bell in her run-down chair, Carla cross-legged on the couch—and tried to sort through the last few days.

"You should have told me," Bell said. She kept her voice calm and even. Losing her temper with Carla would accomplish nothing. "Right when you got here. You should have told me what you're dealing with."

"I couldn't."

"Why not?"

"You're not the easiest person in the world to talk to, Mom." Carla settled her head back against the couch cushion. She seemed fascinated by the living room ceiling.

"How so?"

Carla hesitated. "Because nothing I've ever experienced—no matter how bad—can ever be as terrible as what you went through as a kid, okay? Aunt Shirley, too. And you both survived. So it's pretty lame of me to complain about the kind of shit that's been coming my way."

Bell was startled. She had never considered trauma a competitive sport. And it had never occurred to her that Carla might think of Bell's own resiliency as intimidating.

"You can always talk to me," Bell said. "About anything."

Carla lowered her gaze from the ceiling, but still didn't look her mother in the eye. "I didn't want to disappoint you."

"Sweetie, you could never—"

"I did. I *did* disappoint you. And I've embarrassed you, too. You and Dad. Because I'm a complete and total screwup, okay? I know that. I *know* that." The tears came in a great gush. Bell rose and in an instant was sitting beside her daughter, gathering her in, cradling her head, stroking her shoulder.

"Carla," Bell murmured. "My sweet girl." There was too much to say—there was always too much to say—so Bell said nothing, but she continued to stroke Carla's shoulder and to try to wish her pain away.

Waiting for Sam, they had fallen asleep on the couch, Carla stretched out with her head on her mother's lap. Bell kept a hand on Carla's shoulder. It should have been terrifically uncomfortable for Bell, sleeping whilst in a sitting position, but it was not. Holding her daughter, touching her, keeping physical contact with her just as she had done when Carla was an infant, would make this—despite everything that was going on, despite all the questions about Carla's conduct and choices—one of the best times of Bell's life. She was able to keep her daughter safe, even for just a few hushed hours, deep in a winter's night.

And then Sam showed up. He stayed less than fifteen minutes. Not only did he want to get Carla back, he explained, but he had a full slate of his own meetings to deal with. He politely refused Bell's offer to fill a thermos for them.

"I can get coffee on the road," he said.

"Can't be as good as mine. Mine's strong enough to eat through the bottom of a Styrofoam cup. Try finding *that* at the Highway Haven."

He laughed, and some of the awkwardness vanished. But even as he was laughing, he was putting his coat back on. Sam Elkins was a man in a hurry. He would always be a man in a hurry.

Bell watched them go. The sun was mere seconds from clearing the top of the mountains, whereupon it would fill the world with light but no heat. She stood on the porch as long as she could stand it. Finally the cold was just too much for her, and she went back inside.

She had finished her first cup of coffee—Sam didn't know what he was missing—when her cell rang. Caller ID told her it was Deputy Oakes.

"Hey." His voice had a quality to it that Bell rarely heard from him: a kind of keen excitement. Typically he cultivated nonchalance.

"Morning, Jake. What's going on?"

"Heard back from Leroy." She did not respond, and so he added, "About the car. The one Darlene Strayer was driving."

"Right." She had not exactly forgotten about her request to Oakes to get an expert report on the Audi, but neither was it in the front of her mind. She had assumed—well, hoped—that he was calling about a breakthrough in the investigation of the deaths of Marcy Coates and Connie Dollar.

"And so," Oakes said, "he checked all the usual places—brakes, engine, tires. Everything was fine. Nothing suspicious. Nothing that might suggest any kind of tampering or foul play."

"Okay." *So why are you calling?* she wanted to add, but knew she didn't have to. Oakes would not leave her in suspense for long. He was busier than she was. The county had two deputies who were forced to do the work of five. He did not waste time—neither his own nor anyone else's.

"But Leroy did find something on the rear bumper," he said.

"Like what?"

"Paint chip. From another vehicle. Meaning the Audi might have been pushed from behind. Maybe just a nudge. But a nudge on an icy mountain road at those speeds is serious business. I've already sent off the chip to the state crime lab. Maybe they can tell us the make and model of the vehicle it came from. It's a place to start, anyway."

Bell's skepticism showed through in her voice. "No telling when the paint first got there. She had made a long drive that day. Came over from D.C. Somebody could have backed into her car the week before in a Whole Foods lot."

"True. I pointed out the same thing to Leroy. Without the Whole Foods reference, that is. Wouldn't want to confuse old Leroy. He'd be wondering if there's a Half Foods out there somewhere, too."

"And?"

"And he agreed. Might not be relevant at all. But he thought you'd want to know."

She did. She absolutely did want to know, even though it added another complication to an already puzzling set of circumstances. And even though it tended to validate the fiercely held opinion of Ava Hendricks, whose dark solemn eyes Bell could still picture, as she stared at Bell in the prosecutor's office four days ago, incensed that her lover's death had been deemed an accident.

If Darlene's car indeed had been pushed into the curve, it could mean that the two women—one dead, and one very much alive and very pissed off at Bell for not investigating further—had been right all along.

Someone *did* want to kill Darlene Strayer. And that someone had gotten away with it.

With Carla gone, the house was too big. Bell felt lost in it. She spent a good portion of the morning in an aimless ramble from room to room, wondering how the front hall had suddenly become longer, the doorways wider, the ceilings taller. She tried to figure out how the entire place had gotten so swollen and echoing and empty.

In a bewilderingly short time—less than a week—Bell had become accustomed all over again to her daughter's presence around the house. Carla was not a large person, but she seemed to take up a lot of space.

After Jake's call, Bell tried to settle down and finish some paperwork. She could not focus. Yet drifting around in search of domestic busywork didn't do the trick, either, because it only reminded her of Carla's absence. The house kept right on expanding, inch by inch, memory by memory.

Maybe a change of scene would help. Shortly after noon she packed up her briefcase with the paperwork she had quit on earlier, wrapped herself in the big down coat, tracked down her car keys, and headed to JP's for lunch.

The drive took twice as long as usual. Each night for the past two weeks had brought an impressive dump of new snow, and the roads were still reeling. This winter, Bell reflected as she angled the Explorer into a cleared-out spot in front of the diner, had a relentless feel to it. A sense that snow would be coming down forever, bit by bit, like some sneaky form of torture.

She was the only customer. She decamped in a booth in the back corner. Jackie came by, and Bell agreed to the daily special: bean soup and a basket of corn bread. Jackie nodded her approval and went off to fetch it.

Bell set a stack of legal pads on one side of the table, leaving the other side free for her food. She was preoccupied by a question:

Should she call Ava Hendricks and tell her about Leroy's discovery?

No. Because it proved nothing. It was speculation, not evidence. Evidence sometimes was discovered as a result of speculation, but speculation itself was useless until it could be backed up by facts, by science—by something hard and ineluctable, not a mushy-soft hunch. In the meantime, the ID of the vehicle that had pushed the Audi would have to come—if it came at all—from the forensics lab in Charleston, and that meant waiting their turn. It meant standing in line behind all of the other requests from all of the other small communities that had their own crimes to worry about, and their own prosecutors with hunches.

Right now, Bell thought, they did not have much. They had a paint chip on a back bumper. And they had the musings of Leroy Perkins, tow-truck driver, salvage hauler, and amateur forensic mechanic. Until she heard back from the lab, it was not enough to justify a call to Ava Hendricks.

She got down to work on the ten thousand other issues—give or take—that constituted a prosecutor's duties. She flipped through the legal pad on the top of the stack. These were the notes she had prepared on the Charlie Vickers case for Hickey Leonard. She would be briefing him early Monday morning. Rhonda Lovejoy's grandmother was still in the ICU at the Raythune County Medical Center, rigged to a ventilator, her brain function summarized by a thin green line on a monitor. Rhonda was at her side. And she would stay there, as long as the line did.

"Excuse me."

Bell did not look up. She continued to write on the legal pad, wanting to get a thought down in black and white—or black and yellow, in this case—before it eluded her. "Just leave the bowl right there, Jackie," she said, using her left hand to wave toward the table-top. "Thanks."

Nothing.

Bell lifted her head. It wasn't Jackie.

It was Ava Hendricks.

"They told me I'd find you here," Ava said.

"Who's 'they'?"

"Everyone I asked."

It was plausible. Bell hadn't noticed any witnesses to her arrival here, but that did not matter; in a small town, your habits were as well known to your fellow citizens as if they routinely tracked you on a satellite uplink. There were only a limited number of possibilities as to where you could be. In her case, it generally came down to three: the courthouse, home, or JP's.

The courthouse was closed on Saturdays. Ava had probably gone by her house—everybody knew where the prosecutor lived, and nobody was shy about sharing. That left JP's.

"Care to join me for lunch?" Bell said. She was surprised, but wanted to be hospitable.

Ava took off her coat and hat and scarf. She tossed them onto the bench seat. She was wearing dark green corduroy slacks and a gray cashmere sweater. She scooted into the booth, pushing her outerwear along the seat toward the wall to clear out a space.

"It took me an extra two hours to make the drive this morning," Ava said. There was umbrage in her tone. The look on her face suggested that she blamed Bell for the bad roads, as well as for every other impediment in the known world.

"We've got one snowplow," Bell said. "And one guy to drive it. And he's pretty swamped." She flipped shut the legal pad and put it back on the stack. "I won't even ask about coffee. But the bean soup's pretty good."

"I'm not hungry."

The woman's coldness was as off-putting as always. Bell attributed it to Ava's profession; doctors in general could be an arrogant lot, with neurosurgeons leading the pack. The long years of training, the life-and-death stakes riding on every flick of the scalpel—the arrogance surely had some justification. Still, though. How could someone as rigid and austere as Ava Hendricks have an intimate life? How could she ever let go of herself long enough to love?

Love.

Well, there you go, Bell thought. *Look at me—judgmental as hell.* Ava Hendricks had lost her partner. How could she forget that? Maybe this woman's distant attitude was coming as much from grief as it was from the brain surgeon bit. She was a woman in mourning.

And maybe I'm just as narrow-minded as Rhonda. Maybe I forgot that because I don't quite think of them as having been a couple—a real *couple, that is, like a man and a woman. Maybe Acker's Gap is changing me more than I'm changing Acker's Gap.*

It was a dismaying possibility. Bell moved past it by speaking quickly.

"So if you didn't drive all this way for Jackie's bean soup, what can I do for you?"

"I found something. Something you need to see." Before Bell could respond, Ava was talking again. She was more animated now. "Darlene bought a new cell two weeks ago. It was a different model, with a different plan. But she hadn't canceled the other cell yet. It still works. The data's still on it. I came across it last night when I was— I was putting some things away."

When you were sorting through the belongings of your lost loved one, Bell thought. *When you were touching the only things you have left of her now.*

"What did you find?" she said out loud.

"This." Ava handed her the cell, which she had retrieved from her trouser pocket. "It's a video. Taken at Thornapple Terrace. According to the date stamp, the first one's from a month ago."

Bell pressed the spot on the screen that initiated the playback. At first there was only fuzz and static, a large blue shape and a scuffling sound. Then the cell's angle changed. It moved back, and the blue shape was revealed to be a sweater. Harmon Strayer's sweater. Bell had never met him in person, but she knew right away that this was Darlene's father: Even after the ravages of age and illness, the family resemblance was remarkable. Looking at his face was like looking into Darlene's face—as it might have looked from a distance, and through a frosty windowpane.

He was sitting at a round table in what appeared to be a lounge. His hands were placed on the table; they were pale and wizened, and wrenched by arthritis into painful-looking shapes. The view of the room behind him included other tables and chairs, too, and a sofa.

On the table was a checkerboard. The red and black pieces were arranged expectantly on the squares.

A voice could be heard from behind the cell. It was Darlene's voice, softer than Bell had ever heard it: "Hi, Daddy. You look real good today. Real handsome. Are you ready for Alvie's visit? He'll be here soon. I know you like it when Alvie comes by." There was a pause, and then Darlene spoke again. "I love you, Daddy. I love you so much. I hope you can understand me when I say that. But even if you can't, I hope you can just feel my love. I hope it's like the sun on your face. Even if you don't know what I'm saying, you can feel the warmth of it."

Harmon Strayer looked at the cell. He raised his arm. Bell assumed he was going to wave.

Instead, the old man suddenly let out a terrible bellow. He leaned forward and smashed at the checkerboard again and again. Then he swept the board and its pieces off the table.

"Daddy—Daddy, what are you doing?" Darlene said. The picture wobbled as she leaned forward to try and stay his hand; her hand was briefly visible. "Daddy, stop. Stop it."

The video ended.

Bell looked from the screen to Ava's face. "I'm not sure what I'm supposed to be seeing," she said. "Don't people with Alzheimer's sometimes display inappropriate anger? It's not uncommon, is it?"

"Play the next video. It's two days later."

Bell touched the screen again. This time, Harmon Strayer was wearing a red turtleneck sweater. He was sitting in the same spot, his twisted hands settled on the table. But the checkerboard was not there. He blinked, and then he appeared to grow more apprehensive; he shifted back and forth in his chair, making a moaning sound. He pulled at his bottom lip.

The checkerboard slid into the scene; an unseen someone had

brought it to the table. A pudgy white hand and a pink sleeve came into view, placing the pieces on the squares, one by one.

From behind the camera came Darlene's voice: "Isn't that nice, Daddy? Your friend Marcy is getting the checkerboard ready. They had to move it to dust under it. But now it's back. Maybe somebody's going to play a game later. So it will be all ready for them."

The look that Harmon Strayer gave to the camera—to his daughter, who held it—was hard for Bell to witness. It was filled with startled panic and a clawing, ravening, bottomless fear. She wanted to reach into the video and pull the old man out of there, protect him, shelter him. The pitch of Darlene's voice revealed that she, too, saw all those things in her father's eyes: "Daddy, what's wrong? Daddy, please don't be upset. What's wrong? I'm here, Daddy. I'll always be here. I won't let anything happen to you. I promise, Daddy." The video ended.

Bell put the cell down on the tabletop.

Ava said, "There are several more, very similar to those two. Darlene and her father are in the lounge. Something upsets him. It's like a switch being flipped. He goes from quiet and submissive—to this."

"What do you think it means? Was someone at the Terrace abusing Mr. Strayer? A staff member? Marcy Coates? Is that why he's reacting this way?"

Ava shook her head. "I don't know. But I can't believe that if Darlene knew her father was being physically abused she would have left him there. It has to be something more subtle. And she was trying to figure it out herself. What could be spooking him like that?" She surprised Bell with a baffled, bemused smile. "I mean—like, a haunted checkerboard? Or what?"

The smile completely transformed Ava's face. Her features came alive, and there was a soft sparkle in her dark eyes. And then, a few seconds later, it was all gone; the hard face was back, the closed one, the one that let nothing slip.

"Here you go." Jackie had arrived at the side of the booth. She set down the bowl of bean soup and the red plastic basket of corn bread. "Bowl's hot," she said to Bell. "Be careful." She turned to Ava. "Anything for you?"

"I'm fine." Ava's voice had a slight but perceptible shudder in it, as if even the contemplation of eating in this place was just a notch below repulsive.

"Give a holler if you change your mind," Jackie said. Back to Bell: "Plenty more corn bread where that came from. Got another batch in the oven. Just say the word."

By this time a few more customers had hustled in, stomping the snow off their boots, faces set grimly against the cold. The moment they felt the warmth of the indoors, those faces changed. They relaxed. Jackie left to take their orders.

Ava watched her walk away. When she turned again to Bell, her face was puzzled but still riven with a sort of quasi-disgust. "So how do you do it?"

"Do what?"

"Put up with this place. I mean, you don't strike me as somebody who's all that crazy about bean soup."

"You're wrong about that. Nobody makes bean soup like Jackie's." To back up her words, Bell dipped in her spoon to sample it.

"You know what I mean." Ava frowned. "I used to ask Darlene the same thing. She actually considered coming back here to live, did you know that? She talked about buying a house and having her dad live with her."

"You mean 'live with *us*,' right? You would have come with her, surely."

Ava looked at Bell for several seconds before replying. "We discussed it. And yes—I suppose that's what I would have done. Move here, but keep my practice in D.C. Live here, work there. Which is the opposite of how most physicians do it. I have colleagues who fly into

Charleston once a week, perform back-to-back surgeries for two days, and then fly back home. They live in a big city—a more sophisticated place, frankly—and they work here."

"And then her father died."

"Yes."

"So she never had the chance."

"That's right." Restless, Ava picked a piece of corn bread out of the basket. "You mind? Looks pretty good. Fresh."

"Knock yourself out," Bell said, nudging the butter dish in her direction, and sliding over a knife as well.

"Long drive this morning. Just realized how famished I am." Ava paused to butter and then eat a broken-off section of the corn bread. "This is actually delicious."

"Don't let Jackie hear you say that. She's liable to fall over from shock. The way you've been acting—sneering at the food, glaring at the table like you think it's crawling with germs—well, she's not expecting a compliment. The surprise of it might just take her down."

Ava's tone was a bit sheepish. "Am I really that obvious?"

"Yeah. You are." Bell shrugged. "Look, there's no law against snobbery. And the people around here—they're used to it."

"Don't you mean 'we'? Don't you mean *we're* used to it?"

Bell put down her spoon. This woman was smart. God, yes—she was a neurosurgeon. But she was smart in other ways, too. Ways that Bell had not been expecting.

"I suppose Darlene and I were more alike than I realized," Bell said carefully. "I came back to West Virginia—and from what you're telling me, she might have been getting ready to do the same thing. But I'm not sure you ever make it all the way back, you know? Once you've lived somewhere else? And so you end up caught between two worlds. You don't feel quite at home in either one of them. You're like a tightrope walker who gets to the halfway point on the wire—and suddenly you're afraid to go forward. But it's too far to go back."

Her words seemed to resonate with the woman who sat across the table from her. "When Darlene talked about you," Ava said, "she'd always get around to the fact that she wondered how you did it. Left D.C. Left your entire life behind. And made a new life here. I told her it could not have been as easy as it looked."

"You were right. It wasn't easy. Still isn't."

She did not elaborate. Ava waited a decent interval, and then she touched the cell that lay on the table between them. "So you'll look into this? Keep trying to find out what was going on at the Terrace? And what happened to Darlene?"

"I'll do what I can. But I have to tell you—there are other priorities right now. The aide in that video? Her name was Marcy Coates. She was found murdered last week at her home. Along with the friend who had gone to check up on her. The town's pretty rattled by it. As well they should be."

"I heard about that. When I stopped for gas this morning, I went inside for a bottle of water. That's all anybody was talking about."

Bell nodded. She pushed the bowl to the far side of the table. The soup was good, but she was not hungry anymore. She was thinking again about the photo of Marcy Coates, and about the trusting eyes of an old woman who had worked hard, lived simply and honestly and frugally, tried to take care of her family—and still died a violent and painful death. It was not so much the flagrant unfairness of it all that nagged at Bell; it was the fact that it made no sense.

Logic. It could be a prosecutor's best friend—you always went with the most plausible explanation—or a prosecutor's worst nightmare. Because sometimes the truth *didn't* make sense. You were forced to grope along in the dark, hoping to find your way to the mouth of the cave, to the place where the sunlight was.

She made a quick decision, reversing an earlier one. She had changed her mind about Ava. She deserved to know what Bell knew— precious little as it might be.

"I didn't want to tell you about this," Bell said, "because it's such a long shot, and I don't want to get your hopes up. But we found a paint chip on the back bumper of Darlene's car. From another vehicle."

"Which could mean she was forced off the road that night." Ava's voice was eager.

"Yes. It's a possibility. We've sent it off to the state crime lab for analysis. But Ava—I need to be very clear here. It might be nothing. A false trail. I don't want you to think that—"

"Understood." Ava cut her off. She slumped against the back of the bench seat. She had been leaning forward ever since Bell mentioned the chip. "I'll let you do your job. I know how irritating it is to deal with the unrealistic expectations of loved ones."

"I'll bet you do. Brain surgery—that's got to be incredibly nerve-wracking for everyone involved, for the family members as well as the patient."

"It is. And that's why I have to be so controlled. I had to teach myself to be this way. To not be emotional in critical moments. To not let feelings get the upper hand. Because doing that doesn't help anyone—not the patient, not the patient's loved ones. And not the doctor, either." She smiled. It was a soft smile of reminiscence. "Darlene and I used to talk about that all the time. She thought I was too cold. Too remote. And I told her that she was too impetuous. Wore her heart on her sleeve." Ava paused. "There's an Elizabethan phrase I like. It says that some people are 'a feather for every wind that blows.' That was Darlene."

As long as they were sharing, Bell decided to take a chance. "Your lack of emotion about Darlene's death—it's puzzling, frankly. Especially around here, where the norm for grief is a bit more demonstrative. Weeping, wailing, fainting in public. Shouting for Jesus. That kind of thing." She looked down at the tabletop, and saw that she'd spilled a small beige drop of soup. Then she met Ava's gaze again. "Some people even wondered—well, they wondered if you really cared all that much."

" 'Some people.' Meaning you."

Bell did not answer. Ava reached for her winter garb: hat, scarf, gloves, coat. She pulled them back toward her, smoothing out the gloves, untangling the scarf.

"I'm due back in D.C. tonight," she said. "I'd better get on the road."

"Do me a favor. Forward me those videos. And anything else you find, okay? Diaries, notebooks, photos—anything that relates to Darlene and her father. Even if it doesn't specifically refer to the Terrace."

"I will. There's a ton of stuff. Darlene kept everything. Especially everything related to her dad. She even had his Navy uniform. From World War II. And the letters he wrote home to his mother and father."

Ava turned her body sideways. She started to slide out of the booth. She stopped. She looked back at Bell. Her face showed no emotion, but her voice was unexpectedly filled with it, breaking at certain points, growing hoarse and shallow and then robust again, and then faltering. "I need to say something here. To you—and to anybody who has the slightest doubt about how much I loved Darlene." She swallowed hard, fighting to maintain her composure long enough so that she could finish what she needed to say.

"When I walked out of that surgery on Sunday night," Ava went on, "and they handed me the phone, and someone on the other end of the line told me that Darlene was gone, the bottom dropped out of my world. I could not think. I could barely breathe. I had to hold it together, though, because there were people all around me—my colleagues, the nurses and the other doctors, the hospital staff. I had to be professional." She paused. "I wanted to scream. I wanted to fall on the floor in a sobbing heap—but I couldn't. I had to be steady. I had to keep my emotions in check. For one thing, I still had to go talk to my patient's family. They'd been waiting all day. I had to be strong and resolute, so that they would know their little girl was in good hands.

"But make no mistake. Darlene was my life. *My life.* Is that clear? I don't know if you've ever loved anyone like that. Or if you love someone like that now. If you have, if you do, then you will know what I mean. When she died—*I* died." Another difficult pause. "They called me a 'survivor' in the *Post* obituary. That's the word they used. But if you love someone, you *don't* survive. When they bury the person you love, they bury you, too. This body that you see, this body that's walking around, talking, working, driving, eating food, breathing"—Ava tapped two fingers against her chest—"this person, this one, is not real. I'm a ghost. Do you understand? This is what's left behind. That's all. Not a person—a ghost. Do you hear what I'm saying to you?"

Ava's dark eyes drilled into Bell's. Her voice was pitched so low that no one else in the diner could have heard it unless they were making a deliberate attempt to listen, and no one was. "Can you pass that along to your friends and colleagues? To anybody who wonders if I really loved Darlene? Can you?"

"Yes," Bell said.

Chapter Eleven

The mourners here did not look like ghosts. They looked more like sleepwalkers. They looked gray and exhausted and even slightly stupefied as they made their way under the low brick arch that led from the church door to the long stone steps. There was no rail for those steps, which surely violated several building codes as well as state and federal laws requiring proper handicap access—but few law enforcement personnel had the stomach to take on a house of worship. They would have to answer to their grandmothers, for one thing.

So the Crooked Creek Baptist Church in Norbitt, West Virginia, got away with it. They got away with not updating the century-old crumble of steps, forcing the elderly and the disabled to grab whosever's arm might be close by as they swayed and tottered during their slow downward ordeal.

Bell, sitting in her Explorer, watched a couple of near-spills and almost-stumbles and so-close disasters. She had parked across the street. The funeral had been scheduled to start at ten on this cold, wind-bruised Tuesday morning, thus Bell assumed it would be finished by eleven thirty. Or noon at the absolute latest.

Alas, she had forgotten to factor in the stunning loquaciousness of your average country preacher. She had not reckoned on his affection for his own blowsy gusts of rhetoric, liberally spiced with Bible verses and long excerpts from the more sentimental hymns. A good preacher—even one as old and presumably feeble as Alvie Sherrill— could go three hours without breaking a sweat. So here it was, almost one o'clock, and Bell was still waiting for her chance to mount those treacherous steps herself, in search of Rev. Sherrill.

The brief announcement of the funeral on the church's Web site— Bell had checked Sherrill's schedule—had identified the deceased as Lillian Pauline Strunk, seventy-two years old, lifelong resident of Norbitt.

The funeral meant that Sherrill would be on the premises. A small church such as Crooked Creek would normally be locked up tight on a weekday. But Bell caught a break—even though Lillian Pauline Strunk, to be sure, had not. The funeral meant that Bell could drive over to Norbitt, wait for the conclusion of the service, and then ask Sherrill for a few minutes of his time. The article noted that he would not be attending the graveside service. It was understandable. Having a ninety-year-old stand out in this weather, while they lowered the mortal remains of Lillian Pauline Strunk into the ground, was likely to bring on a second funeral hard on the heels of this one.

The cell video that Ava had shown her was troubling. Harmon Strayer's childhood friend, Bell figured, might have a theory about the source of his buddy's agitation. Yet Bell wanted to come to Sherrill's workplace, not his home; a home visit was too pointed. It raised too many questions she could not answer. Chief among them: Why was she spending so much time exploring the death of a sick old man with Alzheimer's? A death that wasn't even in her jurisdiction?

Monday's activities in the Charlie Vickers trial had been dominated by opening statements. It was Hick's responsibility, not Bell's, but because everything had been dumped in his lap at the last moment, she did not feel right about being out of the office on an investigative whim while he presented the state's case against the slippery and suspiciously illness-prone Vickers.

Minutes after the opening statements, Vickers's attorney announced that—surprise!—the defendant was feeling poorly again. They needed a continuance. The judge granted it. The court could not take the chance that he might truly be ill, and that the trial had worsened his condition. The ensuing lawsuit could put Raythune County in the red for the rest of their natural lives.

Hence the next morning—today—Bell had driven to Norbitt. The trial was postponed for at least a week. Her conscience was clear.

The roads, alas, were not.

After a long slog across back roads cluttered with blowing snow, she arrived at the church. And then she waited. Every fifteen minutes or so she was forced to start the car and warm herself up, cupping her hands around the spot on the dash where the heat came out and cursing winter all over again.

Finally, at 12:57 p.m., the wooden door swung open and the first mourners trudged out, dazed by grief and by the sudden resumption of cold in their lives. The older people—and it was mostly older people—were wrapped in so many insulating layers that they resembled hand grenades with canes and walkers. Some of the younger people raced down the steps to fetch their vehicles from the parking lot next door; they would pick up the old folks at ground level, saving them some painful steps.

Few people were crying. That did not mean they hadn't cared for Lillian Pauline Strunk; it probably meant they recognized that tears would freeze on their cheeks.

How would the grave diggers out at the Baptist Cemetery chisel through the deep-frozen soil? Bell had no idea. She'd heard stories in her childhood about people who died way back in the hollows during fearsome winters, times when the ground was as tough as iron, the roads were blocked up, and there was nothing to do with Grandpa except to keep him in the shed—and on ice—until the spring thaw. She never knew if that was true or not. But it sounded true.

The last burly SUV had just picked up the last fragile load of mourners at the base of the steps. Now was Bell's moment to slip inside.

The one-room church bristled with a thick, insidious cold that had barreled in each time the door opened and squatted in the corners. The requisite altar was at the far end. Six rows of pews were bolted to the dark wooden floor. The windows were regular ones—not stained glass. Stained glass was expensive, and this was plainly not a prosperous church.

It was empty now, except for a narrow-shouldered, black-suited man who was hunched over in the first row, his back to Bell as she moved up the center aisle. His head was bowed. His right hand fitfully massaged his forehead. He was resting or praying, she thought. Or maybe a bit of both.

"Reverend Sherrill?"

He did not jump. He seemed more peeved than startled. He dropped his hand and scowled up at her, blinking. His skin was paper-thin. Wispy white hairs sprouted from his ears and his nose. His eyes were beady, pinched into two slits. His face was severely elongated, as if it had been left too long on a hanger. The shape of that face gave him the look of an old and canny rat.

"Yeah?" he said.

"Sorry to interrupt."

"What?"

"I thought maybe I was interrupting you while you . . ." Bell gestured toward the altar. "You know."

He grinned, sending a sea of wrinkles undulating across the thin concave face. "Nope. Nothing like that. I'm just tired, is all. Long funeral. Used to love 'em. No more. Takes a lot outta me. Folks don't understand that."

"I'm Belfa Elkins. I work over in Raythune County. I'm the prosecutor."

He blinked again, waiting for more. He did not invite her to sit down. She wasn't surprised. Most older people she knew were cautious with strangers. They could not defend themselves as they once could. Wariness was their best weapon now.

"You and I had a friend in common," she said.

"That so?" His gaze had drifted away from her by now, toward the altar, which was little more than a raised platform with a book stand and an open Bible.

"Yes. Darlene Strayer. Harmon's daughter."

Again, no surprise registered on his face. Nothing seemed to rattle him. *Is that,* Bell mused, *what happens when you reach a great old age? Do you just settle back and let life have its way with you, showing no reaction to its twists and its turns?*

"Shame about Harm's passing," Sherrill said. His voice was a sort of gravelly grumble. Bell wondered what it would be like to have to listen to that voice for an hour or three every Sunday. "And Darlene," he went on. "Heard about her, too. Car wreck in the snow. Pretty girl. Once upon a time, she was best friends with my boy, Lenny. They grew up together. Got along real good. Then she went away. College and law school. And then some fancy job. Got a little too big for her britches. Last time I saw her was about three years ago. Right here in Norbitt—she was moving her daddy out of his house and into some institution. He was fading fast. Didn't know his own name anymore. Couldn't remember how to tie his shoes. Lenny went by the house, just to say hello. She wouldn't give him the time of day."

He squinted at Bell. "Her accident was real, real bad, way I heard it. Yeah, I guess Little Miss Smarty-Pants was driving too fast. Probably couldn't handle her car. It was a big one, I bet. She'd have a big one. Had to show off. Had to make sure everybody saw how rich she was."

A second voice cut through the gloom of the empty church. "Hey, Pop. Cut that out. Be nice."

Bell turned. The voice had come from behind her, from someone who'd just entered the front of the sanctuary. An exceptionally skinny man in an ill-fitting blue suit—it was too big for him, the cuffs flapping around his ankles, the white shirtfront billowing, the cut of the shoulders all wrong for his thin frame—shuffled up the aisle. His gait was so herky-jerky that he looked like a reluctant groom.

He stumbled once. His shoes, Bell saw, also were too large for him. He had slicked-back brown hair and a red complexion.

"I'm Lenny," he said, extending a bony hand. Up close, Bell saw that the redness in his face was the adult version of what must have been an almost operatic case of acne in his youth—florid, vigorous. "You've met my dad. So how can we help you?"

Bell shook his hand. Lenny's skin had a slimy feel to it, an adhesive unpleasantness.

"Belfa Elkins. As I was telling your father, I was a friend of Darlene's. We were law school classmates. He tells me that you and Darlene grew up together."

"Sure did. Real sorry to hear about what happened to her."

Bell looked down at Reverend Sherrill. "You visited Harmon Strayer quite frequently, isn't that right? At Thornapple Terrace?"

"Fair amount." The old man smacked his lips. "Whenever Lenny here'd take a notion to drive me over. I stopped driving in 1999. Well—no, I didn't stop. I was *prevented* from driving anymore. Forcibly prevented." He glared at his son, an old grudge smoldering in his eyes. "You help win the war and you save the U-S-of-A and the rest of the free world. But they still don't trust you behind the wheel of a car."

Lenny patted his father's shoulder. "Settle down, Pop."

Quick as a flash, Alvie Sherrill slapped away his son's hand. "Don't you *touch* me. You keep your dirty hands to yourself, you hear?"

Bell was taken aback. The good reverend's nasty take on Darlene was one thing, but humiliating his own son in front of a stranger? At first she wanted to laugh—*this* was the same old man who had just wound up a Bible-infused eulogy in a sacred space not ten minutes ago?—but then she remembered. Age could function like a floor-stripper, scraping away layer after layer of social graces, of polite-ness, digging down until it exposed a grim grain of resentment and irritation at being old and tired and weak. Alvie Sherrill was no dif-ferent from a lot of the old people she dealt with as a prosecutor: bitter and crotchety. Even a preacher would feel the cold in his clicking old bones.

"Okay, Pop," Lenny murmured. "Okay." He turned to Bell. His tone was brusque now. The brusqueness, she understood, was there to cover up his embarrassment, his wounded pride at how his father had treated him.

Some observers, Bell reflected, might wonder why a grown man like Lenny Sherrill stuck around, waiting to be bullied by his father, doing the old man's bidding, but she got it. Bullies started when their victims were very young, and their first order of business was to persuade the victim of his utter and absolute unworthiness. Baby elephants, she had read, only have to be chained for a few short months; they quickly come to believe they can never break free. Even after the chain is removed, they do not leave. They never wander out-side the pinched circumference of their former captivity. For Lenny, she thought, the hook must have been set early, and the tether just got stronger over the years.

"So what did you need to know?" Lenny said. "We're in a hurry here. Got to get my dad back home. More snow coming, they say. Maybe lots of it."

She aimed her question at the minister. "Just a few quick things. Did Harmon Strayer seem upset to you, the last few times you visited him?"

Alvie Sherrill looked at her with almost as much scorn as he had recently visited upon his son. "News flash, lady. Harm had Alzheimer's, okay?" While he spoke his next sentence, he pointed to the side of his head. "Wasn't much going on up there. Big old empty space. Did he get upset? Well, sometimes he got upset when somebody walked by or hummed a tune or turned the page of a newspaper. Other times, he'd ignore everything. No way to predict. Different every time I visited."

During this speech, Lenny had moved into the row just behind the one in which his father was sitting; he was picking up hymnals that the mourners had left on their seats, slotting the leather-bound books, one by one, into the shallow wooden tray hooked to the pew in front of it. The activity distracted his father, and Alvie Sherrill called out: "Land sakes, boy, leave it be! We pay a janitor good money to take care of that."

Lenny stopped abruptly. "Okay," he said. He turned around, almost tripping; he grabbed the back of the pew to steady himself.

"And what's the matter with your damned shoes?" Alvie Sherrill muttered.

"Couldn't find the right ones. Had to borrow some."

"Had to borrow some. Had to borrow some." Alvie's singsong repetition was deliberately mocking. Bell watched Lenny; he hunched over even more, as if trying to shrink the target as his father made fun of him.

"That boy," Alvie went on, turning back to Bell with a sneer of disgust, "would lose his damned head if it wasn't attached." He leaned closer to her. "Want to know something funny? There was a time— way back when he was still in school—when folks around here thought

Lenny might take over for me here at the church. Just like I took over for my daddy. But that didn't work out. No, that did *not* work out." He slid an annoyed glance over at Lenny, for whom Bell was now feeling distinctly sorry. "You either have what it takes—or you don't. My boy couldn't hack it. So I had to stay on. Way past when I wanted to. Way, *way* past." He heaved a weary sigh.

"I appreciate your time," Bell said. She wanted to leave before Alvie Sherrill was inspired to share more of his son's failings with her.

"Come on, Pop. We've got to be going, too." Lenny took Alvie's arm to help him up. The old man let him. "That meeting's going to start pretty soon."

Alvie's face collapsed into a frown. "Meeting?"

"To plan the celebration. To honor you, Pop. Sixty years of service to the church."

Relief eased itself into Alvie's face, smoothing out some of the wrinkles. "That's right. That's right." He gave Bell a sly grin. "You hear that, lady? They're gonna honor me. Sixty years in the pulpit. Longer'n any pastor before me, including my own father. Come spring, there's going to be a big party right here in the sanctuary. Speeches and music and all kinds of refreshments. And a parade, right down Main Street. All for me. Norbitt won't know what hit it."

She let Alvie and Lenny Sherrill leave the church first, the old man clinging to his son's arm. It was slow going. Every few steps, Alvie paused to tell his son that he wasn't doing it right, that he was holding his arm too tightly, or too loosely, or that his pace was wrong.

So how would a child learn to put up with that kind of abuse from a parent, year after year, decade after decade? What would he become in the wake of it? Bell did not like the answer that occurred to her: He would get hard himself. He would become his father times ten—shifty, selfish. And empty. Or he would feel, if he were lucky and brave, the shadow of another kind of life, a life he might live if he were ever able to break free. It would be an odd kind of shadow—one that projected out in front of him, in the direction he was heading, and not behind him, in the direction from whence he had come.

Bell had almost reached the Explorer when she heard a voice calling out to her. When she turned, a heavy woman bundled up in a jumbo brown parka and red plaid hunter's cap—the fleece-lined earflaps clamped her face, giving her a slightly demented look—was crossing the street toward her, moving as fast as she could on stubby legs weighed down by thick wool pants.

She handed Bell a shiny white brochure. On the front were the words THANK YOU REV. SHERRILL FOR SIX DECADES OF SERVICE TO THE LORD!!! in glaring red letters. Below that was a Bible verse.

"Hi, there! I'm Mary Alice McGruder. I saw you coming out of the church. I live right over there and I never miss a thing!" The woman was almost breathless from her brief scamper in the cold. "You must know Reverend Sherrill. Saw you coming out the door right behind him. So I thought you might like to hear about our little shindig. We've been planning it for over two years! It's not for a few months—but we want a nice big crowd! Big as we can get."

Bell took the brochure. She folded it and put it in her coat pocket. "Thank you," she said. No need to let Mary Alice know what she really thought of the grouchy preacher and his skinny disappointment of a son.

Over the years Bell had met many women like this one, women who were not attractive in the only ways that counted in the world, a sin for which the world made them pay in loneliness and isolation. Such women often looked to places like the church to give their lives meaning and purpose.

There were, Bell supposed, worse vessels in which to pour your passions, although she had never personally been tempted by organized religion. She had seen too many scoundrels—politicians, mainly, although a good number of lawyers and judges also made the list—play the God card when it suited them. She found it hard to forgive religion for the slimy things done in its name.

"Oh, yeah," Mary Alice continued, oblivious to Bell's tepid response. "We're pulling out all the stops. There's even gonna be a parade!"

"So I heard." Bell turned, a hand on the door handle of the Explorer. Maybe Mary Alice would get the hint and leave.

No such luck.

"And that's not all!" the woman said. She was practically gushing now. "Maybe you already knew this—but Reverend Sherrill was a war hero. World War II. He was right there on D-Day. We're gonna honor him for that, too. For what he did in the war—him and his two best friends. They're also from Norbitt. We were hoping to have them here to help us celebrate." She shook her head and sighed. "That's not gonna happen now. His friends died. Both of them. They were old, so I guess it wasn't much of a surprise, but still—it's too bad."

"Yes. Well, good luck with the festivities," Bell said, in her best *Let's wrap this up* tone. She was, in addition to being bored, freezing cold. "Have a nice afternoon."

"Oh, it's not just the festivities! We're also having some booklets printed up. With the whole story." Mary Alice's enthusiasm, Bell decided, was keeping her warm, in ways that even those fleece-lined earflaps could not manage. "The story of how three boys from Norbitt went out and sent that old Hitler straight to hell, which is where he came from in the first place, you ask me. We've been interviewing a lot of folks who have known Alvie Sherrill his whole life. Shame we can't include his two best friends. Woulda been really special."

"How nice," Bell said. Now she really did have to go. Thornapple Terrace was on her way home from Norbitt, and she planned to stop in. Bonita Layman had called that morning. New information, the director said. Might be relevant.

Mary Alice was still talking. "Of course, we won't bring up much about his daddy."

Bell released the door handle. A few extra minutes in the cold wouldn't matter. "Why not?"

"Oh, everybody knows about *that*." For the first time, Mary Alice seemed a little reluctant to go on.

"Remind me."

"Well . . ." The woman looked around. The snow-packed street was deserted, but she wanted to make sure. "Nobody much talks about him anymore. But my mother told me all about it before she passed. See, Reverend Sherrill's father was the pastor here back in the 1930s. Until the scandal. It must've been hard for the family—that kind of disgrace."

Gossip was still irresistible, Bell thought, even if it was eighty years old.

"What scandal?" she said.

After another furtive look around, Mary Alice plunged in. "Reverend Sherrill's father was the first Leonard Sherrill. Our pastor named his own son after the man. Anyway, way back in the day, the first Reverend Sherrill had an affair with a girl who'd come to him for counseling. She got pregnant. And this was the 1930s, of course, so it was *unforgivable.* That girl lost the baby, which was a terrible shame, but in the meantime, once word got out, the church board fired Leonard Sherrill. Based on what my mother told me, things got real hard for the family after that. Nobody would hire him to do anything around here. Reverend Sherrill's mother took in washing and ironing to keep food on the table for Alvie and his brothers and sisters." She redid her grip on the stack of brochures, a thoughtful look on her round red face. "Sometimes I wonder if that's why our pastor became a minister himself. To make up for what his daddy did to this town. Preaching wasn't something that came natural to him, that's for sure. He had to work real hard, way I hear it." She arched her eyebrows. "Wish that kid of his was half that ambitious. But Lenny—well, he's got his issues."

"What do you mean?"

"Always in some kind of trouble. Reverend Sherrill's done everything he can do for his boy, but it's no use. Lots of folks say he's part of that gang that's been holding up gas stations. Oh, sure, you'll see Lenny at the church a lot—but that's just to make himself look good."

Bell patted the pocket in which she had stowed the brochure. "Thanks for this," she said.

"So you'll come to the parade?" Mary Alice's voice rose in hopefulness, like a kid standing up on tiptoes to reach the cookie jar.

Not a chance in hell, Bell thought. Out loud, she said, "I'll check my calendar."

Bonita Layman was waiting for her in the lobby. The director of Thornapple Terrace stood by the reception desk, her hands clasped in front of her brown wool skirt. She was frowning. The frown bit deep. It was the kind of frown that came not from simple displeasure, but from dark and troubling thoughts.

"Sorry I'm late," Bell said. She was half-convinced that she might as well have those words tattooed on her forehead, and thus could just point to them everywhere she went. It would save time and breath.

Bonita nodded. "Do you mind coming this way?" She used a hand to indicate the secure corridor. "A member of the staff is waiting to talk to us in the lounge." Before they set out, Bontia turned to the receptionist. "Dorothy, I need that light switch for the lamp fixed in my office. I've asked Travis about it multiple times. Where is he?"

"He was right here just a minute ago." Dorothy looked around. She was perplexed. "I don't understand it. He was working on the front door—the weather stripping is coming loose. Then your visitor drove up, and he just disappeared."

Bell was instantly on alert: Why would an employee vanish when she arrived? It wouldn't be hard to find out that she was a prosecutor; she assumed the staff had gone into Full Gossip Alert seconds after her earlier visit. What was this Travis person afraid of? Once she had finished with whatever Bonita Layman had to show her, she would check on the maintenance man's access to patient rooms. And his work schedule on the days when each of the three residents had died.

The lounge had just been cleaned. Bell did not need a forensic team to tell her so; the evidence was clear. It smelled of lemon Pledge. There were wide stroke marks on the carpet where the vacuum had made its symmetrical swipes. The four chairs had been pushed back under the round table, and the checkerboard was ready to go. The cushions on the sofa had been plumped up.

A short, small-boned woman stood next to the bookcase. The pink smock and white pants told Bell that she was an aide. She was exceedingly nervous; she could not keep her fingers out of the sausage curls that dangled across her shoulders, playing with them, flipping them back and forth. Those curls were a very unlikely shade of red. The Clairol box, Bell speculated, probably called it something like "Come-Hither Crimson" or "Dusky Rose Sunset over Sausalito." She remembered the less charitable name by which she and a friend would refer to that brassy color back in high school, when they'd spot it on store clerks who were plainly trying to hide gray hair: Redneck Red.

"Grace Ann," Bonita said. "Let's sit down." She nodded toward the table.

The woman looked terrified, but she complied. She stayed on the forward edge of the chair, back straight, the living embodiment of discomfort. Her hands were flat on the tabletop in front of her, as if maybe Bell would want to check her for weapons.

Bonita had pushed the checkerboard to one side. "Bell, this is Grace Ann Rogers. She's been working here about a year now. Grace

Ann, this is Belfa Elkins. She's the prosecutor over in Raythune County."

"Prosecutor." Grace Ann breathed the word as much as said it.

Bonita went on. "I want you to tell Mrs. Elkins here what you told me this morning. When I came to you with what I'd found out. I checked the assignment logs, right? And I discovered that Marcy Coates was not originally scheduled to be working with Harmon Strayer on the day he died—isn't that correct?"

Grace Ann nodded. She looked so miserable, so totally distraught, that Bell wondered if she was going to faint or throw up.

"Yeah," the aide muttered.

"So as it turned out," Bonita went on, "Marcy Coates was the last person to see Harmon Strayer alive. Not you. Why did you switch jobs with Marcy that day?"

Head down, Grace Ann delivered her answer to the tabletop. Bell could not make out what she mumbled.

"What?" Bonita said sharply. "You need to speak up, Grace Ann."

The aide reluctantly raised her face, and Bell saw a multi-pack of emotions flitting across it: fear, confusion, doubt, dread. Grace Ann was much older than Bell had first taken her for. She had done all the things a woman could do to camouflage her age—all the things, that is, that a poor woman could do. A facelift was not an option. Instead she had dyed her hair and slathered herself with makeup, from sparkly blue eye shadow to mascara so black and so thick that it looked as if plump spiders were clinging to her eyelids.

"She asked me to," Grace Ann said.

"Did she say why?" Bell asked.

Grace Ann shook her head. "And it didn't make sense. One room's the same as another, really. Once the patients move in here, they kinda blend. Don't have no real personality no more. Just need. Just the things they need, all the time. And they all pretty much need the same things, you know? Sad to say, but it's true." She took a breath. "We come in

and we get our assignments for the day—which rooms we'll be taking care of. Nothing much to pick and choose over. Oh, there's a few
folks around here that you'd rather steer clear of, if you can—Sammy
Landacre is one, because he'll cuss you out as soon as look at you,
and Mavis Henderson is no picnic, lemme tell you—but mostly it don't
matter. That's why I couldn't figure what had gotten into Marcy."

"What do you mean?"

"She was real agitated that morning. She was standing by the bulletin board with the room assignments, and the minute I got there, she
was after me. Asking me to switch with her. She wanted Mr. Strayer's
room. She wanted it bad." Grace Ann's head flipped back down, as if
she feared the tabletop had missed her. Then she looked up again. "I
was real sorry when I heard that Mr. Strayer had died that day. He was
a nice man. And then when it come out that Marcy'd been killed—
well, this has been a terrible time, tell you that."

Bell looked her squarely in the eye. "You're sure that Marcy never
mentioned why she wanted to work in Harmon Strayer's room that
day? Not even a small remark in passing? A hint?"

"I'm sure." Grace Ann's voice was emphatic. "But I still traded
with her. Because you didn't say no to Marcy. Not when she asked like
that."

"She threatened you?" Bell asked. "Is that what you mean?"

"*Threatened* me? No, no, no." Grace Ann was aghast. "You gotta
understand. Marcy was a real good lady. The best. She really cared
about the people here. She hated to see them suffer. Said so all the time.
She'd make them as comfortable as she could, even if she was off the
clock. Pushed herself. And Lordy—she had a hard life at home, too.
Only family she had left was that good-for-nothing granddaughter of
hers, who was always coming around begging her for money. More
and more and more. So what I meant was—you didn't say no to her
because if there was anything you could do to bring a little happiness
to Marcy, you did it."

SORROW ROAD

As soon as Grace Ann left the lounge, Bonita turned to Bell. Her face was grave. "I should have listened to Darlene," she said. "She *told* me there was something going on with her father's death. But I put her off. I thought she was being emotional. Letting her grief get the best of her." She pressed the table with her fist. "I just—I just didn't want anyone telling me how to do my damned job, you know?"

"Yeah. I do." Bell understood that motive very well. It came from stubbornness, and it came from pride. But in Bonita's case, she thought, it also came from talent and ambition, and from having been over-looked a lot of times in the world, when you know you're qualified and you're not given a chance to prove it. And so when you *do* get that chance, you cannot admit to doubt.

"It's hard enough trying to get some respect when you're younger than people expect you to be, running a place like this," Bonita declared. "And then when you add black and female . . ." She closed her eyes and shook her head. When she opened them again, she'd recovered her poise. "I've always felt I have a lot to prove in this job. Muth County, West Virginia, is not exactly diverse."

"Grant you that."

"You should have seen what happened when I tried to check into a motel last year. I hadn't closed on my house yet. So I walk up to the reception desk in the lobby, with my credit card out and my ID ready—and the woman behind the desk says, 'We don't need any more maids right now. But you're welcome to fill out an application in case we have an opening.'"

Bell shuddered. "I don't know how you kept calm."

"No percentage in getting upset. I just politely told her that, no, I wanted a room." Bonita shrugged. She shifted back into professional mode. "Okay," she said. "So what do you think's going on around here?"

"No idea. But I need to be clear—it might be nothing, after all. Marcy Coates could have had any number of reasons—perfectly

241

innocent reasons—for wanting to switch assignments with Grace Ann. And Harmon Strayer's death was most likely the result of age and ill health and Alzheimer's. But I'll make some inquires at the coroner's office. And I'd like to chat with other employees, too, at some point. See if they noticed Marcy Coates behaving out of character. Would you mind giving me a staff roster? And scheduling some time for each employee to meet with me?"

"Funny. That's the same thing I was doing when I found out about the assignment switch—putting together a roster and some interview times."

"Really."

"Yes. For the librarian at the Raythune County Public Library. She called me last week. Wants to send someone over to interview our older staff members. For an oral history thing." Bonita paused. "Hold on. I just remembered the interviewer's name she gave me—Carla Elkins. Any relation?"

"As a matter of fact," Bell said, "she's my daughter." There was pride in her voice. There would always be pride in her voice when she talked about Carla.

Carla Jean Elkins stepped down from a Greyhound bus in the middle of Blythesburg, West Virginia. It was as close as she could get to Acker's Gap, because the bus station in Acker's Gap had closed down five years ago. No other business had taken over that location—the town had run out of reckless fools—so now it was a crumbling building with a gouged-up linoleum floor, cracked windows, and the slithery ghosts of long-ago travelers whisking to and fro.

The station in Blythesburg was even less impressive, although it was still open. It was just a kiosk and a couple of benches on a concrete pad. But it was the only place for many miles to board and disembark, so no one was likely to complain about the lack of deluxe accommodations.

The first thing Carla did when her feet hit the frozen ground was to look up. Just for a second, because there were people behind her, shuffling and wrangling their belongings, also eager to get off the bus.

The sky was clear. The sun was the color of a saltine cracker. Snow had been pushed back into a low dirty-white hedge that ran alongside the sidewalk. It was very cold, and very windy. Carla moved on, clearing the way for the other passengers.

She felt . . . well, how did she feel? She wasn't sure. That was a new thing. Before, she had always known how she felt. Exactly. She could describe her feelings precisely. She could even select the right words for other people's feelings. Her friends would come to her with a hot whirling mess of half-formed thoughts and vague impressions and blunt yearnings, and Carla would sort it all out for them, separating the various emotions, reverse-engineering their moods.

Not anymore. Now she was just as blind and bumbling as everybody else when it came to feelings. She had intended to figure it all out on the long bus ride, but instead she mostly slept. It was not a restful sleep; she jerked awake each time the bus rocked sideways or the driver braked hard, wondering where the hell she was. Then she'd doze off again, head jammed sideways against the seat back, backpack secured on her lap with both hands.

Her dad had offered to drive her to Acker's Gap. *No thanks,* she had said. He'd offered to buy her a plane ticket to Charleston and then hire a limo to get her the rest of the way. She turned him down again. She wanted time to think. She'd only been on a Greyhound bus one other time in her life—she had visited her friend Sandy Lightfoot in Owensboro, Kentucky, the summer after seventh grade, because the Lightfoot family moved away once school was out for the year—and she remembered that a bus ride created an amazing space for thinking. It took a long time, but unlike flying it featured the same old crap out the window that you had seen a million times before, so you did not get distracted by awe. You could focus on what you needed to think about.

Kayleigh Crocker was going to pick her up. Carla hadn't told her mother that she was coming. She wanted it to be a surprise.

Back in Arlington, her dad had fixed things for her. She was not sure how she felt about that. Without him—and had she been, say, a homeless veteran with psychiatric issues or a black teenager with anger management problems, and had she done *exactly the same thing*—she knew the outcome would have been far different.

But Sam Elkins knew everybody in the world who mattered and, in addition to knowing them, he also was owed favors by them, because he had done things in the past on their behalf. So it all happened very quickly, in a blur of insider privilege: the store dropped the charges, the cop withdrew the resisting arrest complaint, and the judge told her to pay the fine and mind her manners henceforth. Those were not his exact words, Carla had explained to Kayleigh when she called her the night before and asked for a ride from Blythesburg to Acker's Gap. But close enough.

And now Carla understood about courts. She had thought she did already—everyone thinks they do—but standing in front of somebody in a black robe, waiting for your entire future to be decided, was a watershed experience. Carla had listened to her mom talk about it, and she'd learned about the court system in her civics class, but the actual *feel* of it—of watching the little mole on the left side of the judge's mouth sort of jump as she spoke, of smelling the aftershave on her attorney's pink shaven jaw, of hearing the brief creak of leather as the deputy standing in the back reclasped his hands and the gun belt shifted on his hip, of realizing that her life was completely up for grabs at this moment—was very different from hearing about it or reading about it. It was like seeing pictures of the circus—and then walking the tightrope. She was scared out of her mind, and she never wanted to be in this kind of place ever again, and she knew exactly where she needed to be.

As they were walking out of the courthouse her father had said, "So, where do you want to go now, young lady?"

Carla's reply: "I want to go home."

And here she was.

"You got a car?"

A pesky old woman had climbed down out of the bus right behind her and then followed her onto the concrete pad. She had long, greasy hair with blond highlights that had grown out a long time ago, leaving the gray parts in charge. She was dressed in what looked like an accumulation of knotted-together dishrags, safety-pinned scarves, and ratty overlapping blankets. She smelled like a dirty bathroom.

"No," Carla said. She hoped Kayleigh would be getting here soon.

"'Cause if you did," the woman said, arching her scraggly eyebrows, "I was gonna ask you for a ride."

"Well, I don't."

The woman sniffed repeatedly. Either a bad cold or drug habit, Carla thought. Smart money was on the latter.

"Okay, well," the woman said. "But if you did, that's what I was gonna do."

The bus had loaded right back up again with the people who'd been waiting on the pad. Carla didn't want to inhale that noxious exhaust when the bus left, which it would do within minutes, so she headed for one of the benches.

The old woman followed her.

Leave me alone, Carla thought, but did not say out loud, because some people only got more clingy after that, bolder, as a kind of perversity took hold of them. Doing the opposite of what you asked became a mission. Whereas if you ignored them, you had a fighting chance of seeing them give up and go away.

"I got bit by a cat," the old woman said. She wriggled her bare right arm out of its nest of materials and stuck it out, underside turned up. An abscess had cracked the scabby white surface and now bloomed like a fierce yellow flower. "Bite got infected. That's why it looks so bad. Them infections get real dangerous. I was in the hospital in Charleston for a week and a half."

Carla scooted to the far side of the bench. *Come on, Kayleigh. Come on.*

The old woman had only bothered her a few times on the ride itself. Once to ask Carla if there was a toilet on the bus. Once to ask if Carla had a tissue. And once more to apologize for the two times she had already interrupted her.

It was not a cat bite. That was obvious. It was a DIY drug portal that had been poked at too many times with a filthy syringe. Carla did not know why the woman had chosen her as the audience for her spontaneous confessions—her fibs, that is—but she had.

Lucky me, Carla thought.

Her one-word, noncommittal answers finally began to wear down the woman, who picked obsessively at the skin around a fingernail and made a few more remarks about the overly aggressive cat. Carla said nothing. Finally the woman left. Carla settled in to enjoy these last few minutes of solitude.

She wanted to think about everything that was ahead of her. One of the most important things was her job, which she was even more excited about, now that she had been away from it for a few days. She couldn't wait to get back to the interviews. She had called Sally McArdle on Monday, and explained what was going on—although she left out some of the more embarrassing parts. You did not lie to Sally McArdle. And Sally McArdle had said, in a curt voice that Carla found far more satisfactory than she would have found a gushy, gooey, sympathetic one: "Okay, fine. Clean up your mess over there and then get back as quick as you can. We need to finish things up."

And then there was Travis Womack.

That was another reason Carla was glad to be back. She had been thinking about him. A lot. It was not a boyfriend kind of thing—at least she didn't *think* it was, because, Jesus, he was *ancient,* he was older, probably, than her *father*—but it was something. She just didn't know what. Do you ever know, though? That's what she was thinking about now, as she sat on the cold bench. Does anybody ever figure out what attracts them to one person and not somebody else? She had discussed that with her mom once, when her mom first started dating Clay Meckling. People talked. Wow, did they ever! Clay was younger than her mom, more than ten years younger, and—this being Acker's Gap—people were on fire with gossip. At one point her mother said to her, "Look, sweetie, we never really know why we like someone, beyond some common interests." Carla had rolled her eyes. *Common interests* was, like, the lamest phrase in the world. Then her mom said: "But in the end, you have to decide if it's worth it. Doesn't matter what anybody else thinks. It's up to you. *You* decide if the person you have chosen is worth all the fuss and the bother, worth changing your life for."

"Is Clay worth it?" Carla had asked her.

"Yes," Bell said, after a pause. "Yes, I think he is. But we'll see."

Carla looked around. She was alone on the little square pad now. The other people who had been on the bus with her and disembarked here in Blythesburg had drifted away. Including the woman with the gross-looking arm and the lie that went along with it.

Lies.

That was the issue, right? Carla had been knocked back by the possibility that Travis Womack used illegal drugs. That he had only *pretended* to be clean that night to throw her off the trail. Maybe he even had an arrest record. She would be seeing him again when she went to Thornapple Terrace tomorrow. And she absolutely *had* to know: Did he have a record? If he had a record, she'd never be able to introduce him to her mom.

Or to consider pursuing—Carla could not even think the word without blushing—a *relationship*. God, no. Not possible.

She pulled her cell out of her backpack and sent another quick text to her friend Brad. Brad Turim. She had already texted him twice during the bus ride.

Brad was the absolute best tech guy on the planet. Carla had gotten to know him when she worked in Web design at a start-up last year. One day the bosses came in and fired the entire design staff. *Boom.* Just like that. Some venture capitalists they'd been counting on had turned out to be not so adventurous, after all, and withdrew their offer. But Carla had kept in touch with Brad—who did not get fired, of course, because the techies never got fired. Somebody had to keep the computers up and running. It couldn't *all* be about social media marketing and PR. Somebody had to know how to actually do something.

She had asked Brad to check out the name Travis Womack. Run it through some databases, the ones that were easy to access—and the not-so-easy ones, too. See what came up. If he had a record, Brad would find it. And then she would know what she was dealing with.

She texted: *Just checking back. Anything yet?*

His instant reply: *Bosses everywhere. Getting 2 it soon*

Carla heard the *toot-toot* of a car horn. She looked up. Kayleigh Crocker waved at her from behind the front windshield of her white Scion, mouthing the words, "Come on!" Carla jumped up, slinging her backpack strap over her shoulder. Despite all that she had gone through in the past several days—hell, the past several *months,* if you counted the panic attacks and the sleepless nights and the crying jags and the complicated wodge of emotions—she was aware of something stirring in her heart right now that surprised her, frankly, with its simplicity, something that felt an awful lot like happiness.

She was home.

Three Boys

April 9, 1942

Lying was a lot easier than Harm had thought it would be.

Lying itself was a snap—he lied routinely to his gullible teachers, and to his even more gullible parents, and he lied to his girlfriends and to his little sister, Rosemary—but lying to an official representative of the federal government? That, Harm had assumed, would be difficult.

It wasn't. It was the same. He stood in front of the man at the recruiting station in Charleston, who gave a quick, bored look at the form Harm had just filled out. "Okay," the man said. He was wearing a uniform, but he did not seem much like a soldier to Harm; he had a belly on him, for one thing, and Harm was pretty sure that a real solider would not have a belly. "Okay, you're fine, kid," the man added. He reached for the knobby black handle of a chunky rectangular stamp. He brought the stamp down upon the top sheet of paper. *Thunk.* He re-inked it on the moist red pad, and stamped the second page and then the third. *Thunk. Thunk.*

"Okay," the man said again.

On that paper, Harmon Arthur Strayer had scribbled this in the blank for AGE: "16 yrs." Alvie and Vic were sixteen, but Harm was only fifteen. He would not be sixteen for another three months.

Harm's heart was beating fast and loud, so loud that he was pretty sure other people could hear it. He had been told that lying to the government meant you could go to prison. What if that was true?

I don't care, Harm thought. *To hell with it.*

The man stood up. He motioned for Harm to join him in a corner of the room. He measured Harm's height—six feet, one inch—and then he weighed him: 157 pounds. "It's a little low, but you'll fill out," the man said. He chuckled. "Once the Navy gets hold of you."

Harm was embarrassed. He had always been on the skinny side, and his chest was a narrow cage of curved bone. After supper that night, when he had told his mother what he'd done, she had cried out, "But you can't! Look at your legs!" His legs, it was true, were like toothpicks, thin and white. Harm's father told her to shut up. "He'll be fine," he said. Growled, really. "He'll leave a boy and come back a man." His father had read that phrase somewhere, or overheard it, and he repeated it several times that night before Harm was able to slip away, finally, to go be with his friends. Harm's father was very big on the whole becoming-a-man business. His own father—Harm's Grandpa Sam—had, Harm's dad had told him, served in World War I. When he came back to Norbitt, nobody recognized him. The gentleness was gone. He was a brute, and people feared him. Harm's father said that with admiration.

In a few days, Harm, Vic, and Alvie were going to get on a bus and travel to the Naval Station Great Lakes in Lake County, Illinois, for basic training. It was near Chicago. That was all they knew. When they asked for details, that was all they were told: "It's near Chicago." As if invoking the name of a big city—a city out in the great world beyond Norbitt, beyond West Virginia—made all other information extraneous.

Well, maybe it did. Because that was why they had decided to join up and go. They wanted to get the hell out of town. Naturally they did not say that—they talked about patriotism and duty, like everybody else did—but there was no future in Norbitt. There was only the past. Teachers in school talked about how old those mountains were, about how many thousands of years had gone into their making. Every time he heard that, Harm thought: *Well, yeah. You only have to look at them to know. Old. Old, old, old. Everything's old around here, and used up.* The roads were old. The buildings were old. *Jesus. Nothing ever changes here. Especially the people.*

Frank Plumley confirmed it: People never changed. That was what he had told them, the single time he talked about what happened along that dusty road just outside Caneytown.

The conversation happened in 1938, about a month and a half after the death of the old lady and the kid. The three boys were sitting on the back porch of the Plumley house, in the same general configuration they had formed on that other day: Vic leaning back against the top step, his legs stretched out in front of him, and Harm and Alvie seated on either side of Vic, like palace guards surrounding the king.

Summer dusk had settled over the town, purpling the world, staining the sidewalks with shadows. From down the block came the squally sounds of the Boykin kids, hollering their way through a game of hide-and-seek—or hide-and-shriek, as Harm had heard Vivian Plumley call it once, irritation in her voice, because the Boykins played it every night, at the top of their lungs. From another direction came the distant sound of a train whistle, a sound that always made Harm a little bit sad, no matter how good he had been feeling before.

All at once Frank Plumley came crashing out of the back door. The smell of alcohol clung to him, as if he had rinsed his clothes in it. His movements were loose and unsteady. A big grin was smeared across his face, like the residue from a jelly sandwich. Harm's stomach clenched in fear. Vic's dad always made him apprehensive, even when the man was cold sober. Drunk was much worse. Drunk made him a monster.

Before Vic could react, before he could move aside and let the old man go down the steps, Frank Plumley nailed him with a vicious, leg-swinging kick that caught him between the shoulder blades. Vic never had a chance. He crumpled up and tumbled down the steps. He landed at the bottom on his hands and knees.

"Get up," Frank Plumley yelled down at him. His voice was loud and sloshy. "You look like a damned dog, you know that? Bow-wow! You gonna bark for me, boy? Bow-wow! Lemme hear you!"

Vic slowly got to his feet. By this time Harm and Alvie had joined him at the bottom of the steps. They were scared, but they wanted to make their allegiance clear. Their friend Vic had been totally humili-ated. Normally, such humiliations came in private. But this one—well, Alvie and Harm knew full well that Vic would take it out on them later and they didn't see anything wrong with that. Just as his father bullied him, Vic would go right on down the line and bully them. That was how it worked. It was a progression, a journey, a certitude, and it was utterly predictable, like the route of that train whose solemn whistle had chastened the world just seconds before Frank Plumley's assault.

A few seconds passed before anything else happened. In that quick interval, something caught Harm's eye. It was in the second-story win-dow, up over the porch. Harm knew whose room that was: It belonged to Frank and Vivian Plumley. The window was open. The motion he had seen was the twitch of the curtain. Somebody was up there. Lis-tening. Watching. He saw the curtain move again. And because there was a faint light up there, from a small lamp on a bedside table, he was able to see her face. It was Vivian. Her face was fluid and shiny. Both of the Plumleys had been drinking. Drinking, and doing other things, too. The idea of that inflamed him.

And then, as he was about to lower his gaze—Harm was afraid

that Frank Plumley might see him looking, and might somehow guess his thoughts—Vivian opened the curtain just the slightest bit more. Just enough for Harm to see the pink silk robe she was wearing. She stared down at him. She put a finger to her lips, and she licked it. The next thing she did—God help him—was to touch her left nipple with that finger, and move the finger in a slow insinuating circle. Harm thought he might explode.

"You know what?" Frank Plumley said. Harm was forced to refocus. "Guess what. Guess what." His words were slurred—*Gethwad, Gethwad*—and they were all on one string. It would have been funny, Harm thought, if it weren't so scary. Drunks on radio shows were always funny: They knocked things over with a crash and a bang, they hiccupped and they sang songs. They were hilarious.

Frank Plumley was not hilarious.

"You're *worse* than a damned dog," he said to Vic. "You're a murdering sonofabitch. You know that, right? You're a goddamned killer."

Vic stood there and took it. He had no choice. Frank Plumley wavered on the top step of the porch, swaying and listing at a dangerous angle, teetering on the edge, and Harm wondered: If Frank Plumley fell and hit his head, if he was bleeding and dying, would they help him? Would they pick him up? Or would they just leave him there to die?

We'll just leave him there to die. The thought shot across Harm's mind like a bolt of electricity. It was exciting and dangerous. And freeing.

Frank Plumley didn't fall. He hitched up his trousers with the heels of his hands and he said, "All I ever wanted was a son. A good, strong boy. And what'd I get? I got a miserable stinking sonofabitch like you. A pantywaist." He pointed down at Vic. He was not shouting anymore. His voice had dropped into a dark running mumble. "Think I *like* cleaning up your damned messes? Think I *like* that? Gonna be paying off that goddamned deputy and that goddamned magistrate for *years,* you know that? No such thing as favors, boy. Only trades. Bargains. And I made a bad one. Tell you that."

And then Frank Plumley's voice dropped even lower, and he uttered the words that would forever alter the destinies of the three boys, but in a way that would not manifest itself for years. In fact they would not, on their own, ever have been able to mark this moment as special, and it was only in relation to each other that they would finally understand its significance:

"You ain't never gonna change," Frank Plumley said with a savage snarl. "Because nobody does. Nobody changes. You're gonna be what you are right now for the rest of your goddamned life. I got your number, boy. Don't you think I don't. Not for one goddamned minute." He leaned over and spat in the yard, sending forth a gooey wad of phlegm that ended up—or a good part of it did, anyway—on his chin. He was not aiming at Vic, but Vic still ducked, which made Frank Plumley laugh. Then he turned around and lurched back into the house, letting the screen door smack shut behind him. Harm's dad once told him that Frank Plumley specialized in the fuck-you exit. Harm's dad even used the word itself. He did not say, "F—you." He said the word.

The three boys were completely still. A dog barked in a yard on the next block over.

Everything was exactly the same as it had always been.

Everything was different.

June 7, 1944

A story had come through the ranks, passed along from hand to hand, soldier to soldier, like a baby rescued from under the rubble. These days, stories always came that way—stories, jokes, rumors, gossip, slogans, dirty rhymes. Harm noticed that. One person gave the story to the next person, and then the next to the next. Stories were passed from shore to ship, from ship to shore, from officer to enlisted man, from one service branch to another, up and down, back and forth. It reminded Harm of how gossip made its way around Norbitt. Person to person, with things added along the way. Things to spice it up.

The story was about Eisenhower. Harm heard it that morning and immediately had to tell Vic and Alvie, because how could he not? It was a great story. And it had Eisenhower in it. So, of course.

Harm told it when the three of them were standing on the deck of the USS *Arkansas,* strung out along the rail, looking at the choppy gray ocean. They were as seasick as it was possible to be—Alvie had thrown up three times already this morning, Harm and Vic once each. No matter how many days they had been at sea, they still got seasick. They may have been officially designated as seamen second class, but they were boys from a landlocked state and the sea was like a germ against which their bodies had built up no tolerance. His Eisenshower story, Harm thought, might take their minds off the woozy dip and rise of the big ship, the chop and bounce and heave. So he motioned them into a ragged little circle.

Harm tucked into his tale like a hungry boy with a plate of pancakes in front of him—although if anyone had proposed that analogy to him right then, if anyone had even murmured the word "pancakes," Harm would have been sick all over again.

It had happened two days ago, he told Alvie and Vic. The night before D-Day. The night before anybody knew how it was all going to work out, when a million things might still go wrong.

General Eisenhower was reviewing the 101st Airborne. The Screaming Eagles, they called them. Parachutists. Each man draped with so much equipment—three knives, one machete, two bandoliers, two cans of machine gun ammo with over seven hundred rounds, one Hawkins mine, four blocks of TNT, one Gammon grenade, and that was just for starters—that they looked like fat waddling bears when they went by, holding their arms out from their sides in stubby arcs.

Eisenhower went up and down the row. He stopped in front of a fresh-faced, beefy kid, a kid who wore all that heavy equipment like it was nothing, like it was scarves and feathers instead of ammo and TNT blocks. He asked the kid—and when Harm told the story to Alvie and Vic, he hammed it up, making Eisenhower's voice booming and stern—where he was from.

"Pennsylvania," the kid stammered back. The kid was nervous, don't you know, because this was, after all, the Supreme Allied Commander. God himself would probably salute General Eisenhower.

"Oh, is that so?" That is what Eisenhower said to the boy. And then he said this: "Well, did you get those big shoulders from working in a coal mine?"

"Yes, sir," the kid replied, confident again, sure of himself. "Yes, sir."

When he finished the story, Harm punched Alvie's arm. Alvie winced and punched him back, but Harm did not care, the story was good: Eisenhower and a coal miner. "Can you beat that?" Harm said. "The night before it all happened. The kid could just as easily have been from West Virginia as Pennsylvania. Think of it—Eisenhower. And, with the shift of few hundred miles, somebody we might've known. Might've grown up with."

Vic and Alvie liked the story, too. Not quite as much as Harm did, but that was okay. The three boys did not always share the same tastes. Vic liked bourbon, for instance, and Harm could not abide the stuff. Too sweet, he said. Alvie smoked Kools, while Vic went for Lucky Strikes. Harm was not particular; he would smoke Camels, Old Gold, anything cheap and handy.

Telling stories was a good way to keep the anxiety down. True, the major assault was over, and the Allies had landed in a sweeping fury of guns and rushing manpower and clever technology and the propulsive power of sheer abundant hope and youth, but that was just the beginning. This battleship, the USS *Arkansas*, all twenty-seven thou-

sand tons of it, was still busy, its Bofors guns and its Oerlikon can-
nons still firing at German positions on Omaha Beach. The *Arky* had
orders to stay right here for another six days, helping to finish what
the Allies had started on D-Day. And Vic and Alvie and Harm were
a part of all this now. No one could take that away from them, ever:
They were *here*. They were part of this great thing, this magnificent
mission.

The motive that brought them here had not been pure—but what
motive really is, ever, when you take it apart and examine it, piece by
piece?—and yet here they were, the three of them. In history.

They had only wanted to get the hell out of Norbitt. Put it all behind
them: the town, Frank Plumley, the strictly sequestered memory of the
accident. But gradually, as they trained and as their bodies grew hard
and as they did what they were told to do, and as they lifted their eyes
from what was right in front of them and concentrated on the horizon,
they changed. They began to realize just how momentous this truly
was. They had always understood how high the stakes were—you
could not read the newspaper or listen to the radio and *not* be aware
of that, God knows—but this was different. Now they were *in* it. They
were *part* of it. No matter how lowly their rank, they were in the
center of something immense. They wanted to live up to that, to be
commensurate with the wonder and peril.

The three boys had never expected to be able to serve together.
They were sure they would each be sent to some different remote place,
and that by the time they retuned to Norbitt—*if* they returned—they
would barely be able to communicate, so diverse had been their
experiences. But, no. Their assignments had kept them together, Vic,
Harm, and Alvie. They had spent most of the war in England, at an
air base; their only combat experience thus far was being on the *Arky*
during D-Day, and really, that did not count because they were
offshore. When they talked about the fact that they had yet to see

close-up combat, they put disappointment in their voices, impatience and irritation, they way you were supposed to do, so that people would not think you were a coward.

A man on the *Arky* who *had* seen combat—real combat—set them straight one day: "Everybody's a coward. You got that, boys? Everybody. It's what you do anyway—it's what you do *while still being a goddamned coward*—that matters. You're here, aren't you? You're here."

Their job for today was to stand on deck and search the water for bodies. They were looking for survivors, for men who had maybe fallen behind during the assault, been dumped out of a landing craft, and were bobbing along now, waiting for rescue. So far they had not found any living men. Just bodies. Those, too, they brought aboard. Those, too.

The *Arky* was an old beauty. Commissioned in 1912, she was the oldest ship in the D-Day fleet. Patched-up, a little rusty, but okay. And the three boys? They were lean and fit and strong—fitter than they had ever been before in their lives and, they suspected, fitter than they would ever be afterward, either.

They looked out across the chaos of ocean that slapped and rubbed and pounded against the shore of Omaha Beach. They scoured every inch of that water for any sign of life. It was tricky, though, because there was so much motion already—the wind plucking wildly at the gray waves, and the gray waves rising and splitting and diving against the gray sky. Trying to find movement within other movement was grueling, and tiring. But they did their jobs.

It was shortly after Harm had told his Eisenhower story that it happened. Harm had turned away from the water—he was still savoring the afterglow of having brought the tale to them, its very unlikeliness giving it its glory, as the general in charge of everything, of all of their lives, plus the fate of nations, had stopped to chat with a damned coal miner, a guy who might have been any one of them—and so he did not see it.

Alvie was the one who saw it. He saw khaki, and he saw motion. But he made the mistake of telling Vic first, and pointing at the undulating scrap on the waves, before shouting it out to the other men on deck, and so it was Vic who sounded the alarm, Vic who got the credit for being alert and observant.

The soldier was faceup in the water about thirty yards off the starboard bow, his arms and legs spread out and twitching, as if he was doing jumping jacks with great enthusiasm. Following the alarm, the deck was swarmed; officers shoved aside enlisted men and other officers, too, shouting out orders, almost hysterical with expectation. Regular order was quickly restored but for a few crazy minutes— minutes that reassured Harm that even the officers were human beings, men with feelings, and subject to intense emotions such as relief and joy—there was no order whatsoever.

And then it was over.

When they hoisted him up it was instantly clear that the soldier in the water was not alive, after all. He was dead. Stone dead. The motion of his arms and his legs had been caused by the heavy waves, not by any volition of living limbs. His body was being rocked and jostled by the sea. That was all. It was just one more body, nothing special. The men returned to their stations. The three boys went back to scouting the water.

That water continued to rise and fall all around them in a ragged dance of which the ocean never seemed to tire, an endless saga of waves climbing and collapsing, climbing and collapsing, like gray peaked mountains created and destroyed again in seconds, crumbling to their doom and then instantly reforming. Harm would have found it hypnotic and even somewhat soothing, if he was not so sick all the time.

The three boys stood on the deck, scanning, searching. As Harm had watched his shipmates haul up that dead body—the skin was greenish-yellow and rubbery-looking—he was smote by a memory, an image he had tried very hard for the past six years to keep locked up and far away from him: the old woman and the kid, dead at the side of that road.

The wind was even stronger now. It had a roar at the back of it, a sound like a tractor engine. Harm had to get right in his friends' faces to talk to them, so close that some of his spittle landed on their cheeks. There was no other way to be heard. "When we get back," he said, shouting each word, giving it a separate weight and thrust and authority, "maybe we should go visit the family of that little girl and the old lady. See how they're doing. After all these years. It's the least we can—"

"You shut the hell up!" Alvie shouted. He wiped Harm's spit off his face with a savage motion, as if even the delivery system of Harm's idea might be contagious. "Just shut up."

"Nobody will know," Harm yelled back, "why we're asking. They won't know."

The wind tore at the words, ripping them into smaller sounds, flinging them around the deck like confetti.

Vic ducked his head closer to his friends, so that he could be heard. "Shut up," he shouted at Harm, not angrily, but in a bossy way, and then he turned back to the water to do his job.

That was the next-to-last time they would ever speak of what had happened that day on the dusty road outside Caneytown, West Virginia. The next time was seventy-one years later, and it would cost two of them their lives.

Chapter Twelve

The first thing Carla did when she arrived at Thornapple Terrace on Wednesday morning was to look around for Travis Womack. She did not want to be too obvious about it. Casualness was key.

She stood by the receptionist's desk. She had given the old woman her name, and the reason she was here. Now it was a matter of waiting for Bonita Layman—she was finishing up a phone call, the receptionist had informed her—to come out and escort her to the area where she'd be doing the interviews with the older employees.

"So," Carla said. "This is a pretty big place. You must have a good maintenance staff." *Smooth, Elkins,* she thought. *Real smooth.*

The receptionist's wrinkled old prune-face twitched. "Yes." She went back to her computer screen.

Carla unhooked her backpack from her shoulder. She set it on the floor. She leaned over, pretending to be checking her gear. Truth was, she had already checked it multiple times out in the Kia, before she even came in. She had everything she needed.

While rustling through the items, Carla said, "I mean, with all these rooms, there's a lot to go wrong. Plumbing, electrical, heating and air-conditioning."

"Yes."

Instead of saying what she was really thinking—*You're a chatterbox, lady, aren't you?*—Carla said, "So what do you have? Five people, six? To keep it all running right?"

The receptionist made one of those snickery sounds in her throat that indicated disbelief at such an outlandishly inaccurate guess. "We have two people on our maintenance staff. Mr. Ford and Mr. Womack. Mr. Ford is the supervisor."

"Oh." Carla tried to act as if she really didn't care what their names were. She zipped the top of her backpack shut, lifted it, and re-slung it over her shoulder. "Are either one of them around? Well, come to think of it, I don't want to bother a supervisor—so maybe that other guy? I just had a few questions about the kind of brick they used on the outside. About its insulating properties."

She'd gone too far.

"I'm confused," the receptionist said crisply. "Are you here to do interviews for a library project—or are you an inspector with the county building department?"

Bonita Layman's door opened, rescuing Carla. The director motioned her into her office. Before she shut the door behind them, Bonita called across the lobby to the receptionist: "Dorothy, the light switch."

"Yes, ma'am. I'll call Travis and send him in."

Score! Carla thought.

But she didn't get to see him, after all. He never came into the director's office, at least not while she was there. Which was not, admittedly, all that long. Bonita Layman gave her a quick summary of the Terrace's history, and then handed her a sheet of paper. It was a list of staff members who were old enough to fulfill Carla's criterion for interviews, and who had agreed to participate.

Bonita took her to the lounge. It was crowded. Two old men sat in armchairs with their walkers angled directly in front of them, as if they needed to be ready at any moment to bolt in order to accomplish some essential errand. In truth, they had not moved in hours, and would likely not move at all for the rest of the day, unless someone came and fetched them. A woman who looked as fragile as glass stood by the window, staring at the snow, one hand on her chin, the elbow of that arm cupped by her other hand. Every thirty seconds or so she would turn and face the room at large and say, "What? What?" Then she turned back to the window.

Carla's attention was drawn to a gentle-looking old man who sat at a round table across from a younger woman. Judging by the similarities in the bone structure of their faces, and by something that rhymed in their eyes, Carla guessed that this was the man's daughter. On the table in front of them was a checkerboard, its pert little squares filled in and waiting for someone to make the first move. The old man wore a plaid driving cap and a soft blue V-necked sweater and beige slacks. He kept his slender, gnarled hands folded in his lap. He had a serene expression on his face. The woman, however, did not; her face looked as if it had been eaten alive by a scowl.

In the chair between them sat a bored-looking aide. She had spilled something on the sleeve of her pink smock, and the only time she came alive was when she frowned and dug at the crusty spot with a fingernail.

Despite the aide's lassitude, Carla felt a definite energy emanating from that table. It was not positive. It had, in fact, a raw and corrosive vibe. It only went in one direction. And it came from Scowler, not Driving Cap.

Got to be a story there, Carla thought.

Or maybe not. Maybe it was ordinary, and maybe they saw this kind of thing around here every day. Maybe the effort of visiting a loved one in the lounge, watching them sink beneath the gray waves of Alzheimer's, would make *anybody* sour and angry, and maybe, after a while, you would start worrying hard about all the money and time and resources he was taking up, day after day, and so you would start to resent him, even though you knew it was not his fault.

"Arlene, this is Carla Elkins," Bonita said. She moved Carla along, directing her into a corner of the room. Two metal folding chairs had been set up there, facing each other. On one of the chairs a plump, frizzy-haired woman in a pink smock had settled herself, her white-clad thighs spread wide and partially rolling off either side of the seat. "Carla is the woman I told you about," Bonita went on. "She's doing a project for the library. Talking to people about why they stayed in the area."

The aide's mumble was low but audible. "Must've been for jobs just like this—a high-paying, fulfilling job of emptying bedpans for minimum wage."

Bonita stiffened. "As I recall, you *volunteered* to talk to her today, Arlene. If you don't care to participate, then you certainly don't have to."

"I'm fine, I'm fine," the aide said. "Just kidding around." She offered Carla a polite, insincere smile that lifted her doughy face for an instant. "Sit down, honey. Tell me what you need to know."

Carla wondered a bit at this sudden change of heart, but then she realized that the aide could put off her duties as long as she was being interviewed. Talking to some nosy stranger was more desirable than emptying bedpans. Only by a slight margin, probably.

Bonita wished them well and left. Carla turned on the digital recorder.

Arlene Lewis had been born and raised on a farm just down the road from what was now Thornapple Terrace. "Was just a big old hunk of woods back then," she said. "My daddy always hoped to buy it, add it to our property, but hell—he could barely afford the monthly payments on the land he had already, much less go out and add more."

She was sixty-nine years old. She'd been married and divorced three times. Carla must have reacted to that news without meaning to—perhaps she had flinched, or raised an eyebrow just the smallest bit—because Arlene laughed at her and said, "Honey, you just wait. Wait 'til you're my age. You'll see. Things get stale, okay? For the both of you. Only thing you can do then is move on. I loved 'em all. Still do, matter of fact. And once I've refreshed myself with somebody new—well, there's no law that says I can't sneak back around from time to time and sample the earlier merchandise. If you know what I mean."

Carla was very much afraid that she did know, and so she hurriedly changed the subject. She asked Arlene when she had decided to make her life here, and not somewhere else.

"That's not something you *decide*, honey. It's something that just *happens*. You always think it's temporary—everything, I mean. Because you can change anything at any time. When you're young, you think you've got all these choices. Well, you don't. My daddy used to say that you don't have to worry about falling into a rut—because the rut's out there looking for you already and it'll get here real soon. No escape. You're stuck before you know it." Arlene said these things with a certain gallant cheerfulness, and not the lugubrious self-pity that such sentiments might inspire.

Before Carla could ask the next question, there was a commotion at the checkerboard table. The daughter was jabbing a finger at the old man. She was not shouting, but her voice had the menacing, escalating edge that was well on its way to a shout: "You *fucker*. I *know* you fucking remember. I *know* it."

The aide tapped the woman's shoulder. Time to settle down. But the woman shook her off and continued to heckle the old guy: "What about me? What about Nelson, wherever he is? What are we supposed to *do,* huh? With the rest of our lives? After what you did to us?"

The woman abruptly broke off her rant, lowered her head, and thrust it in her hands. She was not crying; her grief struck Carla as something that had ranged beyond the ability to be expressed in mere sobs a long time ago. It was part of her being now, fossilized inside the larger universe of everything she did and said and was. In the meantime, the old man gazed serenely across the table. He smiled a tiny little smile.

Arlene turned back around to Carla. She had been watching the drama with a relish that made Carla want to offer to go fetch popcorn. "We get that all the time," Arlene muttered. With a naughty grin, she added, "Usually, though, it's the *patients* who act up—not the visitors." She squared herself in her chair, ready to get back to it. "Fire away."

"What's your favorite childhood memory?" Carla asked.

Arlene pondered the question for a very long time. "I don't remember very much about my childhood. I used to—but I don't anymore."

Carla looked concerned. Her face made Arlene snicker and sweep a pudgy hand around the lounge, where three more patients had wandered in, shuffling along like lost zombies. They stood in a row by the wall, waiting for someone to tell them what to do.

"Oh, honey—not like *those* poor folks," Arlene exclaimed. "Not *that* kind of 'I can't remember.' What I mean is that I don't *want* to remember it, so I just don't. I keep it off to the side of my brain. See, we were pretty poor, and my parents went hungry a lot of times themselves so that us kids could eat. I don't really like remembering how my mother would stand by the table, thin as a corpse although not quite as talkative, and spoon another helping of oatmeal into my brother Leroy's bowl. Leroy would eat it right up. He was too young to realize that my mother was giving him *her* helping." Arlene shook her head. Carla started to point out that she had just recounted a scene from a childhood she claimed she did not remember, but held back. Arlene was an intelligent woman. If there was irony in the vicinity, she would know it. She didn't need Carla to circle it with a Sharpie.

"Memory's a tricky thing," Arlene said.

"What do you mean?"

"Well, take that lady who was sitting at the table over there with Bill Ferris."

Carla looked. The table was now vacant. Both Scowler and Driving Cap were gone. Only the aide remained, still picking at the spot on her smock, digging in.

"That lady," Arlene continued, "comes here *all* the time. Lives pretty far away, but makes the drive, no problem. And it's like she's trying to get old Bill to remember something. But he won't. Like you saw, she gets real mad at him. Got so mad once she went a little crazy. It was way worse than today. We had to pull her off of him. Me and Lester, another aide who works the same shift as I do.

"It's gotten so bad with Bill's daughter now, you know, that Ms. Layman said she can't be left alone with him. Has to have an escort. That's why Peggy's over there. Today was her turn to make sure that crazy lady didn't take a swing at her own flesh and blood."

"If she hates him that much, then why does she have him in a place like this? Gotta be pretty expensive."

"Guess so," Arlene said, bobbing her head. Her frizzy hair bounced up and down like dandelion fluff in a mild breeze. "But it's sure as hell better than having him live with *her,* I bet."

"So does he know her? His daughter, I mean? Does he know who's visiting him?"

Arlene shrugged. Then she grinned. "My medical degree's a little outdated, hon, but okay, here goes. Based on what I see around here, the older memories stick. It's the newer ones that don't get stored. The older stuff—that's generally all they *do* remember. With old

Bill—well, I can't say. But he's not that far along. It's weird that he can seem to remember stuff from forty, fifty years ago. I mean, ask him to tell you today's date, and he'll look at you like you told him to speak French. That's understandable. But the older things—he ought to remember them. Then again, like I said, memory's a tricky thing."

Carla needed to wind this up. She had three other interviews to do before she left the Terrace. But she had one more question. She'd been trying to figure out a way to ask Arlene about Travis Womack without arousing the woman's suspicions. "A friend of mine went to school with a guy who works here," Carla said. "Or at least he *did* work here, last time she checked. She was hoping to get in touch. Guy named—wait, was it, I don't know, maybe Tom? No—it was Travis."

"Travis Womack."

"Yeah. That's it." Carla was terrified that she might be blushing. Her face did feel a little hot. But then again, Thornapple Terrace was overheated, like every old folks' home, right?

Arlene gave her a *listen, sister* look. "Honey," she said, "I'd put you at about twenty-one, twenty-two years old, if you're a day. Travis Womack has got to be pushing fifty. How could a friend of yours—somebody your age—have gone to school with him?"

Carla was too embarrassed to answer, so Arlene patted her knee. "Had a crush on him myself a while back, hon. Don't blame you a bit. It's those eyes. Deep as a river."

Bell sat at her desk. The courthouse was busier today than it had been for almost two weeks. Along with the slightly better weather had come an influx of people with business to conduct here, business they had put off because of the bad roads but could put off no longer. Property tax bills were due; the grumblers with jury duty summonses were entitled to a fair shot at wheedling their way out of it; parking tickets had to be argued over. As Bell had learned when she first undertook this job seven years ago, a county courthouse in a small town was a sort of secular sanctuary, a place where everyone eventually came to plead their case to a higher authority.

Arranged across her desk were the three pages of the coroner's report for Harmon Strayer. At the bottom of the first page, on the right-hand side, was the requisite sketch of the front and back view of a human body. Typically the coroner would have marked what he found on the body he was analyzing, and where: entrance or exit points for bullets or knife wounds, bruises, any sort of abnormalities.

On this report, the sketch was bare. Nothing at all had been marked.

In the general summary at the top of the page, under the heading *Strayer, Harmon Arthur, aged 89 years,* in the box labeled *Cause of death,* was this: *Complications from late-stage Alzheimer's.*

Next she shuffled through a stack of papers at her left elbow. She drew out the coroner's reports for the deaths of Polly Delaney and Margaret Jacks. She found the same omission: The front- and side-view sketches of a human body had not been filled out. And the cause of death was listed as *late-stage Alzheimer's.*

She called out to Lee Ann, who sat at her desk in the outer office: "Can you get me Buster Crutchfield on the phone?"

Crutchfield, the Raythune County coroner, sounded jovial. "Ever since they invented those dang fax machines, I don't get as many visitors as I used to," he said. "You oughta come by and see me now and again, Miss Belfa. Pick up the paperwork in person, instead of relying on those fancy boxes of yours." Crutchfield was seventy-two, and he liked to play the curmudgeonly Luddite. Truth was, he kept up with the latest advances in pathology, and his lab was as up-to-date technologically as his budget would allow. "How're you doin'?"

"Fine, Buster. Hey, I have a question."

"Shoot."

"How well do you know the Muth County coroner?"

"Ernie Burson. Well, lemme see. I guess he's doing a mite better. Still at the rehab place, though."

"What do you mean?"

"Ernie had a stroke about four months ago. Not back to work yet, but he's hopeful."

"So who's been doing his job?"

"The load's shared. County calls upon any physicians in the area who have a free moment or two and are willing to pitch in."

Securing the phone between her ear and an upraised shoulder, she turned to the final page of each coroner's report. She had not noticed it before, but each one had a different scrawled signature—and none of those signatures read: *Ernest T. Burson, MD.*

"Those helpful physicians might very well have been rushed, then," Bell said. "Busy with their own practices. And maybe inclined to wrap up a case as quickly as possible."

"I suppose so, yes. Although I can't imagine that any reputable physician would do shoddy work just because—"

"It happens, Buster," she said, cutting him off. "You and I both know that. A big caseload, a lot of extra work—and the next thing you know, you're not quite as rigorous as you ought to be. It's not incompetence. It's fatigue and expediency." And it happens to prosecutors, she reminded herself, as often as it does to physicians. It happens to everybody.

"Is there something I can review for you?" Buster said.

"I'd appreciate it. I can fax over the paperwork in a few minutes. If, that is, you don't mind the use of newfangled technology." Buster, she knew, expected to be teased. If you did not tease him, he would think you were mad at him.

"I'll overlook it this once." He chuckled. Then he was serious again. "Give me a quick sense of what I'm looking for." He and Bell had worked together for many years, and they had learned to shuttle quickly from jocular to grim as the situation required.

"Three elderly people, all with late-stage Alzheimer's as well as other significant health issues—diabetes, cardiac and respiratory issues. All died at a care facility over in Muth County within the last few months. Given those circumstances, how diligent would a coroner be about searching for evidence of foul play?"

Buster slowly took in a long breath of air and then expelled it, even more slowly.

"I'll be honest with you, Belfa. But if you quote me in public, I'll deny it. If word got out that I was casting aspersions on the professionalism of my colleagues—"

"Not asking you to testify in open court, Buster," she said, interrupting him. "I'm just asking for your opinion. Off the record."

"Okay, then. You're right. They wouldn't be looking. Now, if it was something big and obvious—ligature marks on the neck or any evidence of physical assault—sure, they'd see that and write it down. But overall, no. No, they wouldn't be quite as attentive as they might be if the deceased were young and healthy."

"What would slip through the cracks?"

Buster paused. He was thinking about it. "Well, with a helpless older person, I'd probably be looking for evidence of suffocation. Mucus at the back of the mouth. Trace fibers around the nose and mouth area, from whatever was used to restrict the airway—a pillow, say, or a scarf."

"To look for those things, though, you'd first have to suspect that a crime had occurred."

"Yes. But it's too late, Belfa. If you're trying to build a case, that kind of evidence would have to be collected at the original autopsy. Once the body is released to the funeral home, you're screwed. And if the deceased was cremated, then you're *doubly* screwed. And even if the body *wasn't* cremated, you can't go back and—"

"I know, Buster. I know."

"Does this mean a murderer got away with it?"

"No," Bell said. Her next words would confuse him, but so be it. "She didn't."

Carla had just settled into her Kia. The car was very cold—not surprising, because it had been sitting in the Thornapple Terrace parking lot for the past three hours. Before she left, however, she took a few seconds to savor the day.

She was still excited from the interviews she'd completed this afternoon. Her mind was busy with ways to organize the material. Sure, they could just post transcripts of the individual interviews, one by one, but she also hoped to create other ways to search the archive: train stories, say. Or courtship stories. Stories about the land itself—rugged land that had nourished the people here for hundreds of years. Yet the very things that made that land beautiful were also the things that doomed those same people to poverty and despair. These mountains protected you, but they also isolated you.

The people she'd interviewed knew that—knew it in their bones, because the mountains *were* their bones, the strong framework that underlay all that they did, all that they might do. And yet when outsiders wrote about Appalachia, they assumed that the people here were oblivious to the tragic ironies of the place, to the fact that its major industries—coal mining, and chemical plants that damaged fragile rivers—provided a living, but not a life. Only a half-life. The shadow of a life. The truth was, of course, that the residents knew that very well. They did not just know it—they *lived* it.

Those were just a few of the things that Carla had learned in the course of her work thus far. She looked out the windshield at Thornapple Terrace. It was a graveyard for the past. At times today, she'd had to turn away from the specter of blank-eyed residents who seemed to float slightly above the corridors, helpless and hapless, borne aloft by all the memories that had fallen out of their minds but still followed them, murmuring elusive hints about things they used to know. But the interviews with staff members had rescued Carla, reminding her of why she was doing this: So that even if the individual person lost her memory, there would still be a place for those memories to live.

No Travis sighting. That was the single dark spot on the day. She had really, really hoped to come across him. She still did not understand why she was so drawn to the guy, and maybe the mystery was part of it—she did not even know what kind of music he liked or how he took his coffee—but she wanted to talk to him again. See that lean face and its contemplative expression as he thought about what she'd just said. And then he'd say something, too, something wise but not pretentious.

The *ding!* of an incoming text brought her back to the fact that she was sitting in a freezing car in a quasi-deserted parking lot at dusk. First she turned on the engine, and then she checked her text.

It was from Brad: *U sure u got the name right? Travis Womack?*

She texted back a thumbs-up emoji.

His next text sort of annoyed her: *Double-check name, K?*

Her return text started out with a red-faced, frowning emoji, followed by this: *Right name. What's up?*

There was a small delay. Brad, she imagined, was staring at his tiny keyboard, thumbs curled protectively around it, before he typed his message:

Only 1 Travis Womack in any database: Dead 2010. Motorcycle crash

Three Boys

1950

Harmon Strayer sat in a booth at the Double-D Diner on the main thoroughfare that ran through Norbitt, West Virginia. He sipped at his coffee, trying to make it last. She was late. He did not want to order another cup—he had hoped to have this over and done with in minutes, and if she came and they talked and he'd ordered a second cup, he would have to wait until it was brought to him before he could leave. If the talk was not going well, if he needed to leave, those extra few minutes might be awkward.

He did not look appreciably different from the way he had looked five years ago, when he came home from the war. He was still handsome. He had not put on weight, the way Vic had. Vic was always pledging to lose it. He'd pat his belly, rub it with a satisfaction that made Harm wonder why he wanted to get rid of it. The belly seemed to bestow on him a certain confidence as he walked through the world. Ballast. And it did not affect his overall looks, either. He was still Vic Plumley, dark and dashing and nonchalant.

"Hi." A woman's voice.

He looked up. She stood next to the booth. She'd dressed up for him. She was wearing a white dress with red polka dots—a summer dress, and this was February. But she knew how much he liked her in this dress, because he had told her so; her breasts looked as if they would be spilling out of the top of it any minute. She had put on makeup, fixed herself up. He felt a pang from this evidence of her efforts. Her eagerness. And in the middle of the afternoon, too. Just because he had called.

"Hi," he said back. He gestured toward the seat across from him. "Take a load off."

She slid in, folding her body neatly to do so, tucking the back of her dress under her bottom. He could not help it: He pictured her ass naked, the way it looked when she was walking away from the bed to get dressed, and he was still lying there, raised up on one elbow, savoring the sight of her round, saucy ass. A bit of a bounce to it when she walked.

He shook his head, hoping the memory would slide out of there and leave him alone. Not a good way to begin this kind of conversation.

"Glad you were free today," he said. "To meet me."

"You could've come by the house," she said, and they both knew what that meant. "Frank's out of town all week. Some kind of a sales conference. Somewhere. I don't care, really. As long as he's gone."

"Yeah," Harm said, because he could not, in the moment, think of anything else to say. The picture of her, bare-assed naked, would not leave. He did not think he could get through this unless he got rid of the image. "Look, Vivian—"

"Oh, I don't like any sentence that begins like that!' she said, with a merry, twitchy, nervous little laugh. "That can't be good! 'Look, Vivian' sounds like one of my teachers back in grade school." She flashed him a naughty smile. "Have I been a bad girl, Mr. Strayer?

Have I been a bad, *bad* girl? Are you going to have to take me over your knee and—"

"Stop it, okay?"

The irritation in his voice startled her. Her eyes widened. He thought, for a terrifying moment, that she was going to cry.

But it was the opposite: She was annoyed. She had gone from flirtatious to angry, just like that. Her rapid-fire mood changes had, once upon a time, intrigued him, aroused him. She was like her own little weather system, compact and self-contained; you never knew what you would be dealing with, from minute to minute, and the need to react to that, to turn on a dime, had excited him.

"Okay, then," she said. Neutral now. "What's up?"

What's up? That was her way of saying: *Two can play at this game.* She sounded like a bored gas station attendant leaning in the driver's window. *Check your oil, too, bub?*

"I don't think we should see each other anymore." There. He'd said it.

She did not blink. She did not shriek. She said, "Well, that'll be tough. This is a small town. We're bound to 'see each other,' as you put it, every now and again."

"You know what I mean."

She looked out the window. It was a gray February day. February was not a good month for Norbitt; the dingy color of the sky seemed to leak into the town itself, into the old buildings and the streets.

"Yeah." She turned back to look at him. "I know what you mean."

The waitress showed up. Harm waved her away. "Still making up our minds," he said to her, and he smiled, not wanting her to get the idea that he was in the midst of any kind of confrontation here, because news of that would be all over town in an hour. The waitress smiled back. More importantly, she left.

"So," Vivian said pertly. "How do you want to do this?"

He was not prepared for that. "I don't know what you—"

"I *mean*," she said, "do we just say good-bye right here and now, or do I get some sort of explanation? Did I do something wrong, Harm? Did I pester you, ask you for a lot of expensive gifts? Demand too much of your precious, precious time? Was that it? Or was it something else? Was it—" She stopped. She snapped her fingers. "Is this about that time you couldn't perform, poor baby, and I was a bit on the *needy* side, and so maybe I said something that you found a little *demeaning,* a little *insulting* and *belittling*, you big, strong war hero, you . . ."

"Vivian." He knew about this side of her, the cruelty, the shallowness. He had seen her unsheathe it in front of other people. And when he saw that, he had known it was only a matter of time until she turned on him, too. He understood how selfish she was. In the beginning, it had fascinated him, that selfishness. She was completely devoted to her own pleasure. Single-minded. She would straddle him sometimes, furious with desire, clenching the hair on both sides of his head, moving forward and back with glassy-eyed abandon. The memory of those times could drive him mad.

They had started up before he left for the war. He was fifteen. "I could go to jail for this," she'd whispered to him, at exactly the right moment, and that functioned as a kind of aphrodisiac for both of them, all she was risking. It was just a few times. During his years away, they did not keep in touch. There was too much at stake, with Vic right there beside him, in close quarters.

When he returned, they had resumed it. Harm was now engaged to Dixie Chambers, a girl he'd dated in high school, but that did not matter. That had not changed things one bit. Dixie was a nice girl. She occupied one section of his life, a small, solid, high-walled space that he had carefully prepared for just such a thing: the nice girl he would marry. Vivian Plumley was not a nice girl, and the space she occupied was big and flimsy and makeshift.

Did Vic ever know? Harm was not sure. Sometimes, Harm thought, *yes, yes, he knows. He* must *know.* But other times, he thought: *no, absolutely not.* Vic did not have much to do with his parents these days. He was out of their house. He ran his life as he saw fit. The idea of Frank Plumley laying an angry hand on Vic now—Vic was six feet, three inches tall and, even with his newfound gut, powerful and intimidating—was laughable. More like the other way around. You could easily envision Vic Plumley knocking the crap out of his old man.

Alvie might know. Alvie was sneaky. He watched. He figured things out. He was working in his dad's church now, Crooked Creek Baptist, the same church that had kicked out his father all those years ago. Alvie planned to be a preacher, too, which surprised Harm no end. A preacher? Alvie? Well, okay. To each his own, right?

The important thing was that they had kept the secret of what happened on that dusty road outside of Caneytown. They never talked about it, never even said the word "Caneytown" out loud—never, not even once. But when one of them wavered, and got together with the other two at this very diner, say, or at Sal's, a bar three blocks away, and started murmuring words such as "honor" and "morality," the other two knew what to do. They brought out words such as "family" and "responsibility." And "jail." Now, there was a word for you, there was a real conversation stopper. They talked about all they had to lose if . . .

They did not finish the sentence. They did not need to.

So they had looked out for each other after the war, just as they had done before and during the war. Just as they had been doing all of their lives. No matter what happened to any of the three of them, no matter what choices they made or what roads they walked, they would never tell. They had burn marks on their souls, identical ones, and those marks bound the three boys together forever.

"Fuck you. Fuck *you.* You're a fucking liar, do you know that?"

Vivian was leaning over the table, her voice a strange singsong hiss, the tenor of it not matching up to the viciousness of her words. "You think you can just take off and *go* like that? Is that what you think? Just walk away like I'm some piece of *garbage* that you *fucked* and you *fucked* and then you—"

The waitress was back. She took one look at Vivian's face, and at the way she was leaning over the table, and she turned around and left. She had not even taken her order pad out of her apron pocket.

"You *fucker*," Vivian said, resuming her chant. "You *fucking fucker.*"

Women did not talk this way in Norbitt. Harm was pretty sure they didn't talk this way anywhere. She was coarse and bold, and she'd always been so, only he was not enchanted by it anymore. Harm was glad there was almost nobody else in the diner at this hour.

She settled herself down. "I want to know why," she said, her tone businesslike. "That's all I want from you at this point, Harm. Just the why. Seriously."

He looked down into his coffee cup. He had kept a grip on it throughout her verbal assault. "I can't tell you."

"Because it's a fucking *secret*? Or because you don't know?"

"Because you'll make fun of me."

That surprised her. She had had a speech all ready, a cutting retort for the answer she was sure he'd give. She was sure he was going to say that that bitchy fiancée of his had found out about them and was insisting he break it off, or that he was afraid Vic or his dad would find out and he could not bear their rage and disappointment. She had expected, that is, some boring, predictable excuse, an excuse she could counter with scorn.

"What do you mean?" she said.

He was still staring down into his coffee cup.

"I mean," he said, "that I want to be different."

"Different." She'd intended to echo his word disdainfully, with cynical blackness in her tone; instead it came out, against her will, sounding curious.

"Yeah," he said. "I want to be a different kind of man."

"Little late for that, don't you think? You are what you are. And here's a little clue, honey—the war's over. *Long* over. If it was going to change you, lover boy, that would've already happened. And it didn't. Trust me—I know. I know what you like to do to me—and it ain't reading me Bible verses, you know? So, sorry—no chance for you to be that different man you're talking about. Didn't happen. You can't do it."

"I can try."

That put her over the edge. "Well, aren't *we* the noble fucking saint." She laughed a thin, brittle, low-pitched laugh. The disdain never drifted very far from her. It was always within arm's reach. "Aren't *we* just so all-fired fucking *good*."

He did not answer.

She needed a cigarette, and started to dig in her purse for one. Then she stopped. She'd had enough. She did not need to take this from him. She was a good-looking woman—any man would tell you so, and would pump his eyebrows up and down appreciatively while he was saying it. She could have her pick.

"Just tell me this," she said. She was gathering her things. She might never speak to him again, and so she had to get the information quickly. "Why now?"

Her meaning was clear: You have been back for five years now. What in the world had prompted this sudden see-you-later—when she knew for *absolute certain* that he was still attracted to her, when the sex was still as good as ever?

If he could have talked to her, really talked, he would have told her the truth. But the truth would have made no sense to her, because it was not a matter of words, but of an image, a memory, one that had moved forward to lodge front and center in his brain, like a piece of shrapnel:

A dusty road.

Harm married Dixie Chambers. Vic was his best man, and Alvie was there, too. When Harm first told Alvie that Vic would be his best man, Alvie had nodded, grinned, and smacked Harm's back. *Don't care about that, buddy*, he said. *You know me well enough to know that.* But of course he *did* care, he cared a great deal, and so his response had a pathetic ring to it. By now Alvie was even skinnier, his face long and narrow and flat, his eyes little slits that made him look nervous and paranoid by default.

Alvie had had some trouble since the war ended. The year before Harm married Dixie, he was accused of rape by Lola Pope, a young woman who worked as a volunteer at Crooked Creek Baptist Church. Alvie had continued to go there, too, despite his father's disgrace; neither the Rev. Leonard Sherrill nor Alvie's mother ever went back. The church and its people were like poison for them now. But Alvie stayed.

Lola claimed that, after they had been working late one night on the programs for the revival, Alvie followed her out the door. He put a hand on her bottom. And he said something to her that—well, it shamed her, she said, even though she had done nothing to encourage him, nothing whatsoever. Next thing Lola knew, Alvie was yanking her back inside the dark sanctuary, kicking the door shut behind them. He turned her around and started kissing her. They were slimy-wet, open-mouthed kisses that made her sick to her stomach.

And this all happened in the Lord's house, she added at this point in her statement to the deputy. *In the Lord's own house!* Alvie had jammed his hands up under her skirt, she said, and he fingered the hem of her panties. Then he raped her.

The good news was that Abe Pope, Lola's father, was a veteran.

He had been in the Air Force, in the Pacific Theater. He knew Alvie from the VFW Hall. And frankly, as Abe Pope would say once the beers starting hitting him, that girl of his was not as all-fired innocent as she pretended to be; he'd seen her go out of the house in some out-fits that, if he hadn't been her father—wellsir, you could finish the sen-tence yourself. He had warned her, he had told her about going out looking like a two-dollar tramp. That skirt, for instance, the one Alvie had supposedly put his hand up under? That one? It was so short that Abe wondered why she didn't catch her death of cold when she stepped outside. My God. Didn't the girl know anything about men? *Anything?* Alvie was a vet. He'd saved the world. For God's sake, wasn't he entitled to a little something? So Abe Pope had a talk with Lola. *Vets stick together,* he told her. *It's a sacred bond. You live under my roof, girl, you eat my food, you better understand that.*

And so somehow it turned out that she had been mistaken. Alvie had indeed been alone with her in the sanctuary that night, but no, he did not kiss her or flip up her skirt, and no, she said, he did not rape her. The charges were dropped. It was all a big mistake.

Mistakes happen, don't they? Of course they do.

Two years after Harm married Dixie Chambers, Alvie, too, got married. The woman's name was Bonnie Oliver. The same year, Vic decided to marry his longtime sweetheart, Eva North.

After that they lived in overlapping circles, the three boys and their families. Vic and Eva bought a house on Briarly, one of the nicer streets in Norbitt. Vic was a salesman, and a good one, and his commissions were the kind that made you blink and read the sum again, just to make sure you weren't dreaming. Alvie and Bonnie moved into Alvie's par-ents' house in the old neighborhood; as Bonnie had confided to her friends at the time, it would not be too long until her father-in-law and mother-in-law died and then they would have the place to themselves, free and clear. But there was a small hitch: Rev. Sherrill did not die. Alvie's mother was thoughtful enough to fulfill Bonnie's hopeful prophecy, dying in 1969, the same year Alvie's and Bonnie's son, Lenny, was born, but not the reverend. The Reverend stuck around. Bonnie much preferred Alvie's mother. Yet it was Rev. Sherrill who plugged along, a shriveled streak of gloom and resentment, chewing over past slights until his gums were ground down to stumps.

Harm, too, had some misfortune. Dixie died in 1960, of breast cancer. They had barely had a chance to get to know one another, which made it hard for Harm to mourn her properly—not because he did not love her, but because he did not really know her, and mourning is about specifics. You mourn the sound of a laugh or the memory of how somebody eats a piece of corn on the cob. You don't mourn an abstract thing called "loss." Loss only matters when it is attached to particulars. You can't mourn a concept.

Harm remarried in 1965. Sylvia Branigan was fifteen years younger than he was, and a good choice. She was practical and efficient, a dynamo on housecleaning day, a reliable sounding board guaranteed to espouse the status quo. Four years later, Darlene was born. Harm asked Vic and Eva to be her godparents. And then ten years after that, Sylvia, too, died, of kidney disease this time, and just like that Harm was a single father.

Shortly after Dixie's death, but before he married Sylvia, Harm thought about going to the authorities and telling them what had really happened on that dusty road outside Caneytown in 1938. He should have done it long ago, if he was going to do it at all, but he was too afraid. He would not implicate his friends; he would not even mention their names. He would say only that it was him, not Frank Plumley, who had run down the old lady and the little girl.

But he did not do it. He never called anyone or confessed to anything. And so it was that Harm Strayer henceforth carried a small indigestible pellet of guilt in his gut: Maybe his action—really, his lack of action—was why Dixie had gotten cancer so young. Her suffering toward the end had been terrible to watch. Maybe she had been forced to atone for his sin. It was an awful thought, the kind of thought that turned him inside out with anguish.

A few years later, there was one more moment when he thought about setting the record straight. He imagined walking into the Muth County Courthouse and holding out his wrists to the first person in uniform he came across and telling the whole story. But by then he had remarried, with a child on the way. He had responsibilities. It was inconceivable that he would leave his wife and his child to fend for themselves, so that he could indulge in the luxury of confession. That was how it felt to him at this point: like a luxury, a way to pamper himself. He needed to work. He needed to support his family. That was the priority now.

He never discussed it with Vic and Alvie, but he assumed they felt the same general way by this point. Years had passed. People had forgotten. Frank Plumley was dead—he had been obliterated in a car accident, hitting a bridge abutment at a speed estimated to be 90 mph—and so he could not reap any blame for having lied to save his son and his son's pals. Vivian Plumley was also killed in Frank's car on the night of the crash. Both of them were so drunk that, according to witnesses at the bar they had just left, they had slid and slithered all over the car in the parking lot, laughing and snorting, unable to figure out where the doors were. And then, unfortunately, they found the doors, and they got in and drove away at a high rate of speed.

So the three boys moved on with their lives, never having spoken of Caneytown again since that day on the *Arky* in 1944. They drank beer together, and went to some of the same social events, and their wives were friends; they constituted a sort of volatile Venn diagram, the trio of circles merging and separating, making different configurations along the way.

Darlene was very smart. That was evident early. She studied hard and she loved school. She had short dark hair and, when she was concentrating, she had her father's features, the stubborn jaw, the hooded eyes, and the eyebrows that looked like a harsh *V,* like a black stick somebody had tried to break in the middle but had not quite finished the job. She was a star in school. The teachers predicted great things for her: medical school or law school or an MBA. She would put Norbitt on the map. No question about it.

Lenny Sherrill, however, was not a star. Alvie and Bonnie were embarrassed by him. His grades were terrible; if a teacher called on him in class, he blushed and mumbled. He was as skinny as a soda straw. His acne was a nightmare he was forced to share with the world, a rippling thistle-patch of pustules and scarlet fury. He was shy, and so he did what shy, tall people tend to do: He hunched. He was always looking down.

His report card and his complexion were not the only problems. By the time he entered Muth County Consolidated High School, Lenny was in trouble all the time. He had keyed a line of cars parked on Main Street. He had chucked rocks through the window of the school gymnasium. He was never accused of those things—there was no way to prove it—but everybody knew it was Lenny.

Alvie Sherrill had followed through on his stated intention to become a minster. Alvie was now in charge of Crooked Creek Baptist Church. When the news of his appointment got around Norbitt, a lot of people assumed it was a sort of tribute to his dad. *Ha,* Alvie thought, when he was told of that speculation. The truth was, Alvie hated his father. He did not want to honor him; he wanted to show him up. Last longer in the pulpit than the old man had. Be beloved by his congregation and by the town, in a way the original Rev. Sherrill had never been.

Alvie's old man had ended his days in a nursing home, a breathing mummy who sat in a chair all day long. He still had his mind and most of his memories, which, in his case, was not a blessing: His memories were of betrayal and dissatisfaction, of the ruin of the perfect beauty of a life.

1986

In the alley behind the diner was a small detached garage that nobody had used in a long time. It was a hideout for Lenny Sherrill and Darlene Strayer. They would drive here after school in Lenny's car on those days when they needed to be someplace where no one was telling them what to do, when the last thing in the world they wanted was to be looked at or talked to.

The garage was filled with mice shit and busted furniture and random car parts and spilled motor oil and open paint cans with a half-inch of hardened paint in the bottom, but there was a roof, and the padlock on the door was broken. So it would do. It was a place to come and smoke cigarettes and drink whatever alcohol one or the other of them had been able to procure, and to talk about the indignities of high school.

Their dads had been friends forever. Since long before the two of them were even born. Their fathers' relationship was a bond between them, just like the bond they had forged over their love of Elton John. Lenny knew all the words to "Tiny Dancer." Once, sitting in that garage, he had tried to give Darlene a nickname—Blue Jean Baby. She looked at him and said, "Call me that again and I'll knock your teeth out, buster." He laughed, like she was kidding, but he knew she really wasn't.

Lenny was a loser. Even this early, his loser status made a funky little force field around him. There was a smell, too. The indescribable odor of all the failures-to-be. Darlene, though, was clearly *not* a loser. Her friends sometimes asked her why she hung out with Lenny Sherrill. "I don't *hang out* with him," she said. "We just talk sometimes." Her friends still were mystified. Lori Smallwood asked her if she'd let him kiss her. Darlene laughed. Kiss her? Lenny *Sherrill*? The idea was so totally ridiculous. That wasn't it. That's not what drew them together. It was the fact that she could talk to him. About anything.

Well, almost anything. Today, she had lost her nerve.

She could not tell him. Could not say the words out loud. Not now, not here in their special spot. They had arrived ten minutes ago. It had rained all day but stopped abruptly at three, as if the rain had a precise schedule to keep.

"Come on," Lenny said. "Something's bugging you. What is it? Can't be *that* bad."

"Maybe it is."

He shrugged. "I'm here," he said, "if you want to talk."

"It's kind of hard to talk about."

He shrugged again. "A lot of stuff is hard to talk about." He shifted his feet. "Talk or don't talk. Up to you."

"Don't get mad, Len."

"I'm not mad."

"The thing is, if I told anybody, I'd tell you, okay? It's like—like I know you won't judge me. And you never would, no matter what." She made certain he was looking at her, so that he could see how earnest she was. Her words came fast: "Things are going to happen to us, once we graduate. I know that. I'm going away to college. It's all set. And I'm really excited about it. But listen, Len—I'm coming back. I can help the people in this town. People like my dad and your dad. I can stand up for them. I *know* it. But I need to get a degree. Some power. Or I can't do anything. Once I do that—I'll be back. I want you to understand that. We're friends, okay? That's not going to change. So no matter how bad things get around here, just hang on, because I'll be back. We'll figure it all out, okay?"

He nodded. He believed her. He couldn't find the words, but he knew she understood what he was thinking and feeling.

"So what're you so upset about?" he said. "Give me a hint."

Darlene sighed a long, tormented sigh. "It's—"

"What?"

"Nothing."

"Oh, hell," Lenny said. He started to get up from the overturned paint bucket he was sitting on.

"Wait," Darlene said.

He waited.

"It's just that," she said, "I think I'm in love with Stephanie."

He repeated the name, but he put a question mark in his voice: "Stephanie? From school? That Stephanie?"

"Yeah."

"But she's a girl."

"Yeah."

"Oh."

When Darlene got home that afternoon, she went straight out onto the rickety back porch. Her father was sitting there, on an old rocker. He did shift work at Cray-Loc Plastics and he was working nights now. He was usually home in the afternoons when Darlene banged into the house from school, dumping her jacket and her books, hunting food.

Today she wasn't thinking about food.

Now that she had told Lenny Sherrill, she had to tell her dad. But she was terrified: How would he respond?

She sat down in the lawn chair next to him. The chair was old, and the fraying white plastic strips that constituted the seat were so worn out that they turned mere sitting into high adventure: Would this be the moment they gave way?

Darlene wiggled a bit in the chair, testing her luck. So far, so good.

And then she told him. She told him about how she cared so much for Stephanie that it hurt sometimes.

"If you're wondering what I'm thinking, sweetheart," her father said, "it doesn't bother me one little bit. You're the smartest person I know. You know your own mind. Better than anybody else does, that's for damned sure." A few more trips back and forth in the rocker. "I'm not saying you'll have an easy time of it. Especially not here in

Norbitt. But you know what? To hell with Norbitt. As long as it doesn't hurt anybody else, you do what you're called to do. And you do it proudly."

She wanted to cry from relief and joy, but that would have been embarrassing, so she didn't. She was quiet for a moment, savoring his words. She had heard stories over the years about how her dad had been a nasty guy in his youth, a thief and a brawler and a bully. Selfish and mean. Back then, people said, Harm Strayer was the kind of boy you never turned your back on, if you knew what was good for you. So what had changed him? The war, maybe. That's what some people said. Others said, No, it was after that. Marriage and fatherhood: Those were the things that tamed him.

Darlene did not know about any of that. All she knew about was the man who sat in the rocking chair beside her right now, his big hands on the hand rests, his scuffed work boots set flat against the floorboards of the old back porch. All she knew was that he loved her and believed in her. The sun was just starting to go down, and as it left this world, it flung a strange shadowy beauty across their tiny backyard. Even the shed out by the alley, pieced together by her dad from cast-off lumber and picked-up nails, looked, in this light, mysterious and radiant.

She told him about the grade she had gotten on her English essay: A-plus-plus. The teacher, she proudly added, had called her essay "exceptionally argued, worthy of a legal scholar."

"So maybe you'll be a lawyer," Harm said.

"Maybe I will."

And then they talked about all manner of things, from football to politics to whether or not it was possible to outrun a bear to her father's long-standing plans for adding a bathroom to the first floor of the house. It had always been this way with Darlene and her father. Hours would go by, and they'd still be talking. Their only awareness of the passing of time was the gradual darkening of the sky, and sometimes they missed that clue, too.

At one point Harm's voice grew soft and thoughtful. He said, "Do me a favor."

"Sure, Dad. What?"

"Remember."

"Remember what?"

"This moment. This. You and me being here. Together."

"That's all?"

"That's all." He paused. "That's everything."

Chapter Thirteen

There was always a period of stunned silence in the hours before a major snowstorm came ripping across the mountains, as if the sky itself was shocked to be reminded of its power—the power to make life on the ground a misery. The silence was like a held breath. Everything was suspended in expectation.

This morning was one of those times.

Bell took note of the ominous quiet. She had an uneasy feeling about the day ahead. She had been up and dressed since four, and now she stood on her porch, breathing in the cold, cold air. The sun was somewhere behind the eastern sweep of the mountains, deciding if it really wanted to make the effort today.

Her neighbors' houses were gray lumps set against the slightly lighter gray of the horizon. Snow had been cleared repeatedly from the street and the sidewalks, but never went away entirely, because modest snowfalls had arrived continually on the heels of the major ones. Snow defined the world at this time of year, outlining the contours, keeping a hand in.

She had not slept well. In her head she had assembled some of the puzzle pieces, but that only meant she now knew more profoundly than ever just where the blank spaces were, the places where knowledge ran out and she had to rely on intuition—or as Nick Fogelsong liked to call it, on guesswork. And intuition was not the same thing as knowledge. Having to rely on it was like switching to an auxiliary gas tank during a flight emergency, and discovering that the second tank was dry.

She needed help, and she knew it. So she had called the people she trusted most in the world—well, two of them, anyway, because Nick was off the list, given his civilian status—along with Ava Hendricks. Bell asked them to come by her house today. She promised two things: a lot of coffee and a lot of questions. The time the meeting would commence depended on how soon Ava could make it to Acker's Gap from Washington, D.C. A colleague of Ava's had agreed to take over her most pressing cases for the next few weeks, leaving her free to travel to West Virginia at will.

The silence this morning was a bit unnerving, Bell thought. Usually she relished this kind of natural pause in the world's busyness; usually it was excessive noise that made her anxious. But today, as faint white shoots of almost-daylight slowly materialized in the sky, she was struck by how long this winter had lingered, and how tired she was of snow and ice and cold.

And the questions: She was tired of those, too. Damned tired.

Carla was not sure what she ought to be feeling. Hurt? Duh. Betrayal? Well, that was a tricky one. Could you be betrayed by someone who had never made any sort of promise to you in the first place?

Finding out that Travis Womack was not Travis Womack had jolted her, to be sure. But after thinking about it a while, she decided that maybe it wasn't the worst thing in the world—somebody giving her a phony ID. How many phony IDs had *she* handed out when she was sixteen or seventeen years old, to gain admittance to some bar that

Kayleigh Crocker insisted would be *so* much fun? Or to buy a hard pack of Marlboros, so that she could cough her lungs out and look cool while doing it? Plenty, that's how many.

In a sense, then, Travis-or-Whoever-You-Are had done what she'd done, only for different reasons. Maybe he had a few drug arrests under his real name. That was always a possibility. She wanted to know. No: She *had* to know. Because if he needed help, she wanted to be there.

And so she had green-lighted the plot.

It had started with spending the night at Kayleigh Crocker's apartment. Carla had her mother's blessing—well, not exactly her blessing, and not exactly her permission, either, because she did not really need that, given the fact that Carla was twenty-one. What she had was Bell's reluctant-sounding "okay" on the phone. What she had was her mother's toneless acknowledgment that Carla had informed her of her plans.

It was a practical choice, though. Logistics-wise. Kayleigh lived with her father—her parents had been divorced a long time, and her mom was always either going into rehab or just coming out, so Kayleigh's dad had been the custodial parent since Kayleigh and Carla were in middle school—in an apartment in Wyatt Heights, a small town between Swanville and Acker's Gap. Last night, Carla had her first appointment with a new therapist, one whose office was in Swanville. The therapist's name was Blake Eiler. Her dad had set it up, just as he'd promised the court he would. For the first week, Eiler told her, they would be meeting daily.

Daily. Carla could not believe what she had just heard. But apparently the man was serious, because when she said, "What!?" in a voice that combined outraged disbelief with *you can't make me* rebelliousness, he had ignored that altogether and handed her a slip of paper with the next several appointment times.

One session a day, for the next seven days. Including Saturday and Sunday.

Carla had explained to Bell, during their somewhat tense call, that Kayleigh's apartment was a lot closer to Swanville. So it made sense that Carla could go there after her appointment, and then, the next morning, return to Swanville to hear more words of wisdom from Dr. Eiler, who, Carla further informed her mother, possessed eyes that seemed to pop out of his head on little springs and a speaking voice that sounded like a car engine with a belt going bad.

Spending last night at Kayleigh's had worked out fine. They were not really friends anymore, not like they'd been in high school, and that made it easier. The intensity was gone. They were just people, not best friends with so much at stake in every revelation.

But the proximity of Wyatt Heights to Swanville was not the only reason Carla had cooked up the plan to stay with Kayleigh.

Wyatt Heights was just up the road from Thornapple Terrace. If Carla was spending the night with Kayleigh, her mom would not know her timetable. And would not know that, after leaving her therapist's office, she would be driving back out to the Terrace. She was determined to track down Travis-Whoever and find out what he was hiding—and why.

"The truth doesn't matter."

"What do you mean?" said Ava Hendricks. She was clearly disturbed by what Bell had just said to the people assembled in her living room. In addition to Ava, there was Rhonda Lovejoy and Deputy Jake Oakes.

"I mean," Bell said, "that it's irrelevant. Every person in this room will back me up on this, Ava. It doesn't matter what we *know*—even if we know beyond any doubt that it's true. All that matters is what we can prove."

Ava did not look at all satisfied with the explanation. She sat back against the chair that Bell had brought in from the kitchen to supplement the furniture in her living room. Deputy Oakes had offered her his spot on the couch, but Ava refused. Bell was not surprised. Ava Hendricks was the human equivalent of a hard-backed chair: reliable but rigid.

It was just after 3 p.m. The snow had continued to fall with an almost machine-like relentlessness, but it arrived so gracefully—on soft, lovely flakes that wafted to earth like feathers—that it was hard to take it seriously. Local weather reports were using phrases like "total accumulation may top twenty-six inches or more," but it was hard to associate blunt numbers with the delicate white ballet outside Bell's living room window.

"That's why I wanted everybody to come over—away from the courthouse, away from all the distractions," Bell said. "I want to go over what we know so far—what we *know,* not what we suspect or what we hope for. And then, Ava, I'd like you to give us a summary of the letters you brought. Darlene's letters. I know they're very personal, but I'd never ask you to share them unless I thought they were significant to our work here today. And I assure you that my staff is discreet."

As she said the word "discreet," Bell shot a quick meaningful look at Rhonda. Rhonda would be able to translate that look as skillfully as a simultaneous interpreter at the United Nations: Nothing said here could join the pile of gossip that Rhonda routinely assembled throughout the day, which she then sorted into categories and shipped out to interested parties.

Rhonda nodded, but she did not have to. Bell knew she would respect the request.

It was good to have Rhonda back. Last night Grandma Lovejoy's vital signs had improved. She was removed from the ventilator and was now breathing on her own; she would start physical therapy soon. It would be a long, slow road, but as Rhonda noted, her grandmother was stubborn and prideful, traits that usually presaged a successful rehabilitation. Her first complete sentence to her granddaughter had been about her friend Connie and Marcy Coates: Any progress? Rhonda knew she was referring to the investigation into their deaths. She squeezed her hand and said, "You bet." The old woman smiled.

Rhonda did not waste the days at Grandma Lovejoy's bedside. She had made calls, scribbled down information, kept in touch with Jake Oakes. She had tapped her network of sources. She was ready to contribute.

First, though, she looked around the living room. "Where's Carla?"

"She's with a friend," Bell said. "She'll be home later. Okay, let's get started. Jake, what do we have?"

Deputy Oakes looked down at the clipboard on his lap. "Got the results back on that paint chip from the state crime lab. That paint has only ever been used on one model—a 1998 Peterbilt eighteen-wheeler. I checked, and there are one thousand, four hundred and twenty-seven of them still traceable."

"That's going to be a hell of a search," Rhonda muttered.

"We don't have to go door-to-door," Jake shot back. The two of them had turned fact-gathering into a competitive sport, and Rhonda's comment was the equivalent of trash talk. "Or garage-to-garage, in this case. I put every single name associated with the accident—the paramedics who responded at the scene, the staff at the Tie Yard Tavern, the employees of the gas station that sold the deceased her gas that day—into a database to see if there were any hits. Any link between anyone associated with the deceased and a name on a title or lease for an eighteen-wheeler."

When she heard the phrase "the deceased" repeated twice, Bell looked at Ava. No reaction.

"And?" Rhonda said.

"I got one." Jake thumped the clipboard twice with a flat hand, like someone giving a head-pat to a spelling bee champion. "Felton Groves."

"The trucker who found Darlene," Bell said. "Who called the cops to the scene."

"You got it." Jake did not look triumphant. "I should have checked into him more thoroughly at the time. But he was helpful and cooperative—and you know what happens when somebody's friendly. You skip things. You don't mean to, but you do. It's the nasty ones who make us meticulous. Good thing the bad guys don't know a surefire method of fooling cops—be nice."

"What's the connection?" Bell said.

"That's where I come in," Rhonda said. "Jake asked me to do a background search on Felton Groves. Because—and I'm quoting you accurately here, right, Jake?—Jake's about as good in front of a computer as I would be in the driver's seat of an eighteen-wheeler."

"Connection," Bell said.

"Groves is broke," Rhonda replied. "That accident he told us about, down in Georgia? The one where he says he came across a van in the ditch and a bunch of dead kids scattered around? He didn't 'come across' it. He caused it. Went left of center. Served twenty-four months for involuntary vehicular manslaughter in Georgia State Prison in Reidsville. Once he was out, that's when his troubles *really* began. He was sued by relatives of the dead family. He's paying off a four-million-dollar settlement for wrongful death. The only jobs he can get now are short-hop hauls in undesirable locations—like, say, the mountains around Blythesburg."

"So this tells us," Bell said, "that Groves was an ideal candidate for recruitment—by somebody who wanted to make sure Darlene didn't make it down that mountain. Groves needed money. And he had the kind of vehicle that could easily run a smaller one off the road. Having Groves be the one who found the body was a nice touch—it threw us off the trail." She pointed at Deputy Oakes. "Jake? Anything else?"

"Plenty." He went back to his clipboard. "Got that warrant and pulled Lenny Sherrill's cell records. He's made ten calls over the past three months to the number you told me to check."

Bell looked at Ava. "It was your home number in D.C."

"So Lenny Sherrill," Ava said, "was the one making the threatening calls to Darlene. Her old friend from Norbitt."

"Looks that way. He had his number blocked so it wouldn't show up on your caller ID. And he must have used a voice changer."

"But why would he threaten her in the first place?"

"Still working it out," Bell replied. She gestured toward the briefcase Ava had set on the floor next to her chair. "Would you mind sharing with the others what you found in Darlene's letters?"

Ava shuffled through several before she came to the right ones.

"Harmon wrote to her constantly," she said. "College, law school, her first years as a federal prosecutor—all through that time, he'd write these wonderful notes. When she was lonely or sad or scared, she'd read them. Over and over again. And she kept them all." Ava paused. "She told me once that if it weren't for her father's letters, she would never have gotten sober. He never knew about her struggles with alcohol—she was very careful to keep that from him—but his letters saved her life."

She tapped the top letter on the stack.

"This is one of the last letters that made any kind of sense," she said, "By this time, Harmon was suffering fairly significant symptoms of Alzheimer's. I explained to Darlene what would be happening. How things were going to progress." Ava paused again. Her pauses had a kind of gravity to them, as if, even when she was not speaking, important concepts were being conveyed.

She held up the piece of lined notebook paper and read from it. "'My dearest Darlene, I've been having those spells again. Times when I can't. I don't know the word there I was trying to write. I'm sorry. I don't want you to worry. I am so proud of you! So glad that. So glad. Darlene, I am losing my mind. I have already lost it, I think, and only find it again from time to time. Darlene, I. When I find it, I try to do all that I need to do, before it. Darlene. We did something bad. Vic and Alvie and me, too. We were all. Darlene, I was eleven years old and about to be twelve. Vic was twelve. Alvie. The car. Nobody meant for it to happen. Nobody. Nobody's fault. Everybody's fault. It was. Oh, Darlene.'" She set down the paper. "It runs off into a sort of gibberish after that."

"What happened?" Jake asked. "What do you think the three of them did?"

"I wondered the same thing," Bell said. "And whether it might be relevant to what's happening at the Terrace. Harmon Strayer was born in 1926. The year he's talking about would have been 1937 or 1938. So Rhonda checked the archives of the weekly newspaper that's been published in Norbitt since 1878. Rhonda?"

"Finding the details of a car accident within a two-year window wasn't as hard as you'd think," Rhonda said. "Not a lot of cars back then, period. At least not in Norbitt." She took a deep breath. "So I found it. An elderly woman and her granddaughter—Gertrude and Betty Driscoll—were killed by a Ford pickup and buried in the Silent Home Cemetery near Caneytown. A man named Frank Plumley was cited for reckless driving. No criminal charges. He paid a fine."

"Frank Plumley," Bell said, picking up the story, "was the father of Vic Plumley. And according to what I was told at the Terrace, Vic Plumley sometimes visited Harmon Strayer. Vic was killed last year by a hit-and-run driver. That driver is still at large."

Ava was relatching her briefcase. "What does any of this have to do with Darlene's death?"

"We don't know for sure yet," Bell said. "But it looks likely that Felton Groves and Marcy Coates were hired to get rid of people that somebody else wanted out of the way. Groves and Coates both needed money. They had access to Darlene and her father. That access made them valuable. Groves was bribed to run Darlene off the road. He needed money to pay off his settlement.

"And Marcy Coates," Bell went on, "needed money to pay for her granddaughter's drug rehab. Lots of it. She traded shifts to make sure she'd be taking care of Harmon. The earlier death—Margaret Jacks—was a trial run. A way to see just how meticulous the coroner was going to be with bodies that came from the Terrace. Once the answer came back—not meticulous in the least—then Marcy was free to go after Harmon. And she killed Polly Delaney to divert attention from Harmon Strayer's death."

"That doesn't sound like the Marcy Coates my grandmother told me about," said a clearly dismayed Rhonda. "She didn't know Marcy as well as Connie Dollar did, but still. A murderer? That sweet old lady?"

Jake spoke up. "I don't think Marcy Coates would've considered it murder. It was something else. Yes, it benefited her. But would she have gone out on her own and, say, killed somebody just for the hell of it? No. Never. This was different. These were sick old people who didn't have a lot of time left, anyway. Who were suffering."

"So we're supposed to cut her slack?" Rhonda said. Her tone included a good deal of incredulity.

"Think of it however you have to," Jake answered. "I'm just saying that the context is crucial. You can't judge every action by a single standard of right and wrong."

"Funny thing for a deputy sheriff to say," Rhonda shot back.

"You got my job title right," he said. "But I'm a human being first and a deputy second, okay? And it seems to me that—"

"Okay, you two," Bell said, interrupting him. "Cut it out." Lately she had begun to see their mild quarreling as a sort of mutual flirtation. Usually it amused her, but not now. This wasn't an episode of *The Bachelor*. It was a murder investigation. "I had Buster Crutchfield look over the coroner's reports for the three deaths at the Terrace. They were pretty superficial and slapdash, he said. A lot of things could easily have been missed. There's no way to go back and confirm those specific details now, of course—it's way too late—but it does round out the picture of what might have happened."

Ava looked as if she was processing a million pieces of information in a nanosecond, like a supercomputer in a charcoal-gray cardigan. She raised a finger, ready to ask a question, but before she could start, Rhonda's cell rang. She listened and nodded. When she ended the call and turned to the group, her eyes were bright.

"That was Kirk Avery." Her voice bounced with excitement. "The bartender at the Tie Yard. The one who was working on the same Saturday, Bell, when you and Darlene were there. I asked him to keep an eye out for the man who was drinking with Darlene that night—the night she doubled back to the bar."

"And?"

"And the guy just showed up again. Got the kind of face you don't forget, Kirk says, even though nobody knows his name. Semi-regular. But this is his first time back since the accident."

Bell moved so quickly that she startled Deputy Oakes, typically a fast mover himself.

"Come on, Rhonda," Bell said. "I'll drive."

"Hold on, hold on." Oakes stood up, affecting his best *I'm a deputy and you're not* pose. "You two aren't going anywhere. We've been getting reports all afternoon. Storm's a lot worse. They're shutting down the interstate in both directions."

"Not taking the interstate," Bell said.

"Not my point." Oakes glared at her.

Bell glared right back. "Jake, you know as well as I do that most of our so-called 'evidence' so far is pretty skimpy. It's all theory and conjecture. Rhonda's filing for a warrant to pull Groves's financials, to track the payoff, but that's going to take a while. Unless we can get somebody to confess, or we dig up some actual evidence, we're shut down. This could be our chance. And there's no telling how long that guy will stay at the Tie Yard tonight. We've got to get out there."

Oakes grunted. She was right, but he did not like it. "I'd come if I could. But with these roads the way they are, and with the number of accidents that we'll surely have, I don't see how I can—"

"You're needed in Acker's Gap," Bell said. "Sheriff Harrison would have my head if we took you out of commission right now."

Oakes grunted again. "You stay in touch."

Bell nodded. She turned to Ava. "Make yourself comfortable here. I insist you spend the night. Plenty of room."

"I'd like to go with you," Ava said. "This is the man who had a hand in killing Darlene, isn't that right? I think I should be there."

Bell smiled. "If our intention was to go out there and string him up like a piñata, I'd say, 'Sure.' I'd even let you have the first whack. But that's not how it works. We're going to talk to him. That's all. You need to stay here." She indicated the staircase. "Spare room's the first one on your left. Sheets and towels in the linen closet at the end of the hall. My daughter, Carla, will be home soon. I'll text her and let her know you're here."

Ava nodded. While the other three people in the room put on their boots and heavy coats, she appeared to be waiting to speak. Finally, when Bell, Rhonda, and Deputy Oakes were ready to go, she took her opportunity.

"Darlene never had a lot of friends. She had too many secrets. Her alcoholism, our relationship—she felt like she had to keep the world at arm's length, so that it wouldn't judge her. And once her father died, she felt more alone than ever. Yes, she had me—but that was all. She was the loneliest person I've ever known." It was a difficult thing to say, and Ava needed a few seconds to recover her poise after she said it. "If she could see this right now—see the three of you, moving heaven and earth to find out what happened to her and her dad—I think she'd be surprised. I think she'd be moved. And I know she'd be grateful."

Carla parked the Kia in the side lot. The snow was really picking up now. Her drive had included a few slides that might have ended disastrously but did not, and so in addition to her relief at arriving here she felt a certain perverse pride: *I made it, dammit.*

This was crazy. Even Kayleigh Crocker thought it was crazy, and Kayleigh was usually the passionate cheerleader for any sort of wild, outlandish behavior. "I don't know, Carla," Kayleigh had said, as Carla was leaving the apartment. "I'm not sure you should do that."

Carla had given her friend a brief, highly edited rundown on the situation: older guy (she did not say how old), who had given her a fake name (she did not mention that he had taken the name of someone who had died in a motorcycle accident), and who she had not known very long (she skipped over the fact that it was a single twenty-minute conversation in her car in the Driftwood parking lot). And now, Carla explained, she was compelled to find out what the hell was going on. Why did he lie to her? To his employers?

Her plan was to drive out to Thornapple Terrace and find him. She would simply ask him why he was hiding who he really was. It was only four p.m. Even with the heavy snowfall and the slickening of the roads, she would be back in Acker's Gap by dinnertime. No problem.

The mission reminded Carla just a little bit of her quest for a can of Diet Dr Pepper on the snow-laden day she had driven back to Acker's Gap: It sounded silly on the face of it. Nobody else in the world could possibly understand. But *she* understood. She got it. She had to do this. She had to know who he really was. And then she could let it be. She didn't want anything from him—just an explanation.

She would not go to the reception desk this time. She had learned her lesson. She would go to the maintenance building. If Travis—or whoever he was—was not there now, he would be there shortly. All she needed was a few minutes with him. Just long enough to get an answer. She would assure him that she had no intention of ratting him out—she would never do that—but he had helped her, and if he was in some kind of trouble himself and needed help, she could return the favor.

She had a new text. It was from her mother. Carla read it quickly: *Working 2 nite. Houseguest in spare room FYI.* She didn't reply to it. She had more important things on her mind right now.

The door to the building was unlocked. It was a large, square, aluminum structure and its insides had the feel of an airplane hangar: no windows, pristine concrete floor. It was filled with items carefully segregated into specific areas: spare bed frames, extra dressers, and rocking chairs; electrical cables wound tightly on wooden spools; shovels, ladders, buckets, and hoses; a long tool bench with an array of serious-looking tools, from jigsaws to miter boxes; a riding lawn mower and two snowblowers.

Carla did not see him at first. And then she did: He was over by the tool bench, his back to her, working on something. He had not heard the door open because he was making noise himself, pounding nails into the end of a board.

Without even seeing his face, and even though he was dressed in ubiquitous light gray coveralls, she knew it was him.

Before she could speak, he finished with what he was doing, and he turned. He took off his goggles. She would never forget the look on his face—surprise, mingled with a happiness he could not hide, and then the dissolving of that happiness into annoyance.

"Hey," Carla said.

"What the hell are you doing here?" he said. His voice wasn't nearly as harsh as the words were.

"Needed to talk. You're not Travis Womack." She did not say it accusingly. She said it with a sort of bemused wonderment. "So who *are* you?"

"You need to get out of here," he said. "Now."

"Just tell me who you really are. And why you lied about it. Are you in some kind of trouble? Because if you are, I can help. My mom's the Raythune County prosecutor. We can go talk to her, and if there's a way to get you out of—"

"Listen to me," he said. He walked several steps toward her. The building, she realized, was not heated. He must be freezing in only the coveralls.

When he got close enough to reach out and take her arm, he did. He did it gently, and then let it go again. "Carla, I really need you to go. I don't want anything to happen to you."

"Just tell me what's going on and I will," she said. "I'll turn right around and leave. I know it's none of my business. But the other night— you saved my life, okay? That's what it felt like. I don't mean because of that asshole who wouldn't leave me alone. I mean because of our talk. The things you said—and the things you *didn't* say, too, like: 'Hey, Carla, grow up.'" She smiled. "And so I want to repay you—if I can, I mean. If there's anything at all I can do." She took a deep breath. She had been talking very fast, making her case. "So just tell me why you're using somebody else's name. And after that, if you still want me to go away, I will. I promise. And I'll never tell anybody about this."

There was such compassion in his eyes, and such bottomless sadness. She wished he would touch her again, take her arm.

He had not answered, and so she spoke again. "You're a good man. I know that."

That seemed to snap him back to the here and now. "Really." His voice was sarcastic and sharp. "Really—that's what you know. You know that for sure."

"I do."

"Oh, yeah? Well, what do you think I'm about to do? This 'good man' you think you know? Listen, Carla. I stole a guy's name from a headstone I saw in a cemetery. Everything I've done was for this. To be here, right now. I've waited for the perfect moment and it's time. If the storm gets as bad as they say it will, this place'll be cut off for at least a day or two. Nobody going in or out. So this is it."

"I don't—"

"Now that I've told you, Carla, I can't let you go. I don't want to hurt you—but you have to stay out of the way. I have to do this."

"Travis." She had forgotten all about the fact that the name was a fake. She wanted desperately to reach him. "Travis, please, I don't understand."

"Of *course* you don't understand." His voice shook a little. "You weren't raised by a monster. A monster who brought strangers home to have sex with you and your sister—while he sat back and counted the money. A monster who locked you in the closet for days—lying in your own pee and shit after you couldn't hold it anymore. And then when he opened that door and he smelled what you'd done, he dragged you out by your hair and he held you down on the floor and he lit a cigarette and put it out on your arm. And then he lit another cigarette and did the same thing. And another and another. And then he switched to the other arm. Now he's here—and he doesn't *remember* it. He has Alzheimer's. So what can I do? He doesn't remember, so it's like it never happened.

"And that, Carla," he said, bitterness giving way to anguish, "is the worst part of all. He's forgotten all about it. I can't even get in his face and tell him what he is—a *monster*. A fucking *monster*. Janie has been trying that for months now. Trying to get him to say what he did. So that our lives are *real*. So that our suffering *matters*." He shuddered. "She doesn't know that I work here. She hasn't seen me in years. I keep a lookout for her car, and when I see it, I disappear. Last week, when I spotted her car, I had to pretend to get sick and slip out the back. And a few days before that, I saw a strange car in the lot and I thought it might be hers. It wasn't—it was your mother's." He shook his head. "The staff tells me what Janie does in there with him, yelling at him, over and over again. It's her way. It's just not my way. And this . . ." He lifted the board, the one he had just embellished with nails. "I don't want Janie to know about this. I don't want her involved. I'll take the consequences. She's suffered enough."

He rolled up his sleeve. His arm looked like uncooked meat riven with fissures and divots. The scars from burns and infections and neglect raged from his wrist to his shoulder.

"My name is Nelson Ferris," he said, "and I'm going to kill that bastard."

Three Boys

Alvie had brought the checkerboard again. The stiff cardboard was folded in half, and so after pulling it out of the paper shopping bag he opened it. He set it in the middle of the table. He did this with a bit of a flourish, the unfolding and the placement. Then he reached into the bag again and pulled out the little round pieces, one by one. Each time he thrust his arm down into the bottom of the bag to retrieve a piece, the paper bag rattled.

At each rattle, Harm twitched and blinked. He hated the sound.

Alvie saw that, of course. It made him go slower, making the noise last even longer. Milking it. He liked the power he now had over Harm Strayer. He would reach into the bag, ostensibly to dig around for another round piece, but it was really for his own deep satisfaction: seeing Harm react with that twitch, that blink. Fear and confusion in his cloudy eyes. It was a small, exquisite torture that Alvie could inflict on his old pal. And it left no marks. No one would ever know. It was just Alvie and Harm in here, two old friends.

Harm had gotten all the breaks. Well, no—Vic had gotten lots more breaks than Harm, more breaks than anybody, but Vic was so far out of Alvie's league that Alvie did not think of Vic in relation to his own life. Vic was not a standard against which Alvie could measure himself. The differential was too great.

But Harm—well, Harm, was still on Alvie's level. So he could compare. They were two boys. Two boys from Norbitt, West Virginia. And Harm, everybody liked. Everybody looked up to. Why? For years, Alvie had tormented himself with the question. It was like biting down on a sore tooth, over and over again, just to feel the pain: Why did people like Harm so much? He was a fucking factory worker. Blue collar, all the way. Never did anything else, never dreamed of doing anything else.

Whereas *he* had actually read some books. Studied. Not in a formal way, because the church did not care about any of that when hiring a pastor. They did not ask about degrees—only about whether you were married and had a family. They wanted you stable. But he still read books. Books about motivating yourself to work harder, to size up your enemy and defeat him. How to *succeed*, in other words. How to be a winner.

And then there was Harm Strayer. His old pal Harm. A man who had skated by on his looks and his line of bullshit and on—what else? What else made people gravitate to Harm Strayer in a way they had never gravitated to him? Maybe pity. Harm had buried two wives, and people felt sorry for him. Raising his little girl on his own and all.

Well, Alvie had known sorrow, too, and nobody ever seemed to be extending any kindness *his* way. Nobody ever said, "Sorry your boy's such a good-for-nothing loser, Alvie. Too bad." Because that was another thing: Harm's girl, Darlene, was smart and focused. She was going places. You could just tell. She worked hard, and she had not taken the kind of shortcuts that Lenny specialized in: stealing things, cheating people when he thought he could get away with it. Losing job after job because he was lazy and stupid. He would get hired, then call in sick for the first week. When he finally showed up again, they'd tell him to leave. *And while you're at it, don't come back. Ever.*

It was as if Harm was rubbing his nose in it, in what a bum Lenny was, just by having a daughter like Darlene. Go *ahead,* Harm probably said to himself over the years, secretly snickering. *Go ahead and compare. Put them side by side: Lenny and Darlene. I dare you.*

There was no comparison. None at all.

The kids had been friends for a while, in junior high and high school, his Lenny and Harm's girl, Darlene. It was not a boy-girl thing—Alvie always had his suspicions about Darlene, her with that short hair and those dungarees, because every woman he knew cared deeply about her appearance and Darlene did not seem to give a rat's ass about that—but it was a steady, solid friendship. Darlene helped his Lenny. For a time, when they were spending a lot of time together, Lenny's grades ticked up a bit. His attitude improved. He even straightened up when he walked, losing that pathetic, *please don't hit me* hunch of his. But then Darlene went away to college and that was that. Lenny slid back down into his old loser self. It was like she had given him a vision of another way to live, another kind of person to be, and then, just when he was starting to believe it might be possible— she left.

Bitch.

Alvie rattled the bag. He had a few more pieces to go. After he had gotten out the last one, he intended to reach over the table with two hands and crunch the bag in Harm's face, hard and long. Really make that fucker squirm.

Somebody else had come into the lounge.

It was an aide, one of those fat old ladies in their pink smocks and their too-tight white pants and ugly white shoes. Alvie smiled and held up the bag. "Gonna play checkers," he said. "Harm here loves his checkers."

The aide had come in to retrieve a cane propped up in a corner of the lounge. One of the residents had left it there. She picked up the cane, and then she looked over at Alvie, and then down at Harm, who sat in the chair with his arms around his shoulders. He was shuddering.

"Doesn't seem to me like he likes it too much," she said dubiously.

Alvie laughed. "Old Harm here don't know *what* he likes anymore. He'll come around. You watch." He was silently willing her to leave, but he knew that if he showed that, if he revealed how much he wanted to see the last of her fat ass, she would probably stick around. People were perverse like that. Did what they could to go against you, every damned chance they got.

He looked closer at the woman. She was standing a little cockeyed. She had a problem with one of her hips. Her named tag said MARCY.

She's the one, Alvie thought. *When the time comes—and it's coming, oh, yes, it's coming—she's the one I'll tell Lenny to pick.*

He remembered seeing her not just here at the Terrace, but in town one day. In Norbitt. He had recognized her then, even though she wasn't wearing that damned pink smock. The bad hip gave her away. She had been trying to feed coins into a meter and she dropped a couple, probably a nickel and a penny, could not have been much more than that, and when she tried to lean over to fetch them, her hip must have seized up on her, because she jerked and stood up straight again, her free hand going to her hip. She rubbed at it, and then she tried once more. Again, the hip misbehaved. It was only on the third try that she was able to pick up the coins from the sidewalk.

Anybody who works that hard for a nickel and a penny is poor, Alvie remembered thinking. *Really poor.* As poor as his family had been when Alvie was a kid, after the church fired his dad because the Reverend Leonard Sherrill, Mr. Morality, Mr. *I'm Better Than You Are,* couldn't keep it in his pants.

Anybody that poor would be an easy target.

"Just the same, sir," Marcy was saying. "Why don't you put the bag down and see if it calms him?"

"Sure." Alvie set the bag on the floor. He took the seat across from Harm. He spread out his arms, as if he was blessing the checkerboard, the table, his old buddy. "We're just fine, ma'am. Appreciate the concern for good old Harm. You have yourself a nice day now, you hear?"

Marcy stood there for a few more seconds, fingering the cane she had just retrieved, eyes on the checkerboard. She did not want to seem as if she was staring at the visitor, keeping tabs. But she needed to make sure things were really okay here. Tammy, the housekeeper, would be coming in momentarily to dust the blinds; if not for that, Marcy would not have left. She did not like this old man. He came here frequently, to sit with Mr. Strayer, and each time he did, she liked him less. There was a slipperiness to him. A sliminess. She could not define it past that.

"You, too," she said, because that was what you were supposed to say when someone told you to have a nice day. One of the other aides had told her that he was a preacher. Seemed unlikely, but okay.

When she moved her eyes back in his direction, he was looking at her, too, just as intently. The two of them seemed equal at that moment, balanced. Yet they were not equal at all, because she did not know what he knew: That she was, in effect, looking into the eyes of her executioner.

This had not been a good visit. Harm just sat in the chair, refusing to look at Alvie, refusing to speak at all. *You stubborn sonofabitch,* Alvie wanted to shout at him. *You tell me what you remember. Tell me what you might say.*

Finally he gave up. Good days and bad days: that's what people with Alzheimer's have, Alvie had been told. Up and down. Can't predict.

At first he had not given it a thought. Not a single thought. He was not worried at all. Why should he be? Harm Strayer's mind was gone, swamped by what the newspaper articles said were these little fuckers called plaques and tangles—sticky shit your brain can't shake off, plus squiggly things that worm themselves into the nooks and crannies between all the brain crap up there.

Bottom line: If you get it, you're screwed. There was no cure. Once that train starts heading downhill, you can pull the lever all you want, but it's not stopping.

Harm's decline had not been gradual. Apparently it was different for everybody—Alvie had read that, too, in those articles he found about Alzheimer's—and for Harm, it was *whoosh*, *boom*. Game over. His brain was a mushy blob.

Which was actually pretty good news for Alvie. First, it was nice to see Harm Strayer *not* get a break. Good to see the odds finally catch up with Mr. Goody Two Shoes, Mr. Oh I'm So Perfect. And second, it meant Alvie would never have to worry about Harm shooting off his mouth about Caneytown. Alvie had worried about that—oh, yes he had. He'd worried about it since 1945, when the three of them came back from the war and Harm started getting a little strange. Nothing big—just more thoughtful than he'd been before. Slower to act. Alvie knew that Harm was one of those men who brooded, and dithered, and sat on his back porch thinking. No telling what he might do, if things broke a certain way in his head.

Vic, he never worried about. Vic was smart. Vic was a winner. He understood there was nothing to gain—and everything to lose—from coming clean about Caneytown. Vic had moved to Bluefield and opened up a string of car washes. He had made a shitload of money. When he visited Norbitt, he came in a BMW. New wife every ten years. New house every three. Or maybe it was the other way around.

Anyway, Vic was okay. Harm—he was the real threat. Harm was the loose cannon. The one who could destroy all three of their lives by letting his guilty conscience get the best of him, and then dragging them down into the same pit.

Well, they didn't have to worry about that anymore, did they? No siree. Harm was down for the count. He had started his fade a few years ago, and then it speeded up. Six months ago came the end of the line. He got lost on Main Street, and a deputy drove him home. When they got to the house, Harm looked at the deputy and said, "Where are we? Who lives here?" The next day he walked out of the house in only his underwear. The day after that he started calling people and when they said, "Hello?" he said, "Hello?" back. When they asked why he'd called, he said, "Did I?"

And then he almost set the house on fire. Put an empty pan on the stove, turned on the burner, left the room. Forgot all about it. By the time the boys from the fire department got there, the flames were eating up the kitchen curtains. They barely got Harm out in time.

That was it. Darlene drove in from D.C.—she had an Audi, a fancy one, and just the sight of that car put Alvie in a bad mood—and packed up her dad and took him to Thornapple Terrace.

Fine, Alvie thought. *We're in the clear.*

But maybe they weren't.

Because Alvie had read an article last year about Alzheimer's. And it said something he'd never known before. Turns out that while people with Alzheimer's can't remember things they learned recently, they *can* sometimes remember old stuff. Stuff that has been in their brains for a long time. Stuff that has settled in for the long haul. Stuff from way, way back.

Stuff from, say, 1938.

Right after reading that article, Alvie began driving over to the Terrace once, twice a week. He would bring the checkerboard. Sit there in the lounge with Harm.

The checkerboard was part of Alvie's plan to smoke out his old friend. Alvie would pick up a game piece. Harm would sometimes imitate the gesture and pick up one, too. Then it was Alvie's turn again. Then Harm's.

Alvie figured that if Harm was more up to snuff mentally than he was letting on, he would slip and show it during a game of checkers. Harm loved checkers. Darlene had tried to teach him chess once, when she was in high school—Lenny told Alvie the story, just the way Darlene had told Lenny—and Harm had smiled, shook his head. "Don't like to do that much thinking," he said. "I like to play a game where I can shoot the breeze with my friends and play at the same time." For all that nice-guy talk, though, Harm had a competitive streak when it came to his favorite game. Alvie knew that firsthand.

So Harm might not be able to help himself. If he was not as far gone as he seemed to be, if the memory of Caneytown still lived in his brain in the same place it lived in Alvie's brain—dead center— then Harm might tip his hand in a game of checkers. Make a smart move before he could stop himself. And that would give Alvie the perfect opening to ask him outright: *Do you ever start mumbling about the old days, Harm? Telling the folks here about Caneytown? You wouldn't do that, Harm, now, would you? Because Vic and I—we've got a stake in this, too, you know. We've all got a lot to lose.*

Especially him. Especially Reverend Alvie Sherrill. Especially now. The church was planning a big celebration in his honor next year. Sixty years in the pulpit. A hell of a lot longer than any other minister in town—or in the county, either—had been doing the job. And best of all, it was a hell of a lot longer than his old man had made it at Crooked Creek.

This was going to be Alvie's day. His moment in the sun. He would take their gifts and their good wishes, he would smile for the pictures and say grace at the big meal, and he would ride in the parade in the convertible Cadillac Eldorado that the president of the bank, Sherman Beamer, was loaning the church that day, and all of it might just barely begin to make up for everything he had suffered over the years. The slights, the insults, the murmured remarks he'd heard even though he was not supposed to.

Rat Face. Beanpole. Pencil Dick.

All of that would go away. The nicknames, the sneering, the pity. He had waited for this. He had waited patiently while Vic Plumley got the girlfriends and later the worldly success, while Harm Strayer got the sympathy and the respect, and Alvie Sherrill got . . . *bupkis.*

Now, finally, he had his chance. He was old, he was tired, he took ten pills in the morning and another ten at night, he had terrible arthritis and a leaky heart, he had a good-for-nothing son whom he'd been bailing out of trouble and making excuses for ever since the kid filched his first piece of Bazooka from the Rexall, but by God—he would make it to his special day. His father never had such a day. God, what a laugh! His father, in a parade. No. *He* was getting the parade. He had beaten the old bastard. Beaten him good. And he would stay beaten—no matter what Alvie had to do. No matter what he had to order Lenny to do. *No matter what.*

Nothing was going to go wrong. Nothing could interfere with his golden moment.

Except, maybe, a sick old man with a dying brain and a big mouth.

The parking lot was never crowded at the Terrace. As Alvie Sherrill walked through the glass double doors and headed toward the red Chevette, he held his gray overcoat closed tightly at his throat—the cold was brutal on this early December day—and he reflected on all those empty spaces. Once they put you away in a place like this, people forgot about you. And why not? Why *should* anybody visit? It's not like you're going to sit around and discuss world affairs. The people who lived at Thornapple Terrace reminded him of the frozen-food section at the supermarket: row after row of bundled muteness. No sign of life.

Lenny had driven him over here, like always. He was asleep in the car. Alvie could see his son through the front windshield, splayed in the driver's seat, head thrown back, eyes closed, mouth open. Alvie couldn't hear the snores but he could imagine them—clotted, wet-sounding messes.

The wind was a pinching one, as quick and mean as a terrier's bite. Alvie tried to pick up his pace. Hard to do with arthritis and scoliosis and every other damned ailment that went along with being an old fart. He was glad he had both hands free to keep his collar clutched shut. He was not carrying the checkerboard; he'd decided to leave the checkerboard in the lounge. Why keep toting the damned thing back and forth when he could just . . .

"Alvie Sherrill. What the hell."

Alvie turned. He had instantly recognized the voice, but did not believe it.

"Vic," Alvie said. Now he believed it.

For here was Vic Plumley, looking much thinner but still prosper-ous in a double-breasted camel hair coat that went almost all the way to the ground. He was bald, and the hanging flesh on his face looked like the skin of an overripe banana, complete with crowded-up brown spots—but Vic was Vic. He still had the old Vic Plumley aura, the roguish charm that Alvie had spent most of his life in awe of.

"How're you doing, you old bastard?" Vic said. There was a qua-ver in his voice now.

"I'm fine, Vic." Alvie felt himself shrinking down ever so slightly. Why did this happen every time Vic was in the vicinity? Alvie felt like a worm that some kid had poked with a stick. He coiled inward, mak-ing a circle out of what had been a line. Protecting himself from Vic's hearty, heartless charm.

Vic was talking again. "Still can't believe you're a fucking preacher, Alvie, but hey—stranger things've happened, am I right?"

"Yeah."

Vic suddenly adopted his concerned look. Alvie remembered

how well Vic had been able to do this, even as a kid. He would get nabbed for something and then, quick as you please, his face would crumple up, his eyes would grow solemn, and his mouth would droop into a sad little downturned half-moon. Next thing you knew, the teacher—or cop or storekeeper or whoever had caught Vic doing something he should not have been doing—would feel sorry for *him,* for Vic, for the perpetrator and the ringleader. The crime would be forgotten. They would want to focus on this poor sad boy. And on cheering him up, persuading him that things were not so bad, after all.

"So," Vic said. "How's he doing? You come by and see him a lot, right?"

"Yeah."

"And?"

"Hell, Vic, he's got Alzheimer's. How do you think he is?"

Vic looked even more stricken. "God, Alvie, you're right. Stupid fucking question." He brightened. "Hey—you said 'hell.' Thought preachers didn't curse."

"Hell's an important word in my business, Vic. Use it all the time."

"Ha! Good one, Alvie." He thrust his hands deep into the pockets of his coat. "Cold out here." He looked around the lot. "On your way home, are you? That your boy, over there in the car?"

"Yeah."

Vic nodded. "I don't get up here very often. Stay pretty busy in Bluefield. But I miss you guys, you know?"

Alvie did not believe him. Vic was always working an angle. This sentimental, *poor me* pose was an act on behalf of something Vic was after. Some scam.

"I've got to be heading out, Vic," Alvie said. He wasn't biting. Not this time. "Things to do at home." When they were kids, Alvie was never the one to leave first. He was always the one being left. This felt good—telling Vic he would have to say whatever he wanted to say because Alvie had plans.

"Right, right," Vic said. He moved his weight from one foot to the other. "It's like this, Alvie. With you being a preacher and all—well, I wanted to tell you . . ." He shook his head. He cupped a hand around the back of his bald head. "It's like this, buddy. I don't have a lot of time, you know?"

Alvie had known Vic Plumley his entire life. He had seen him drunk, high, prideful, furious, conniving, horny, and hell-bent—but he had never seen him humble.

He was humble now. Vic Plumley looked down at the concrete. When he raised his head again, there was fear in his eyes.

"It's my damned colon, Alvie. Started there, anyways. Spread everywhere. Bones, liver, the works. I've got a couple of months, tops. Miracle I'm still walking around." There was no self-pity in his voice, which surprised Alvie. He was sure that self-pity had been Vic's first reaction to news of his fate. And Alvie wished he had seen that part, the part where Vic whined and moaned about how it wasn't fair, it wasn't right. Everybody else in the world might get cancer but not *him*, not Vic Plumley.

Vic was still talking. "So that's why I'm here. Want to see Harm again. For the last time. He usually doesn't have much to say, but sometimes he surprises you, right? Starts talking about the old days. The *Arky*. And other things." He rubbed at a spot under his nose. It might have been the cold that was making it run, or it might have been something else. "And—hey, there's one more thing, Alvie."

"Yeah." Alvie was aware that he still had not said anything about Vic's revelation that he was dying. No condolences, no expressions of surprise and regret. Some preacher he was.

"I've been thinking," Vic said. "About Caneytown."

The three boys had rarely spoken the word out loud in seventy-six years. If it came up inadvertently in conversation with friends, if someone was asking for directions and one of the boys needed to say the name of the town in order to be accurate, they would sidestep it, using another phrase, some all-purpose euphemism: "That little hole-in-the-wall just past Redville" or "Oh, you know that little place I mean," and the other person would say, "Oh, yeah, sure I do" and name it themselves, sparing them, sparing the three boys from having to say the name of the town.

Vic had always been Alvie's last choice for who was going to crack first. For long, long years Alvie had thought that he himself was the most likely one to fall. Not because he was a moral fussbudget—no, because he was a chickenshit. And a blabbermouth. He knew himself better than anybody else did. Harm was next on his list. The next-most-likely to turn them in. Harm, too, was weak.

But Vic Plumley? Vic would hold out forever, Alvie had thought. Vic was tough. Vic knew the score, knew how the world worked.

"Yeah," Alvie said.

"And, well—I think we ought to do something. Talk to somebody. Admit what we did. For our own peace of mind. I mean, they're not going to do anything to us. My God. We're closing in on ninety years old. But it would mean a lot, I think."

Alvie nodded.

"It's time, Alvie," Vic said. "You know it just as well as I do. We've had decent lives, all three of us. Harm's not so good anymore, but he had some fine years. That girl of his—a real firecracker. Fun to read about her. But we're old now. And yeah—this'll change how they remember us. That's okay, though, right? Because it's the truth. And you know what, Alvie? I don't want to end up like my old man. He was a liar and an asshole. Never told the truth. Always twisted things to suit how he wanted them to be. Sure, he made a lot of money. But that's all he did. He didn't have anything that mattered. Nothing." He looked into Alvie's eyes. "So it's time, right?"

Vic pulled a hand out of his coat pocket. Alvie realized that Vic wanted him to shake his hand. He complied. He had no choice. Vic held onto Alvie's hand just a few seconds too long. Alvie, uncomfortable, tried to pull his hand away. Vic would not let him.

"Right, buddy?" Vic said. He needed Alvie to agree with him. Say it out loud. Seal the deal.

You fucking bully, Alvie thought.

"Sure," Alvie said.

Vic grinned. "Good. Good. Well, I better get inside. Need to see old Harm." He nodded at Alvie. "I'll be in touch, okay? And in the meantime, you think about it, okay? About how we ought to do it. The two of us go in together, or one after the other? Just think about it, buddy. I value your judgment, you know. Always have."

Vic turned. He bent his head and walked a slow, crablike walk toward the entrance to Thornapple Terrace. Alvie did not waste any time watching him go. He was already sliding into the passenger seat of the Chevette, crunching up his spine to do so, and shaking Lenny's shoulder to rouse him.

"What?" an annoyed Lenny said. "What?"

"Shut up." Alvie checked his watch. "Take me home. And then I want you to get another car and take a little drive tonight. A car that's not registered to you. Can you do that?"

"You mean steal one?"

"That's up to you. Whatever you have to do, do it."

"Drive where, Pop?"

"Bluefield."

Chapter Fourteen

Bell had forgotten just how crummy the Tie Yard Tavern looked from the outside when it wasn't nighttime, when the place was clearly, drearily visible: rotting roof, stained cinder block walls, slushy parking lot constantly garnished with glass from beer bottles smashed against those cinder blocks in fury or boredom or both. Like every bar, its charms were not aesthetic, but anesthetic.

It was still early—not yet 6 p.m.—but the roads were already at the edge of unmanageable. The thick snow made a wall as it fell, a wall that Bell's Explorer had to cut through again and again. Finally she turned into the parking lot.

"You'd think this weather would keep a few folks home," Rhonda murmured, surveying the rows of snow-covered, car-shaped lumps.

"For a lot of them," Bell said, "this *is* home."

They wanted to be discreet, thus Rhonda had called Kirk and asked to be let in the back door. Getting to that door was an ordeal; the owner of the Tie Yard Tavern was not, it was safe to say, a neat freak. Every item he had ever bought at a garage sale was stacked and wedged at the back of the building. Bell and Rhonda had to do as much climbing as they did walking.

"Any such thing as a fire code in this county?" Bell muttered as she scooted around an old wringer washing machine and moved a trash barrel to get to the door.

"Sure there is," Rhonda said, engaged in her own clumsy waltz with a rusty bicycle and an upright piece of PVC pipe. "I bet the fire chief's inside right now, having his fifth beer. You can ask him about it."

Kirk the bartender met them at the back door. He turned out to be a middle-aged man with a nasty scar that ran diagonally from his right eyebrow all the way down to the left side of his chin. The slash must have been gruesome, Bell thought, and it was clear he'd had neither the time nor the cash to get it stitched up properly. His skin, as it aged and shrank back, had pulled and fussed at the long cut, so that now his whole face was implicated in the wound. His hair was a dirty mop of gray. He was skinny everywhere except in the gut, which meant his physique matched that of two out of every three adult males in these parts.

"When we get to where we can see the bar," Kirk said, "he's the second guy from the end." He led them through a narrow, poorly lit tunnel that smelled like piss and beer. It occurred to Bell that those substances were really one and the same, because beer was, in effect, piss in the larval stage. "Hasn't been here since the night he sat with that gal and kept her drinking," Kirk added. "Noticed him right away. Seems keyed-up."

"He's here alone?" Bell asked.

"Yep, near as I can tell."

They paused before a pair of waist-high white louvered doors that swung inward and provided access to the bar. The place was drowning in loud music and louder laughter. Here, nobody fretted over an approaching storm or plunging temperatures or the need to stock up on bread and milk. There was only noise and booze and the comfort of a willed oblivion.

Kirk put a hand on one side of the door, ready to pull it toward him. "You gals okay on your own? I gotta get back to work."

"Thanks, Kirk," Rhonda said. They watched him over the top of the doors as he returned to his dominion, fending off the shouts of those who had had to wait—shockingly—a good three minutes for a refill.

Bell quickly spotted the man at the bar. "It's him," she said.

"Like you thought."

"Yes."

"So what do we do now?" Rhonda said.

"When in Rome."

"Huh?"

Bell pressed the edge of the louvered door. "We buy him a beer."

Lenny's face when he first saw Bell was like a balloon being filled by a faulty pump. It got big with shock, then went back to its normal size as he realized the necessity for playing it cool; it puffed up a little more after that as he took some deep breaths, holding them too long before exhaling.

He sat in front of his beer, a gloomy hunch to his bony shoulders.

"You're that judge from Raythune County, right?" he said. "Last time I saw you was in church."

Bell slid onto the stool next to him. Rhonda took the one on the other side.

"It's prosecutor, not judge," Bell said. "And that's the first time anyone's ever said that they remember me from church." She laughed. "Buy you another beer, Lenny?"

"Sure." He looked uneasy. This time, it was more than just an aversion to law enforcement. The Tie Yard Tavern was not the sort of place where people bought each other beers. Any beer bought for somebody else was automatically one less beer for yourself. Do the math.

"Lenny, this is Rhonda Lovejoy. She's my assistant."

He gave Rhonda a brief sideways swipe of a glance, and then came back to Bell. She signaled Kirk that Lenny would be having another.

"Whadda you want?" he said.

"I need your help," Bell said.

"My help."

"Oh, yes. You see, Lenny . . ." Bell paused, because Kirk had just set a sticky-looking bottle of Budweiser in front of her, and she had to push it down the line to Lenny. "It's like this. Darlene died pretty close to here. She was run off the road. Hit a tree and died instantly. Do you remember that, Lenny? I'm sure you do. She was your friend, after all. Tragic story, don't you think?"

"She wasn't run off no damned road," he muttered. "She was drunk off her ass. Everybody says so." He kept his eyes forward.

"That's what we thought at first, too, Lenny. But we were wrong. Her car was forced off that road."

"Forced." He flung up his head and twisted it sideways, peering at her. Under the bar lights his skin looked even worse than usual, redder and shinier and flakier, as if an ancient disease were reawakening under the surface, a roused dragon. "Nope, that ain't the way it happened."

"Oh, yes, Lenny." Now that Bell had his eyes, she intended to hold onto them. "And I think you know that. You were here that Saturday night with Darlene. You sat and drank with her. You knew she had a problem—you knew she shouldn't be drinking. But you needed her to be impaired. So that when that truck came along and bumped her car, she wouldn't have the reflexes to save herself."

"That's a lie." He said it mildly, like someone ordering fries at a drive-through window.

"We have witnesses, Lenny. People who saw you in the bar that night, buying her drinks. Why'd you do that?"

"Me and Darlene, we go way back."

"So that's all it was. Just some drinks with an old friend."

"Yeah." His face was in lockdown. No emotions were allowed in or out.

"Okay, fine," Bell said. "Let's move on. We know you placed several calls to Darlene's home. You used a voice changer. You told her to stop asking questions about her father's death."

"Didn't do no such thing."

Bell let out a *don't make this harder than it has to be* sigh. "Once again, Lenny, we have proof."

He shrugged. "Don't matter. No big thing. So maybe I made some calls. No law against it."

Bell raised an eyebrow at Rhonda, who had been waiting for the signal. Her turn.

"Hey, Lenny?" Rhonda's voice offered its *just between us* lilt that Bell admired. A lot of very sly people had admitted to some very bad things while relaxing in the shade of that voice. "Remember the night you went out to Marcy Coates's house? You needed to shut her up. Isn't that right? I bet she was threatening to turn you in. Was that it? Marcy was a good woman. She took your money, because she wanted to help somebody else, and because the people she took care of at Thornapple Terrace were so far gone, anyway. And then she smothered Harmon Strayer—just like you'd told her to. She used a pillow, maybe. And put it over the old man's face. He was helpless, and he died right away. Just like the other two. But she couldn't stand it. Couldn't live with herself. So she called you and said she was going to go to the police. No way *that* was happening, Lenny—right?"

Rhonda leaned closer to him. His elbows were locked tight at his sides and he was looking straight ahead, at the rows of liquor bottles lined up on stacked shelves at the back of the bar, avoiding her eyes. The room was hot and crowded, and the thumping music never stopped, but it was as if they were, at that moment, the only two people in the world: the skinny haunted man and the woman on the next stool over, murmuring into his ear, telling him truths he already knew.

"Lenny," Rhonda said. "You had some trouble that night, didn't you? There was another woman there. Marcy's best friend, Connie. They ran. You had to chase them out of the house—after you'd killed the dog. You chased them into the snow. You got them—but you made a mistake."

"I don't know what you—"

"We found your shoes, Lenny," Rhonda said, interrupting him, but doing it gently, almost reluctantly. "The ones with blood on them. From when you walked over to the bodies to make sure Marcy and Connie were dead." It was a long shot, but she had seen much longer ones pay off, so why not?

A tremor ran through Lenny Sherrill's body, top to bottom. "You *couldn't* have found them," he said, his words rushed and bunched. "I buried 'em. I buried 'em that very night. Only pair I had. Nobody knows where I put 'em. *Nobody*. So there's no freakin' way you could've—"

He stopped.

Rhonda was silent. She leaned away from his ear and put her hands on the bar, as if she had to steady herself in the wake of this revelation, to deal with the momentousness of what he had just revealed.

Lenny changed. He seemed to droop. It was as if he was letting go of something he had been holding onto so tightly for so long that he'd forgotten what it felt like to not be holding it. Now that he was free, he realized it felt pretty damned good.

He looked first at Rhonda, then at Bell. He touched a couple of fingers to his chin, where the stubble had to fight for room to sprout between the acne scars. He knew what he'd done. He knew.

And instead of getting mad, or backtracking on his story, or claiming they had not heard him right, or threatening them in the way he was used to doing when things went against him, he nodded. His voice sounded thoughtful. And a little relieved.

"You didn't really find my shoes, did you?"

Bell shook her head.

Lenny nodded again. He sat up a little straighter. "Got it," he said. He slapped a hand on the wood. The impact made a funny sound as flesh hit the gathered wetness of a bar at this time of night, when the sloshed beer and the spilled whiskey were so abundant that desperate drinkers down to their last dollar had sometimes been known to take a quick lick.

Lenny had made his decision. "None of this was my idea," he said. "I've been doing what that old bastard tells me to do for my whole damned life." He finished off the beer they had bought for him with a long, soulful slug, head thrown back, Adam's apple bobbing. When he finished, he wiped his mouth with his sleeve. "You tell me where I need to sign and I'll sign. I'll do whatever I have to do."

Bell recited his Miranda rights. She asked if he wanted to keep talking to them. He did. She asked if he wanted an attorney. He didn't. He started to say something else when his chair was bumped hard by a passing customer, a man with long black hair tied back in a pony-tail. Lenny tipped forward on his stool.

"Sorry, bro," the man said, his voice a slurry mumble. "Sorry 'bout that. Oh, hey, Lenny—didn't see it was you. How you doin'?"

"Hey there, Jeff," Lenny answered. "How you doin'?"

By way of reply the man lifted his empty glass, which he handed over to Kirk for a refill. "Better soon," he said, winking at Lenny. They both laughed and then the man moved on to wait for his drink at a spot farther down the bar.

Bell leaned back on her stool so that she could see Rhonda. She nodded. Rhonda nodded back and began texting Deputy Oakes. She was asking him to come pick up Lenny Sherrill.

Lenny hunched over the bar, shoulders raised high, head sunk between them. He was lost in his own world now. Bell wondered if he even heard the raucous music overhead, the punchy bass notes so powerful that they could serve as unofficial defibrillators, the electric guitars rolling out in fuzzy bursts of static.

"A few more questions," Bell said.

"Fire away," Lenny said. "Got nothing to hide no more." He took a deep breath. "First good clear breath of air I've had in forever. Feels better already, you know? Being out from under my old man. Free of that SOB."

He cocked an elbow on the counter and faced Bell. He knew his life was about to change immensely—he knew what he had done, and knew he would be called to account for it—but there was satisfaction in that as well as anxiety, because the old life was hateful and painful and nothing he had ever chosen. And the new one—well, no one knew what the new one might bring, least of all Lenny Sherrill. Only that it would be different.

That day at the church, Bell had sensed this about Lenny: Out of all the things he wanted to be—tough, cool, strong, a player—the one thing he *didn't* want to be was anything like his father, Alvie Sherrill. It was Lenny's single redeeming feature. Bell had counted on it. But she also knew that Lenny could not escape that fate on his own. He needed a hand.

"Where did you get the money to bribe Groves and Marcy Coates?" Bell asked.

Lenny shrugged. He was an explorer at the mouth of a cave, deciding how far to proceed. Checking his flashlight. Calculating odds. Okay: Just go.

"Me and some buddies, we been holding up gas stations all over the county. Works real good. Saved every penny of my share for this— to get those folks to do what my dad wanted 'em to. That church—it don't pay him shit. So I had to help."

"How did you know Darlene would be here that night?"

"She told me."

"She told you?"

"Yeah. We'd been getting together to talk sometimes, when she was back in Muth County to visit her dad. Like in the old days." He looked down. He did not like this part. "My dad told me to keep in touch with her. Then she told me that she was coming to the Tie Yard on Saturday night to meet an old friend. She meant you, I guess." He changed his position on the bar stool, shifting his bony butt in a doomed attempt to find some comfort. "So I got here, too. Stayed out of sight. Watched you two from over there." He jerked his head in the direction of a booth in the corner, across the room from the one in which Bell and Darlene had sat.

"And after that," Bell said. "Once she'd left at the same time I did—how did you get her to drive back?"

"I called her. She'd given me her cell number when her dad was first getting sick. Asked me to keep an eye on him when she couldn't be there." His mouth twitched. "She was driving down the mountain. I told her I was real bad off. Told her I was thinking about killing myself. Just getting a shotgun and doing it. I knew that would get her back here. She was softhearted that way. When she got my call she pulled over into a patch of woods. Turned off her lights and waited for you to go by. She told me about all that, once she'd gotten back. We sat at the other end of the bar. Right over there." He scooted the empty bottle around on the soaked coaster. Bits of wet cardboard were tearing off. "She always felt guilty about leaving Norbitt."

"Darlene was your friend, Lenny," Bell said. She said it quietly, forcing Lenny to lean in to hear her. She needed him close for the next few questions. "So why did you want her to die?"

"I didn't. It was my dad."

"But you went along with it."

"My dad—he runs the show, okay? You don't go against him. Not if you know what's good for you. He said Darlene was asking too many questions at that Thornapple place. Things that oughta just be left alone."

Bell shook her head. "I don't buy it. You do a lot for your dad—but causing the death of your best friend? No. What's the real reason, Lenny?"

"I told you."

"And I said I don't believe you."

The standoff wasn't much of a standoff. A petulant Lenny shoved away the empty bottle that he'd been playing with. It nearly capsized.

"The bitch *left*," he said. His voice was bitter. He kept his eyes on the bottle. "Just up and left. Went away to college—but promised to come back. Went to law school—and did it again. Swore she'd be coming back. But she never did." He nodded grimly to himself. "What happened to her—she *deserved* it."

"Because she left you."

"No." Lenny shook his head. "Because she left me alone with *him*."

Bell was just about finished. She would have to do this all over again at the courthouse, and by that time, Lenny might very well have changed his mind about that lawyer. She had a few more things she wanted to know before Deputy Oakes arrived.

"And the drinking binge? Darlene had been doing so well. Carried her sobriety chip with her." Bell wanted to add: *And so not only did you kill her, but you also made sure her last moments were filled with shame and self-loathing.*

Lenny looked away. It was as if he had heard the addendum.

"Wasn't too hard," he said. "I knew how to do it, because I knew her better'n anybody else. All I had to do was start talking about our dads. And about the old days. The days that ain't coming back. That kind of thing, it liked to tear her to pieces. Thinking about the past can open up a hole in some people that's so damned big they can't find nothing to fill it. They try, though. They try and they try. That's how they get to be drunks."

Bell received Carla's text about twenty minutes after Deputy Oakes arrived and began the familiar ritual with Lenny Sherrill: cuffs, another Miranda, perp walk through a thickening haze of determined snow that was already ankle-high. Jake did not want any trouble from the bar crowd—liquid courage and the current epidemic of anti-cop sentiment being a troublesome mix—and so he handled everything through the back door, discreetly. He draped Lenny's coat over his shackled hands and led him out to the Blazer. Most of the clientele in the Tie Yard Tavern did not even realize what was happening.

By now Bell and Rhonda were outside, too, standing beside the Explorer. The snow was falling even faster now. The wind had a spiteful streak. They waved at the Blazer as it went by, Jake hunched over in his seat like a ship's captain lashed to the wheel, Lenny Sherrill in the back, his face unreadable behind the glass in the brief flash of visibility afforded by the sole light in the parking lot. Jake's intense focus was necessary; he had a long drive back to the Raythune County Courthouse. Most of Lenny's crimes had occurred in Muth County, and Bell would have to sort it all out with Steve Black, but that was down the road. Right now, they had their man—or one of their men, because she was already contemplating ways to charge Alvie Sherrill as well as his son. For a moment, all was well in the world.

And then she read Carla's text:

Hey, mom. I'm at TT. All fine. C U later

"Problem," Bell said.

"What?"

Bell held up her cell and waggled it. "This isn't okay. Carla's trying to tell me something."

Rhonda leaned over and read the text. "Sounds pretty straightforward to me. She says she's fine."

"Right. That's the problem. 'All fine' is not something Carla would text if everything *was* fine."

"Because?"

"Because she's the daughter of two lawyers. And whether she was at Sam's house or here with me in Acker's Gap, she grew up hearing both of us say the same thing, over and over again: 'Never answer a question that hasn't been asked.' I didn't text her and ask if she was fine. She volunteered the information. Something is definitely amiss."

Rhonda tucked a gloved hand up under its opposite armpit. She was shivering. "Could we maybe discuss this *inside* the car?"

The heater took a while to warm up. While it fought the good fight, Bell read the text several more times. She texted back: *What's going on??*

In five minutes, when there had been no reply, she called Jake Oakes.

"We're driving out to Thornapple Terrace," she said. "Just wanted you to be aware in case we need backup."

"You can't do that." Jake was adamant. "Can't get out there. Not now. Roads're totally covered. You can't even see where there *was* a road anymore."

Bell did not care what he said. She was going. All she could think about were the similarities between this night and the one four years ago, when Carla had been kidnapped by a man who called himself Chill. He was a pathetic, two-bit hoodlum, but he was a pathetic, two-bit hoodlum with a gun—and that changed everything.

It was all happening again. Carla was in trouble, and Bell was trying desperately to get to her. No, not trying: She *would* get to her.

"Bell? Did you hear me? Don't do it," Jake barked at her. "I've got a buddy who's a deputy in Muth County. I'll call and get him to go by the Terrace. Check things out. But you can't go. You'll never make it."

"Watch me," she said. She ended the call. The bravado was less about convincing Jake Oakes than it was about convincing herself.

She turned to Rhonda: "You don't have to go. I can drop you off somewhere on the way. At a relative's house, maybe. I know you've got 'em everywhere."

Rhonda rubbed her hands in front of the dash heater. "Maybe it's a measure of the basically nonexistent social life I've had lately," she said, "but right now, I can't think of anything I'd rather do than drive through a blinding snowstorm to get to an old folks' home. Let's go."

It was the hardest trek Bell had ever attempted. She had driven through snow before, and she had driven over ice, and she had nearly rolled an SUV once when tornado-force winds gripped the vehicle like a gang of hooligans trying to upend it, but this was different, by several orders of magnitude.

As Jake had warned her, the road had simply vanished. No magician could have done a better job of it. In lieu of a road, there was a minefield of white across which the Explorer churned, and the trick was to go fast enough not to get stuck in the rising snow but slow enough to keep from spinning out. At one point, Bell was suddenly going sideways; she had tapped the brake and her rear wheels took offense. They skidded dramatically to the right in a lively swoop, producing just the kind of feeling, she thought, that people pay good money for in amusement parks. Had any other cars been present, they would have been doomed. She had no functional control of the Explorer, except to will it to go in the right direction.

But there were no other cars. Who else would be dumb enough to drive in this weather? Thus the very recklessness—or foolhardiness, as Bell knew Nick Fogelsong would dub it—of the mission tended to make it safer. They were alone out here. Sliding along sideways was fine.

"I guess I'm going to have to rethink some things," Rhonda said, "about love and marriage, you know?"

"What?"

Bell was frantically trying to keep them upright and moving forward—and alive—for at least a little while longer. Yet Rhonda seemed oblivious to the peril. *She has more faith in my driving abilities than I do,* Bell thought. *God help her.*

"I was looking at Ava Hendricks tonight," Rhonda went on. "I mean, goodness. She's an attractive woman. Even more than what her pictures show. I wanted to say to her, 'Honey, you could have any man you wanted in Acker's Gap.'"

Bell was about to suggest that that really wasn't much of a compliment, but she had to deal with a sudden crisis. The Explorer had hit a patch of black ice. It felt as if it were levitating. The vehicle was not being steered anymore, in any real sense; it was skating all on its own, indulging in a series of wild loops. Bell kept only a minimal touch on the wheel and hoped for the best. At long last the tires seemed to find the road again. They were moving forward.

"I don't understand it—but it has to be true," Rhonda said. She was unfazed by the near-disaster. In fact, she seemed barely aware of it. "Ava and Darlene must have really been in love. They had choices, both of them. And they chose each other."

Bell nodded. Rhonda's sudden conversion to tolerance was a bit too abrupt to be entirely sincere. Maybe her assistant would indeed work her way toward an acceptance of the idea that people could live as they pleased. But Bell was the boss, and Rhonda knew her feelings on the subject, hence this little speech reeked of expediency. Still, Bell told herself, it was better than nothing.

After a few more miles Bell took a guess and twisted the wheel and hoped she was heading into the parking lot of Thornapple Terrace. Rhonda had tried Carla's cell multiple times. Nothing.

The building in front of them was barely visible through the continuing onslaught of snow, portions of the brick emerging now and again when a gusting wind cleared out a brief area of clarity. A few lights were on inside.

Before they could talk strategy, Bell's phone rang. She put it on speaker.

"Mrs. Elkins, this is Kayleigh Crocker. I've been trying to call Carla. So I got worried and thought maybe she'd contacted you."

"Kayleigh, what's going on? What do you know?"

"Nothing, Mrs. Elkins. Carla and I barely got a chance to talk last night. I don't have any idea—"

"Cut the crap." Bell's voice was as mean as she could make it. "There's no time. I got a text from her an hour and a half ago. Said she was at Thornapple Terrace. Why the hell would she be going there, Kayleigh? Tell me everything you know. *Now.*"

Kayleigh was crying. Bell did not care. She listened as the young woman took a few kittenish sniffles. Then Kayleigh said, "There's this guy she likes. An older guy. He works there."

"What older guy?"

"Just somebody she met. At a bar. And then she found out that he'd given her a fake name. So she was driving out there this afternoon to ask him about it. Please, Mrs. Elkins, I told her not to. And I'm sorry I didn't try harder to stop her or—"

"Just sit tight, Kayleigh. I'll take care of it."

Oh, Carla, Bell thought. *Carla, Carla.*

Her daughter's passion and impetuosity were so much a part of who she was.

But they also got her into trouble on a regular basis. *Would I,* Bell wondered, *want her to be otherwise?* A sedate, predictable Carla Elkins would not be her little girl. She would be somebody else's little girl.

Bell would stick with what she had. With Carla—and with everything that went along with her, including, at the moment, a mysterious and possibly dangerous scenario unfolding on the other side of the cascading snow.

The building was now officially invisible. Snow dominated this world, and as was its kingly prerogative, it was erasing all boundaries, taking over everything.

"So what's the plan?" Rhonda said.

"Well, we don't have any idea what's going on in there. So let's go in quietly and be ready for anything."

They fought their way out of the Explorer—the wind desperately wanted to rip off the opened doors—and bent their heads, trudging toward what they hoped was the front door of the Terrace. Bell tried to shut off her mind during the journey, and stay focused on remaining upright against a wind intent on knocking them over and dragging them away, but she could not. She was envisioning all the terrible things they might discover within: injuries or, God forbid, fatalities; a crazed gunman with a grudge; mayhem and peril.

But when they got inside, it was not like that at all.

There was a small couch in the corner of the lobby, and an armchair, and that was where the people were. A soft silence permeated the room; it was not the kind of silence that occurs in the aftermath of violence, that shocked, freeze-frame stillness, but rather the silence of weariness and resignation.

Sitting on the couch was an old man. Bell knew she had seen him before. Yes—it was the old man at the reception desk the day she first visited here. The one in the driving cap. Right now he was in his pajamas, a pale green flannel pair with white piping on the sleeves. His hands were folded in his lap. He looked perfectly content. Next to him was Carla. She was obviously surprised to see her mother and Rhonda when they entered, but she did not jump up or call out. She waved them over, putting a finger against her lips to indicate they should move quietly.

An older man in gray coveralls sat in the armchair. He had pulled the chair around so that it faced the couch. He was holding something in his lap. As Bell came closer, she saw that it was a flat board with a circle of nails protruding from one end. Clearly, a weapon.

Yet the only violence right now was occurring outside the large window just over the couch. The storm was at its peak; wild gusts of snow were hurled against the glass by a manic wind, in profound contrast to this tidy pocket of calm.

"Hi, Mom. Hi, Rhonda." Carla spoke slowly and carefully. "Nelson, it's okay if I talk to them, right? I can tell them what's going on?"

The man in the chair—Bell remembered him now, he was the maintenance man here, the one who was fixing the sprinkler head on the day of her first visit—nodded. His head was tilted slightly forward. There was a compressed energy about him, a sense of coiled power, especially in his hands. The hands that held the board.

"Okay, then," Carla said. "Mom, Rhonda—this is Nelson Ferris. And this is his father, Bill."

Nelson did not acknowledge them. His focus was locked onto the old man.

One of Nelson's fingers twitched, the board shifted in his lap, and the atmosphere immediately changed, tensed up. But it was only that: a finger twitch.

Bell's impulse was to rush forward and grab the board from Nelson Ferris. But something in Carla's demeanor told her to hold back. Her daughter was not acting like a victim. Despite all evidence to the contrary—despite the presence of an obviously distraught man with a crude weapon—Carla seemed to be in charge.

"Everything's fine," Carla said. "Everything's okay."

"If everything's okay," Bell asked her quietly, "then why didn't you return my calls? Or Kayleigh's calls?"

"Nelson didn't want me to," Carla said. Bell thought she understood her strategy now: Make Nelson Ferris believe he was safe, that no one was challenging him. "And like I said in my text, it's all fine."

Bell looked around the lobby. "Isn't there a security staff on duty? Where are they?" She had been visited by a sudden ugly vision of a guard tied up and tossed in a closet somewhere.

"At night," Carla replied, in the serene, unruffled voice that was rapidly persuading Bell that her daughter would make an excellent hostage negotiator, "the security is handled by maintenance. Nelson—or as they know him here, Travis Womack—is in charge of things tonight." She gave her mother a look that Bell immediately translated as: *Be cool. I've got this.*

I've trusted her this far, Bell thought. *In for a penny, in for a pound.* They waited.

Bill Ferris sneezed. He examined the clear goop in his hand as if he had no idea where it had come from. Then he smiled.

"Look at him," Nelson scoffed. "Pretending to be out of his mind."

Carla leaned forward and touched Nelson's knee. When she did that, Bell felt a jet of panic in her stomach. What if this man abruptly decided to swing that board? It was all Bell could do not to grab her girl and head for the exit.

"Nelson," Carla said. "I don't think he's pretending, okay? He has Alzheimer's. You know that." She looked up at Bell. "We've been sitting here for a while. We just needed a little bit of quiet time. Nelson has to figure some things out. He woke up Bill in his room and brought him out here. Now he has to choose."

"I'm going to kill him," Nelson said. His matter-of-fact tone concerned Bell far more than a raging snarl would have.

"No," Carla said. "No, you're not. That's not who you are, Nelson— I *know* it's not. That's not who you want to be. That's not—"

"You don't understand," Nelson cried out. He gripped the board harder. Bell realized that every muscle in her body was tensed to spring. If he so much as lifted that board half an inch, she would go after him, getting between that weapon and her daughter howsoever she could, no matter the price.

"I'm trying to understand," Carla said. "I'm really trying. But he's sick, Nelson. He doesn't know who you are. You've been working here for months, going past him every day, and does he ever seem to know you? Does he show the slightest recognition?"

Nelson did not answer. He stared at the old man. The old man was smiling, as if it were the most natural thing in the world to be sitting in his pajamas in the lobby after midnight. His face looked rinsed clean of thought.

"Nelson," Carla said, "let's take him back to his room, okay? My mom and Rhonda will help. This doesn't have to get any worse. We can just help him up and—"

"No," Nelson said, interrupting her. He shook his head. "Do you know what he did to my sister and me? The horrible fucking things he did? It won't leave me alone—it's with me every day. It's always right in front of me. I can't forget." He was struck by the irony and he laughed. "He can't remember. And I can't forget."

"What do you really want, Nelson?" Carla said.

"I want him to know what he did. I want him to remember it the way *I* have to remember it—every day, every hour, every fucking *minute*. Because if he can't remember it—how can I hate him? How can I hate this . . ." Nelson nodded toward Bill Ferris, who had a whimsical look on his face, as if he were strolling in the park on a sunny day. ". . . this *blob,* this thing that doesn't know its own name? How can I hate *this*? This man isn't the one who did that to us, who made my childhood and my sister's childhood an absolute fucking nightmare. The man who did that is gone. He escaped." Nelson gave Carla a look of piercing anguish. "He got away. He never had to pay for what he did."

"That's right, Nelson," Carla said quietly. "You said it yourself. This man isn't the one you hate. He's not the one you want to kill. You don't even know this man. And he doesn't know you."

Nelson looked at her, and then he looked at Bill Ferris. His fingers slowly relaxed their grip on the board. It slid out of his lap and hit the floor with a brief clatter. He slumped over in his chair. He was crying, but it was such a noiseless and subdued kind of crying that only someone standing close to him would even know he was doing it.

Carla rose from her seat. She picked up the spiked board, keeping it well out of Nelson's reach, and she handed it carefully to her mother, who would safeguard it. Then she moved over to stand beside Nelson's chair. She took his head in her hands. She held his head while he cried. He cried very quietly. He was crying for his lost childhood, and for all that he might have been if he had had love in his life, all that he would have done if once—just once—he had come into a room as a little boy and had known by the light in someone's eyes that they were glad to see him.

Chapter Fifteen

A week had passed since the night at Thornapple Terrace. The cold had finally broken. It was a temporary reprieve. Bell knew that. She was determined to take advantage of it, though, and enjoy this relatively mild day and the nearly clear roads.

She asked Carla to come along. She did not tell her where they were going. Carla, of course, asked several times during the drive.

"Be patient," Bell said.

They traveled along a narrow two-lane road that went up and down like a sine curve. Farms, or in some cases what was left of farms, spread out on both sides of the road. Bell could sense Carla's growing puzzlement, and she could also sense that it was gradually giving way to irritation. Mysterious errands were only fun for the person in charge, the person who knew where you were going.

The legalities were still being sorted out. Felton Groves had been located and arrested three days ago in Valdosta, Georgia, and would be extradited to West Virginia to face felony charges for vehicular assault on Darlene Strayer and for a accepting a bribe to commit a felony. Lenny Sherrill had been transferred to the Muth County Jail;

he would be arraigned for the murders of Vic Plumley, Marcy Coates, and Connie Dollar, and for conspiracy to solicit the murders of Darlene and Harmon Strayer. Alvie Sherrill was also in custody for accessory to murder. Muth County Prosecutor Steve Black had agreed to drop charges of attempted kidnapping against Nelson Ferris, if Ferris underwent mandatory inpatient treatment for post-traumatic stress disorder at a mental health facility. Bell had requested that, knowing she would pay the price later for Black's granting her the favor: insinuating phone calls from the prosecutor, the kind that left Black with a wide swath of deniability—and left her with an intense desire for a shower.

Well, so be it, was Bell's rueful thought at the time she made the deal. *Sam Elkins—and Frank Plumley, God knows—aren't the only ones who understand the necessity of bargains.*

Bargains. The word made her think about Clay Meckling, and the unspoken but clearly understood limits of their bond. They were in a committed relationship, yes, but the truth was that she had kept him at arm's length for almost four years now. He did not complain—well, sometimes he did, but Bell had mastered the art of deflecting questions that involved the future. Their future. Yet she often wondered how long they could dance this careful dance.

Did she want to marry Clay? No. She did not want to marry anyone. Clay knew that and accepted it—or at least he said he did. For now.

Carla spoke again. Her voice revealed a troubled mind. She had visited Nelson Ferris in jail the day before, and heard more details about his early life.

"So many horrible fathers," she said. "Seems like that's all we ever hear about. Aren't there any good guys out there?"

"Sure. Harmon Strayer was one."

"Yeah. *One.*"

"And your dad. He and I may not be together anymore, but he's a great dad, right?"

"Yeah, okay. That's two. But how about *your* father? Or Bill Ferris? Or Alvie Sherrill? Seems like all you ever deal with are the selfish assholes. The ones who wreck their kids' lives. And other people's lives, too."

"That's because of where I'm standing."

"What do you mean?"

"I'm a prosecutor, sweetie. Selfish assholes are my stock in trade. Comes with the job. I mean, the good guys don't often cross my path— not professionally, that is. I get the bad guys. Sometimes that makes the world seem pretty lopsided. Out of balance."

"So what do you do? To restore the balance, I mean. So that you don't get, like, really, really depressed. What do you *do*?"

Her daughter had a real knack for digging to the crux of things, Bell reflected. She recalled how Carla had expertly defused the situation with Nelson Ferris in the lobby of Thornapple Terrace. And now she was using her skills on her family.

"I do this." Bell swept a hand toward the windshield, indicating the breadth of the land that held them, land that unrolled like a dark carpet at the foot of a somber mountain range. This territory was battered and wind-torn, still suffering from repeated maulings by the severe and prolonged winter, but when the sun struck it at a certain angle, you could envision the spring to come. You could imagine the way those fields would fill up with growing things, the way the woods would jump to life. "I get out of the office," Bell went on, "and try to remember that there's a whole world out here. Filled with decent people. People who love their children. People who try their best to take care of them."

"Yeah. I guess you're right," Carla said. "I mean, those are the kind of people I've been meeting on my interviews. I really love talking to them. I go to Collier County tomorrow. It's all gone by so fast." She swiveled her head around repeatedly, trying to get a sense of their location. "So where *are* we?"

"You'll see."

Carla uttered a theatrical sigh and let her head flop back against the seat.

"Mom?" she said, after a minute or so had passed. "I want you to know something." A pause. "I'm going to be okay."

Bell glanced at her, and then retuned her eyes to the road. She did not interrupt. A faux-casual *Tell me more* would, at this point, have had precisely the opposite effect, and Bell knew it.

"I wasn't okay before," Carla continued. "I was about as far from okay as it's possible to be and not be like Nelson—out of control, I mean, with my emotions running so far out in front of me that I couldn't get hold of them and bring them back. At least I still had a grip. Well, *sort* of. Until that day at the mall." She hesitated, waiting for the words to settle out in her mind so that she could select the right ones. "I think that's what I sensed in Nelson, you know? Somebody else who was so good at holding it together, at fooling people into thinking he was just this guy. But I—I got it, you know? First time I met him, it's like I had this quick glimpse into his soul." She laughed. "*Whoa.* That's pretty lame. Like you can peek into somebody's soul after a few minutes in a bar."

"In a bar, it's not the soul that most people want a peek at."

"Mom." Carla laughed again. Then her voice grew somber. "Just want you to know that I'm getting there. I really like the new therapist Dad found for me. He's weird as hell, but I like him. And I'm going to keep in touch with Nelson. I know he'll be okay, too. Takes time, though."

"It does."

They traveled a few more miles. Finally Bell turned onto an unpaved road, its entrance almost lost amidst the wild woods trying to enfold it, reclaim it. She knew where to go because Rhonda had helped her by making calls, by checking records. By doing the thing that only Rhonda could do this well: linking the past and the present through the difficult, unforgiving geography of this place. Finding the right road into that past.

As they turned, Carla read out loud the message on a small wooden sign almost completely engulfed by unruly bushes and out-of-control vines. CANEYTOWN 3 MILES AHEAD, it said, in flaking red letters, along with a skinny arrow.

Bell drove for another ten minutes or so. She had to go slow, to preserve her tires and her shock absorbers.

At last she saw it, off to the right in a white tangle of woods. The words SILENT HOME CEMETERY were spelled out in wrought iron across the top of an arch. Seasons of hard weather had turned the arch a distressed-looking gray. Bell drove under it and parked along the rutted lane.

She and Carla climbed out. The markers here were small and unassuming, with none of the fancy granite angels or mammoth marble praying hands that Bell had seen in cemeteries that were the permanent resting places of the more affluent. These headstones were so thin and spindly, and rubbed raw by wind and by rain, that on the oldest graves—some dated back to the mid 1800s—the writing was unintelligible.

Bell opened the back of the Explorer. She took out a pair of small, tidy bouquets. The flowers were pink and delicate. It was still much too cold for flowers to survive outdoors for any length of time, but Bell did not mind; longevity was not what she was after.

She moved along the rows. Carla trailed behind her. Once Bell found the graves she was seeking, she stopped. She knelt down on the frozen ground and placed one of the bouquets in front of the headstone where the faint letters read GERTRUDE ELOSIE DRISCOLL. 1865–1938.

She handed the second bouquet to Carla. Carla knelt down in front of the grave next door, placing it against the headstone reading BETTY GERTRUDE DRISCOLL. 1933–1938.

They stood up. They walked a little farther down the lane, mother and daughter. They did not talk. The sky somehow felt closer out here than it did in town, not in a meddlesome, overbearing way but in a way that seemed to offer a strong opinion about the need to connect things, to knit separate elements into a larger timeless whole. Between the earth and the sky were the mountains—gray, distant, brittle-looking in this temperature, still tipped with frost. The mountains had been here a long, long time. They would last even longer than the memories did, all memories, the good and the bad, the wounding ones and the healing ones, too.

On a summer day in 1944, three boys gazed out across the choppy, nettlesome ocean. It was gray in every direction: gray sky, gray sea, gray beach, gray horizon. The same gray as the mountains back home. They had never been here before, but they were in familiar territory.

Even in the midst of this tumult and uncertainty, their lives seemed to spread out before them, rich with promise. An immense vista drew them forward, whispering its secret promise of tomorrow. They had done their duty, and they had survived.

The war was winding down. Soon they would return to West Virginia and pick up the stories of their lives. Along the way they would try to forgive themselves for the things they had done, the shameful things, the things that were unworthy of them and the great gifts they had been given—the gift of being alive, the gift of possibility.

They had started out wild. Wild and selfish. They were troublemakers. They were imperfect. They made mistakes. They had a past— oh, Lord, did they ever. But when it counted, they were there. That was what they would tell themselves in the following years, when life sometimes looked bleak, when they suffered failures and setbacks and disappointments, when they doubted themselves: *I was there. The call went out, and I raised my hand, and I was there.*

Three boys.

One of them was different, and for him, all roads were narrow and dark. But the other two believed that the road ahead would always look brighter and wider than the road behind. Those two were changing, and they were growing. It would take them a long, long time, it would take them decades, but they would get there.

The three boys came home from the war. They settled down. They took care of their families. They lived and they loved and they dreamed and, for as long as they were able, they remembered.

Acknowledgments

From this remove, the profound sacrifices of the men and women who fought in World War II are difficult to fully appreciate. In the prime of their lives, they left familiar circumstances to plunge headlong into a distant conflict whose outcome was far from certain. To help me come a bit closer to the experience of D-Day—a core moment in this novel—I studied many histories of World War II including, most fruitfully, *D-Day: The Normandy Landing in the Words of Those Who Took Part*, edited by Jon E. Lewis. The anecdote about General Eisenhower comes from this splendid oral history.

I also drew upon the recollections of my late stepfather, Donald C. Weed, who, like the three young men in this story, was a wide-eyed kid from West Virginia who joined the U.S. Navy after Pearl Harbor and served on a vessel assigned to search for bodies in the waters off Normandy. The memory of spotting a possible survivor was his.

To better understand Alzheimer's, another facet of this novel, I returned to a book I have read multiple times, and that always strikes me anew with its grace, its thoroughness, and its abiding humanity. The book is *The Forgetting: Alzheimer's: Portrait of an Epidemic* by David Shenk.

Turn the page for a sneak peek at
Julia Keller's next novel

Fast Falls the Night

Available August 2017

Copyright © 2017 by Julia Keller

Danny

12:04 A.M.

The woman asked to use the bathroom. Danny Lukens was 99 percent sure of what she wanted it for—and it had nothing to do with the usual uses to which bathrooms are put. He said yes, though, because it wasn't worth arguing about. He had a long night still ahead of him. He had just started his shift. He didn't want any trouble.

"Okay, thanks," she said.

Her speech wasn't slurred, which surprised him. Then he realized that he shouldn't have been surprised. The slurring would come later. Right now, she was honed to a clean, brittle edge, polished to a gloss of pure longing. No wonder the "Okay, thanks" had come out intelligibly. She was too sharp, too attuned to her life and its attendant miseries. Slurring—not only her words, but also her world—was the goal, not the current reality. In a few minutes, she would be able to relax into the newly made mess of herself. The beautiful ooze.

"Back there," he said, pointing. "It ain't locked."

Whatever she did in the bathroom was her business. Not his.

She nodded and moved away from the counter. He took a quick mental snapshot with his sideways glance, just in case she trashed it and his manager asked him for a description of her to give to the sheriff.

As if, Danny thought, *they'd be able to find her again if she didn't want to be found.* Addicts were ghosts. They drifted in and out of people's lives, just as they drifted in and out of their own lives.

He sort of knew her and he sort of didn't. He had seen her before, most likely, but he didn't have a precise recollection of it, and they all ran together in his mind, anyway, the faces and the skinny bodies. She had been in here before; again, he didn't remember it, but the odds favored it. This was a small town. Not that many places to go. She wore cutoff denim shorts and a too-tight black T-shirt with the word PINK splayed across her chest in—*Duh,* Danny thought—pink letters. She was very, very thin; her arms and legs were like tiny white PVC pipes. She had a long narrow face, scraggly blondish hair with black roots, and dead eyes. Her eyebrows were charcoal smudges. She was barefoot. She was—how old? Danny couldn't guess. Maybe eighteen. Maybe forty.

Did it matter? It did not.

Until she came in, he had been alone since his shift started at 11 P.M. Chuckie Purvis, the guy with the shift before his, had reported that it had been slow all night. Which was strange, really, for August. Usually August nights brought an unbroken line of customers: smart-ass kids, say, out for midnight rides in dusty pickups, buying gas and beer, shedding waves of look-at-me bravado, slapping a fake ID down on the counter like the winning card in a blackjack game. Or truckers craving a can of Red Bull and a flap of conversation. Or sometimes it was deputies from the Raythune County Sheriff's Department. They had a habit of stopping in, too, at intervals throughout the night, propping a black-holstered hip against the front counter and slowly unwinding the brown wrapper from a Snickers, alternating bites with observations about how anybody in their right mind would've gotten the hell out of this state a long time ago. No question about it. Once the last chunk of candy was chewed and swallowed, they would use the tip of their tongue to pry out the nut pieces from their back teeth.

The Marathon was a natural gathering place. It was the only station in these parts open after 11 P.M., except for the Highway Haven up on the interstate. The Marathon was closer to Acker's Gap, the county seat. At one time there had been a Lester Oil station even closer, but it shut down last year, the front glass window replaced by sheets of yellow plywood. The pumps and the underground tank had been hauled out, leaving open holes and a trough gorged with trash and rainwater. Husky weeds had colonized the long cracks in the asphalt.

The Marathon, though, was still going strong.

Danny's favorite deputy was Jake Oakes. He liked Charlie Mathers, who had retired a while back, well enough, and he didn't mind Steve Brinksneader, Charlie's replacement. Jake, though, was the best; he was the one Danny most admired, most looked forward to seeing during his shift—or any other time, for that matter, which was weird, because Danny wasn't the kind of guy who liked authority figures. That had been his whole problem back in high school, and the reason he had to drop out: He couldn't stand it when somebody tried to tell him what he could and couldn't do. In study hall one afternoon in his junior year, he spat at Mrs. Pyles, the civics teacher. She had told him to quit talking and do his work. Witnessing him being called out that way, some of the other guys laughed at him. That was *not* okay. And so when Mrs. Pyles marched down the aisle in his direction, surely intending to repeat her reprimand, he stood up and sent a ginormous wad of spit right in her eye. It was worth everything that came after—being expelled for the rest of the year—just to see the look on the old bitch's face, the shock and the fear. By the time the school year rolled around again, he was out on his own. To hell with her. To hell with all of them.

Jake, though, he respected. He never made Jake pay for his Snickers. Yet so far tonight there had been no sign of Jake. No sign of anybody. Just this woman. Danny didn't see a car outside, which meant that wherever she had come from, she had walked.

It had been a strange summer. The heat never really settled in. Throughout June and July and the first two weeks of August the weather seemed to be in a sort of trance, a holding pattern, as if it was waiting for a secret signal to let loose and intensify, prompting a moist and insistent misery. That is what usually happened. Not even the cooler air in the mountain valleys was any match for the sudden descent of the wipeout heat of August. This year, though, things were different; temperatures remained moderate. And yet people could not quite trust the moderation. They waited nervously for that final blast, for a day when a red, pitiless sun stuck to the sky like a wet lollipop on a sidewalk. It was like expecting a call with bad news and listening always for the phone to ring.

Danny looked toward the short hallway leading to the bathroom. He wondered how long he should give her—the station only had the one bathroom, and both women and men had to use it—before he fist-knocked on the door and muttered, "Hey," followed by, "you okay in there?"

Chuckie Purvis had gotten in trouble last month for not checking on a trucker whose name turned out to be Gil Trautwein. Trautwein had stumbled in through the double doors at about 2 A.M. on a very busy night, lurching past the counter and into the bathroom. According to Chuckie, he was sweaty, disheveled, grimacing, and he clutched at his shirtfront, mumbling about how "goddamned awful" he felt, and how it must be the flu. Forty-five minutes later, after several other customers had come up to the counter and complained that the bathroom door was still locked, Chuckie unhooked the key from the bent nail under the counter and went to investigate. The bathroom door could be secured from the inside with a little push-button lock, but the key overrode the button.

Chuckie had knocked, called out, knocked again. Silence. Then he shouted. More silence. Finally he used the key. He found the trucker curled up on his side next to the toilet, pants puddled around his ankles, his skin the color of sliced beets. Apparently he'd had a heart attack or a stroke or a seizure—Danny never heard any confirmation about which it was—and he damn near died. Chuckie called the squad. The paramedics hauled the trucker out of there on a rattling gurney. Later Chuckie got an earful from the regional manager, Brady Sutcliffe, and now the instructions were clear for all employees: Give them twenty minutes in the can and then go check. No matter what you find, do not touch them.

Like you have to tell us that, Danny thought. *Like some guy passed out by the shitter is so freakin' irresistible.*

He liked this job. He liked the fact that he had regular company—customers coming and going, unless it was a night like tonight, with that odd stretch of nothingness until the girl came in—but he never really had to get to know anybody, and they didn't know him. Mostly you were your own boss. Danny had never had a serious problem on his shift. Chuckie had once been held up at gunpoint—what was it about Chuckie and bad luck?—but it turned out that the guy's gun was a fake and the deputies caught him down the road. He was a meth head and stupid to boot. If he'd had a real gun, Jake Oakes told Danny, he'd have blown off his own pecker. He was that dumb.

So maybe it's my turn for some trouble, Danny thought. *My number's up.*

He stood in front of the bathroom door.

"Hey," he said. He started out with a mild tap, using a flat hand and not a fist. What if she was—well, sick with some kind of female thing? Something embarrassing?

If that was the case, then she could tell him so. Through the door. He would be able to hear her plea for privacy.

"Hey," Danny repeated.

He waited.

"Just need to know," he said, raising his voice, "that you're okay in there."

Nothing.

Now he pounded. He made a fist and he rammed it against the gray metal door. Four times—*boom boom boom boom*—in quick succession.

"Come on," he said. "Don't make me get the key, okay? Just tell me you're okay and I'll leave you be."

Nothing.

Danny was pissed. He liked things to go as planned. His pleasures were simple: He enjoyed standing behind the front counter, arms crossed, looking out through the glass toward the gas pumps. He liked to watch the bugs nosing in and out of the wedge of light dropped by the bulb up on the high pole at the edge of the lot. He liked it when somebody pulled in and bought their gas with a credit card and then pulled out again without even looking his way; he and the customer were like two people stuck on separate islands, never acknowledging each other. Night after night Danny was on his own here, and he was totally in charge, yet there was very little to do, which was the perfect combo: authority without duties. He also liked having his days free to do as he pleased. That suited him just fine.

And now: this. The woman in the bathroom. Doing God knows what.

Okay, so maybe God wasn't the only one who knew. Danny had a pretty good hunch himself. She was skinny and from the look of her, she was well on her way to being dope sick. He knew the signs. Heroin was as common as stray cats around here. It was swiftly replacing the pain pills, because heroin was so much cheaper. Sure, it was also a lot more dangerous—but you couldn't argue with the math.

He had to get her out of his bathroom. Had to get her moving on down the road, even if that road led nowhere. At least it wouldn't be here.

"Last chance," he yelled at the door.

Nothing.

Danny returned to the front counter. He was bending over to find the key on the bent nail when it occurred to him that it was high time for Deputy Oakes to pay him back for all those free Snickers. He would call Jake, make it his problem. He knew Jake's schedule. He was working tonight.

Fourteen minutes later, a black Chevy Blazer with the county seal branded on its flanks pulled up in front of the glass. The vehicle juddered and then was still, as if a cord had suddenly been snipped. Danny watched as Jake Oakes unfolded himself from the driver's side. He was a big, black-haired, sturdy man, and his brown deputy's uniform made him look even bigger; the fabric fit tightly across his chest and his taut stomach, and snugly encased his thick thighs. It was a hot night but Jake Oakes always looked cool and sleek, no matter what the temperature was.

"Evenin', Danny," Jake said. He had gotten the greeting out of the way before he even reached the counter. He showed Danny his palm, wiggling his fingers. "Gimme the key."

Danny retrieved it. He had filled in the details for Jake during the phone call: A woman wouldn't come out of the bathroom. Possible overdose. "On my way," Jake had barked back, sounding abrupt, almost mean. Danny had known him long enough not to take offense. Jake was a nice guy, but when he was focused on his job, nothing else mattered.

Danny followed him down the corridor.

"Ma'am, this is Deputy Oakes." Jake stood in front of the door. He kept his voice at an ordinary, business-as-usual pitch. Danny figured that Jake didn't want to scare her if this wasn't a situation, if she was just hanging out. "You've got thirty seconds," Jake said. "Tell me you're okay or I'm coming in."

The only noise was the hum of the refrigerated case on the other side of the wall, the one with the assorted six-packs and racked cans of energy drinks.

Jake did not wait the full thirty seconds. He thrust the key in the lock.

"Coming in," he said. He twisted the key as he grasped the doorknob, pushing at the metal door with a meaty shoulder. Danny leaned to the left so that he could see around the deputy's broad brown back.

She was lying faceup in the middle of the floor, her head partially blocking the round gray drain in the center. Her limbs extended straight out from her body, stiff as sticks. Her face was a bluish color. Her mouth was slack; foam leaked from one side of it, glistening on her chin. Her black T-shirt had rolled up, exposing both her concave belly and a wet red sore next to her navel. The syringe had slipped out of the swollen wound and rolled into a lane of cracked grout separating the yellow tiles.

"Damn," Danny said in a whisper. There was more awe than shock in his tone.

Jake dropped to his knees and checked for a pulse, thrusting two fingers up under her flaccid chin. He used a thumb to prop up her eyelid. The pupil was dilated. He didn't bother yelling at her or shaking her shoulder or slapping her face to revive her. She looked to be long past the point at which that sort of intercession would be effective. He did the only thing he could, Danny figured, under the circumstances: He used his radio to call the paramedics, keeping his voice low and calm, his description specific and succinct.

He had seen this before, Danny knew. Many, many times. They had talked about it, on one of the few occasions when their conversation turned serious. Talked about how Jake and the other deputies handled more overdoses these days than car accidents.

Now they waited for the squad.

"Look at her left wrist," Jake said. He stayed where he was, kneeling on the sticky floor beside her. "Must be left-handed. Left wrist's clean. Right arm's a mess. She uses the left to inject herself." He waved his hand toward the prime access spots: ankle, belly, groin, thigh, between the toes, under the fingernails.

Danny squinted. Her left wrist was indeed white and delicate, like a fluted piece of fine china. The rest of her was filthy and nicked with scars and ablaze with oily dark sores, but not that left wrist. It looked like the wrist of a little girl.

Jake was muttering again. "Such a waste. Such a fucking goddamned waste."

Danny shrugged. Jake didn't usually talk like that. In fact, Jake had told Danny that you couldn't get emotional about these things. Anger and sorrow were useless. Worse than useless: They made a person sloppy. You took your eye off the ball and you couldn't handle your job. If by some miracle this woman lived she would, Danny knew, be doing this again another night, in another dirty bathroom. Again and again. And so would all the others. Rinse and repeat. It wasn't worthy of anybody's grief. Nothing was ever going to change. There was nothing special about any of this, Danny told himself; there was nothing special about this woman, or about this night.

He was wrong.

Bell

1:58 A.M.

She couldn't remember the last time she had slept through the night. Surely at some point she had experienced a golden, unbroken road of sleep—everyone had, right? At least once? As a child, perhaps? As a teenager, when she had exhausted herself by a constant headlong flight from anything that threatened to touch her, tame her, hold her back? There must have been a night when she slept long and seamlessly and well. But she had no memory of such a thing.

Bell Elkins placed the bookmark in her book and closed it. Had anyone asked her just then, she could not have come up with a single detail about the plot of the paperback with the shiny, curled-back cover currently perched on her right knee, the story she had allegedly been absorbing for the past hour. Nor named a single character. Her eyes had moved methodically over the pages, but nothing stuck. Late-night reading, reading undertaken in lieu of sleep, could be like that. It was empty, pointless motion, a surface activity that never engaged the depths of her mind. Busy work, aimed at passing the time.

And speaking of time: What time *was* it?

She looked up at the wood case clock on the mantel. She had sensed that it was after midnight because—well, because even without a clock she could always feel when midnight slipped by, like a dark wind brushing her cheek. But after that milestone, the rest of the night fell back into a blur.

The clock settled the matter. Not quite two.

She was disappointed. She had hoped that more of the night would have vanished by now, without her having to know about it. That was the trouble with insomnia—along with all of the other things, of course, such as the fact that it left her weary and grumpy during the subsequent workday. It made her hyperaware of the passing of the minutes, the hours. Time was a great problem for Bell Elkins. She had trouble chopping it up into its constituent elements—past, present, future—because time to her was a continuous black ribbon and she couldn't figure out where to make the cut.

One night, she had watched the second hand on that mantel clock perform its dutiful loops until she realized—startling herself—that twenty-four minutes had gone by. She had been thinking about the past. She did that a lot. The process always reminded her of washing out a filthy bucket, one crusted with mud and sticks and sadness. She scrubbed it and soaked it, and then she filled it with water and swirled the water around in it, and then scrubbed it and soaked it again, over and over, knowing—well, hoping—that sooner or later it would rinse clear.

She could not identify the precise origin of tonight's insomnia. Sometimes it was easy. She was a county prosecutor, and there was always something to worry about. Always a case pending, always a judge to be placated or a jury to be persuaded. She was always facing a can't-put-it-off-any-longer decision about whether to charge a certain defendant and, if she charged her or him, what that charge ought to be. She always had to balance the probability of success against the expenditure of resources—because Raythune was a small, poor county. Her staff consisted of two assistant prosecutors and one secretary. They had to count every paper clip.

But the sleeplessness that bedeviled her at present might not be about work at all. There were other possibilities. She lived with a constant sense of apprehension, a kind of itchy, nervous, fluttery buzz that, at some point, had been inserted under her skin without her knowledge or consent. Her older sister, Shirley, lived with it as well. They had discussed it many times. Neither had been able to shed the vestiges of a violent past, vestiges that included a fear-induced vigilance. And vigilance was a hard habit to break. Relaxation felt dangerous. If they let down their guard, they were asking for trouble—and they would have no right to complain about that trouble, either, after the fact, because they had made themselves vulnerable. And they had done it voluntarily.

Then again, her restlessness might emanate from the ongoing quarrel she was having with her boyfriend, Clay Meckling. "Boyfriend" was a ridiculous word. But the other words didn't work, either. "Partner" was jumping the gun. "My guy" sounded like a 1950s song lyric. "Gentleman caller" was ludicrous and Victorian. "Lover"? Not lately. Neither one of them had been in the mood. Not while Clay's challenge still echoed: *So what's the deal, Bell? I want to marry you. I've said it until I'm tired of saying it. If you don't see that happening, you need to tell me so.* He didn't want to wait anymore. She couldn't blame him.

But she also couldn't get herself there. By all rights, she should cut him loose, let him find someone else. Someone who would make him happy.

So why didn't she do that?

It was 2:03 now.

She unhitched her gaze from the clock so that she could look around the living room. She liked everything she saw. Other people might not understand that, given its degree of dishevelment, from the battered brown couch to the coffee table with the nicked edges to the lamp with the frayed and cockeyed plum-colored shade to the cracked and slanting hardwood floor, and then on to the low arch, its beige plaster chipped and flaking, that linked the living room and the foyer, and over to the weather-warped front door. The sole item of furniture in the foyer was an antique desk—"antique" being a nicer way of putting it than "older than dirt"—and sitting in the middle of that desk was a stout manual typewriter with CORONA stamped above the top row of keys in dull gold. The typewriter was a gift from Ruthie Cox, who had been her best friend in Acker's Gap. Ruthie died last year, leaving Bell the beautiful machine. They had shared a wariness of technology, an unease about the liberties it took in so many lives.

This house always seemed smaller at night, and pugnacious in the way of all runts, as if the corners drew themselves in ever so slightly to make a tighter seal against the pressure of the dark. The house had her back. It protected her. If the house could somehow figure out how to keep her anxieties on the other side of its walls, it would do so. She was sure of it.

This was the first house she had ever owned by herself. The others had been jointly owned with her husband—now ex-husband—Sam Elkins, and they were in various upscale sections of the Washington, D.C., area, where she had lived during her marriage, and where Sam still lived. This house was considerably smaller and shabbier than any of those. And it happened to be located in Acker's Gap, West Virginia, not some fancy suburb in Virginia or Maryland. But she didn't care. She reveled again and again in the simple forthright joy of the realization that this was *hers*—all of it, every nail, every plank and stone, every tile and joist and dusty corner, every scratch and stain, everything from the faulty furnace to the disintegrating roof to the lopsided front porch to the rickety back stoop. She didn't care about any of those flaws. She cared about the fact that this house belonged to her. And to no one else.

So things weren't altogether terrible. She had much to be grateful for. Her daughter, Carla, had ended a period of restlessness and enrolled at George Washington University. She was undecided about her major—which was another way of saying that she was majoring in everything. Her emails to her mother were filled with the verbal sunbursts that came from a newly awakened and continually challenged mind. Bell knew better than to tell her how much she loved those emails and looked forward to receiving them. That would make Carla far too self-conscious.

Her gaze switched back to the mantel clock: 2:05 A.M.

She heard a train whistle in the distance. It was a stretched-out, lonely sounding moan that tailed off into a sigh of solemn wistfulness. Something clunked against the roof; chances were, it was a black walnut released from the tree that hung over the back half of the old house. On late-summer mornings she would find the fist-sized yellow balls dotting the yard. Sometimes the hard shells split open from the impact of the long fall, and chips and shreds of black nut meat littered the grass like the visible remnants of her dark dreams.

The minute hand shifted: 2:06 A.M.

She had returned to Acker's Gap eight years ago, law degree in hand. It was a rescue mission. Her hometown was in trouble, slammed by unemployment as the coal mines shut down, one by one, and ripped up by drug addiction and stunned into lethargy by—the worst foe of all—hopelessness. By the cast-iron conviction that nothing would ever go right around here. It wouldn't because it couldn't. It couldn't because it wasn't meant to. It wasn't meant to because—well, look around. Just look around. Could you doubt it? The circular logic of despair kept the people dizzy, turning around and around on the same small patch of muddy ground instead of moving forward.

She lived her life amid lives that didn't seem to matter to the outside world. Lives that didn't seem to matter, either, to the people who were living them. And that was one of the chief reasons why Bell had come back, and why she had chosen to run for prosecutor. The highest compliment you could pay to a place and its people, she believed, was to insist on justice. On the rule of law. To say to the dark anarchical currents that were always threatening to overwhelm this area: *No. I won't let that happen.*

She had done her best. Yet West Virginia still had the highest rate of drug overdose deaths in the nation. Raythune County Sheriff Pam Harrison would stop by the prosecutor's office every few days and share a grim statistic or two, just in case Bell had dared to let some optimism trickle into her mood. Newly emboldened gangs of drug suppliers continued their regular sweeps through the mountains, sowing their poison in the creases in the land, tempting discouraged people with a quick and easy bliss. A few days ago, a bedraggled old man— he had a scraggly beard and a too-big Army jacket and droopy pants and a lost look in his bleary eyes—had been hanging out in front of the courthouse, and when Bell went by he grabbed her by the sleeve and shouted in her face, "It's coming! It's coming!" She shook him off, but it was unsettling. She had never seen him before, but the old man seemed to be channeling her own grave apprehensions and clinging doubts. He reminded her of a soothsayer from a fairy tale, the kind she used to read to Carla when her daughter was a little girl, only far more sinister. His warning was strange and vague, but it matched up with Bell's growing sense of dread about Acker's Gap, her feeling that some final, terrible reckoning was at hand.

The clock hand jumped forward again: 2:08 A.M.

For a time, when she worked with the former sheriff, Nick Fogelsong, she had believed they were making progress. Then the heroin took hold. But she didn't give up; she fought back. Hard. She was still fighting, every damned day. She did what she could to help the new sheriff, Pam Harrison, hunt down the suppliers, and get help for the addicts—but she had no answer for the despondency that made people reach for drugs in the first place. Sometimes she felt as if she was knee-deep in rapidly rising water on the lower deck of the *Titanic,* bailing it out with a rusty teaspoon.

If people did not care about their lives, about their health and their future, you could not make them care. Could you?

A glance at the mantel: 2:10 A.M.

Two days ago, she had received a phone call from an old friend in D.C. Elaine Mitford was a classmate from Georgetown University Law Center. Intimidatingly smart. Formidably successful. Dazzlingly well-connected. With two other classmates, Grady Fiske and Abigail Mc-Elroy, Elaine was starting her own firm. She had leased office space on K Street. Prospects were bright. She wanted a fourth partner. "Mitford, Fiske, McElroy and Elkins—how does that sound?" Elaine had said, putting a lively curl in her voice, a brisk shiver of enticement.

A year ago, maybe even a few months ago, Bell would have turned her down flat.

But now . . .

"Let me think about it," Bell had replied.

"Really?"

"Really."

"Not to pressure you, but we need to move quickly." There was even more excitement in Elaine's voice. "God, Bell—this would be *terrific.* Frankly, I didn't think we had a shot. If you're serious, though, I'll send you a detailed proposal."

"I'm serious."

Am I really ready to jump ship? That was the question she couldn't shake tonight. It blocked every path to sleep. She thought about Clay. She thought about a lot of things. Finally she made a bargain with herself: She would put off a consideration of Elaine's offer for another day or so. And then she would make up her mind for good, having let all the probabilities and contingencies and pro-and-con arguments move around in her head unchaperoned for a short while.

She didn't want to give up on West Virginia. Yet sometimes it seemed to her that the mountains were slowly closing over her head, the peaks meeting and sealing. If she waited too long to leave, she would be trapped. When she had that vision, she had trouble catching her breath; she felt a little faint, a touch claustrophobic. Maybe the solution was simple: She needed to get out while she still could.

READ THE ENTIRE
Bell Elkins Series

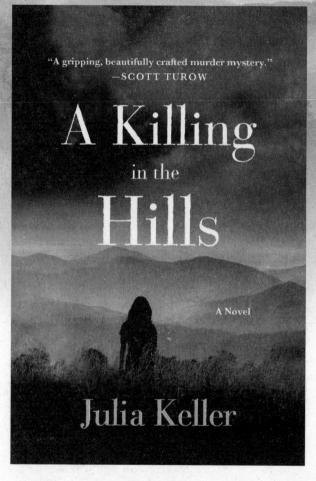

"A gripping, beautifully crafted murder mystery."
—SCOTT TUROW

A Killing
in the
Hills

A Novel

Julia Keller

Bitter River
Summer of the Dead
Last Ragged Breath
Sorrow Road
Fast Falls the Night (August 2017)